Tempted By Monstrous Lovers

TEMPTED BY MONSTROUS LOVERS

A MONSTER & PARANORMAL ROMANCE ANTHOLOGY

GENEVIEVE BRANDON MINDI BRIAR LISA EDMONDS

S. C. GRAYSON ELISSE HAY KRISTIN JACQUES

DESIREÉ M. NICCOLI HOLLY ROSE MEGAN VAN DYKE

JEM ZERO

EDITED BY
LISA EDMONDS

CONTENTS

Authors' Note — vii
Content Notes — ix
About the Stories in This Anthology — xiii

SEED AND BONE — 1
Genevieve Brandon

HER VELOCIRAPTOR LIBRARIAN — 51
Mindi Briar

THE KINGS' BRIDE — 99
Lisa Edmonds

BRIDE OF THE FOREST — 167
S. C. Grayson

THAT ONE TIME I LET THE HERO SUCCUMB TO HIS EGO
AND MOVED IN WITH THE MONSTER — 213
Elisse Hay

GIRL DINNER — 287
Kristin Jacques

MEAT CUTE — 347
Desireé M. Niccoli

PSYCHOPOMP IN BLOOM — 385
Holly Rose

BRIDE OF THE DRAGON PRINCE — 447
Megan Van Dyke

JUST ONE SIP — 517
jem zero

Content Notes for All Stories — 587

AUTHORS' NOTE

All stories and art within this collection (including the cover and interior art) are original human creations.

The authors and artists associated with this volume stand with human creatives and against the use of derivative artificially generated text and images produced and marketed as human art.

CONTENT NOTES

This collection includes violence, death, explicit consensual physical intimacy, and other material that may be triggering or distressing to some readers. Please read safely.

A complete list of content notes for each story is available at the back of the book.

DEDICATION

To Flavia and Bojana—
For breathing beautiful full-color life into our dreams and desires;

To monster and paranormal romance lovers—
May you always find something irresistible lurking in the dark;

And to our wonderful readers—
Thank you all.

ABOUT THE STORIES IN THIS ANTHOLOGY

In the mood for something in particular? Browse the collection!

All authors request readers to review the content notes included at the back of this volume prior to reading.

Seed and Bone by Genevieve Brandon

For seven years, Lady Sylvi has desperately sought the truth about the fall of the royal family and her cursed childhood friend Elias. After escaping the grasp of a wicked man and his equally evil family, Sylvi runs to the desolate land of Espa Brus, hoping to find the demon boy who captured her heart all those years ago.

Her Velociraptor Librarian by Mindi Briar

Rakish adventurer Claudia returns to the city to record her adventures at the Great Library. Sparks fly when she meets grumpy velociraptor librarian Minerva, who just might have a wild side waiting to be unleashed.

The Kings' Bride by Lisa Edmonds

In this gothic why-choose romance, apothecary shop owner Aveline's desperate flight from her kidnapper leads her to the cursed ground of Geed-hollow, den of monsters who hunt unwary travelers by night. Instead of doom, she finds salvation—as well as a chance for vengeance on the true monsters among us and at last a home filled with love.

Bride of the Forest by S. C. Grayson

The forbidden forest has always called to Esmeray, a celestial witch, but she's kept her wilder instincts in check while raising her younger sister. Now her sister is fully grown and has come into her own power, and Esmerey can follow the call of the full moon into the shadows to find the mysterious god of the forest who waits and watches—and who hungers for his bride.

That One Time I Let the Hero Succumb to His Own Ego and Moved in with the Monster by Elisse Hay

Cassandra knows how epic quests turn out, not that anyone will listen to her advice. Forced into a Gorgon hunting expedition, she flees the hot headed hero first chance she gets, and runs straight into the arms of a monstrous beauty. Medusa is fierce, independent, and just might be the first person to listen to her, if Cassandra can keep her wits about her.

Girl Dinner by Kristin Jacques

After an epically bad breakup, med student Daphne is determined to keep her head down when her intentions are derailed by Celeste, an eldritch cosmic entity hiding in a blonde bombshell, with an appetite for undergrads. Will Daphne be her next meal, or will she wine and dine her way into Celeste's tentacled embrace? *Check content notes before reading

Meat Cute by Desirée M. Niccoli

Lady Leviathan awakens from a centuries' long slumber, and her home, the ocean, has become a living nightmare. When she rescues a deep sea mermaid trapped in a net, hunger for connection and revenge put them on the hunt, wrecking ships and wrecking hearts.

Psychopomp in Bloom by Holly Rose

The only psychopomp with a human soul is fascinated by humans living their lives, an opportunity he chose not to take ages ago. But when he accidentally appears to a beautiful florist and falls for her, his gentle, loving heart begins to learn what it means to be human, even if he risks breaking her heart—and his own—by following the edicts set down for his kind.

Bride of the Dragon Prince by Megan Van Dyke

When hardworking cheese-maker Briannis is selected as the next dragon's "bride" (a.k.a. sacrifice), she fears the worst. But what she finds is a cursed prince with a heart of gold who believes she's the key to his freedom. A retelling of The Frog Prince.

Just One Sip by jem zero

Shard, a displaced cosmic entity, has become infatuated with an ill-mannered stripper named Rooney, whose risk-filled lifestyle compels Shard to do everything within his power to protect his jewel—a challenging task, even for a being with Shard's abilities. Unfortunately, Rooney doesn't want a guardian, no matter how sexy, and Shard will need to learn boundaries before Rooney allows him past his hard, glittery exterior.

SEED AND BONE

GENEVIEVE BRANDON

CHAPTER

ONE

THE ESCAPE

Dead leaves and sharp twigs dug into the soles of Sylvi's tattered slippers, piercing the soft skin around her ankles and between her toes. The cool, damp air had long since seeped into her flesh during her days traversing the Wretched Woods beneath the mountains. Had she not lived among the snowy peaks her whole life, she might have succumbed to the persistent ache in her limbs and cold in her lungs, but her years smothered beneath heaps of snow and ice made her hardy enough to survive the unforgiving forest during her desperate escape.

Or, she supposed, what *remained* of the forest.

Sylvi staggered to a stop and propped herself against the trunk of a dying pine, chest heaving. Her hands trembled, and her stomach growled in persistent protest. The escape hadn't been planned. She hadn't squirreled away provisions or worn practical shoes. Bone-deep fear had inspired her miserable run from an impending wedding and wandering hands. Somehow, despite the lack of planning, she had managed to not only survive the wilds, but also the relentless pursuit of her betrothed's guard.

Her nose wrinkled at the thought of her supposed husband-to-be.

Viggo. A handsome man with cold, violent hands who wanted to conquer the continent one massacred clan at a time. She'd rather perish in the cursed lands of Espa Brus than suffer a life chained to him any longer.

The early rays of sunrise spiked through the gnarled remains of the forest ahead, and Sylvi pulled in deep breaths as she slumped against the pine. A decade prior, she had ridden through this same forest with her father filled to the brim with fear of the keep nestled along the coast of the fjord beyond the forest. Now? Well, now she willingly ran to that very place.

Because if everything had gone to plan all those years ago, the land wouldn't be dying. If she had married the cursed boy from the forests, the mountains wouldn't have been conquered by morally corrupt vermin like Viggo and his miserable family.

If the entirety of the royal family hadn't been slaughtered by the very demon they made, everything would be different.

If her father hadn't forced her to leave Elias behind—

Sylvi gripped the crumbling bark, wincing as splinters dug beneath her nails, and forced the thoughts of *if only* away. Thinking that way would not erase what had already been taken. The only thing to do now was attempt to understand what had happened in Espa Brus all those years ago.

With her bottom lip between her teeth, Sylvi dug into the well of magic within her bones and allowed it to flood into the pine. The trees up on the mountain had been full of life still, but this one wasn't dying as she previously believed. It was *dead.* The further from the mountain she ran, and the closer she traveled toward the hold of the fallen royal family, the less life she found in the trees. The energy from the trees had been the only thing keeping her alive in her mad escape, and now that resource was gone.

The silver lining—if there could be one—was the surrounding death meant she was almost to the keep. Her dread at the distance between herself and her destination was almost heavier than the cold burrowing into her bones.

Sylvi focused on the terrain ahead. The aftermath of a landslide gave her a clear view of an old road below through the broken trunks and splintered timber. Most merchants never traveled through Espa Brus anymore, and the path had long since been overtaken with fallen tree limbs. But beyond that road, she would see the coast and ocean inlets. Castle Mourem, the old seat of the former royal line, would loom like a giant beside the water.

All she had to do was make it there. Back to the place where her last happy memories lingered in stone corridors and courtyard gardens.

"Oi! I see her. Just there! Arve, the bitch is in the trees."

"Drat." Sylvi glanced over her shoulder, only to be greeted by the bobbing flames of magic in the distance. Unfortunately for her, Viggo's clan possessed powerful fire magic, which was uniquely effective against the plant magic she'd inherited from her mother. It also gave them unlimited access to light, and she so desperately needed the dark. She'd lost them a few times over the past days, but they always found her again.

Arve, Viggo's brother and commander of his personal guard, would never let her rest.

Quick, hard footfalls in dead leaves forced her away from the pine and into a staggering run down the slope heading closer to the fallen keep. The pursuit had gone on for several nights, and she'd had yet to experience the blissful relief of a moment's rest. Fatigue pulled at her limbs, and an endless ache hung deep in her chest. What remained of her wedding gown hung in tatters at her knees and her golden hair had long since darkened with mud and grime. Her stomach cramped with a hunger so fierce that magic from the earth would no longer sustain her, and the little rainwater gifted by the sky had left her thirsty for more.

The only instinct driving Sylvi forward was the hopeless yearning for something better. If she only ran faster, tried harder, perhaps things could be different. Perhaps she would find answers at the castle.

Maybe Elias wasn't dead.

If she didn't make it, she would only have a life tied to Viggo and his horde of fire magicians to look forward to. That miserable existence wouldn't be much of a life at all.

"Idiot woman," the sharp voice of Arve called out. "The dead of Espa Brus cannot save you!"

Heat scorched the backs of her legs and the ground shook beneath her feet. Weakened by hunger and exhaustion, Sylvi stumbled and pitched forward. Her face smashed against the ground, pushing forest undergrowth between her chapped lips, and her torso twisted painfully. She rolled in a furious heap down a knotted, root-turned hill, body smashing into exposed rocks and felled tree limbs.

Agony splintered down her arms as she clawed at the ground. It wasn't until her body caught nothing but air that she gained clarity, and even then, she could do nothing until her form crashed into the ground again, finally still against flat earth.

Stunned and disoriented, Sylvi pawed at the dew-covered grass. The roll down the hill likely bought her some time as Arve and his partner took careful, measured steps to chase her down, but the time gained was vanishing the longer she lay helpless.

"Where did you go, Lady Sylvi?" Arve called out. "Stop this foolish waste of my time."

Dazed, she pushed herself from the ground. Sharp, fiery pain shot up her left arm, and she cradled it close.

"Lady Sylvi…" Arve taunted, voice pitched into a song. "Lady Sylvi, my brother awaits you. What sort of wife leaves her husband on their wedding day?"

With tears pricking her eyes, she spun on panicked feet, frantically searching for the looming keep she knew stood close—

There.

Her heart stuttered as the stone crags of the ancient gates parted the thick fog rolling through the fjord. Tall and adorned with rusted pikes, it still took her breath away, just as it had the first time she saw it at nine years old. Castle Mourem echoed her home in the mountains insofar that it was a beastly thing made of stone and iron, but instead of being nestled in ice and snow, the bulk of it partially bathed in the water of the inlet. Once the home of thick ivy and families of seagulls, the residence now sat lifeless, no greenery to be seen. The still waters of the sea lay beyond it, a dreary backdrop to an already despondent place.

Blood flooded her mouth and dripped from her lips. The desire to reach the keep, to survive without Viggo, gave her the strength to keep moving when all she wanted was rest. She ignored the burn in her arm as it jostled against her side. A broken arm wouldn't much matter if she were caught.

The humiliating trip back to the mountains, the nights trapped beside—or under—Viggo in his cold bed, would pale in comparison to the pain she felt now.

Reaching the castle became something more than hope as she cleared the last line of dead, gnarled trees. Haloed by the rising sun, the dark and forbidden castle of her memories became more clear. No red banners hung from the parapets, and the once-bustling town around it lay in shambles, charred skeletons of a time since past in a kingdom that had fallen to a curse no one understood. The dissonance between her memories and her reality would have brought her to her knees another time, but in the present, she had no choice but to push ahead.

Run, run, run.

Heat brushed the backs of her legs. A ball of fire crashed into the forgotten, rotted remains of a house's frame. Wood exploded around her. Shards of splintered pine cut into her ankles, biting into the soft, exposed skin. She stumbled, regained her balance, and continued, pushing toward the gate.

Her vision clouded. Were these to be her last moments? Even so, Sylvi found herself strangely detached. Like a puppet on a string, she was powered by a master greater than pain. Fear guided her now, pulling her legs up and down and up again—

—Until her strings were cut.

Sharp agony bit into her palms as they collided with debris-covered cobblestone, and a resounding crack filled her ears. She might've screamed, but the pain shooting up her arm kept her from hearing it. Flames batted ever so closely to her face, beckoning her closer in a bid to end the misery eating her alive.

"Oh, hells. We're going to give her back to Viggo broken." Now that they were closer, she recognized the second voice: Tor—Viggo's cousin. "He's going to be furious."

"Bones heal, you fuckwit." Arve bit out. "Sylvi, you wretched woman, stop this nonsense."

Sylvi heard the footsteps behind her, but she couldn't stop. She pushed to her knees and crawled toward the gate, dragging her weary form along the overgrown cobblestones. The dead grass before her erupted into flame, and she froze before it with a quivering chin.

"If we bring her back broken *and* burnt, Viggo will have our heads! You might be his damned brother, but I have no such protection." Tor's voice, shrill and panicked, echoed in the empty expanse around them. "She's the last of her line. Sylvi's magic ends with *her*. Viggo—"

"Exactly, Tor. She's the *last*." Arve scoffed. "It's better to bring her back broken and burnt than never bring her back at all then, isn't it?"

"I dunno. I just think you could be more careful—"

"Fine, you useless idiot. I'll grab the bitch and we'll get to go home."

The fire billowed before her, the final obstacle before the remains of the gate. If she crawled through, she would burn. If she turned away, if she left the castle and marched back to Viggo, she would still die. One way or another, she would never live again.

A shadow fell over her and booted feet emerged in her periphery. Fingers tangled in her hair and yanked, giving her no choice but to look at the man holding her head aloft. Arve, with his painted face and shorn scalp, stared back.

"You've put me through days of trouble, Sylvi." His light eyes, stark against the black paint smeared across them, sent a bolt of resignation through her. Arve looked so much like Viggo, especially in his hatred, it made her stomach churn. "What did you think you'd do, eh? Find salvation in a haunted castle?"

She inhaled deep. "I'd hoped."

"Death lingers here. No salvation to be found." Arve shook her just enough to send a bite through the hair at her temples. "Two steps closer and you would've belonged to the Demon of Espa Brus."

"Perhaps the Demon of Espa Brus is a fate easier to stomach."

"Perhaps you're a stupid woman." Arve released her hair. "I ought to do my brother a favor, I think."

"And kill me?"

"Maybe. Sounds a bit too simple though." Arve pressed his booted foot into her chest, easily sending her battered body to the ground once more. "Maybe something more...thorough."

The warmth of the fire touched her scalp. It was so close. So, so close. All she would need to do is heave herself back just a few inches and she could be free of all of this. Of Viggo and Arve. Of her dying mountain and the endless famine.

Of her relentless guilt for her family's abandonment of the monster boy in the cage the fateful night everything changed.

Arve stepped closer, heedless of the growing flames. He reached forward, fingers outstretched and curled, seeking her throat. "Now, hold still—"

"Goddess save us! It's the demon!" Tor cried. "Arve—"

A sharp, frantic scream rent the surrounding fog. Arve jerked back, eyes wide as blood streaked across the bridge of his nose and along his throat. A hulking shadow, a malevolent mountain much like her home, hung over Arve, looming.

Fire erupted in Arve's palm as the shadow grew taller still.

A man she believed she'd never see again darted between her and her captor.

Horns. Hair like blood.

The last image to grace her consciousness was that of Arve's head separating from his neck.

And she smiled right as the world went dark.

CHAPTER

TWO

THE BEFORE

The eldest prince of Espa Brus lived in a too-small cage the first time Sylvi met him. He'd been naught but a boy, wearing nothing but a ripped tunic and trousers, and the blanket beneath his legs was so thin it should not be called a blanket at all. He ignored her arrival entirely, too invested in the chicken leg someone must've dropped into his cage, and she wondered if his father, King Iverr, noticed his son sneering at him from between the iron bars.

"Welcome, Lord Sundem." Iverr glanced at her from the head of the large table. The gold thread of his red robes glinted in the light of the nearby fire. He'd decided to call them into a council chamber to meet, and given the lingering goblets of wine scattered throughout, she suspected another meeting had just concluded. "I trust the wait wasn't too unbearable? The council had many opinions about our recent accord with those Vithian dogs, and it took some time to address them all."

"No trouble at all, Your Majesty," her father had said, as if he hadn't been cursing King Iverr and all of House Mourem for their time spent standing in a cold reception room under the watchful eye of the castle steward. "The honor you bestow upon my family is great, and I understand your council's hesitance concerning our negotiations."

"Honor? Bah! A curse. Call it what it is, Peder." Iverr curled his lip as he observed his caged offspring pick his teeth with a clean wishbone. "If you must suffer the blight of my house, I would prefer you do so without needless flattery. I owe you that much."

"I will do as you command, my liege. Just as I did all those years ago in the war against those aforementioned Vithian dogs." For the first time since they'd left home in a packed carriage with far too many dresses and hair ornaments, her father laughed. He stroked his beard before dropping a hand on her shoulder. "This is Sylvi."

She met the king's stare with one of her own and subconsciously pulled her cloak close. Many rumors about King Iverr had reached their hold in the mountains, and none of them had been flattering, at least to her. According to her father, Iverr was a visionary with a spine of wrought iron, unbreakable in the thick of a fight. According to the wives of visiting nobles, however, the king was nothing more than a philandering blowhard desperate for relevance and to save his small kingdom from complete annihilation.

Lips pursed in displeasure, she allowed herself a glance at the crown prince in the cage. Given what the man had done to his son, Sylvi was inclined to believe the stories. Who condemned their own child the way Iverr had condemned his?

"Hello, Sylvi." Iverr studied her, and the weight of her father's hand on her shoulder intensified. His fingers dug into the fur curtained around her neck, a quiet threat. She had one task and her father had no intention of seeing her fail. "Are you prepared to save a kingdom?"

Unsure what that meant, but equally certain she wasn't meant to say so, Sylvi nodded.

"Good, good." He motioned to the cage. "Go along. Meet your fate then."

A firm push between her shoulder blades by her father sent Sylvi stumbling toward the caged prince on slipper-covered feet. Fire crackled in the hearth, rivaling the racing beat of her heart in her ears as she neared. While she had only seen nine winters in the mountains, she was smart enough to know the boy in the cage was not simply a boy. The stories of his birth had traveled far, finding even her in the peaks despite the snow and icy roads. The rumors of his early days had grown alongside her like a playmate—a horror story to frighten her and other children into compliance.

Sylvi saw the stories in him. Allegedly, if the rumors were to be believed, his mother died moments after his first shriek and his father stuffed a demon inside him shortly thereafter. Demons were allegedly plentiful in the forests of Espa Brus, all believed to have wicked grins and horns. As she crept close, malice shone in the boy's eyes and in the way his lips parted to display pointed, glinting teeth. Small horns poked through his deep red hair, and she found herself wondering what they would look like when he was a man.

It wasn't until she crouched by his cage that he looked at her, with the remains of the chicken leg dangling from his fingers.

"Hello." Her blood cooled when his red irises bore into her deep blue stare. "I'm Sylvi."

The boy didn't move, not even to breathe. Red lashes fanned against pale skin, and fire danced in the shine in his eyes.

Unsure how to respond to the unnerving way in which he stared, Sylvi glanced up to Iverr. "Your Majesty, what is his name?"

"Depends." Iverr shrugged, lip curled as he glanced down at his son. "Elias is the name of my son. The demon? Well, he's never revealed it."

Her brow bunched as she returned her attention to the caged boy, surprised to find he still stared at her. "The demon?"

"The demon is all that's left, girl." A pause. "Until you succeed in breaking Elias's curse, of course."

In a fleeting moment, the boy's eyes infinitesimally widened, as if his father said something profound and altogether unexpected.

"But until the moment he is free...the boy is simply Demon." Iverr scoffed and turned on a booted heel. "Peder, would you care for a drink? You've traveled quite far for little gain."

"Serving you is gain enough, my king," her father said, although he didn't sound terribly convincing. "However, I would be quite grateful for a drink."

"Of course." Iverr motioned toward the hearth and a small table with a brass decanter sitting atop it. "That's the least I can provide considering the circumstances."

Alone with the prince and uncertain how to proceed, Sylvi decided to settle on the wood floor across from him, legs tucked beneath her. The fur lining of her cloak brushed against her jaw as the boy continued to stare with nary a breath, and the warmth of the fire suddenly wasn't enough beneath the weight of his intent gaze.

Since they'd somehow fallen into a silent game of watch and wait, she allowed herself to observe him further. Most of him was human, from the look of things—at least, for now. One of her aunts had passed along the rumor he wouldn't look human forever if the curse remained. Sylvi decided there were far too many rumors when it came to Prince Elias, and she was tired of trying to decide which ones were real.

A portion of his neck and one of his hands were quite obviously not human, which did lead *some* credence to her silly aunt's gossip. About half of his throat and almost the entirety of his left hand no longer possessed human flesh, but instead a deep burgundy, scaled skin, and two of his fingernails had turned slate gray and unnaturally sharp, like claws. Weapons, if he wanted them to be.

"Hello, Elias," she whispered. "In case you didn't hear me before, I'm Sylvi...Lady Sylvi Sundem."

The boy stared, silent still. She knew she was supposed to be speaking with him, being friendly and all, but how could she when he wouldn't speak in return?

"According to your father, I should not call you Elias, but I am unsure what else to call you." Sylvi glanced to the older men by the fire not-so-subtly watching them from the corners of their sharp eyes. "I think your father is rather ridiculous. Demon? I shall not call you that. It's heartless."

When no response came, she watched the prince twist in his cage to watch the older men. It wasn't until he craned his neck to better sneer at their fathers standing before the ablaze hearth, drinks in hand, that she noticed a thick, glistening scar carved across the width of his throat.

Could Elias speak, even if he wanted to?

"They aren't over here, you know. You can ignore them." She wrung her hands in her lap. "They're probably talking about something boring anyway. My father is very boring. I imagine your father is boring too. No imagination, either of them."

Elias glanced at her briefly but shortly returned his attention to the older men again. His upper lip peeled back, revealing sharp teeth, and he wrapped his hands around the iron bars, ire visibly mounting the longer he watched them.

"Elias?" Sylvi glanced between the fireplace and the caged prince, panic climbing in her throat. "Please ignore them. If you don't at least pretend to like me, my father will be very angry."

The boy's grip on the bars faltered and his angry snarl slowly fell away. His glanced back at her, brow pinched.

"Thank you," she said, deeply meaning it even though Elias hardly looked thrilled about the prospect of speaking with her. Failing her father was rarely a painless experience. "I saw your neck, you know. I suspect you can't talk." She continued wringing her hands, unsure what to do with them. "It's all right, you know. If you can't talk, that is. My father says I talk far too much—he slapped me for it just this morning, in fact—so I imagine I can talk enough for the both of us."

Elias stared at her, red eyes unblinking, and hope began to fight for air within her.

"How about this?" She smoothed her hair, hands trembling with something between fear and hope. Failure was not an option. "I'll ask you questions. Tap on the floor twice if your answer is yes. Tap once for no. I think that would work. It's more intentional than a nod, especially when several things are happening in the room. What do you think?"

Suddenly, in that warm chamber nestled on the hard floor, Sylvi found herself intensely desperate. She had a profound awareness of her shortcomings—far too chatty, far too thin, and far too needy. Her father reminded her each day of every way she failed their family. In that moment, that long, heavy moment, there was nothing she wanted more than to speak with someone who didn't loathe the sound of her voice.

Elias reached for the floor and tapped once with a sharp nail.

Twice.

Relief swam through her, and a smile twisted her lips. "Thank you for tolerating my nonsense, Your Highness."

His head cocked to the side and his brows drew together again.

"If I talk far too much, you can tell me, you know? Well, that is rather silly of me to say, considering the plan we just worked out. I suppose you can *show* me." Sylvi held up her hand, palm out. "Just do this, and I'll stop."

When Elias did nothing in response, only continued to watch her in clear confusion, she decided to continue talking lest he lose interest.

"Your Highness, do you have magic?" she asked, curious. After a short moment, Elias tapped twice. "Excellent. I do as well. It is my mother's magic, you see. Her clan can do beautiful things with plants. She was sent to the mountains to help end a famine there. That is how she met my father."

Elias's brow smoothed. He held out his hand, and for a moment she feared she'd said one word too many. But instead of holding it out in a plea for silence, Elias turned his palm to the ceiling and bent his fingers in a quiet beckon.

Her eyebrows lifted in surprise. "Oh. Do you want to see it?"

Two taps.

Pleasantly surprised, she reached for her belt and removed the pouch tied to it by leather strings. "My mother told me pushing beans and seeds to sprout was a good way to practice. If I give too much, I could hurt myself, you see. This forces me to be careful." She opened the pouch and plucked out a small, white bean. "Watch closely, Your Highness."

Sylvi cupped the bean between her palms and called upon the warmth in her veins. With a slow and controlled push, she sent her magic into the bean and opened her hands. A vibrant, green sprout emerged from the bean and curled along the soft golden glow encasing her fingers.

Eyes wide, Elias leaned closer to the bars to observe and pride warmed her cheeks. Everyone loved her mother and they all flocked to watch her revive dying trees and fields of crops. No one had ever thought *her* and her boring beans amazing before.

"What of your magic, Prince Elias?" she asked, voice low. "What is it you can do?"

He flinched and quickly tapped an iron bar once. *No.*

"Don't be like that. It's not fair to keep secrets." Sylvi kept the bean sprout cupped in her hands and gave him a look. "You know why I am here, yes?"

Despite his lips being pursed in a pout, he shook his head.

"Well, you silly boy, I will be your wife one day." When his mouth dropped open, she laughed. "Please don't look so disappointed. I am rather nice, I think, once you get to know me. However, more to the point, you are simply *not* allowed to keep secrets from your betrothed, and I am desperate to know what sort of magic you can do."

Despite the look of utter terror on his face, he tapped the floor, resolute. *No.*

It was her turn to pout. She puckered her bottom lip. "That is very unkind, you know."

Elias's gaze shifted to the ground, but he made to no move to acquiesce to her demands. And why would he? She was just a strange girl who appeared seemingly out of nowhere. He did not owe her that vulnerability.

"I understand," she said, after several long moments of continued silence. "It is hard to be unguarded, isn't it, when you have nowhere to safely fall afterward? I bring my father great shame. My mother loves me, but she is never home. There is always a village suffering in the mountains, you see."

Sylvi cut a glance to the fireplace, feeling the heavy weight of her father's gaze on her. His hard look, while unsurprising in the wake of her one-way conversation with Elias, sent a chill down her spine.

"I realize my openness is strange, and oftentimes, it is obnoxious." She curled her fingers around her sprout, relishing in the soft pulse of her magic along the plant. "But I will continue to be this way for I know of no other way to be."

Elias watched her in that unnerving manner of his, and she was unsure what to do in his continued quiet. If he refused to engage with her, this whole marriage enterprise was largely worthless. She did not wish to eventually marry someone who could not tolerate her personality or answer her questions.

"I suppose I'll—oh!" Sylvi flinched at the abrupt movement of his hand through the bars. "What is it?"

Elias reached for the sprout, the two claws on his hand glinting in the firelight.

"Do you want this?" When he continued trying to swipe the sprout, she laughed. "Well, all right then. Here you are."

With amusement twisting her lips, she slipped the sprout into Elias's palm.

The bright green of the sprout leeched away, and the stem curled into itself, thinning and twisting as it shriveled. Elias never looked away, never faltered in his search of her face, while the plant died before them, hanging limp along his fingers.

Death.

Her brow pinched in thought. Not only did Elias have to bear the burden of his curse, but he also carried the weight of significant shame for his magic. How could one boy suffer so much?

She lifted her hands, stopping just short of touching his. "May I, Elias?"

Instead of tapping, Elias slowly nodded. She cupped her hands around his, unperturbed by the sharp edge of his claws grazing her skin. The crushed sprout, draped limply between his fingers, called out for her magic, and she gave it.

"Life and death are linked," she explained. "A cycle. That's why I have to start with something small. My mother said if I tried to revive an entire rose bush this young, it would drain me utterly. If I practice, I will be able to bring a whole garden back one day when I'm older. But now? It's not the right time to try. I'll die if I do." Sylvi uncovered Elias's palm, and the sprout now sat whole and new. "I work in life, and you in death. I work in seed, and you in bone. I think we could be a good match, you and I. What do you think?"

Elias stared at the sprout in his hand before meeting her gaze with a look so profoundly sad in its surprise and earnestness that it broke her heart.

Then, without breaking eye contact, Elias—the Demon of Espa Brus—tapped the floor twice.

CHAPTER

THREE

THE REUNION

The soft embrace of blankets greeted Sylvi upon waking. In the quiet dark surrounding her, body aching at a level she had never known to exist, Sylvi could not bear to open her eyes. Instead, she cataloged every strand of fur pressed against the exposed skin of her neck and legs, every fiber grazing her broken arm and cut feet. If she didn't acknowledge the world around her beyond this, she could ignore the problems that undoubtedly awaited her beyond the warmth. She could enjoy these moments of comfort and security—her own world separate from the one that had fallen apart in a moment of fear so consuming she could think of little else.

The sudden recollection of Arve's head hitting overgrown cobblestone, however, created a swell of warmth beneath her breastbone, and she opened her eyes.

Given her last memory, Sylvi was somewhat surprised to wake up in a familiar chamber in her tattered dress. She sat up, awe-struck, and allowed the blankets to fall around her waist. Broken arm cradled close and smothered beneath thick furs, she stared, mouth agape, at the space before her, hypnotized by the memories invading her mind.

The room hadn't changed much in the years since she'd last seen it. A painting of snow-covered trees still hung above the bed, curiously free of the cobwebs draped in the rafters and along the tops of the armoires. A shelf packed with books and trinkets originally from her mountain home loomed along the right wall, across from stained-glass windows and thick curtains. A vanity with a hairbrush and a circlet still sat in the corner, freshly cleaned and free of dust, as if she hadn't left them in the dark of the night to escape the castle with her father all those years ago.

Sylvi pressed a hand to her lips, closed her eyes, and inhaled, thankful for the grounding scent of the fire crackling in the hearth. Regardless of her feelings in the past, of how she had fled the future she mourned, she had reached Castle Mourem. And, if the shadowed form at the cursed gates meant anything, she had also seen Elias.

He wasn't dead.

Overwhelmed and hands trembling, she considered her new circumstances. Viggo's demand that she travel from her mountain home to his clan stronghold had been a surprise, and the lack of time to prepare left her at a strange sort of mercy. Her father, her only surviving family, had died only days prior, and the period of mourning had not passed. It wasn't proper to ask a woman to travel so soon. Not that Viggo was a man bound by any code or morals beyond his own.

Perhaps the demand shouldn't have been a surprise, considering her father had been the only obstacle between her and Viggo. The patriarch of the Barem clan had been inquiring after her hand for years, desperate to bring her magic under the control of his family. After the royal family was thought to be completely massacred, and her betrothal to Prince Elias consequently nullified, Viggo would ride to their mountain hold several times a year, bearing all sorts of gifts and gold. Sylvi had made a consistent habit of sending him away, but it didn't matter.

Her father's refusal to give her to Viggo, especially since he had intended to give her to an alleged *demon* initially, was the only sign she needed to know he was a bad man.

Sylvi lowered her aching body back onto the bed, lip tucked between her teeth. Viggo *was* a bad man...and now he was a bad man with a slain brother. He would never allow the person who killed Arve to survive. Or her, for that matter. He would come to the castle. Perhaps not today or tomorrow, but eventually he would come. His desperation for her magic and revenge for Arve's death would call the warlord to Castle Mourem like a siren's song.

The beat of her heart within her injured arm increased, and she swallowed down the nausea overwhelming her stomach. She was physically in shambles, starved from days on the run in the elements, and nursing a broken arm in a castle with a being that might be more demon than man. But if she left, she would be at the mercy of a vile cretin bent on revenge for Arve's death. Neither place seemed safe, but what else was she to do?

Perhaps her effort to get to the castle was more foolish than she initially believed. Even though she now knew he *was* alive, Elias might be too far gone.

Shame swelled within her at the thought. Elias had been good to her as a child. Given her current accommodations, he was likely still the same boy. Older and probably less human than he had been as a child, but still the same boy yearning for a world much kinder than the cage he lived in.

But what had she done to that boy, if not led a true monster—Viggo— to his doorstep?

"We will be all right," she whispered. Tears welled along her lashes and her lip quivered. "Everything will be all right."

Filled with remorse, pain, and regret, Sylvi wept. The night, her quiet companion, welcomed it.

THE FIRE HAD LONG SINCE DIED WHEN SYLVI AWOKE AGAIN. PAIN AND COLD HAD settled deep in her bones, compelling her to stay burrowed in the blankets.

But the rays from the sun streaming through the stained-glass windows called to her and provoked her into moving.

Lying in bed would not solve any of her many problems.

Her arm, lightly bandaged and splinted while she slept, throbbed in a deep, desperate pain, and she held it close. If she could find some life—a tree or some grass—she could borrow some life from them to begin to heal. It would be a slow process, but it would be better that allowing her bones to knit on their own. Her future was uncertain and she couldn't allow herself to be hindered by a broken arm.

The thick, wooden door leading to the outside corridor loomed ahead, and her pulse quickened. Someone, presumably Elias, had brought her to her old room. A part of him did not want her dead. She hoped that part of him continued fighting the monster within that compelled him to kill his family that fateful night.

Her thoughts strayed to the potential for finding signs of life as she padded across the room on bare, aching feet. The trees around Castle Mourem had long ago fallen to the strange curse plaguing Espa Brus and the blades of grass had gone with them. The ground had taken upon the evil of the demon, if the rumors were to be believed, and anything growing from it had died the moment the royal family perished.

If healing was not possible, if there wasn't a single sign of life in the gardens or halls, then she would simply have to hope Elias's demon was feeling generous enough to let her stay until her arm was whole again, or until she could find another way to escape Viggo's reach.

The castle hadn't changed since the night she left. The same tapestries hung on the walls, and moth-eaten rugs lingered along the floor. Sylvi noticed sconces outside the castle's many doorways, but no torches occupied them. It was as if Elias had lived in darkness since his family passed. Maybe he had.

The iron door leading to the dungeons beckoned her forward. Unlike the rest of the corridor, the doorway was free of cobwebs and the door hung slightly open. Cold swiped at her skin as she pulled it wide and her breath passed through the air in a cloud.

Elias had always lived in the dungeons before. Even though his father was dead, she somehow doubted he'd take the king's former chambers. She'd never known Elias to have a shred of respect for his father or the mantle he held. While he was technically the king of Espa Brus now, she realized with a start, the throne was never anything the boy in the cage ever wanted.

Grief tugged at her heart.

All Elias had wanted was love.

She stepped down into the curling stairs. The cool draft and smell of damp stone brought back flashes of childhood experiences of visiting Elias when he was locked away. King Iverr had always shut him inside his dungeon chamber for days when his curse visually progressed. Each time a finger shifted from man to monster, Elias would be sequestered for weeks. When the scales reached the underside of his jaw, weeks more.

As she reached the dungeon corridor, it suddenly occurred to her that perhaps she had it all wrong.

Maybe *Elias* had wanted to kill his family and the demon simply didn't stop him.

Unsure how she felt about that realization, Sylvi pressed on. Answers wouldn't suddenly present themselves. If she wanted to understand what happened that night, she'd have to ask Elias.

If her father had prepared her for nothing else, he had prepared her for this moment, at least.

Elias's cell was at the end of the corridor. The door, the only one made of solid iron, hung open in invitation. Arm still cradled against her abdomen, Sylvi approached, bare feet silent against the stone. Beyond a steady *drip drip* of water echoing along the damp stone, no sounds reached her ears. Elias had always been able to move like an assassin in the dark, however. The lack of noise meant nothing.

She held her breath and stepped into the doorway of his former cell.

In her youth, she had never seen inside. Her mind had conjured images, of course, in the hours she spent outside it, talking to him and pushing drawings beneath the door. She had hoped during those conversations that the interior was more livable than his usual cage.

The reality was worse than she'd imagined.

The cell was cramped and chilled...and exceedingly empty. Blankets were piled in the corner, and a small table with an oil lamp sat against the left wall. An open wooden chest took up another corner of the room.

She edged forward to the center of the space. Had he always lived like this? Alone in an empty cell?

The soft sound of footsteps in the corridor sent her heart flying into her throat. Despite her fear, she inhaled deep and steeled her nerves. If Elias wanted her dead, he could've left her outside the gate or taken her head along with Arve's.

She would have to trust that their childhood relationship, however one-sided it oftentimes felt, would keep her alive.

While the shadow along the ground at the gate had hinted at his size, Sylvi wasn't prepared for the large, looming form Elias occupied now. Towering just inside the doorway, his head well above its frame, he watched her with uncertainty in his eyes.

The curse had taken over the left side of his body, covering his arm and spreading through the open front of his black tunic to the front of his throat. Scales crept past his jaw, edging close to his left eye, and his ear no longer bore round edges, but instead came to a point. Horns, once small enough to hide if one tried, now curled along his scalp, a frame against his blood-red hair.

And between his hands, nestled inside a large, bronze pot, was something she never expected.

All moisture vacated her mouth at the small pear tree.

"How?" Sylvi had planned on saying something much more profound the first time she saw Elias again, but all she could see was the one plant in the kingdom that hadn't died being held by the monster who allegedly killed them all. "I thought..."

Hesitant, she stepped closer, but Elias didn't move. He watched her, his unnerving stare unchanged despite the years since she'd last seen it. Elias knew much of her relationship with plants, more than anyone else since her mother passed. The significance of this gesture, of his willingness to bring her the one thing that could truly help, was not lost on her.

The leaves were soft and full of life. Clusters of pears hung from hearty branches, and they called to her. She felt the throbbing in her broken arm even in her teeth, but now that she had means by which to heal, all her pain and sense of helplessness could stop.

She allowed her magic to seep into the leaves. The plant gave to her almost the moment she asked it permission, sending heat into her skin.

All too soon, she had to withdraw her hand. Her arm, while less painful, was far from healed. However, the plant was the last in Espa Brus. Killing it for her own gain, no matter her injuries, would not do.

"Thank you," she whispered, both to the tree and the man who held it.

Unable to distract herself with healing any longer, Sylvi forced her gaze to meet Elias's own. He watched her, expressionless, before setting the brass pot on the floor.

Before she could ask any of her many questions—*How are you alive? What happened that night? Why did you kill your father?*—Elias pressed the backs of his fingers to her cheek, and the warmth settled her somewhat erratic heartbeat. This was Elias. He had never harmed her before. He'd never even tried. She believed, perhaps foolishly, that fondness hadn't left him, no matter his curse.

It is yours.

A soft gasp brushed her lips at the sound of his voice filling her mind. In their time together before, Elias had never communicated beyond taps and nods. How...?

She searched his throat for the scar that once lingered there, only to find it had been covered entirely with the same scaled flesh that now engulfed his left arm.

Confused, but hopeful, she licked her chapped lips. "What is mine?"

The plant. He glanced at the pear tree. *You grew it from seed in your hand.*

Her memory traveled back to the small bag of beans and seeds she once carried on her belt. "You took care of it?"

The corner of his mouth quirked. He tapped her forehead twice—*Yes*—before allowing his fingertip to rest against her skin.

Come with me.

CHAPTER

FOUR

THE GARDEN

E lias led her from the dungeon, keeping in step on her right and matching her slow pace.

Trapped in a strange limbo between her old life and this new one, Sylvi tried sifting through her many warring emotions—grief for the time they lost, hope for the time they still had—attempting to make sense of them and the questions she wanted to ask. But there was no easy way to ask any of them, so she continued cradling her arm and thinking on the unbelievable.

Famine had taken Espa Brus in the months following the death of the king, and given the cursed ground, most people living within its borders had long since moved on. It was only within the last year that the curse had spread further across the continent, breaking into the mountains where she lived in the north and desert region in the west. There seemed to be no end to the curse.

And yet, in the heart of it, a lone pear tree thrived.

The mysteries of the curse were not coming together neatly. Not yet.

The one thing she did know, however, was the certainty in her bones that Elias was still Elias. He was no demon remade or a boy lost to the curse.

He was just Elias, the boy—now the man—she was destined to wed since her ninth birthday.

"I mourned you, you know." The words left her easily, and she glanced up at him, remembering the first time they met. With no shortage of nerves, Sylvi lightly grabbed his forearm, unperturbed by the scales beneath her palm. Her broken arm, still blessedly numb thanks to the pear tree's healing, allowed her to drop her other arm to her side. "It was awfully rude of you to let me assume you were dead."

Elias's lip curled in distaste. *As if I would allow anyone to kill me.*

"I didn't mean literally dead, you silly man." The Elias she had grown to know would not have torn his father's heart from his chest unprovoked, and she had feared the demon within had finally won. "I thought you had succumbed to the curse. That you weren't whole any longer."

I am hardly whole. A heavy pause weighed between them. *I have never been whole.*

"Nonsense. You seem whole and present to me." He tensed beneath her hand, but Sylvi ignored it. "You'll be pleased to know that the years away have not broken me, and I am still far too chatty."

I am...pleased.

Her cheeks warmed and she failed to fight off a grin. "I also wanted to say thank you for taking care of Arve. He was foul person."

Was he your husband?

"No," she answered quickly as they turned down a long corridor, one she remembered leading to the great hall and courtyard. "However, his brother, Viggo, was forcing me to marry him, and I may or may not have run away from the ceremony."

Elias's frame shifted, on edge. *I will kill him as well.*

She grimaced. "I admire your enthusiasm, Elias, but there is no need—"

His head will join his brother's on a pike outside the gate.

"You are being rather dramatic." Sylvi patted his forearm lightly in reprimand before gripping it firmly once more. "How are you able to speak to me like this? If you made me create that ridiculous tapping system for no good reason, I will be quite cross."

I am uncertain. Each time the curse progresses, I'm given more gifts by the darkness. Elias bent his arm and settled her hand at the crook of his elbow. A quick glance revealed a faint blush overtaking the human flesh of his face. *Our chats were the only attempt anyone ever made to communicate with me. I do not think you appreciate the enormity of what you did for me back then, Lady Sylvi.*

A comfortable silence fell between them, and she found herself leaning into his warmth as they walked.

She did not think Elias appreciated the enormity of what he'd done for her either.

THE DOOR TO THE COURTYARD WAS SOMETHING SYLVI WOULD NEVER FORGET NO matter the amount of time that had passed.

King Iverr had never let his son out of the castle. Confined to the cage or the dungeons, the four years their relationship grew had always been on the other side of iron. The only concession the king had made in her time at Castle Mourem was to have Elias moved to the courtyard. Still enclosed in his cage, but outside in the sun.

She ground her teeth. With age, she saw what Iverr had done. He'd given a stupid girl with grand ideals a concession, an illusion of power in a situation she did not truly understand. After months of begging, determined for Elias to drink in the sunlight, Iverr had given in to that single request. She never asked for anything else until the night everything fell apart, and likewise Iverr never gave.

"I haven't seen it in so long," she said, somewhat nervous, and ran her hand along the deep grooves carved into the wooden door. "What do you wish for me to see here?"

Elias glanced down at her but remained silent. Now that she knew he could communicate beyond taps, she found herself annoyed.

Patience. His mouth stretched into a smirk. A devious one, just like when they were young. *You will soon see.*

Her eyebrows lifted. "You can read my mind?"

Perhaps.

She hummed and turned up her nose. "I do recall informing you some years ago that it is unacceptable to keep secrets from your betrothed."

He stilled again. *Betrothed?*

"Yes, you silly man. Of course." If Elias thought she was ever leaving his home again, she would have to have a word with his demon. Short of him killing her and removing her from the worldly plane entirely, Sylvi knew she was in Castle Mourem to stay. They'd already missed so much time. "Unless you married another?"

I did no such—

"Did you enter into a contract with another noble house?"

Elias gave her a narrow-eyed look. *You know I did no such thing.*

"Since our marriage contract was never officially dissolved, I suppose we are to wed." Sylvi smiled, and she meant it. Having been moments away from marrying a truly vile man, the prospect of marrying her childhood best friend brought warmth to her otherwise chilled body. "If you wish to have me, of course. If freedom is what you wish to have instead, I would never deny you that."

Before he could come to any sort of conclusion, she decided to show him a bit of mercy. Elias had never been particularly forthcoming with any emotion beyond anger, and it was likely his brain left him entirely in the wake of her hopeful, and likely delusional, proclamation.

She tugged on his arm. "I would like to see the courtyard now."

As you wish. With eyes like rubies, shining with an intensity she'd never before seen, Elias opened the courtyard entrance.

The land outside Castle Mourem had been a sea of death. No plants lived anywhere nearby, and they had been dead for so long, their remains had become one with the dirt. Skeletal trees stretched all the way to the horizon, jutting into the sky in haunting memory. It was this image that Sylvi imagined beyond the door.

Instead, she was greeted by a sea of green.

Ivy crawled up the trellis along the courtyard walls, the ends falling from the top in a leafy waterfall. Lilac and potentilla shrubs, full and lush, filled the courtyard with soft purples and yellows. Heat burned the backs of her eyes at the sight.

She crouched down, loose soil pressing between her toes, and felt along the flowers of a mature lilac shrub. Her magic slipped into the plant, asking for permission to take, and it gave. The warmth flooded her arm, focusing on the break close to her wrist.

"How...?" All thought left her mind, replaced instead by intense confusion. All the plants grew in brass pots, which likely contributed to their survival, but she still had too many questions.

Elias did not answer her feeble attempt at asking, and the low hum of the plant's magic flowing into her body filled the space instead.

After receiving magic from two lilacs and one potentilla, Sylvi stood to her full height, pain-free and heart swollen in gratitude. There had to be at least thirty plants in the courtyard, and all of them had thrived in her absence. "I don't understand. How are all these plants alive when the rest of the kingdom can grow nothing?"

His hand slipped along hers, and she gripped his fingers.

You. A heavy pause filled the silence and she could not breathe. *I cannot kill you. Any part of you. And I would stop anyone who tried.*

"You've tended to all of these plants for seven years?" Sylvi's chin quivered, her heart and mind overcome.

She had lived in the mountains since they'd fled the castle, wondering all the while if Elias not only lived but thought of her. If he did survive and his demon hadn't swallowed him, had he thought she abandoned him? Did he think she ran in fear of him? Had he thought her a heartless teenager, running away from the only friendship he'd ever had?

Even if he had thought those things, she realized, he had never given up on her return. If he thought she would never go back to him, the lively garden around them would likely be dead.

It wasn't until he brushed her hand with his thumb that she remembered his new ability. He'd likely heard everything running through her head just then.

I have never stopped hoping you would return, Elias said, voice soft in the confines of her mind. *The only true life I know, have ever known, has been you.*

Sylvi smoothed down the front of her new gown, strangely light. Her time in the courtyard and walking Castle Mourem had been something she'd only dared to hope for in her dreams for so long, she had to keep pinching herself to make sure she wasn't asleep.

The garden was real.

Elias was real.

Elias. She ran her fingers through her hair, self-conscious. In the years since the fall of the Espa Brus, he had certainly grown up. Sure, he had literally grown taller and filled out his frame, but emotionally? Elias had never been so composed...so assured. Confident, even, but with an air of vulnerability that reminded her of the boy he'd once been.

She arranged her hair over her shoulders—now loose and clean thanks to a well-deserved bath—and adjusted the skirts of her gown. Elias had given it to her, an old relic from his mother's armoire.

What did he think of her?

Did he find her beautiful?

The moonlight poured into the room through the stained-glass, attempting to coax her to bed and sleep. But sleep would not come easy this night, she knew, for her mind could not settle. How could it in circumstances such as these? Espa Brus was not lost. Elias was still whole. The curse could still be broken.

She could still have the ending she'd wanted since she'd met the boy in the cage.

Sylvi ran her fingers along the glass and the outside chill bit back. The people of the mountain had pitied her in the four years she traveled between them and Castle Mourem. They did not understand how her father could commit her to wed a cursed boy, no matter their duty to the king. When her betrothal was announced, it was as if she'd died. A funeral for a living girl, a quiet goodbye in the snow.

They did not know Elias. They did not know her. He had been her closest friend and she did not fear him. She had loved him—she'd told the king as much the night everything changed.

And now that Elias was a man? She feared those feelings had only grown stronger with absence and time.

I cannot kill you. Any part of you. And I would stop anyone who tried.

The garden came to mind again. If Elias could not kill any part of her, including the plants she'd made when they were children, that was presumably a new development. He had killed the first bean she'd grown into a sprout for him, after all.

Then again, this inability to kill any part of her could simply be a choice, which made more sense to Sylvi. He'd chosen to kill her sprout when they were nine because she'd asked after his magic. Elias never killed anything else she grew after that, once she'd wedged herself so far into his life he never had a chance.

"He didn't know me when I grew the first sprout," she whispered to herself and looked at her palms. "So Elias could kill me, truly, if he wished to..."

But he wouldn't kill her. Others? They would receive no such mercy. Arve and Tor had found out the hard way.

I cannot kill you. Any part of you. And I would stop anyone who tried.

Something about Elias's statement hung on the edge of her subconscious. His reluctance to kill her she understood. They had been close once.

But to give into his demon and kill *for* her...to become the demon he loathed? Why would he feel the need to make that declaration—

Cold gripped her body and squeezed. The mystery of that fateful night swelled within her.

Maybe there was more to the king's death that she previously believed. Maybe Elias had been trying to tell her something.

Sylvi licked her lips, mouth dry, and set for the door. Elias might have saved her from Arve, but there were too many questions without answers. The unyielding need to *know* was making her jump to conclusions, and she'd rather get the truth from him instead.

Once upon a time, they had been all each other had. But before she allowed herself to welcome him back into her heart, she needed to know the depths of his.

THE CURSE

As luck would have it, Elias was not in his quarters, nor was he in the courtyard garden. His absence forced her to search the estate with bare feet and determination, and after hours had passed in the dark corridors, Sylvi came to the conclusion that Elias had gone away.

She found the kitchens hadn't been used in quite some time. Years, even. Since she'd only eaten from the fruit bearing trees since she arrived, there was a good chance he had gone to hunt. With the land dead, the animals would be further out. It might be some time yet before he returned home, if that was in fact what he'd gone to do.

She pursed her lips. If the kitchens hadn't been used in so long, did Elias even need to cook his meat anymore? An important question, if he allowed her to stay.

Deciding that the question of Elias's meals would have to wait until his return, Sylvi returned to the courtyard.

The moon hung low and full. Something akin to magic tickled her skin beneath it, teasing her closer and closer, until she settled on the ground beside some lilacs. The soft scent brushed her nose and she inhaled deeply.

If the land of Espa Brus was well and truly cursed, how could this court-yard be so beautiful?

Sylvi ran her fingers along the loose ground, the soil still damp from an afternoon shower. If the curse on the land flowed through Elias, and he said he could not kill any part of her, could she grow something here? Something new? The idea had manifested the longer she thought on Elias's confession. If the curse was directly tied to Elias's magic, it stood to reason that he would allow her to sow the earth with hers. Unless it was some subconscious decision, or he didn't have any control over the cursed magic once it was in the land.

Lip between her teeth, she sighed. The only way to find out was to try.

Perhaps she should try now.

With a deep breath filling her lungs, Sylvi dug her fingers into the dirt. The same dark magic she'd felt in the forest lived here, thrived even, and her magic shrank from it.

"Stop being so fickle," she told herself. She'd bribed her magic before, back when she lived in the castle. It tended to listen, if she were kind enough. "The magic? It's only Elias. He would never harm us."

Her next push went further down her fingers, and the one after that even more so. A soft hum rumbled in her throat as she worked, desperate to know. To try.

When her magic finally listened, the earth sang too.

Elias's magic, heavy and forbidding, bowed to her as she expanded through the soil. Her eyes widened, matching the now frantic pound of her heart. The further her magic tunneled, the realization that Elias spoke true became more apparent.

Not only would he not kill any part of her, but he would allow her to go anywhere she pleased.

A soft gasp shook her throat as something soft pressed along her legs. Grass, strong and thick, sprouted along the courtyard ground, surrounding her body in a living blanket. She withdrew her hand from the dirt and stood, eager to allow the spread as she sent magic through the soles of her bare feet. The grassy patch expanded, stretching toward the lilacs and the west wall of ivy.

She laughed.

And laughed and laughed.

When her heart grew light and her body swayed, she withdrew her magic. Unsteady and giddy, she tried to steady herself on the grass, dancing on weak legs.

Until she hit something quite solid.

Sylvi tilted her head back, finding Elias there. How long had she been in the courtyard garden?

Had he been watching her?

Capricious and delightfully merry, she leaned back, allowing him to catch her mid-fall. "Hello, Elias." She cocked her head, and her hair tumbled over her shoulder. "Did you notice the grass?"

I did.

"It's lovely, don't you think?" It wasn't until that moment that she realized some flecks of red on his cheek. Blood-colored flecks. Her body and mind, still alight with glee, did not register the seriousness of such a sight. "Did you go hunting?"

In a manner of speaking.

"Did you find your quarry?"

His head is outside the gate.

"Oh." She pursed her lips and allowed Elias to set her to her feet. Suddenly worried, she gripped his arm tight. "Was it Viggo?"

Elias nodded. *He foolishly approached my land. I removed him from your life.*

Her heart leapt at this. A part of her felt terrible for her undisguised joy, but a larger portion remembered Viggo's rough, forceful hands and lips. She scowled, wishing she was back under the heady elation of her accomplishment instead of remembering Viggo. "He was a loathsome man. The continent is better for his demise."

Are you better for it?

"What a question. Of course I am." Catching the question within his question, Sylvi decided to get to the key part of her quandary from earlier that evening. She had no idea how long she had spent healing the courtyard, but her realization from before remained...and perhaps became more important in the wake of her feat in the garden.

Sylvi tugged on Elias's hand, coaxing him to sit beside her in the grass. He made no effort to fight her, bending easily to her whims if only to make her happy. "You truly meant what you said. Your magic didn't fight mine at all."

Her companion looked rather uncomfortable in the grass, but the blades didn't wither away beneath him. His brow pinched, clearly confused by this phenomenon. She stroked his human hand. It was scarred, but large and strong, and she wondered how his palm would feel against her cheek.

I said I cannot kill you. Any part of you. That includes your magic, he said eventually.

"Is that why you killed your father?"

Elias's demeanor shifted in the wake of her searching question, as if he were frozen in the mountain's icy lakes. Eyes, red and wide and staring far away, back to the night everything changed, sent a pulse of grief straight to her heart.

His non-answer was, in fact, an answer.

"Your father threatened to kill me, didn't he?" Sylvi needed no verification, but asked the obvious anyway. "I told him I loved you that night... before he died, you know. It was after he locked you away the night your arm shifted again. I tried to petition him to get you out of confinement."

When Elias continued to say nothing, she turned to face him. His distant stare persisted, although one who stumbled upon them might think he gazed deeply at a potted apple tree.

My father made a deal with a forest demon when my mother fell pregnant. He was losing the war with Vithia and he needed a miracle, Elias said, absently tracing the place where the scar on his neck used to be. *He slit my throat upon birth, gave the demon's power a host, and the demon's curse infected the Vithian army. They fell in days. However, even after the war was won, I remained permanently changed.*

Horror seeped into her. Iverr had slit his own son's throat? "I don't understand. Why would he threaten to kill me?"

The demon's terms, Elias clarified. *The curse would remain in Espa Brus until a sacrifice was made of one who loved me.*

Cold swept up her spine and she shivered. Had her father known that would be her fate when he brought her to Castle Mourem?

The timing of the massacre made sense, considering the contents of the curse and her confession of love in the hours before. "Your father told you that he would kill me. That would be the sacrifice. *I* would be."

In all her time knowing Elias, she had never known him to show emotion beyond anger. His father brought it out of him much like her magic did to flowers, and the other times he attempted complete indifference.

But now, for the first time in the years knowing him, shame turned down his mouth. His eyes, still very far away, would not meet hers, intently boring into the night. A beautiful, pleasing burn ignited in her chest, filling her from head to toe.

"Well, I am very clearly *not* dead." She scooted closer on her knees and placed a hand to his cheek. "Look at the grass, Elias. It came back, and I am not dead."

I do not understand the ways of demons.

"When I give to the earth, my magic becomes it. I am slowly giving myself to the plants...the ground..." She held his face between her palms, mouth slowly splitting into a grin. "Remember what I told you the night we met? My mother made me start learning with beans and seeds for small plants because if I tried to do something larger, I could give too much. To break the curse, you need a sacrifice of one who loves you. Using my magic is a sacrifice, Elias. A slow one, but still a sacrifice."

He glanced at her, albeit reluctantly. *You might be able to fix the ground... the trees...but you cannot fix me. The curse will never truly break.*

She sat back on her calves and gripped his arm with both hands. "Fix you? There is nothing to fix, you silly man."

I am a monster.

"A monster? Not to me. I love every part of you. I have since we were thirteen." She leaned in and gave him a look. "Your horns are also very handsome. I'd wondered for years what they would look like on you as a man."

A deep flush overtook his face.

She laughed, and he blushed deeper. "Why are you so surprised?"

Because I am hideous. Half a man. And you are so beautiful, I cannot bear to look at you sometimes. You're so bright in the dark.

"And you, my love, are grounding in the sun." Sylvi put a hand to his cheek once more, pleased when the tension left his body. "I could have married Viggo. He left me little choice in the matter." Elias tensed beneath her palm, but Sylvi continued. "But all I wanted, all I have ever wanted, was the first person who did not find me too burdensome. Too loud. Too much. All I wanted was you, so I ran on a whim and a hope. You are handsome, Elias." She stroked his face, not missing how he leaned into her fingers. "I wish you could see you as I see you."

Sylvi paused, feeling both shy and unusually bold. She had kissed men before. In the years she'd mourned Elias, she tried to move on. But they were never right. Never him. Viggo had forced himself upon her, never more than a harsh kiss and a grope, but hardly a pleasant memory.

Now, she had Elias beside her, watching her like a parched man in the desert staring at an oasis. He'd listed closer, closer than he'd ever been, silently waiting for her to do something.

Deciding to lean more into bold, Sylvi rose up on her knees, meeting him eye to eye.

Then, accomplishing a feat she'd only dreamed of, she pressed her lips to his.

CHAPTER

SIX

THE RITUAL

Elias froze beneath her, nary a breath shaking his chest. Had he ever imagined a kiss? Had he wondered if he would ever have the chance? Had he ever wondered what it would be like to kiss her?

When Elias didn't move, disappointment sank deep, like an anchor attempting to pull her to the ground. Inadequacy mounted inside her chest like the insidious disease it was—had always been—and Sylvi slowly lowered herself to the grass, breaking away.

"I'm…I apologize." She kept her gaze low, unable to meet his eyes. Perhaps if her shame swallowed her whole, she could pretend her foolishness never happened. "I just thought…well, it doesn't matter, I suppose. I truly hope you can forgive—"

Elias pressed a finger under her chin, and he gently guided her attention to his face. His eyes, wide and intently focused on her own, sent a bolt of heat low in her belly. *Stop.* After a moment of contemplation, a frustrated grumble shook his throat. *I am uncertain what to do.*

"I just do what feels beautiful." Her voice sounded weak and far away,

"I wanted to kiss you. I have since we were thirteen. I thought you wanted..."

The chance that she had done to Elias what Viggo had done to her...her eyes burned in remorse at the thought. Elias had already had so much taken from him. What if she had taken more—

What if what feels beautiful to me is not human? The question, one with considerable consequences if she weren't careful, cut through her worries. Worries he would have undoubtedly heard roaring through her mind. *What if what I feel truly belongs to the demon? I do not wish to harm you.*

"Oh." The relief billowing throughout her body allowed her to fully relax against Elias's hand. She had not interpreted him incorrectly. She had not taken things too far. "Well, what is it that you feel, Elias?"

With eyes wide and shining, Elias stroked her chin with his thumb. *I am unsure. What does one call an incessant need to be near you? To be drawn to you like a rose to the sun? What do I call unceasing gratitude? A willingness to surrender to you, even though I have never been allowed to surrender anything in my entire life?*

Sylvi fought the searing heat of tears behind her eyes. The first time she'd met Elias, all she had wanted was for someone to enjoy her. To hear her voice and rejoice in it. Never asking for silence, never pleading for space.

And now, despite the obstacles that dotted the seven years since they separated, they were in the courtyard garden surrounded by plants she grew from death and Elias tended in life. They truly were opposite sides of the same pewter coin, forever a cycle, chasing each other head over heels through the years.

A kiss? Elias continued, voice rough. *I have wished for you to return since the day you left. I regretted never trying to kiss you the last time I saw you. I wished things were different, that you would return to me. But I always asked myself, why would you ever want a half of a man?*

Heart pounding, she blinked away the blur smeared across her vision. "Elias, if you wish to kiss me, then I implore you to do so. Immediately."

He moved quickly, as if the invitation was all he needed to shift from his place of noticeable discomfort in the grass. In a swift moment, he cradled her face between his hands, the sharp nails of his left gently grazing her temples.

His lips, as she suspected for years, were quite soft when they met hers again.

The world slowed and stilled. Warmth, like the crackling of a fire in a hearth, spread from beneath her ribs, wrapping her body in a cocoon of comfort, a safety she'd never before experienced but frequently dreamed of. The longing she'd held for years, the fear of never knowing this, of knowing him, leaving her in a sudden rush, like the tide receding from shore.

Desire filled that space, demanding she deepen the kiss. She leaned into him, clinging to his tunic with white-knuckled hands, and coaxed his mouth open. Elias did nothing at first, likely unsure what she was attempting to do, but when she slipped her tongue inside, meeting his with a moan, he responded eagerly.

And then, like that had been all the approval he needed, he moved. His hands dropped from her face and felt along the curve of her hips and the slope of her neck. She stood higher on her knees, granting him more space to caress, subconsciously asking for more of his fevered hands as she slipped her own into his mussed hair. When he grazed the side of her breast with his thumb, the thin fabric of her nightgown no match for the warmth and friction of his enthusiastic exploration, she gasped, wishing he'd have taken things a step further.

A deep moan echoed from him and into her mouth, and he did as she wished. It occurred to her suddenly that Elias could hear her thoughts, so when she unbuttoned the top of her gown, allowing him access to her breasts, he did as she wanted, running his rough fingers over her nipples as he lowered her to the grass. His lips found her neck, searching for her pulse, and he kissed beneath her jaw.

She ran her hands up his muscled chest, suddenly hating his tunic and everything it was hiding. When he didn't respond with immediacy, she decided to be direct, voice breathy. "Elias, I need you to do something about this."

Elias pulled back, eyes burning intensely. *I'd rather not.*

"I wish you would." Sylvi smiled up at him, pleased to see him haloed by stars and moonlight. "But if you'd rather not, I will not question it."

They stared at each other, the thrum of *what if* growing to a fever pitch. A moment of vulnerability, an extension of trust, hung there too—a cruel reminder that Elias had known nothing but shame and revulsion his whole life. Why would he be eager to potentially relive it?

A willingness to surrender to you, Elias said in answer before he rose to his knees and unfastened the leather belt at his waist. He tossed it aside, face somewhat drawn as he reached for the back of his tunic. He maneuvered out of it with a single tug, revealing a chest both demon and man. He leaned back to her and pressed a soft kiss to her lips. *How the mighty Demon of Espa Brus has fallen.*

Sylvi giggled against him and ran her hands over his chest, palms meeting flesh and scales in equal measure. "You're still quite fearsome. You murdered someone and stuck their head outside the gate naught but an hour ago."

Elias kissed her harder, parting her lips with his tongue. *And I would do it again if you asked it of me.*

His fingers moved expertly over the remaining buttons of her gown, and anticipation held her captive as pleasurable aching grew at the apex of her thighs. When the backs of his fingers grazed the sensitive skin there, she groaned into his mouth, arching into him, searching for sweet friction.

Despite a lack of experience in pleasing women, Elias followed her lead, seemingly eager to please. When she lifted her hips, desperately seeking him to release her from the pleasurable torture wracking her body, he answered. An overwhelmed feeling, a sensation of simultaneously falling and melting, brought a sigh of relief as he slipped his fingers along the soft, wet flesh.

Sylvi wasn't sure what guided him: her thoughts or her body. In her every wish, he complied. His fingers moved deftly, as if he'd touched her like this a thousand times. They would slip in and out of her, slowly bringing her closer with every careful, intentional stroke. Closer to what? She did not yet know. But she wanted to. She was about to.

When her breathing increased, and her heart soared, he increased his tempo, curving his fingers on the very place the made her gasp and tremble. His lips found hers again, swallowing her desperate pleas as she became overwhelmed with the heat building in her body, threatening to spill over.

The moment it happened, where she felt both detached from her body and immeasurably whole, a breathy cry split the air, the only thing she could do to control the uncontrollable urge to do it all again. The control slipped almost immediately. It wasn't enough. She needed more of him.

Sylvi turned, shucking her gown from her arms, and gently pushed Elias to roll onto his back. He caved to her silent demand, growing almost desperate in his own movements. The two of them made quick work of his trousers, their mouths inseparable in the knowing of what waited for them. Days ago, her fate had been tied to Viggo, who'd sworn to take her the night of their forced marriage even if she begged him not to.

Now she was being lovingly worshipped by her first love, and the reality of it set her afire.

His cock, as it turned out, had already been claimed by his shift. Unlike his chest and arm, however, his skin was still soft to the touch, albeit hard and ready beneath her palm. Just large. Fit for a demon hoping to conquer a willing woman.

Sylvi broke their kiss as she lowered herself onto him. While she'd never lain with a man, she knew her body was made for this. For him. Thanks to Elias's diligence, she was ready, and she took him inch by inch.

Something full and warm burned behind her eyes in that moment as a completeness she had never experienced consumed her utterly. He swept his hand along her cheek, and she trembled, both eager for more and desperate to memorize his face as he took her in.

A pleased hiss left his mouth, and their lips met again, a collision of passion the likes of which the castle had never witnessed. Tonight, in that place, upon the land of King Iverr's forever damned legacy, surrounded by the labor of love born from their childhood hopes, Sylvi defied her fate, lived despite it, and brought her cursed lover back from the edge of loneliness and despair. The demons of the forest—seers and prophets all—had known this moment would come. Planned for it, and set the stage.

It was a role she accepted wholeheartedly.

Elias wrapped a hand around her back and thigh, claws lightly pressing into her skin. He rolled her back onto the grass, and she hooked her legs around him. His thrusts started slow, painfully slow, before speeding up, matching her drive as she edged closer and closer to sweet release once more.

He grabbed her wrists, holding them above her head, and pressed them into the grass. She welcomed his kiss, whimpering as the ever-growing warmth swelled between them.

And when they reached the height of their mutual ecstasy, they fell apart together in the garden they made. Elias held her close and swallowed her cry with his mouth, possessing her, owning every inch of her pleasure. He followed her swiftly, quickening his pace, only stopping once he reached his own release, filling her in both body and soul.

Sylvi wrenched her wrists free from his hands and drew him close, pressing a soft kiss to his lips.

Elias was no demon, and she no savior. They were simply man and woman, Elias and Sylvi, who found love in a place and time no one expected.

In the haze of the after, surrounded by the fruits of their labor in a cursed land, Sylvi basked. Elias collapsed, cradling her against chest as it heaved with deep, rasping breaths.

Thank you for returning to me. Elias pressed a soft kiss to her brow. *For breaking my curse.*

"Thank you for waiting for me." Sylvi smiled, warm. "I apologize for the delay."

His eyes, so full of warmth, of *love*, were a far cry from the sneering boy in the cage. *I will give you whatever you wish. Whatever you wish, whenever you wish it.*

Her eyes watered, and despite her joy, tears broke through her lashes.

The ground beneath them called, itching against their joined hands. Sylvi's magic, full and brimming, poured from her and into the ground. The vibrant grass expanded beneath them, creating a thick, verdant blanket from trellis to trellis.

"I work in life, and you in death. I work in seed, and you in bone," she said, repeating the words she had said to the boy in the cage after she'd brought the crushed sprout back to life. "I simply wish to be together until we are both old and gray and the earth reclaims us both."

With something like a smile, soft and lovely, touching his lips, Elias pressed his brow to hers. *As you wish, my dear.*

About Genevieve Brandon

Genevieve Brandon is an author of warm, comforting romance. In another life, Genevieve wrote urban fantasy under another name, but she has since shifted her focus to all things romance.

When not writing, Genevieve is exploring the world with her husband and children or spending time with her two dogs.

Find Genevieve on Instagram at @genevievebrandonwrites

HER VELOCIRAPTOR LIBRARIAN

MINDI BRIAR

CLAUDIA

I fight my way down a crowded sidewalk, jostled on every side by elbows, bags, tails, and spikes. A dilophosaurus-drawn wagon rattles through a puddle, splashing my boots.

This is why I hate the city.

Out in the wild, it's just me and my companions, no other civilized company for leagues. Sure, it does get a tad lonely—especially when Cassian and Eudora need alone time and send me to "gather firewood" for hours—but it beats having to duck swinging brachiosaurus tails and getting cursed at by sweaty-faced men when I stumble heavily into the corner of their food stall.

The Great Library of Balexonia comes into view as I round a corner. I have to admit, the city's centerpiece is a stunning architectural feat. What started out as a palace in the monarchist Dark Age has evolved over time into a celebration of artistic expression and shared human/saurian knowledge.

Centuries ago, the law-defying marriage of King Cyrus to his stegosaurus queen Nyla was the beginning of the end for the ancient kingdom's warmongering and power-seeking. Saurians, who formerly shunned human ideas of agriculture and city-building, were welcomed into our walls. It was primarily plant-eaters who forsook their wild ways, although a handful of carnivorous saurians also chose to give up hunting for a soft life in the city.

A few generations of mingling with the herbivores' peaceful culture—plus their genius for plant husbandry leading to years of abundant resources—shaped us into the egalitarian culture we know today that celebrates art, beauty, and pleasure above all else.

In said culture, it's customary for each person to present a piece of art to their community on ten-year milestone birthdays: ten, twenty, thirty, and so on. These art pieces serve to track an individual's growth and allow their loved ones and neighbors to celebrate and remember them long after they're gone.

The Great Library maintains a catalog of all artistic contributions, updated yearly. And, though the tradition isn't technically mandatory, they tend to get testy and send a hundred pigeons with passive-aggressive reminders until the citizen caves and slaps together something the librarians can record.

Ask me how I know.

At first it was impressive how the birds kept finding me, even when my cartography team was in the middle of absolutely nowhere. Then it was annoying—like the time we were hiding from a sabretooth cat and the messenger pigeon blew our cover. After what must've been the seventeenth one, Eudora looked at me and sighed. "Maybe you should go, Claudia. We were almost done scouting this coastline anyway."

My thirtieth year is almost over, but I've been avoiding the inevitable trip back to civilization to create and register the art representing my third decade.

Mainly because I still don't know what I'm going to make.

"Just do a nice map," Cassian urged me, on the last night before I parted ways with my cartography team. We were sitting around the fire, sharing a bottle of whiskey Cassian had been carrying around for months for "a special occasion." I was flattered that my departure rated cracking it open.

"Yes!" Eudora, her massive pterosaur wings folded into a comfortable roost, leaned against her human husband, eyes half closed in contentment. "Do a map. That represents what you spent your twenties doing, after all."

It's true that I've spent the better part of the last eight years tramping through the wilderness and swaying on ship decks mapping coastlines and outlining lakes. But the actual *drawing* part isn't my forte. Eudora, our aerial surveyor, guides Cassian's hand as he sketches out the curves of the land. I'm mainly there as their hired muscle, scaring off feral tyrannosaurs, hungry sabretooths, and curious liopleurodons. They'd protest I do a lot more than that—Cassian taught me a fair bit about map-sketching during the months after he broke his arm falling out of a tree—but any map I'd try to draw on my own would look woeful next to his masterful designs.

"Well, what did you do for your ten and twenty?" Cassian asked when I shot down the map idea.

I poked the fire with a stick. "For my ten, I barely even remember. I think I made a mosaic out of glass? It was supposed to be hung in the front of Dad's shop, but then my brother cut his hand on one of the pieces I didn't sand down well enough, and they put it away in storage. Then for my twenty..." I stopped, wincing.

"What?" Eudora insisted.

"I wrote a poem," I mumbled, cheeks flushing from more than just the fire. "Don't laugh."

Cassian, to his credit, only laughed a little bit. "What was it about?"

"Comparing the moon to a woman's tit? I don't know. I was nineteen, all right?"

Eudora lost the battle not to laugh. She tilted her head back, exposing her long neck and the wicked-sharp length of her beak, and screeched hilarity to the night sky. Cassian elbowed her, but even after she settled, she couldn't stop chortling deep in her throat, little *chuk-chuk-chuk* sounds that sounded very close to human laughter.

"I think you're a lovely writer," Cassian told me, with generosity I wasn't sure I'd earned. "I've seen your letters. They're..."

"Descriptive," Eudora said, with another *chuk-chuk*. "That one you sent your brother about the dysentery epidemic in Lower Valeria..."

I buried my face in my hands. "I was trying to make him laugh. Probably no one else will ever read that. I can't write about *shit* when it's going on record for all of civilization to read for the rest of time."

With a grin, Cassian said, "Sounds like you're fucked, then."

The next morning, the two of them tramped off into the wilderness with their newly hired temporary guard, a gruff triceratops with a broken horn and tail armor inlaid with long, spear-like spikes. That left me to hire a pterosaur flight back to Balexonia and, somehow, pull a work of art out of my ass worthy of representing a decade of my life.

Now, as I approach the Great Library, nerves writhe in my gut. I still don't have any idea what I want to make, except for excuses. On the way here, I decided I should try going through my family's archives for ideas. Maybe some long-ago piece of art will inspire me.

If plagiarism wasn't grounds for public shaming, ostracism, and expensive fines, I'd consider straight-up copying somebody's ancestor. But supposedly the librarians always find out—or so say the rumors.

Even my toned thighs feel the strain as I climb the seemingly unending stairs through the terraced garden in front of the library. I spot a cluster of volunteer gardeners spreading fertilizer. A diplodocus, feet planted several tiers down, bends their neck to delicately nip a shrubbery into the perfect shape.

Gardening can be art, I recall. I've heard of people submitting a new strain of sweeter, cross-bred fruit, or a perfect rose bloom from the bush they've tended for a decade. My friend's grandfather, for his eighty, presented a tiny potted tree he'd spent decades shaping and pruning.

Still, the idea doesn't call to me, just as map-drawing didn't. I continue the climb, relishing the burn in my legs and lungs.

Somewhere in this library, there's got to be a spark of inspiration waiting for me to find it.

MINERVA

"ANOTHER ARCHIVE REQUEST." ALEXANDER, MY FELLOW LIBRARIAN, SLIDES THE pigeon message across my slant-top reading desk with his weird little human sausage fingers. In the process, he rumples the ancient scroll I'm meticulously copying. A corner crumbles away, and I make a clicking sound low in my throat, a warning.

I promised the head librarian I would stop growling at my human colleagues. They make it so hard, though.

"Why don't you pull it yourself?" I ask through gritted teeth.

"But it'll take me an hour to find it," Alexander says. "It'll take you five minutes. You're so good at this, Minerva. It's like you have the whole archive memorized."

I place my pen down very slowly before turning to face him. "I. Am. Busy."

"C'mon, Minnie, do it for me?"

"If you call me Minnie again, I will conveniently forget why my ancestors chose to cease hunting humans."

Alexander's throat bobs, and I catch a whiff of fear-sweat. "P-please, Minn—erva?"

I slide the pigeon message back to him with a single claw, careful not to let any of my wrist feathers brush against the scroll. "Run your own archive requests, Alexander. You'll never excel if you don't practice."

As he scurries away, guilt nibbles at my stomach. Was I too harsh on him? Maybe. But between the mountain of aging documents needing to be copied and this year's township reports that I still have to file, I don't have time to do basic fetch work—no matter how quickly I can complete it.

An hour later, I'm putting the finishing touches on my copy work, relieved that the original scroll held out long enough without crumbling. The door creaks open again and I sense a human's breathing in the room behind me.

"What, Alexander?" I ask without turning around.

"Hi," says an unfamiliar human female voice. "I think I took a wrong turn. This isn't the archives."

I whip around, startled. The woman holds up her palms in apology. *A patron? How did a patron sneak in here? They're not supposed to access the archives unescorted.*

Through narrowed eyes, I size her up. The natural light from the window highlights her tanned skin and throws gold highlights into her braided brown hair. She's surprisingly attractive for a human.

No. I need to stop using that qualifier. According to the head librarian, it's speciesist. She's beautiful, full stop. Unconventionally so—she wears the clothing of a peasant man, rough-woven trousers with a creamy linen shirt tucked in. The sleeves are rolled up, revealing thin pale-pink scars against her tan. I catch myself inhaling her scent, curious if it will reveal more about her. She smells like sweat, trees, and woodsmoke. A tinge of pterosaur. She recently flew in from the wilds, then. A traveler of some kind.

"I'm Claudia of Rume," she says with a crooked half-smile.

The silence stretches out a beat too long before I say, "Minerva Deft-claw. Senior Librarian. The archives are down the stairs, not up. And you should have an escort."

"Oh, I did. Fellow named Alexander. He was hovering too much, so I snuck off when his back was turned." Claudia grins conspiratorially. "Sorry to barge in on you like this. Can I just say, your script is the neatest I've ever seen?" She gestures to the pages pinned to the drying rack. I'm suddenly and irrationally self-conscious at someone seeing the book unbound and in pieces like this. "And that illumination you copied—I have a friend who's an artist, but even he could learn a thing or two from your work."

Well, this Claudia of Rume certainly knows how to flatter. My feathers rise involuntarily with pride before I shake myself to flatten them down again. "This area is off-limits to patrons. You need to go back downstairs."

Claudia doesn't seem in a rush to do so. She takes a step forward, admiring my scriptorium. Large windows let in plenty of natural light, allowing me to work from dawn to dusk. Against one wall, a cupboard stands open, revealing my overflowing to-be-copied queue.

Normally, the cupboard wouldn't contain quite so many crumbling documents. But our best human copyist just gave birth a month ago, and most dinosaur librarians lack the fine motor control to hold a pen properly.

That means the work has been falling entirely to me. Small wonder I'm snappish.

"I'm curious," Claudia says, casually running a finger along my drying rack. "This might be rude, but how did you decide to become a librarian? It's just that, well, not to stereotype, but most people of your—uh—"

"Species," I fill in, folding my arms. "Don't chicken out now. You can go ahead and say it. Most velociraptors live in the wilds and prey on the weak. Our *natural state.*"

"Whoa, now, I wasn't going to say *that,*" Claudia backpedals. "It's just that all the velociraptors I've had the pleasure of meeting have been sailors, explorers, builders, stuff like that. Outdoorsy types."

"Well, as you can see, we're not a monolith," I say tartly. "Some of us like to read."

In truth, the stereotypes she references aren't far off. My father ran in a wild pack and my mother worked in a lumber mill. Two of my nestmates followed in her footsteps and became lumberjacks. My oldest sister, last we heard of her, was captain of a pirate ship.

There are reasons why I don't talk about my family much.

"I like to read too," Claudia says, "when I get the chance. Out in the wilds, there isn't much opportunity. Books and scrolls are hard to carry."

I take the bait. "Out in the wilds? What brings you to the Great Library, then? Desperate to do some reading?"

Claudia huffs out a little half-laugh. "My thirtieth birthday is in a few weeks. The pigeon notes were starting to get annoying. I'm here to do my civic duty and make art."

"It's customary to present it to your family and neighborhood first," I point out.

Grimacing, Claudia says, "All right, you got me. I haven't come up with anything yet. I came here to browse the archives and get some ideas."

"That sounds like something Alexander can help you with," I tell her pointedly.

"Alexander is annoying."

I can't disagree.

"Hey, are you busy?" she ventures.

"Yes! Very!" I sweep a clawed hand toward the shelf containing my copy queue. "Now I'm going to have to insist that you leave. This area is full of highly fragile documents, and patrons are not permitted in—"

"Excellent. Then you'll show me the way to the archives?"

I cross my arms, annoyed at this woman's attempt to distract me. My feathers bristle underneath the loose toga I wear draped across my upper body. Saurian culture doesn't require clothing, but some of us choose to wear it as a sign of assimilation into human culture. Gets itchy when my feathers prick up, though.

"Fine," I say. "I'll escort you downstairs. Then I really must get back to work."

CLAUDIA

The librarian's footclaws click against the stone steps like a rich woman's high heels. She carries herself like one—proud, confident, more than a little uptight. In fact, I'm pretty sure I've seen a merchant's daughter swish her hair the exact way Minerva swishes her tail. I hide a smile behind her back.

Women like this are my weakness. I've had plenty of enjoyable liaisons with rugged fighters, covered in scars and muscles, but my sweetest dreams are about the bossy ones with soft skin (or...feathers) and a sharp tongue. I love driving them wild. In more ways than one.

"What section are you hoping to browse today?" Minerva asks, turning her head so she can look straight at me with one of her jewel-green eyes.

"Art presentation records for the township of Rume." I don't know if my ancestors have any great inspiration waiting for me, but it's somewhere to start.

"There are two different archives for that," says Minerva. "One is the scroll library, which records a written description of every art piece presented in Rume year by year. The other archive holds original art pieces donated by patrons."

My eyebrows shoot up. "You mean I don't have to wade through dusty old scrolls? Yes, please!"

"I thought you might be interested." Minerva's tone is dry. She thinks she's figured me out already: all muscles, no book-smarts. I'm going to enjoy proving her wrong.

She leads me to a subterranean level of the library, pitch-dark until she opens a cage mounted on the wall and tosses in a handful of worms from a pouch she carries on her chatelaine. The outline of a creature takes shape, glowing ever brighter as it snares the worms with its tentacles and stuffs them into its central mouth. It looks something like the squishy, many-armed anemones I've found in coastal tidepools.

"Natural light source," Minerva explains, watching me run an awed finger across the cage's metal bars. "Less harmful than fire and doesn't give off smoke to damage the scrolls. It's called a cave coral. Watch your fingers —it's quite venomous." When I whip my hand away, she chuckles deep in her throat. "Don't worry. They move very slowly, if at all. Just take care not to touch their excretions."

She moves along the wall, dropping worms to a line of cave corals in wall sconces until the whole room is lit almost as well as the ones aboveground. The pinkish glow illuminates a room crammed with shelves. They're labeled by year and township, the closest one dating back almost a hundred years ago.

"Rume's archives are this way." Minerva removes one of the coral sconces, holding her short feather-frilled arm aloft to cast the light on the shelves in front of us.

As we retreat deeper into the stacks, I give the receding glow of the cave corals a longing backward glance. "Quick question. How long does the glow last?"

"An hour or so. You can feed them again if it becomes dim." Minerva tilts her head to the side. "Don't tell me a brave explorer like you is afraid of the dark?"

"Of course not," I scoff. It's more the stuffy enclosed space. I'm not used to being underground. Having got accustomed to sleeping with the night sky as my ceiling, it's hard to imagine ever going back to a life indoors.

Minerva raises the cave coral lantern and points at a painted label hooked on the lip of the shelf. "Here we are. Year 28 of the reign of Cyrus the Third—that's what 28C3 stands for—and the name of the artist, Ovidia of Rume."

I peer at the art piece from more than a hundred years ago. It's a strange and slightly unsettling mask, shaped from clay to resemble a crying face. "She must have been going through something," I joke.

Minerva nods. "Sometimes the scroll archives include the artist's justification for why they chose to make what they did. If you'll be here for a few days, perhaps you can find the corresponding scroll."

She hands me the sconce. It's heavier than I was expecting. "If you need further assistance, come upstairs and find the library runners. I'll leave you to it."

"Wait," I blurt. "You're just going to leave me alone down here?"

Minerva says, "I told you I was busy. I must get back to my copying work. You're more than capable of reading labels for yourself, are you not?"

"I..." *Don't want to be left in the dark.* "You didn't give me any extra worms, in case the cave corals go dim."

"Oh. Yes." Minerva rummages in the belt pouch, but comes up with only two more shriveled grubs. "I'll get more from the storage cupboard."

She bustles back down the aisle and heads for the stairs. I follow, sconce in hand, noticing the mesmerizing sashay of her tail and the impressive speed at which she moves. If this were the forest, no stone floor for her claws to click against, she would be a silent, deadly foe.

Except her prey would probably be some plant she wants to study. I smirk, imagining her pouncing on a specimen. Maybe she'd employ an eyeglass to observe it up close. Never mind that velociraptors almost never suffer vision impairment.

She stops by the supply closet door. When she turns, she catches the tail-end of my amused expression and lifts her chin in a regal display of annoyance. "I meant for you to wait there."

"I wanted to see where the coral food is," I say innocently. "In case I run out."

She chuffs through her nostrils, but lets me into the supply closet. Most of the storage space is filled with a stack of crates labeled with "DONA-TION." Minerva gestures to a shelf bearing a large pile of cloth pouches. "Dried bugs of all sorts. The corals prefer fresh ones, but they'll accept a few rounds of the dried stuff. You probably won't want to stay down here longer than an hour or two, just in case."

I raise an eyebrow. "In case what?"

"In case they get overfull and go to sleep. They won't light up for several more hours after that."

"Maybe I should just use an oil lamp instead," I say.

"*Absolutely not.*" Minerva whirls on me, her tail lashing. It catches the edge of the door and swings it softly shut behind us, leaving us alone in the cramped space with the coral sconce between us.

I meet her eyes square-on, and she softens a little. "Fire of any kind is forbidden in the Great Library. You could be lifetime banned for endangering our collection."

"Fine, fine!" I hold up my hands in surrender. "No fire. And no over-feeding the corals." I reach across her, deliberately leaning a little closer than socially polite, and snag one of the pouches of coral food. "I'd better get started on my research then."

"Yes. I think that's best." Minerva reaches for the door handle.

Then rattles it. Then pushes on the door with all her considerable strength.

"Oh no," I murmur. "Tell me you have the key."

"Of course I have the key." Minerva lifts her chatelaine. "The problem is, this room only locks from the outside."

MINERVA

I PUSH ON THE DOOR AGAIN, MY HEART STARTING TO RACE. THE AIR FEELS SUDDENLY thick in this tiny closet. These old doors stick in the frames sometimes—maybe one more good shove—

"Whoa. Hold on. Let's just think for a minute." Claudia's voice breaks through the fog of terror clouding my brain. "You're going to hurt yourself if you keep throwing yourself at the door like that."

She's right. My feathers are already smarting from being crushed, and I've probably bruised my shoulder. With a whimper, I sink into a roosting ball, tucking my limbs under me and coiling my tail as tight as I possibly can.

Claudia folds into a cross-legged posture next to me, placing the coral sconce between us. "That's right," she murmurs. "No need to panic. We're fine. The room's not airtight, so we'll be able to breathe. We've got plenty of coral food, so we won't lose the light. Now. Let's think this through. Will someone notice we're missing soon?"

I pull in a long breath through my nose, tamping down the panic. "When they close the library and you haven't signed out, they'll come looking. We never leave patrons lost in the stacks."

"And maybe before that, someone will need coral food," Claudia points out. "So, a couple of hours at most." She bites her lip, looking up to the ceiling as she thinks. "There's a tiny crack under the door. What if we slide something under there, to tip people off that we're trapped? Can we write a note? Do you have any parchment?"

"No." Then, after thinking for a moment, "We could dump out one of the bags of coral food."

"Good idea!" Claudia says brightly. "We don't have any ink either, but maybe blood...?"

I shake my head quickly. "Not a good idea." I may have strong control over my ancestral hunting instincts, but in a small space like this, even the scent of my own blood mixed with my overactive fear response could trigger something dangerous.

Claudia thinks for a few more moments. "Oooh. Let's see if there's anything interesting in the donation boxes. Charcoal or paint or—"

I growl my outrage. "You want to damage a piece of art?"

"I want out of this closet," Claudia says. "Don't worry, I'm not going to destroy anything if I don't have to. Help me pry the lids off?"

Reluctantly, I detach a long, flat key from my chatelaine and wiggle it under the nailed-down lid of the top crate. It loosens without too much effort, allowing Claudia to fit her small fingers into the gap and wrench the lid off.

She's so strong. My nostrils flare; her light sheen of sweat fills this enclosed space with her scent. A sudden, unbidden fantasy plays in my mind's eye: Claudia slamming me against the wall, sinking her blunt human teeth into the downy-feathered skin at the base of my neck. My footclaws flex, and heat builds in my core.

No. Stop it. That is hardly professional.

I snap back to the present moment, where Claudia has wasted no time rummaging through the crate to unearth its contents. These items are part of a bulk shipment from a township called Valeria, so each crate is packed with a variety of discrete items bundled in rags.

There's a delicate glass vase, which Claudia holds close to the coral-light to admire. Then a lovely ceramic tea set, glazed emerald green. "It matches your eyes," Claudia murmurs, almost absentmindedly, raising one of the teacups next to my face. My heartbeat trips over itself.

The second crate is crammed with protective reed tubes that contain rolled-up paintings, poetry collections, and biographical stories. Claudia searches the bottom of that crate but finds not a single charcoal pencil.

Then Claudia opens the third crate, and pulls out...a sculpture.

It's about the size of her forearm, carved and lovingly polished from what appears to be some kind of gemstone. The shape is cylindrical and gently curved. Both ends are rounded smooth, with one end rather wider than the other. In the coral's glow, it has a crystalline glimmer, although its surface is smooth to the touch. Claudia runs her palm up and down it thoughtfully, and my heart nearly stops.

"What do you suppose this is?" she murmurs. "Rather abstract, isn't it?"

My throat constricts. All I can utter is a faint growl that sounds more like a squeak. I know *exactly* what that is. I have a few just like it, hidden in a box under my bed.

Seeing Claudia run her hands over it like that is *doing things* to me. Things I am not accustomed to have happen around other people, whether human or dinosaur.

As she smooths her fingers over the bulbous end, it suddenly seems to click. She bursts out laughing. "Oh, you have got to be kidding me. They donated *this* to a library?"

"We get all kinds of donations," I choke out. "Not all of them end up on display."

Claudia smirks at me. "I'm surprised they didn't want to keep it for private use."

"Most likely, they did." My feathers prickle with embarrassment. "Donations like this are usually left to the library when the original artist passes away and their family chooses not to keep their creations as family heirlooms."

Claudia drops the crystal phallus back into the crate as if it's bitten her. But then she laughs again. "There are some things we don't need to know about our dear departed grandparents. Oh, here! I found something!"

The crate has yielded a stray charcoal stub, probably broken off from the pencil they were using to scratch DONATION on the outside. It's only about the size of Claudia's thumbnail.

She empties one of the pouches of coral food, pinches the charcoal between her fingers, and bends close to shape her letters onto the cloth.

After a moment, she holds it up for my inspection. *HELP. OPEN DOOR,* it reads in blocky, smudgy print.

I nod. "That'll do."

She stuffs the cloth under the crack in the door, then dusts off her hands. "And now, I suppose, we wait."

MINERVA

We're silent for a few minutes. Claudia busies herself with repacking the donation crates, taking care to rewrap everything in rags. When that's done, she finds a spot of bare wall to lean against, her knees up to her chest. I fold myself into a roost, needing the comfort. It's getting harder to ignore my surroundings now that I don't have the task of looking through the crates to focus on.

"Hey," Claudia says. "Are you well? You seem...uncomfortable."

"Obviously, this cupboard isn't where I intended to spend the rest of my day," I say acidly.

"No, it's more than that." She gives me a considering look. "You really freaked out when the door locked behind us. You were trying to bust it down with your bare claws."

I shuffle my arm feathers, looking anywhere but into her eyes. "I don't like enclosed spaces."

"But you were needling *me* about being afraid of the dark?" Claudia lifts an eyebrow, her smile telling me it's a gentle tease. "You were right, by the way. I may be a big, strong, brave adventurer, but I can't stand having four walls and a ceiling separating me from the sky. Makes me want to break down the door, too."

Trailing one claw through the crack in the floor stones, I say, "Many of my people have a deep hatred of being caged. I've gotten comfortable living inside human buildings, but it's the locked door that terrifies me. It's like…" The words bubble out before I can stop them. "It reminds me of a time when I was a child. My siblings locked me in a farmer's vegetable cellar. I was there for days before someone found me."

Claudia's jaw drops. "Minerva…"

I turn my head away from her. If there's one thing I can't stand, it's being pitied.

But turning away from the light toward the locked door makes my muscles tense up. Reluctantly, I turn back.

Claudia's not even looking at me. She's examining her left hand, holding it up to the light. "Wanna know how I got this scar?"

"Was it embarrassing?"

"Totally," she says, flashing a grin. "You see, there was this beach covered in razor-sharp shells, and three hapless explorers who didn't see the spinosaurus fishing around the bend until it was too late…"

Claudia launches into recounting a series of mishaps. One story blends into another. The cave coral dims low, so I sprinkle it with another helping of dried bugs. Claudia hesitates, but I urge her to keep going. Her adventures with her colleagues Cassian and Eudora are riveting, and she has an impeccable sense of comedic timing. Before I know it, we're both laughing.

"I can't believe you thought you needed inspiration for your thirty-year art presentation," I say. "Just write down some of these stories! Not only would the library be proud to display them, but I'm sure you could get the microraptors over at Balexonia Press to distribute them for the public. People love funny travel memoirs."

But Claudia shakes her head, fiddling with the end of her braid. "I don't know. I don't have much of a filter when it comes to my stories. What if people think they're too vulgar?"

I sit up on my haunches. "Most people? They'll *love* that."

"Not my family." Claudia swallows hard. "For my twenty, I wrote an erotic poem for a woman I was infatuated with at the time, and my parents...they didn't like it. They said I was *crass* and *an embarrassment.* They complained that their friends in Rume society were talking about how they hadn't raised me as a proper lady. So..." She lets out a long, heartfelt sigh. "I left. Started picking up mercenary work in different towns and never went back. Rume didn't want me as I was, but I couldn't change for them."

Now it makes sense why she didn't seem interested in presenting her thirty-year project to her township first. "Family," I mutter. "Always our worst critic."

"Tell me about it." Claudia sighs again. "You didn't see any wine in those crates? I don't usually talk about this sober."

"I don't talk about my family at all," I say, examining my foreclaws. "But if it makes you feel better..." My breath comes short. I can't believe I'm about to tell this story to another sentient being. "I used to love taking long hunting trips in the forest. Deer and rabbits, of course," I add hastily, "not humans. Anyway, remember my awful siblings who locked me in the cellar? They were my half-siblings, in truth. Mother had me much later. I came from a different mating than the one that produced their clutch. They didn't see me as a real nestmate, only as a competitor for Mother's time. They killed the rest of my clutch in their eggs, but I survived because my egg rolled underneath the hay." Deep breath in. Out. "One day, when I went hunting, my siblings followed me. They attacked. I only escaped because a tyrannosaur heard the commotion and came looking for an easy kill. We all ran, them in one direction, me in another. I never stopped running until I made it to the city. I was barely out of my adolescence."

Even my fellow librarians have no idea. I never told them that I lived in the temple poorhouse for weeks, shunned by humans and herbivores alike, until my daily wanderings took me into the library. I remember how enchanted I was by the peaceful gardens out front, the glimmering glass windows of the reading room. I remember thinking, *My family will never look for me here.*

By the following week, I'd talked myself into my first job running errands and reshelving manuscripts.

"Smart move," Claudia says, when I pause for breath. "You're probably right. Boneheads like your siblings would never be caught dead in this place. Even if they did attack you here, lawkeeping is a lot more strict in the city than in rural townships. If they think putting you in the cellar was torture, imagine how they'll like prison."

"I'm sorry," I mumble. Now that I've blabbed everything, shame washes over me in sickening waves. "I shouldn't have dumped all that. I don't know why I—"

"I started it," Claudia says ruefully. "Hey. Minerva. Look at me."

She scoots closer, reaching out a hand to touch my arm lightly. It's just a bare brush of fingers against feathers, but the tingling spreads through my whole body.

"Bad shit happens to people." Claudia's gazing into my eyes now, nose inches from the tip of my snout. "To me, to you, to everybody. I promise, this doesn't make me think less of you. The opposite, in fact. You're a survivor. A fighter, except your weapon is knowledge." Her smile is slightly crooked. "Me, I just use regular old knives and crossbows."

I let her hand run down the length of my arm to take hold of my clawed one. "Don't let your small-minded township stop you from writing," I say. Even a whisper feels loud in this intimate space between us.

She leans closer. I breathe in her scent, heart pounding...

And then the door flies open, letting in a rush of cool air. Claudia jerks backward. I surge to my feet, nostrils flaring in a relieved gasp.

"What is this?" Alexander brandishes the HELP note, badly smudged from being shoved under the door. "What were you doing in here, Min—oh, gods, is that a *patron?*" He narrows his eyes at Claudia. "Hang on, you were the one who disappeared on me earlier. Were you two—"

"Kissing," says Claudia breezily.

I gasp my outrage. "We were *not*. I was trying to show her where the coral food was, and my tail—"

"Oh, don't be shy, sweetheart." Claudia runs a hand across the downy feathers on my cheek. I *shiver*.

"She's joking," I tell Alexander sternly. "Do not believe a word she says."

He gives me a suspicious look. "Well, escort her out," he says. "Sundown is in twenty minutes, and we're about to start clearing the stacks."

I chuff through my nostrils, prickling all over with embarrassment and something else. Something uncomfortably like *arousal.*

Maybe half of why I'm so indignant about Claudia's lie is that I wish it weren't one.

CLAUDIA

STARING AT THE WOODEN BEAMS OF AN UNFAMILIAR CEILING THAT NIGHT, LISTENING to the murmur of voices through the inn walls, I can't stop thinking about Minerva.

She's got the most gorgeous feather patterning I've ever seen—sapphire blue streaked with reds and greens. And those *eyes*, greener than the shallow sea, sharp and perceptive, and the way she watched me when she thought I wasn't paying attention...

That's a lady who *begs* to be teased. Whose outrage sparks like desire, whose annoyance feels like flirtation. I always did pine for the princess type, and she's not just a princess, she's a *queen.* The way I'd worship her, if she'd let me...

Restless and horny, I toss my covers off and reach for the cup of water on the nightstand. Then I change my mind and pull my pack toward me. I rummage to find the oilcloth-wrapped wooden box containing my precious letter-writing supplies: wood-pulp paper and charcoals. An expensive luxury on the road, but it was the only way I had left to connect with my brother.

He'd been my only supporter during that last, awful fight with my parents. They may have been embarrassed by my earthy humor and lack of verbal filter, but Demetrius loved my poetry. Even after he wed a sweet local girl who may as well have been tailored for him at a shop called Appease-

Your-Parents Bespoke Marriage Prospects, he never stopped sending me letters and eagerly encouraging me to write back.

It's already been weeks since my last missive. I owe him another, but it's with a wider audience in mind that I flatten out a sheet of paper on the wobbly nightstand. I whittle my charcoal pencil to a fine point, pull the candle closer, and begin to write.

MINERVA

THE DOOR OF MY SCRIPTORIUM SLAMMING OPEN STARTLES ME ENOUGH TO DASH A catastrophic blot across the page I've just spent fifteen minutes transcribing. I whirl toward the intruder, a threat to bite Alexander's head off on the tip of my tongue, but it's not the junior librarian. It's Claudia.

My heart misses a step and tumbles down my ribcage.

"Look at this!" She's grinning ear to ear, brandishing a sheaf of the kind of flimsy paper people use for pigeon messages. Her fingers are smudged up to the first knuckle in charcoal dust. There's a smear of the stuff across her cheek.

"Might I remind you that patrons are *still* not allowed in this room?" I say waspishly.

Claudia ignores me. "I wrote the full story of my encounter with the spinosaurus on the beach. And as I was writing, I thought of at least three more stories I could write down. I just imagined I was telling them to my brother, or to you, and the words wouldn't stop coming! Talking it through yesterday made it all make sense. I've always loved writing. Cassian and Eudora and my brother tell me I'm good at it. I can't believe I let my parents get in my head for so long. Who cares if they think I'm embarrassing? I'm going to write a travel memoir so juicy that they'll never be able to show their faces in town again."

I can't stay annoyed when her brown eyes sparkle this way. "And to think, you found all that inspiration in a closet full of dead worms."

"Don't forget the crystal phallus," says Claudia mischievously. "I found that item *very* inspirational."

My feathers prickle. I shake myself, trying to convince them to lay flat again. "Does this mean you'll be staying at the Great Library for awhile yet?"

Claudia shuffles her papers, her small flat teeth denting her lower lip. "Actually, I was hoping to ask a favor. My penmanship isn't so great." She shows me her charcoal scribbles. It's not the worst handwriting I've ever seen—local officials whose job it is to record important documents seem to love writing in barely decipherable scrawl—but it doesn't even approach aesthetically pleasing. "I noticed your lovely script yesterday. Do you think you could teach me some of your tricks? When I bind this all together into a book, I want it to look nice."

I'm alarmed at how quickly I want to say yes. My copy queue grows by the day. Burning any amount of daylight on tutoring a patron's penmanship would have sounded like an egregious waste of my time yesterday morning.

But then I spent hours in a closet with this woman. Somehow, her stories, her scent, her eyes, and her laugh have overridden all reason. She occupies my mind as thoroughly as crumbling historical texts usually do.

"Meet me in the reading room one hour before sunset," I tell her.

She grins, and my heart stutters again.

CHAPTER
FOUR

ONE WEEK LATER

As soon as the light streaming through the scriptorium window starts to dim toward dusk, I clean my pens and close my inkwell. Excitement fizzes like fermented fruit in my stomach. It's time.

For the past week, I've been saving the last hour of daylight to help Claudia with her writing. It's quickly becoming the hour I look forward to the most.

Alexander smirks as I pass him on the stairs. "Time to visit your sweetheart, eh, Minnie?"

I make sure to "accidentally" whip him with the end of my tail as I pass.

Cresting the stairs, I pause as always to admire the vaulted reading room on the top floor of the library. With four glass walls providing a stunning view of the city, the reading room is this building's main tourist attraction. The room's natural lighting is great for reading, but the constant murmur of visitors violating the quiet-room rule and getting shushed ruins it for me.

The reading desks in the middle of the room are suffused with the golden glow of oncoming sunset. Most of the guest patrons are glued to the windows, *ooohing* and *ahhhing* at the brilliant horizon.

But at a desk in the corner, scribbling away like the most dedicated scholar, there's Claudia.

Her knee is bouncing as she skims over her last few pages, checking her own work. I watch her finger trace lines across the page as she reads. A triumphant smile tugs at the corner of her mouth. Something twists low in my stomach. Like hunger, but not quite...

When she looks up and meets my gaze, her eyes light up in a way that only intensifies my craving. She waves me over and holds up the page she's working on to display her work.

A beautifully bawdy illumination sketch, depicting a human man and a pterosaur engaged in a romantic embrace, takes up the top half of the page. The lower half is covered with Claudia's much-improved script, using quality ink instead of smudgy charcoal. If I'm not mistaken, this is her finished copy of the story of the time that her friend Cassian and his wife Eudora had their clothing stolen by a rodent looking to line its nest. It still needs color—I don't lend my precious colored inks to anyone else, not even Claudia—but her drawing is quite skillful. Good enough to make my feathers prickle when I get close enough to see the details she's drawn.

"Oh *my*." If I could blush like a human, my skin would be tomato red. "That's...ah...very passionate."

Claudia sucks on her lower lip, holding the drawing out to cast a critical eye over her work. "Is it too much?"

"The presses won't be able to print fast enough," I say firmly, pushing down my embarrassed reaction. There's no law against erotic artwork, and it is, in fact, one of the more popular art forms in Balexonia. My shyness around mating-related topics is a product of my own inexperience, and I refuse to shame Claudia the way her family did.

She flashes me a smile that's genuinely flattered and also ever-so-slightly sly.

"Wait. Are you teasing me?" I demand. "I am not above eating a human, however tame you might think I—"

"I'm counting on it," Claudia purrs.

I hiss in a breath, blood rushing south. A couple of the traitorous feathers on my neck stand up before I shake them back down. "You can't say things like that to me in public!"

"Why not?" She reaches out and deliberately draws a line down one of my arm feathers with her soft fingers. My skin feels electrically charged. Preening is intensely familial and, between dinosaurs not bonded by blood, is considered a romantic overture akin to a human kiss.

If she's close friends with a pterosaur, I have a feeling she knows this already.

"I had a different idea for tonight," Claudia says. Her tone stays low and sultry. "What if, instead of working on the project tonight, we go out for a drink? I found a bar a few blocks away that accommodates all species."

I gulp. This is very clearly a date invitation. I've been both hoping for and dreading the moment Claudia asks ever since the two of us were trapped in that closet. It's undeniable we're attracted to each other, and yet...

Unlike my mother and siblings, unlike *most* raptors in fact, I've never been interested in casual sex. I'm already considered something of an odd bird for exclusively desiring women. While bisexuality is common in predator cultures, where mature raptrixes tend to hunt and raise young in single-sex groups, not having *any* interest in mating with raptors even during a heat cycle is considered unusual.

But romantic inclinations are even more so.

That was the main reason my siblings felt I ought to be destroyed. They believed my shy little crushes were signs of weakness. That my capacity for affection would weaken our mother's family line, even though I protested often that I had no interest in procreating. Certainly not if it meant mating with one of the stupid, brutish raptors who courted my sister during her heat cycles.

I don't want Claudia just for a night. If she's soon to disappear back to her adventures, I'd rather not know what I'm missing. Because I *will* miss her. This last week has been the brightest of my life. I hadn't realized how lonely I still was, even here in the library surrounded by colleagues who respect my work. I've never let any of them *know* me. There's no one I get drinks with after work, and certainly no one I bring home to my little single-room apartment.

If Claudia can't stay, it's better if she just leaves me.

All this emotion stays locked in my throat. Unsurprisingly, my upbringing left me ill-equipped to communicate my feelings.

Claudia catches the indecision in my long pause, and her face falls. "If you would rather keep this professional, I understand."

Her disappointment stabs me like a knife to the ribs. "I'd love to go out for a drink," I choke out. It doesn't have to be anything more than that, does it?

CLAUDIA

I *KNOW* I'M NOT MISREADING THE CURRENT OF LUST THAT'S BEEN BREWING BETWEEN us. I know when a woman wants me. I *especially* know what it looks like when she thinks she shouldn't want me and does anyway. I can't count all the times I've been cast as the bad girl, the unsavory element tempting well-mannered young maidens to misbehave.

Except I don't think that's quite what's bothering Minerva. I also don't think it's the fact that I'm human. I've caught her checking me out from across the table enough times to be sure of that. No, it's something else that holds her back, even as the pupils of her eyes dilate when she watches me walk.

I can't imagine what she's waiting for. I've been trying to seduce her for a week. It usually doesn't take this long—most of the time, I have a girl in the palm of my hand (in more ways than one) by day three. My ego's taking a bit of a hit here.

I'm also running out of excuses to keep asking her for help. My penmanship has already improved massively, especially since she lent me some proper pens. Charcoals are hard to write neatly with. Plus, with Minerva's help, I've started using the drawing skills Cassian taught me for a whole new purpose: illustration. I never thought the pictures of my companions I liked to sketch by firelight would interest anyone—I usually just fed them to the fire, unless Eudora noticed and rescued them for "sentimental reasons." My parents never let me read books with pictures, so it never occurred to me that art could be part of a story.

I took the three stories I've completed so far to show the microraptors at Balexonia Press yesterday morning. Just as Minerva predicted, their acquiring manager, Scipio, bubbled over with excitement at the prospect of publishing them. He was fairly jumping up and down on his perch when I spread them out on the desk.

I'd promised he could buy the rights to print them, but only if he helped me make two bound copies of my collected stories. One to donate to the Great Library...and one to send home.

My parents will probably burn it. I don't care. I want them to know who I am now. I want them to know that I'm proud and happy, even if they hate it.

I turn my head to look at Minerva again. Although she could easily outpace me with her powerful thighs, she keeps her gait slow at my side as we weave through the evening crowd on the streets. The wind flutters through her feathers and lifts the hem of her toga. Her chatelaine jingles when she moves, as elegant as any fine lady's jewelry. She holds her tail politely steady, careful not to hit any passersby.

We round the corner to the multispecies bar, and I groan. There's a line snaking out the front, all the way down the street. It must be payday, when the Ruling Council officials hand out everyone's weekly living allowance.

Balexonia City works differently than the rural towns. Most people work trades here, just like farmers and smiths and lumberjacks, but a great number of city-dwellers are employed as artists, philosophers, and other bureaucratic jobs (like librarians) that don't easily translate to payment. As such, the Ruling Council provides every citizen with small, basic lodgings and a weekly handful of coins for food and necessities. Payday often leads to a splurge, especially at food stalls and breweries.

As we pass the large double doors, I crane my neck to peek inside. The barn-sized building is packed tight with dozens of species. A brontosaurus leans their long neck in through a window to sip from a bucket-sized tankard, while long tables are hip-to-hip with human patrons. I spot a couple of stegosauruses and triceratops lined up at the bar drinking through straws, while tiny microraptors sit between the spikes on their backs and sip from shot glasses. A parasaurolophus draped in a tasseled shawl croons a haunting melody. Up in the rafters, a flight of pterosaurs gnaw on a plate of what are hopefully plain old non-sentient chicken legs. (Eudora has informed me in no uncertain terms that it is extremely insulting to suggest that this might constitute cannibalism.)

This isn't exactly what I had in mind when I pictured taking Minerva out. I was thinking a table to ourselves, dim light, a drink or three, and then...

"Looks a little busy tonight," Minerva calls over the noise of the crowd.

"Yeah." I grimace. "On second thought, shall we go somewhere else?"

"I know just the place," says Minerva.

Exactly what a traveler loves to hear from a local. I smile. "Lead the way!"

She waves me toward a side street. Trotting to keep up with her powerful stride, I follow her down side streets and narrow alleys until we arrive in a lovely wooded park with gravel-lined paths.

"If we hurry, we can catch the tail end of the sunset!" she urges. I break into a jog, just about keeping pace with the tail she holds high and steady behind her. The footpath winds through a grove of trees, passing a large open-air gymnasium field scattered with weights and exercise toys for dinosaurs of various body shapes and sizes. Finally, the path ends in a circular track around what's either a large pond or a small lake.

There are a handful of people enjoying the sunset's reflection on the water. Mostly couples, I notice, watching two humans interlock their hands, and a woman loop her arm around a triceratops' neck.

"I come here a lot during the warm season," Minerva murmurs, folding her legs into a roosting posture on the lakeshore. I sit next to her, close but not quite touching. "At lunch hour, it's much more crowded. Children everywhere. At night, though...it gets so beautifully quiet."

"Is it safe to be here in the dark?" I ask. "No cave corals to light our way."

Minerva chuckles low in her throat. "I've never worried about my own safety—I'm the most dangerous thing here." She tilts her head, her eye twinkling at me. "Who better to find their way in the forest at night than a crepuscular hunter?"

My heartbeat quickens. There's a little thrill of fear, chased with excitement. "Am *I* safe?"

She pauses before replying, "I'm hurt that you have to ask."

"What if I don't want to be safe?" I whisper, leaning closer. I repeat the preening touch I gave her earlier, sliding my clawed fingers through the feathers fanning from her arm. "What if I want this crepuscular hunter to catch me? To..." I drop my voice and lean close to the downy feathers that protect her earholes. "*Eat* me?"

She pauses so long that I think I might've finally overstepped and ruined everything. Then she murmurs, "Don't flirt with me unless you mean it."

"Of course I—"

"I don't just mean finding me attractive," she says, her words tripping over each other. "I mean..."

"Feelings," I finish, when Minerva trails off. I place my hand on her cheek, fingers trailing trustingly close to sharp-toothed jaws, and turn her face so that she's forced to meet my gaze. "You mean feelings."

Closing my eyes, I press a lingering close-mouthed kiss to the tip of her snout.

I feel Minerva go utterly still. When I open my eyes, she's staring at me with a wretchedly hopeful expression.

"I can't be other than I am," I whisper, leaning my forehead against the side of her face. "I hate the city, and Cassian and Eudora are out there waiting for me. But I don't want to walk away and never see you again." Raising my head, I smirk at her. "You're a bossy, persnickety, maddening raptrix, but to be honest, I'm even worse. I've no doubt you'll tire of me. But until you do, I promise to come visit for at least a few days out of the month. Because you, Minerva Deftclaw, are the sort of woman one rearranges her life for."

Softly, Minerva reaches out. Her claws hook in the tie at the end of my braid, pulling it off. Working from the bottom, she preens my braid until my hair hangs loose, at which point she pulls me close and rakes both hands through the long, thick, dark mass that I'm far too vain to cut. Her nostrils flare as she scents my scalp.

I dig my fingers into the soft, downy feathers that line her neck and chest. Then I lean forward and bury my face in it, inhaling her scent in return. She smells of ink and dust and the wild tang of rainstorms in summer.

The sun has dipped all the way below the horizon, and the last stragglers begin to wander away. We're nearly alone, but Minerva still rises to her feet and pulls me with her.

"We can go back to my place," I murmur, still nuzzling her neck. "The inn's not the most private, but—"

"I have a better idea," Minerva says. Her voice is a low rasp that sets my skin tingling. "You said you don't mind a little danger, yes?"

"Mm-hmm..."

Her lips, her teeth, are so close to my ear that I can feel the huff of her breath. "My people are hunters. This holds true for our mating rituals as well. When we claim someone...we like to make a game of catching them first." She chuckles low in her throat. "In a traditional pairing, a raptor chases, and a raptrix flees. But I've never been very traditional."

My heart thuds faster. Gods, I've never been so aroused in my life. "Are you telling me to run?" I manage to ask.

"I'm telling you that if I catch you—" Minerva drops her voice very low, the barest hiss of a whisper. "I'll *eat* you."

"Not if I eat you first." I dart in close and bite her on the side of the neck, just very lightly. In my admittedly limited experience with dinosaur women, that move always sends them feral.

Minerva is no exception. Her head drops low, her body gathering into a coiled bundle ready to spring. I let out a taunting laugh, stepping a few paces away from her, though my body clamors to keep touching...

And I run.

MINERVA

No scent has ever intoxicated me like Claudia's sweat on the night breeze. While I wait for her to get a fair a head start, my body trembling with the urge to chase, I dart behind a tree and divest myself of my toga and chatelaine. Clothes will only slow me down.

It's been too long since I came to this park at night and just let myself run. The energy builds up inside me, a sweet ache not unlike the urge to mate. The moment I can no longer hold back, I unleash the hunting instinct in my taut muscles. Springing forward into a sprint pushes my body to a glorious burn.

My feet pound into the soft groundcover. Despite the vicious power my body contains, I can keep near-silent when I want to. Claudia can't say the same. Even far ahead of me, I can hear her breath growing ragged. Her scent intensifies with the heat she's giving off. I let her catch a hint or two of my pursuit—a cracked twig, a rustle as I leap over a bush.

She changes direction. I chuff with satisfaction. She's now heading right where I want her.

In a far-back corner of the park lie the remains of an old gazebo that was abandoned after a tree fell and destroyed its roof. Over the years, a shelter of bramble vines enclosed its sides, all but hiding the structure from view. I discovered it years ago on one of my late-night runs, and have kept it my little secret.

I herd Claudia directly into its dead-end embrace. Her exclamation of frustration when she finds her way blocked by the vines sends a thrill of arousal through me. I approach, not bothering to mask the sound of my movement. Savoring the sight of her, panting and emanating the most delicious scent, cornered in a trap.

"You knew this was here," she accuses. "You tricked me."

I chuckle deep in my throat, letting her see my teeth in an imitation of a human smile. My powerful leg muscles coil for a jump.

I pounce.

Claudia buckles and falls, catching herself on her elbows as I loom over her. There's a tang of fear in her scent now, shamefully delicious. I don't *really* want her to fear me. But the pretense of being a predator is...

Well, I've never been so turned on in my life.

"Clothes off," I rasp, "or I'll rip them."

A spark of arousal lights her eyes. In the dim, I catch the bright flash of her smile. "Yes, madam librarian."

She has her suspenders down and blouse over her head in the blink of an eye, baring her small unbound breasts. Lifting her hips, she wriggles her trousers down, then gives a breathless, high-pitched laugh as they get caught on her boots.

I bend and catch one of her bootlaces in my teeth, pulling the knot loose with a twist of my head. As my claws work the tightened laces loose, I repeat the motion with the other knot. She toes the boots off and shimmies the trousers after them, and then she lies before me utterly nude.

Such delicate, smooth skin with barely a fuzz of hair to protect it should make a human vulnerable. The part of me titillated by the predator/prey roleplay loves having her sprawled below me with nothing to protect her. And yet, at the same time, I marvel at how someone can contain the fierceness of a tyrannosaur, the adventuring spirit of a pterosaur, and the cunning of, yes, a velociraptor, all within the compact, beautiful form of a human woman. She embraces her earthy humor and rakish ways like no woman I've ever met. She writes with an empathetic yet humorous under-standing of humanity I can only dream of.

There's no denying it anymore. I'm falling in love with Claudia.

Just as I'm thinking it, she reaches up and strokes the downy feathers of my cheek. "Gods, you're beautiful," she whispers.

The predator/prey pretense melts away. She pierces right through the armor of sharp teeth and claws, seeing straight into the soft parts of me that long to be cherished. I drag my claws through her loose hair, wishing I could nip and bite her neck as many saurians do to show affection. I don't want to hurt her, though, so instead I dart out my tongue and lick the side of her neck.

She shivers and lets out a soft moan. Heat drenches my core to hear her vocalize her pleasure. I want *more*.

I flick my tongue against her nipples, working my way down to the patch of hair between her legs. She arches her back and gasps, "Have you— have you been with a human before?"

"No," I say. "I may have read some erotic texts, however..."

She laughs, then moans again. "You're...ahhh...going to have to show me where the library hides those."

"As it happens, I have my own...personal collection."

Claudia rakes her fingers down my chest, her eyes on fire. "Now I'm even *more* interested in seeing these texts."

"Allow me to demonstrate what I've learned." I dip my head back down, then pause. "You will tell me if something feels wrong?"

"Of course." Claudia strokes me again. "And when something feels *right. Ohhhhh.*" As my tongue finds the source of her musky scent, her voice trails into a breathy gasp.

My extensive perusal of erotic literature featuring human women has informed me that, while they enjoy penetration, the way to drive them truly wild is to find a small pleasure nub that rests just above their opening. As I explore her sex with my tongue, Claudia's hips move, tilting up as if to encourage me in the right direction. I know I've found the right spot when she lets out a short, high-pitched cry and begs, "There, there, please, more."

I'm unused to using my mouth for such a delicate task. A velociraptor's maw is made for pain, not pleasure. Yet her joyous cries are so fucking sweet and delicious, her flavor a sensual wine I would prefer to any other, that I apply myself with the same precision that I've trained for my scriptorial work. Claudia's cries become louder, until I'm almost afraid someone will come investigate. And for some reason that turns me on even more, imagining some hapless human or dinosaur stumbling into our grotto and watching the absolute magic we're making. Claudia wet and trembling under my tongue, her smooth pale skin glowing in the moonlight, and I the lucky predator who gets to feast on such a perfect woman.

"Minerva, I'm going to come, please don't stop—"

I keep lapping at her nub until she convulses under me, fragrant moisture seeping from her opening. She pulls me close, kissing and biting my neck, and I'm startled by how desperate I am for the contact.

In fact…I pause briefly to catch my breath, huffing out my nostrils as I take stock of my body. My cloaca clenches in heated longing. My feathers have been standing on end for some time, a mating display to impress potential partners. My scent has grown sweeter, barely detectable to other species but irresistible to velociraptor males.

I've gone and triggered a heat cycle.

"Curse it," I pant.

Claudia lifts her head. "Minerva? Are you well?"

With a short laugh, I say, "Too well," and quickly explain.

"That's hot," is Claudia's reaction. She pulls me close, reaching for the base of my tail, where my opening burns for her touch. "Can I help? When this happened before, what do you do?"

"Hide," I admit, closing my eyes.

"You don't seek out relief?"

I take a deep breath and admit, "I have not mated before."

Her head snaps back up. "*Never?* Minerva, I—"

"It's different from human culture," I say quickly, before she gets tangled up in the frankly ridiculous notion of virginity. "My people don't often mate for partnership reasons. It's a procreational transaction. And when a raptrix goes into heat who doesn't want children, she simply sequesters herself during the cycle and...takes care of it."

Her eyes gleam with interest. "And what do you do to take care of it?"

I huff out a breath. "Read my erotic books, and..."

"And?" Claudia's fingers delve deeper, breaching my opening. "I've been with a few saurians before. You can't come without penetration, can you? How does that work if..."

I groan, then pull away from her to scrabble for the jewelry box I keep hidden deep behind a growth of vines in this secret grotto. I never dare take advantage of it when I'm in a heat cycle, but an outdoor run does excite me, and on occasion it's nice to have an object of self-satisfaction ready when the urge takes me.

Opening the lid, I reveal a phallus with much the same dimensions as the one we found in the storage closet. Mine is polished wood, not crystal, but it's thick and long with just the right amount of curve to hit the sweet spot inside my cloaca that's necessary to get me off.

Claudia hisses out a breath. "Oh, clever girl," she whispers. "I *knew* you figured out what the crystal one was way too quickly."

She runs her hand over its curve, then plucks it from my claws and drags its tip down the side of my flank. She smooths her fingers after it, still imitating partner-grooming in a way that makes my legs feel weak.

"Show me how you like it," she whispers.

I've never been this vulnerable with anyone else. Bracing against the rickety, thorn-choked gazebo railing, I lift my tail and present my opening.

She slides up close behind me and begins to circle my tight cloaca with the thick end of the phallus. "Tell me if there's anything you don't like," she says. One hand sinks into the feathers at the nape of my neck as she slowly presses the toy inside me.

I purr with relief and pleasure. "Please don't stop. Deeper, *faster*."

"Oh, sweetie, you're fucking beautiful," Claudia murmurs in my ear. "You're doing so good. Look how eager you are. Gods, I could eat you up." She bites my shoulder, and I clench involuntarily, my purr turning into a growl.

Then she twists the toy ever so slightly, pushing it in deeper, and she hits the spot that turns my vision to stars. I don't even know what comes out of me after that, but I'm pretty sure it's some embarrassing combination of begging and moans, and all the while Claudia keeps up the dirty praise in my ear.

When she bites me again, this time at the back of my neck next to where she's got her hand fisted in my feathers, I come harder than I ever have in my life.

I sink to the ground, boneless, and Claudia moves with me, wrapping her arms around me and leaning her head into the crook between neck and back as I settle into a roost.

"You're amazing," she says, muffled, her lips pressed to my feathers.

Me? I'm going to be fantasizing about this whole encounter for years. From the chasing, to the eating, to her fucking me from behind while telling me I'm a good and clever girl, she's unwittingly played out a dozen fantasies I didn't even realize I had.

"Ah, the thing about heat cycles, though," I say when I recover enough mental capacity to speak, "is that my scent is going to attract any male velociraptor in a several-mile radius. So I should probably go back to my room and lock the door."

"Mmm." Claudia nuzzles her face into me again. "Can I be with you inside the locked room? Because I have a bunch more ideas I want to try out. Like both of us using that toy at the same time."

"A velociraptor's heat cycle can last up to a week," I warn her. "Do you really want to be trapped with me for..."

"I was already on board. You didn't have to convince me further."

I lunge out of my roost and flip over to pounce on her, raking my tongue down her neck again. "Also, I can go about five rounds in a row without getting tired. *You'll* be exhausted by the time I'm done."

"Oh no, as much sex as I can physically take? How will I suffer this hardship?" Claudia laughs. "Listen, if I die, I die. There are worse ways to go than being...*eaten*...by a velociraptor."

CHAPTER

SIX

CLAUDIA

It's a good thing Minerva has a large stock of pens, ink, and paper in her apartment, because I wouldn't have gotten any work done on my story collection if she didn't.

She has a decent stockpile of food in her cupboards, plus a barrel of water for drinking and bathing, so it's day three before I even have to leave to get supplies. Despite her worries of exhausting me, she actually spends a large amount of time during the day sleeping, while the nights are hot marathons of trying out the various ways two extremely different species can get each other off. I sleep plenty, too, but when I'm awake and she's not, I write.

By the time her scent returns to normal, I've very nearly finished the collection. I take an afternoon off to visit the public baths with her, enjoying a long soak while she rolls around in the dust baths and then settles in for a preening session. Then we both return to the library: Minerva to fret over her ever-growing queue of manuscripts to copy, and I to collect the rest of my writings so I can finally compile the entire volume.

The following day, I wake early to bring the manuscript to Balexonia

Press. Scipio eagerly accepts the thick stack of paper and tells me that the formally bound copies will be ready in a month, after which they can start distributing the individual stories as flimsy paper-bound serials. "We'll put your cut of the profits aside and have it ready for you whenever you visit town," he promises.

"I have a feeling it will be often," I say, ignoring the pang I feel at the idea of leaving Minerva even for a few weeks.

When I get back to the inn, I find a pigeon-message waiting for me. Cassian writes that he and Eudora really miss me and would love to have my company on a new expedition they're planning. They'll be voyaging to some northern island rumored to harbor an endangered population of mammoths. Apparently, they're escorting a team of botanists and biologists with very little experience in the wilds, and they could really use my help protecting the group from any potential predator threats.

They'll be there for three months.

It sounds amazing, and I want to go with almost my whole being... minus my heart. Which I'd be leaving here.

Crumpling the message into my pocket, I gather up the writing supplies that I borrowed from Minerva and head to the library to return them.

Barging into her scriptorium doesn't have the same naughty thrill as it did the first few times. I think wistfully back to our first few interactions, how fun it was to rile her up and make her huff with annoyance. Now, she looks up from her work and her eyes light up, but gods curse it, that's even *better*.

I can't leave.

But I'll be miserable if I stay. Not with her, of course. But I'll regret missing out on another adventure, and I'm afraid that it'll make me start to resent Minerva. Not that she'd ever deserve it.

She deserves a life of peace and safety after all she's been through.

For once, the words won't come. So I simply hand her Cassian's letter and watch as she reads it.

When she's done, she looks up, and the light's gone out of her eyes. Her head feathers droop. "You're leaving."

I cup her cheek with my palm. "Not because I want to. Gods, the last few weeks have been…I don't want you to think I'm running away from you, Minerva, because I'm not. I just…I have to…"

"I understand," she says softly. "This is who you are. Always has been. It shines through in every one of your stories. You love that life. I won't get in the way of your dream."

Closing my eyes, I press a kiss to her forehead. "I'm sorry," I whisper. "I'll come back. I promise."

ONE WEEK LATER

"What happened to you in Balexonia City?" Eudora asks in an undertone. We're watching the biologist team load crates of supplies onto the ship, assisted by a sailor team of hadrosaurs. "You've been weird and quiet since you got back. Is everything all right?"

I've been trying to find the right time to tell Cassian and Eudora about Minerva, but every time I try to explain, the words stick in my throat. I miss her so much, it's almost a physical ache in my chest. Even though all three of us are excited about this journey, I've lain awake every night and thought about running back to the Great Library, breaking into the scriptorium, and throwing myself into her arms.

It'll only be a few months. Then you can go back and see her. Your book will even be done by then. That's what I keep telling myself, but it doesn't soothe the ache at all.

"I'm fine," I mutter.

"Well, if you ever need to talk…" Eudora lets the offer hang for a moment, waiting to see if I'll take her up on it. Then she pats me on the shoulder with her wingclaw.

I heave a sigh and approach the botany team, intending to offer to help load their stuff. If I stay busy, I can't think about Minerva, right?

"Hey there, Rufus," I call to the lead botanist. "Need any help with—"

The stegosaur turns toward me and says, "Oh, hello, Claudia! Yes, this is one of our guides. Claudia, meet our last-minute hire, an artist who's going to be compiling a book of plant species for us. Her name is—"

My jaw drops as Rufus steps out of the way and reveals a familiar feathered form. "*Minerva?*"

Rufus rears his head back in surprise. "You two know each other?"

I'm running to her before I even consciously decide to move. I throw my arms around her neck and bury my face in her feathers, inhaling her ink-and-rain scent. "You're here! *Why* are you here?"

"The city felt too quiet and lonely without you," says Minerva. Her feathered arms pull me in, locking me under her long chin. "I thought I could use a change of pace."

"But..." I pull back to look her in the eye. "You love the city. The library. It's your home. I can't take you away from that."

"You're not. I'm not leaving it forever," Minerva says. "I asked to take a sabbatical. The library is very interested in the work these scientists are doing, and when I pitched the idea of going along as a representative to record the expedition's findings, the head librarian jumped at the opportunity."

"But your copying queue..."

"I put Alexander to work on it," she says mischievously. "He needs to practice his penmanship."

"You know it's not going to be easy," I warn. "The wilds can be danger-ous. Bad weather, choppy water, pred—"

"You were *not* just going to say predators." Minerva glares at me. "I may be a librarian now, but have you forgotten how I grew up? I can defend myself. And anyone else who might be in danger."

"You're right. I'm sorry." I stroke the side of her neck, giddy with relief that she's *here*. For at least three months, we get to be together. After that... who knows?

Plans can be rearranged, after all.

ABOUT MINDI BRIAR

Mindi Briar's favorite book as a child was *Commander Toad in Space*, an early sign that she was destined to become a gigantic nerd.

She lives in the Seattle area with her husband and three cats, two of whom are named after punctuation marks. She will be your friend if you offer tea, or if you want to talk about Star Wars. She is the author of the Halcyon Universe sci-fi romance series.

Find Mindi's books and learn more at mindibriar.com.

THE KINGS' BRIDE

A LORDS OF NIGHT TALE

LISA EDMONDS

CHAPTER ONE

AVELINE

Tears blurred my vision as I ran through the trees. Twigs and branches, left leafless and harsh by winter's chill, slashed at my cheeks, chin, and forehead.

I clenched my jaw and wiped the blood on my sleeve. The gamekeeper and his baying hounds were far enough behind that they might not hear my harsh breathing, but I couldn't hide my scent or the sound of my bare feet crunching through dead leaves. The dogs were closing the distance with terrifying speed. Without any spells or potions, I had no way to prevent them from tracking me—not even a handful of herbs that might confuse them. I'd simply seen a chance to run and taken it.

I wouldn't make it to nearby Rivertown or even out of these woods before the hounds found me, but I refused to be captured without a fight. They might tear me limb from limb, or simply corner me until the game-keeper came to tie me up, throw me over his shoulder, and take me back to Forbright Manor. Which fate would be worse? Probably the latter. Death by hounds would be horrible, but my chains at the manor would certainly lead to a longer, more lingering, more miserable end.

You will not cry, Aveline D'Corsay, I told myself, even as dread and exhaustion made my chest tight and my breathing raspy.

Hot blood trickled down my chin. I'd bitten my lip too hard trying not to make a sound.

You will not cry now, or when the dogs find you, or if the gamekeeper drags you back to Forbright like a freshly slaughtered deer. You will be strong like your mother, so when you see her in the next world you can stand proud and say you were never defeated.

No daughter of Mariane D'Corsay, healer and priestess, would cry because of a man or in the teeth of the beasts he owned.

This deep in the forest, no lights guided my way. Worse, I didn't know this area well, other than the village of Rivertown lay to the south and east. My instincts drove me to run in the direction of the moon. A day shy of fullness, it shone through the barren branches, bright and cold in a nearly cloudless sky. I let it be my beacon away from the manor. Any other destination would be better. A village, a hut, a cave...I would accept any of these as a refuge. Even the river, in whose icy, fast-moving waters I could choose my own end.

The cold had stolen all sensation from my feet and hands. My numb foot caught on something unseen. I fell hard and hit my chest and face on fallen branches.

The forest went silent and still. No baying of hounds. No whistle of wind. No rustle of leaves. Not even my own ragged breaths because all the air had been knocked from my lungs.

Icy terror rolled through my body from my feet to the top of my head.

Nobles the gamekeeper had trained his hounds to go quiet as they closed in on their quarry. Sir Henry Forbright told me so just two nights ago, and he was quite proud of it.

"They course in full throat, naturally," he'd said, toasting me with a goblet of wine as I sat at the dining table to his right, tied hand and foot to a chair. "But I told Nobles I want prey to hear and *feel* the cold silence of death just before the hounds get them. Deer or rabbit, fox or girl, they'll know death has come by the quiet."

I swallowed a sob and scrambled to stand.

Moonlight revealed my bare feet to be bloody messes. Just as well I couldn't feel them. I might lose them to infection or frostbite if I lived. If I didn't live, well, the condition of my feet hardly mattered.

I took off again, limping on my twisted ankle. With this injury, whatever slim chance I'd had of escape had dwindled to nothing.

Ahead, to the left, I caught sight of an enormous dark shape that wasn't trees. Some building made of stone, decaying with age.

I could all but feel the hot breath of the hounds on my back. I veered toward the dark pile of fallen stones without any thought of what I might do if or when I reached it. I simply wanted to run *toward* something instead of away.

Emerging into the clearing, I found a crumbling bridge and beyond it, ruins of a manor now little more than a pile of broken stone and a single tower.

My gut contracted and I stumbled, nearly falling. *Oh, Goddess—please, no.* My desperate run had not brought me to Rivertown, but instead to the cursed ground of Geedhollow, ruins of an old manor built at an ancient crossroads. Unmarked grave of a practitioner of the darkest of dark arts who, according to legend, had been slain by his own unholy beasts. A den of monsters who slept deep in the ruins by day and hunted and ate travelers and foolish thrill-seekers by night. I had seen it only once before during a walk with my mother, from a distance and in daylight.

Twigs and branches snapped behind me. Icy fingers of dread ran down my spine. I glanced over my shoulder. A half-dozen shadows flashed through the trees, heading directly for me.

The hounds. Oh, Goddess, the hounds. Nobles would be right behind them.

With no choice but to run ahead, I gathered my skirts, bit my bloody lip to block out the pain in my ankle, and limped for the ruins.

I made it only a few steps before an enormous weight landed on my back. The hound sank its teeth into my shoulder as it took me to the ground.

With a shriek, I landed on something painfully hard but brittle enough to snap and break under the combined weight of my body and that of the dog. The sound was a kind of meaty crunch. My chin hit something, and liquid—stinking, wet, and cold—splattered my face. My eyes flew open.

I was face-to-bloody-face with a broken skull, its jaw hanging by shreds of tattered flesh. I'd landed on a human carcass—or what remained of one. Another corpse lay a few feet away, this one mostly intact except something had torn out its belly. Horror stole the breath from my lungs.

The dog shook my shoulder in his jaws. Others sank their teeth into my legs. The rest circled me, growling, waiting for their chance to bite and tear. I screamed, the sound high-pitched and full of agony. The bloody skull's mouth gaped as if it screamed along with me.

Goddess, please don't let this poor soul be the last sight I see before I cross the Veil...

Something enormous and snarling slammed into us. The lead hound was suddenly gone, its teeth ripped out of my shoulder. Hot blood sprayed my face—mine or the dog's, I didn't know. The hound's yelp cut off abruptly.

Another impact, and the dogs chewing on my legs were gone too. Yelps, growls, and snarls filled the cold air, along with the stomach-churning sound of breaking bones and ripping flesh. And in the distance, a man shouted in alarm, his words indistinct.

Dizziness threatened to sweep me away. With a groan, I tried to push myself up, intending to get to my knees and then maybe to my feet, but my arms and legs didn't seem to want to obey.

Trembling violently and sick to my stomach, I managed to roll off the corpse. I ended up on my side, where I could finally see what was happening around me.

My breathless scream died in my throat.

Forbright's prized hounds lay in pieces, scattered across the grass around two enormous black beasts more than twice the size of oxen. The last two dogs died in the monsters' jaws, their crushed bodies flung aside with chilling snarls that sounded like they came from the bowels of Hell itself.

One beast took off into the forest in pursuit of Nobles, whose shadowy form was crashing through the undergrowth back in the direction of

Forbright Manor. The other turned to stare at me, its eyes glowing bright red.

My chest heaved with shallow, ragged breaths. A sudden ringing in my ears nearly drowned out all other sounds. Darkness closed in, but I fought to stay awake.

I didn't want to be eaten. I didn't want my bones to lie on this bloody frozen ground until I decayed to nothing, like these unfortunate men who'd ventured into Geedhollow for unknown reasons and become a meal.

For a moment, just a moment, I wished I'd walked past that unlocked window and waited for another chance. Maybe one would have come tomorrow, or next week, or a month or a year from today. Or never. But I wouldn't be here, bloody and alone, staring into the eyes of a hellbeast.

Hard on the heels of that thought came a stab of shame. I wouldn't regret my decision, even now. I would *not*. Courage had driven me from the manor tonight, not cowardice or foolhardiness. The courage that had coursed through my mother's veins ran through mine as well, and no woman of our line would succumb to fear—especially at the end.

The creature returned from the forest at a thundering gallop that reverberated through the frozen ground. From its jaws, it dropped something heavy and round that rolled to a stop at the other's feet: Nobles's head, his expression frozen in terror.

The hounds' deaths sickened me. They had been trained from birth to hunt and kill on command and had never known anything else. It was not their fault, but they had killed people before and could not be cured of their bloodlust.

Nobles, on the other hand, could burn for all eternity. My only regret was that he seemed to have died quickly.

The monsters approached, heads lowered and nostrils flaring, their thick black fur matted with blood.

While their heads and faces reminded me most of wolves, they were not lupine. Their scythe-like incisors and sharp teeth appeared designed for tearing flesh and their claws were terrifyingly long, like those of a bear or wolverine. Strangest of all, each had a pair of long, curled horns reminiscent of rams. Each horn bore a gold ring. One of the horns on the beast closest to me had been broken off halfway.

My breaths gurgled in my chest and my side ached. I might have broken ribs. And surely my legs were mangled, and my shoulder too, and frostbite might have claimed my feet and hands. I certainly couldn't feel them anymore.

Even so, I didn't give up, and I didn't look away, even as the monster with the broken horn came within biting distance of my face. Its hot breath smelled of viscera.

The beasts wore thick gold chains around their massive necks. From each dangled a round amulet made from black stone carved with runes I didn't recognize. Were these monsters the familiars of some sorcerer or wizard?

With a numb, bloody hand, I reached up to clutch my own amulet before remembering my mother's precious gift to me still lay in Forbright's fireplace where he'd thrown it. My arm fell back to my side.

The monster with a broken horn crouched beside me. I raised my chin and met the creature's glowing gaze.

"I hope you choke on me," I rasped. "And may my flesh leave you hungrier than you were when you found me."

The other beast raised an enormous paw larger than my head. Gore dripped from its claws. I braced for a killing blow.

Instead, all my pain receded and soft warmth washed over me, banishing the cold. I exhaled in a long sigh. *Thank you, Goddess.* She had granted me a gentle death, at least. Soon I would be at my mother's side, at peace, and beyond Henry Forbright's reach forever.

I slipped away into the dark.

VOSTEN

Our bride has come.

We knew her by her sweet and fiery scent even before we touched her, before she looked on us with defiance and without fear.

And when the chains around our necks broke, the warlock's curse lifted and we became men once more. Our long nightmare and loneliness finally came to an end.

Sitting naked on the blood-splattered grass next to my broken chain, I cradle the human woman who has freed us and marvel at her beauty, her strength, her perfection—even as I rage at her terrible wounds and wish I could slaughter the hounds and their master again and again and again until all my fury is spent.

Her long hair is the color of the richest tea, her skin soft and fair, her strong body forged by hard work. She wears a fine gown, but it is ill-fitting, as if it is not her own. She is also painfully thin and smells of suffering. Her wrists and ankles show signs of having been bound with rope. This beauty has been kept as a prisoner, perhaps by whoever sent these hounds after her.

My brother cups her poor bloody feet in his trembling hands. Her eyelashes flutter and she moans. Thank the Goddess, she does not wake. We must take her home and tend to her injuries, but I am transfixed.

"Vosten," my brother rasps. We have not used our own voices in centuries. His eyes reflect the same awe and disbelief that fill my heart. "Is this real? Am I dreaming?"

My voice is just as rough when I say, "No, we are not asleep."

Gently, I kiss her forehead. Toved does the same and lets his lips linger on her skin.

She sighs in contentment despite her injuries and the horrors of the hounds' attack. Is it possible she knows she is now safe in our arms? I hope so, with all my heart.

Toved rises. I do the same, careful not to cause her more pain by jostling her too much. She is a treasure, a wonder.

"Nothing will ever harm her again," my brother growls. "I swear it on my life."

"As do I," I say, and the vow is solemnized.

Toved picks up the heavy chain necklaces that imprisoned us. "We should take these cursed chains with us and keep them hidden away," he says, his eyes dark with pain and anger. "No one else should suffer as we have suffered."

"Bring them," I tell him. "And let us go home."

Toved and I walk side-by-side past the ruins that sheltered us for so long. Our steps are uneven and ungainly. Our bodies struggle to relearn how to move in this form. We have not walked on two legs for what feels like eons. I am glad to no longer have monstrous claws or a furry hide, but my bare skin feels alien and strangely vulnerable.

Toved stumbles and curses. "How long will it take for us to remember how to be men instead of beasts?" he asks.

I do not know, but I *will* remember. An elder brother must always be strong, even if he is older only by minutes.

"Our people need us to be men," I tell him. "And our bride needs us as well. So we will find our way as best we can, as quickly as we can." I nod at the woman in my arms. "By caring for her and listening to our hearts, we will find our way."

I say it with certainty, so he accepts it. He knows I keep my word.

The bridge beyond the ruins has refused us passage since the warlock laid the curse upon us, but now as ourselves we will be able to cross its threshold and go home. My heart warms for the first time in centuries.

And someday if this fearless beauty will have us as her beloved *sulhai*, perhaps even her husbands, all our long years of suffering will have been worthwhile.

Our bride has come.

CHAPTER

THREE

AVELINE

I dreamed of unending comforts and tender care.

Gentle hands bathed me in hot water, dried my body and hair, and tended to my wounds. Low voices little more than rumbles ebbed and flowed through the darkness. Strong arms cradled me against a warm chest and then settled me into furs so soft and deep that the mere thought of ever leaving this bed made me weep.

Someone dabbed away my tears and pressed their warm lips to my forehead not once but twice, each kiss as gentle as the brush of a feather.

Cool water passed my lips, and warm broth, and herbal medicines. Sharp pains, lingering aches, fever, and chills came and went in turns, all muted by the medicines, hot or cold baths, cool cloths, and the comfort of the furs in which I lay.

Most soothing of all was the strange but wonderful sensation of lying nestled between two enormous bodies who smelled like warm stone and cradled me as if I were a child.

I'd never in my life felt so safe, even when my mother was alive and no one dared threaten us. Not even Henry Forbright, who believed his name and wealth entitled him to anything or anyone he wanted.

The thought of Forbright—the sickness his name conjured in my stomach and the worry he might yet find me—finally roused me from my long rest.

With a contented sigh, I opened my eyes...and blinked several times, waiting for what I saw to make sense.

I lay on my back in a bed of furs, in a splendid cavern lit by torches along the walls and a chandelier of larger ones far overhead. The air was cool, sweet, and fresh, and not at all cloying or damp. Goddess above, where could I possibly be?

I took a deep breath to settle my stomach and flinched. My ribs were sore. At least it was an ache and not the sharp pain of broken bones.

I turned my head and stared.

A man knelt on the left side of my bed, holding my hand clasped in both of his. His gaze was as rapturous as if he beheld an enormous diamond or some great wonder, which made no sense at all.

I say *a man*, but he wasn't—or at least he wasn't human. Even kneeling, he was clearly a giant more than eight feet tall, and so muscular that he might have been carved from marble. He also had a pair of horns on the crown of his head, each decorated with a wide gold ring. One of his horns was broken at about the halfway point, and its jagged tip appeared to be dipped in gold.

On the other side of the bed, an identical giant also knelt, his hands cradling mine, his gaze as elated as his companion's.

I should have been terrified, or at least apprehensive, or even angry that I'd been spirited away. Maybe it was their worshipful expressions that kept me from being paralyzed with fear, combined with the realization that they'd likely saved my life and tended to my injuries too. If they wanted me dead, they could have already killed me, or simply left me to die in the jaws of the monsters of Geedhollow.

Their black hair was very, very long and styled in many braids that glimmered with gold threads. And their skin was an inhuman gray-blue, with large patches of what looked strangely like dozens of small, smooth stones embedded into their flesh. I could see almost every square inch of their enormous bodies, since they wore only long, crimson loincloths clasped at their waists with a large gold medallion of some sort. They seemed entirely unbothered by their lack of clothing.

I was no twittering maiden scandalized by bare skin. Since early childhood, I'd joined my mother and her coven in nude rituals dedicated to the Goddess. As an adult, I'd invited select men—usually travelers passing through the village who I would never see again—to my bed. But my unfamiliar surroundings, the giants, and the strangeness of their attire made my stomach begin to roil.

I wore a nightgown that covered me decently, but that was little consolation. I dimly recalled someone—presumably these giants—removing my own tattered and bloody clothing, washing me clean, and then re-dressing me before putting me in bed. What right did these strange men have to see my nakedness? Hadn't I fled the manor to keep possession of my own body?

Slowly, so they didn't interpret my movement as a prelude to an attack or an attempt to flee, I extricated my hands from the giants' grasp. Their hands were very hot, or perhaps I'd gone cold.

My chest tight with growing wonder, unease, anger, and a dozen other conflicting feelings, I gritted my teeth and pushed myself up until I sat with my back propped against the headboard.

Now that I was awake, I expected the giants to stand, but they remained on their knees. So their size didn't frighten me?

"Where am I?" My voice was rough. "Who are you?"

"Our Lady, you grace our home," the giant on my right said, bowing his head. He had an accent I couldn't place, and his voice was very deep and rumbled as if it rose to his throat from the bowels of the earth. "We are your kings."

That both answered my questions and did not answer them at all.

By all accounts, the king, for all his royal blood, was a human man and no giant. And he didn't share his throne with another. Was I no longer in my own country?

Travel beyond the borders of my homeland couldn't explain this, though. Giants were mythical. They didn't roam any country on Earth—at least not anymore. I didn't understand how anything I heard or saw was possible, but I wasn't dreaming.

And why were the giant's tone and position so deferential? If these men were kings, shouldn't they demand I grovel before them? My confusion grew by the moment.

"Please, Your Majesties, explain how I came to be here," I said, bowing my head.

My hosts leapt to their feet, moving much faster than I would have thought possible for such enormous men, and sat on the bed on either side of me. They took my hands again, their expressions earnest.

"Our beautiful Lady, you must never bow to us," the giant on my left said. His voice was not quite as deep, but more sonorous.

A fragment of memory surfaced of this voice singing to me when I was very sick with fever. A gentle hand had dabbed my forehead and wrists with a cool cloth, and warm lips had trailed soft kisses over my fingertips.

My stomach contracted. Not with pain or fear, but with a sharp pang of longing. I hadn't known such comfort since I was a child, when I'd fallen deathly ill. My mother had cared for me night and day until the fever broke.

I didn't understand anything about my circumstances, including the giants' apparent devotion to a humble human stranger.

Only then did I notice they wore jewelry in their nipples. The man on my left had simple piercings with a thin gold chain that ran between them, and the other's each had a finely made golden ring. Their noses also had small gold rings between their nostrils. I had never seen such jewelry on either a man or a woman.

Like my mother had been, I was a tall woman—so much so that some would-be suitors had been put off as much by my height as my profession. But beside these men, I was as small as a child.

"Please explain," I repeated, looking from one to the other, my hands trembling in their gentle grasps. "And please, may I know your names?"

"I am Toved," the giant with the broken horn said, bowing his head.

"And I am Vosten," the other giant added, with a matching bow. "We yearn to know the name of our beloved."

Beloved? Was that a misunderstanding about the meaning of the word?

No, these giants—these *kings*—certainly treated me as if I were dear to them.

"My name is Aveline D'Corsay," I said. "Like my mother and grandmother before me, I own the apothecary shop in Halston." My voice faltered. "Or at least I did."

Forbright had held me prisoner at the manor for six days before my escape. I had no idea how long I'd been here. In the wake of my escape and the deaths of Nobles and the hounds, had my captor burned my shop and home to the ground as he'd threatened to do more than once? Had I lost everything?

Suddenly trapped in the terrible memory of being chased and attacked by the hounds and coming face-to-face with monsters, I gasped for breath and let out a tiny sound.

Both Vosten and Toved's nostrils flared and their dark eyes glowed red.

"You have nothing to fear," Vosten grated. "No one will ever harm you again, our beloved Aveline. We swear it."

I barely heard him. My breath caught in my chest. *The broken horn...the glowing eyes...*

"Goddess above," I whispered. "You're the monsters of Geedhollow."

I yanked my hand from Vosten's grasp and reached once again for my amulet, seeking comfort and protection, but it was still gone—left behind in the manor's fireplace.

Toved held on to my hand gently but firmly and raised it to his lips to kiss my fingers. "We are men, not beasts. Vosten and I are brothers. We are the kings under the earth."

Vosten did not try to reclaim my other hand, but he put his own on the fur next to mine. "Long ago, we ventured to your land and were captured and enslaved by the warlock of Geedhollow, whose name we do not speak." His expression turned grim, and his eyes seemed to fill with dark memories. "Our master died by his own hand during a ritual, but his curse on us did not die with him. My brother and I lingered, forced to live as bloodthirsty creatures."

The ruins of Geedhollow had existed for centuries. My stomach contracted. How long had Vosten and Toved lived in that cursed state?

"The warlock told us the curse would be lifted by the arrival of a human woman of great wisdom who did not fear us." Toved rested his enormous hand gently on my arm. "He did not believe any such woman would come to Geedhollow. Nor did he believe he would ever die. He was wrong, for here you are and he is long since ash." He kissed my hand once again, and now his eyes glowed softly in adoration rather than in anger. "You freed us, Lady Aveline."

"How so?" I asked, confused. "I have no memory of breaking any spells."

"Our chains broke when you looked upon us with defiance." Now Vosten did take my other hand. They both seemed to want—or *need*—my touch as much as possible. "Finally, as men, we were able to return home. Treating your wounds is so very little compared to what you have done for us, but it is far from the only reason we chose to care for you."

Their devotion to me was obvious. If what they said was true—and my instincts told me it was—I was not in danger with them.

"You said you are kings under the earth," I said. "Are we underground, then?" I gestured around the room. "In a system of caves?"

Vosten tilted his head. "It is...difficult to explain. We are in a realm different from your own. We are not below. We are *beside*."

This explanation was not as strange or incomprehensible or unbelievable as it might have been to someone else. My mother had taught me from a young age that the Goddess watched over many realms, and ours was only one of them.

"But how did we come here?" I insisted.

"Our kind travel between realms using doorways under bridges," Toved explained. "Humans call us *trolls* because of this, though we have never understood the true meaning of that word."

Every account of trolls I'd heard or seen described them as ugly, vicious, and monstrous, twisted by greed and gluttony. The only similarity I could see between that and the men before me was their enormous stature and their horns. And regarding their method of travel...

"There are no bridges near Geedhollow," I protested. "The closest bridge is in Rivertown. And surely you would have been seen!"

"There are no *intact* bridges," Vosten said gently. "But our Lady Aveline, like a crossroads, once made, a bridge is always a bridge, even when it no longer appears to be so to human eyes."

I pictured the ruins of the warlock's manor. "So that ancient stone bridge is the doorway to this place, and my way back home?"

Both flinched a little at the question, but Vosten gave me a nod. "Yes."

"Wait," I said, frowning. "You were in my realm for a very long time. What became of your kingdom in the meantime? Did your people not think you were long dead?"

"That is the magic of such doorways," Toved said, caressing my hand in a way that felt very good. "When you return, it is to the same time as when you departed. Our people did not know of our captivity or torment until we let it be known what had happened to us."

It was my turn to flinch. If I walked through the doorway, it would be that horrible night still. The bodies of Nobles and his hounds would be waiting...and Forbright would come hunting for me. My stomach churned.

To distract myself, I glanced down at my nightgown. "I'd like to see how badly I'm hurt."

Almost moving as one, they rose. How enormous and beautiful they were.

Captivated by the patches of strange texture on their skin, I reached for Toved's leg before I caught myself and pulled back my hand.

"You are welcome to touch me anywhere you please, our Lady," Toved said, moving closer to the bed. "If you are curious, yes, it is stone. Our kind come from the mountains."

Cautiously, I ran my fingertips over Toved's massive thigh. The texture reminded me of stones worn smooth in a river, though some along the outside of the patch were rougher on the top and edges. And they were very warm—as warm as his flesh.

Fascinated by the stone, for a long time I didn't notice that he shivered every time I touched him. When I met his dark gaze, his expression was tender and desire shone in his eyes. Goddess, he was magnificent. They both were, especially in the torchlight. Perhaps I had no business thinking of kings in such terms, but if I was not mistaken, they looked on me in much the same way.

"Does our flesh distress you?" Vosten asked.

"No." I rested my trembling hand in my lap. "It's beautiful."

"There is no beauty here that compares to you." Toved reached for my furs. "You said you wish to see your healing injuries?"

"Yes, please."

Gently, they pulled back the furs and piled them near the foot of the bed. My white nightgown was lovely and soft, with short fluttery sleeves, a square neckline, and a ruffled hem. It covered me to just below my knees. Most in Halston would have called it immodest, but I found it beautiful.

Vosten and Toved turned to give me privacy. Their backs proved as exquisitely sculpted as their chests and shoulders...and their loincloths were no wider in the back than the front, meaning I saw a great deal of their hips and buttocks. *Goddess, do you tempt me, or bless me?*

"You don't need to turn away," I said. "I'm decently covered." And perhaps more to the point, they'd already seen me undressed.

Modesty was a frivolity that had never interested me—and too often I saw it weaponized against girls and women in my village. Like my mother, I had no time for blaming girls or women for the inexcusable behavior of bad men.

As they sat again on either side of me, I slipped my gown off my shoulder to examine the area savaged by the lead hound. The wound wasn't bandaged anymore and was well on its way to healing. I would have a scar there for the rest of my days, though—a reminder of that terrible night.

Gingerly, I ran my fingertips over the mark and hissed in a breath at the flare of pain. "How long have I been here?"

"Six days and nights," Toved said. "We have done our very best to heal your wounds."

This much healing in just six days? I stared at my shoulder in wonder. Their medicine was much better than anything I had access to back home.

"I think I remember being sick," I said. "Was I?"

"Yes." Vosten's expression turned grave. "Your injuries became infected, and we think you were undernourished and weakened by mistreatment."

He plainly wanted an explanation for my condition, but I didn't feel ready to discuss my captivity. Instead, I drew my nightgown up to bare my legs to mid-thigh. These bite wounds were deep but less savage than the one on my shoulder. My feet were still healing, especially their soles, but I hadn't lost my feet or hands to frostbite, which was perhaps the biggest miracle of all.

Thanks to these men—these kings—I was alive. If Henry Forbright and his hounds had gotten their way, I would be a corpse now, or at the very least a terribly injured prisoner at the manor. I took a shaky breath and closed my eyes.

The brothers rumbled. "Our Lady Aveline," Toved said, clasping my hand in both of his. "Please, may we comfort you?"

I'd had little peace since my mother's death three years ago, and certainly none since Nobles hit me on the head and carted me off to the manor. I'd lain awake night after night in my locked bedroom wishing for solace of any kind. And in the forest and on the bloody grass of Geedhollow, I'd begged the Goddess for comfort.

What if Vosten and Toved *were* the gift and blessing I'd yearned for? What if I was the gift and blessing they had waited and longed for too?

"Yes," I said, my throat tight. "Please."

As Vosten smoothed my nightgown back in place, Toved covered me with a silken fur.

When they settled in on either side of me, I glimpsed what was covered by their loincloths. I very studiously did not stare—not that I thought they would have minded. They seemed entirely unselfconscious. Their manhoods appeared very human-like, though much larger than I was used to, in proportion to their bodies. The glint of gold might be piercings. How... intriguing.

I distracted myself by studying the golden threads braided through their hair that caught the light from the torches and glimmered.

Lying on my back with each man on his side facing me felt awkward, but I didn't know which way to turn. I found myself looking at Toved for help.

Gently, he turned me so I faced Vosten, then moved closer so my back was against his chest. He was so wonderfully warm. Almost instantly, the knot in my stomach began to fade.

Vosten slipped his hand under the fur to cradle mine. My hand felt cold, especially compared to his heat.

"Our Lady Aveline—" he began.

"I don't have any title," I protested. "I'm just Aveline."

"You are not *just* anything, our Lady." Toved's voice was kind but firm. "No one so fearless and fierce may say they are *just Aveline*."

A jolt of memory: my mother, many years ago, suddenly angry at a customer who came into the shop to find me at the counter and demanded to see Mariane D'Corsay and not "just" her daughter.

No one refers to Aveline as just *my daughter,* my mother had said, her mouth a thin line. *Aveline is the embodiment of all our ancestors' joy, knowledge, power, and wisdom. There is no* just *about that.*

The customer left the shop with a bottle of herbal tincture and a lesson learned.

"You can choose your own title when you are ready," Vosten said, smoothing hair back from my face.

Their reassuring closeness and the warmth under the fur had me growing more drowsy by the moment. "Thank you," I murmured.

He drew my hand from under the fur and kissed it. "You need rest. We will stay by your side so you may sleep without fear and dream of only beautiful things."

That might have been the most tender sentiment anyone had ever said to me. I curled my fingers around Vosten's much-larger hand and squeezed.

He squeezed back and looked over me. "Sing for our Aveline, brother."

Toved sang. I didn't know the language, or what exactly the song was about, but his deep and resonant voice sounded wistful as it rolled over me and filled the room.

I let myself drift on the melody, and very soon I was sound asleep.

CHAPTER

FOUR

TOVED

Aveline. Her name is as sweet as honey on my tongue.

My soul finds peace when I am at her side. Even before the warlock trapped and cursed us, I never knew such contentment. We have cared for her only one week, but already she is in my blood. She is written on my heart.

I am not sure which has better claim to easing my nightmares and soothing my hurts: our return to our home or Aveline's reassuring presence and sweet scent.

So much about our homecoming has been jarring, painful, and bitter-sweet. We found our rooms and realm exactly as we left them nearly three centuries ago when we ventured through the bridge doorway and fell into the warlock's web. Relearning to live as men instead of beasts presents never-ending heartaches and challenges.

It will be a long time, I think, before we can make peace with our long torment. But at least as my brother and I comfort Aveline and see to her healing, we also heal ourselves.

Whatever ordeal she suffered before we met, she is exhausted both body and soul. After waking only briefly last evening to speak with us and examine her healing injuries, she has slept for another full night. Dawn is now only minutes away. With it comes the promise of another day in her presence. The likelihood she will wake soon and bless us with her voice and attention fills me with joy.

"She smiles in her sleep," I murmur as Vosten braids her hair, his touch as light as a feather. We keep our voices low. "I am glad to see it. I do not want her to dream of the hounds or their keeper."

He growls. "We must find out who set them on her. That man worked for someone. Who sends a pack of hounds to hunt and slaughter a woman?"

My time as a beast haunts me, but it taught me there are reasons to embrace the part of myself that is vicious. Our people are peaceful...until we are not. Until we are wronged, or see a wrong being done.

Rage threatens to steal my reason. I hold in my snarl and temper my fury because Aveline lies beside me and I do not want to disturb her rest.

"Only a monster would do such a thing," I say, my voice quiet but harsh. "Such a man does not deserve to live."

"We will track her scent through the forest when we have the opportunity." Vosten ties the end of the braid and lays it over the fur that covers our bride. "We will find her tormentor and see he pays for his crime. Whether our Aveline stays with us or chooses to return to her home, she must never fear this man again."

My brother—elder by four minutes—is strong. His voice does not shake, but his jaw tightens when he speaks of the possibility Aveline may not stay. I avoid saying any such thing aloud for fear I may speak that heartbreak into being. I do not want to think of how empty this bed would be without Aveline in it. Neither does Vosten, but he at least can bear to mention it.

"We can only offer our hearts," Vosten says as if he heard my thoughts. He knows me as well as he knows himself. He divides out the next section of Aveline's beautiful hair and draws a comb through it. "The choice must be hers."

Watching him braid mesmerizes me. Since childhood, he has possessed our people's gift of weaving love and care into our hair, and now he braids his devotion to Aveline into her beautiful tresses along with the golden threads that signify she is a treasure to us.

Her hair is even longer than ours—much longer than any human's we have ever seen. She could not have known our ways, and yet I believe it is a sign we were meant to meet, to love, to share our lives. My heart would not be so full if it was not so.

But Vosten is right, as always—the choice must be hers. We have no right to call her bride or wife unless she calls us her beloved *sulhai* or husbands.

"She will be hungry when she wakes," Vosten says, glancing up from his task. "We must have food ready, and tea."

"I will see to it." Very reluctantly, I slip from the bed, careful not to jostle Aveline. She makes a little sound of protest. I freeze.

"Even when she sleeps, she knows we are near," Vosten says, pausing to touch Aveline's hand and stroke her fingers to reassure her. She murmurs and snuggles deeper into the furs. "In her heart, she knows she is safe with us," he adds and returns to his task. "There is no greater compliment than that, brother. And no greater reason for hope."

Hope sustained us for the long centuries of our cursed existence. Hope fills me now, holds me up, sends me from the bedroom to the kitchen to ask Liva, our cook, to prepare us a full meal to share with our Aveline. She is happy to make whatever we want. She has been singing since we brought Aveline home. Joy and hope has filled our household.

But on my way back to our bedroom, I think again of Aveline's injuries and the shadows that linger in her eyes. Alone in the stone hall and out of earshot of our sleeping bride, I let out the snarl I held in before. The growl rolls down the hall and through our mountain dwelling. Before the curse, I seldom made such a sound. I seldom had reason to do so. Now I hold rage in my bones—rage that only wanes when I am near our beloved Aveline.

I have only been away from the bed for a few minutes, but I already yearn to hold her again. This aching need is a new sensation. In all my years, my arms never felt empty until we met our bride. Now if I am not cradling or touching her I feel bereft, and dark memories of the warlock's curse threaten to pull me into abyssal depths of pain and despair.

I hurry to rejoin my brother and Aveline and fill my arms again.

CHAPTER

FIVE

The next time I woke, I did so with a smile.

As they had lain when I fell asleep, Toved was nestled behind me with his arm around my middle and Vosten faced me. They must have risen at some point, though, because Vosten held a steaming mug of tea. I also smelled food.

My stomach growled very loudly. My cheeks heated.

With a chuckle, Toved sat up so he could smile at me. "A ravenous creature is in our bed, brother. We must feed her so she does not decide to feast on us instead."

What a feast they would be...

My stomach growled again. Now my face was on fire. I wanted to pull the furs over my head.

Vosten rolled smoothly to his feet, treating me to another glimpse of the bare skin under his loincloth. "We must take better care of our Aveline and ensure she never again goes to sleep hungry."

"I was too sleepy to eat before," I protested. I didn't want them to feel as if they'd failed to be good hosts.

Trays laden with bowls and mugs waited on the table next to the bed. As hungry as I was, I had a more immediate need to address.

Only then did it occur to me that for the days and nights of my illness, they had cared for my most basic needs as well as my wounds. I hadn't considered that when I woke the first time. The realization was embarrassing—humbling and humiliating, even—but it was also another example of their devotion.

Toved spoke. "You will want to relieve yourself, I am sure." He rested his hand on my shoulder. "I worry you will find it difficult to stand on your own after so long in bed. Will you let me help?"

I managed a small smile. "Thank you."

Vosten busied himself arranging the food as Toved helped me get to the side of the bed. He steadied me as I stood. My legs trembled and the soles of my feet were sore, but I stayed upright.

Gently, Toved guided me with his hands under my elbows to a room off the bedchamber, where I was startled to find a truly enormous bathtub carved from stone, a washbasin with a pitcher of hot water and a beautiful mirror above it, and a lavatory with the sound of rushing water below. All were more elegant and civilized than anything in my village—and designed for giants' use.

To my amazement, the brothers had found ways to adapt the room to my much-smaller size: three sets of wooden steps and a removable seat for the lavatory.

Toved helped me arrange my nightgown so it was out of the way but still modestly draped and left the room, drawing a curtain across the doorway to give me privacy.

Alone for the first time since arriving in this realm, I propped my elbows on my thighs and let my head fall into my hands.

Kings. I was the beloved guest of *kings*. Twin brothers, no less, who were beautiful and kind and giant in every way. Who wanted to keep me safe, had cared for me tenderly, and were waiting in the next room to serve me food before showing me their home and realm. What had I done to earn such a blessing from the Goddess?

Cursing under my breath at the pain in the soles of my feet, I rose and tottered down the little set of stairs. A step at a time, I shuffled to the basin to wash my hands. Even with the steps, I was barely tall enough to see myself in the mirror.

Only when I saw my reflection did I realize someone had combed my hair while I slept and plaited it neatly to match how Vosten and Toved wore their hair: in six long braids entwined with golden threads. I stroked the braids, admiring how they shimmered in the torchlight.

While my hair was lovely, I looked and felt anything but. My skin was pale, my eyes too large, my bones too prominent. Forbright's relentless pursuit had diminished my appetite and caused me many sleepless nights long before my six days as his captive, during which I had eaten almost nothing and slept even less. The fact I'd been able to run as far as Geed-hollow from the manor despite my condition attested more to my will than any kind of physical strength.

I must have looked more than half dead when Vosten and Toved found me. Why they found me so captivating, I had no idea at all.

When I pushed the curtain aside, both brothers waited for me, each holding a tray with food and mugs of tea. Their expressions lightened when I appeared, as if my mere presence made them happy. Despite my heavy heart, I couldn't help but smile back.

"Would you like to eat in the garden?" Toved asked. "The sunlight and fresh air might help restore you."

"I would love it," I said, then remembered my wobbly legs and bit my lip. "Can I hold your arm?"

In answer, both men offered their forearms for me to hold. I walked between them from the bedroom, down a series of short corridors hewn from solid rock, and through an archway into a marvelous garden.

Instead of a stone wall, vibrantly colored trees formed the perimeter of the garden of flowers, plants, and grasses I didn't recognize. The sun was warm, though, the breeze was cool, and the air was filled with a thousand wonderful scents.

"Shall we sit in shade, our Aveline?" Toved asked, smiling down at me. "Or in sunlight?"

Our Aveline. Strange how much I liked that phrase. "Sunlight, please," I said.

They led me to an enormous wooden table with long benches clearly designed for their own height. Vosten set his tray on the table as Toved lifted me onto a cushion.

As they sat—Toved beside me the same way we lay in bed, and Vosten opposite us—I looked over the meal. Soup, stew, vegetables, even fruits, and wonderfully hot and aromatic tea.

Vosten and Toved piled three plates high with food. Vosten set one plate and a bowl of stew in front of me, along with a three-pronged fork and spoon. They watched me expectantly, their plates untouched as if waiting to see if I liked my food before they ate.

I reached first for a mug so large I had to pick it up with both hands. The tea was perfect—a little sweet and rich in flavor.

I'd eaten almost nothing at the manor and only liquids since. While some men in my world frowned at a woman with a healthy appetite, my every mouthful seemed to make my companions happier, so I filled my belly without shame.

Even as hungry as I was, I couldn't eat more than a fourth of what was on my plate because there was so much, but I ate every bite of the stew in my bowl. When I scraped my spoon to gather up the last of the broth, Toved rumbled appreciatively and reached for a ladle to serve me more.

"No, no," I said with a laugh, covering the bowl with my hand. "I'm so *very* full."

Toved caught my hand and kissed my knuckles. "Your laugh is wonderful. We are so glad to hear it."

"I haven't laughed in a long time," I said, more to myself than to them. I forced a smile. "And I haven't eaten nearly so well in a long time either."

We left the trays and dishes on the table and moved the seat cushions to make a bed in the shade under an enormous tree. I settled in between them with a little groan.

Toved took my hand, his brow furrowed. "Do you feel pain?"

"Oh, I'm sorry. No." I chuckled. "I'm just a bit too full."

"Do you need a fur?" Vosten asked. "It is much cooler in the shade."

Their sweet attentiveness made my heart flutter. "I'm fine."

When we were all comfortable, Toved squeezed my hand. "Our Aveline, we do not want to spoil your mood, but will you tell us why that man and his hounds were chasing you?"

My stomach knotted. "It's a long story," I said, which wasn't actually true. I owed them an explanation but I didn't want to relive my time at Forbright Manor, or think about anything but this gorgeous garden and these beautiful men.

Vosten caressed my cheek with his fingertips. "We will not insist, but perhaps you will feel better if you do not keep the story locked in your heart where it will fester."

"We know you were held against your will," Toved said. His thumb stroked the side of my hand. "We understand what that is like."

They had endured centuries of miserable, cursed life at Geedhollow. My heart ached for them as much as theirs hurt on my behalf. I hated what the warlock had done to them, but it did help to know they could empathize with my treatment at Forbright's hands.

I leaned against the comforting warmth of Vosten's palm. "All right."

I told them the whole story, from Forbright's initial advances to his threats and then how Nobles had kidnapped me on my way home from my shop. I described my days of captivity, including how Forbright had taken my most treasured possession—my mother's amulet—from around my neck and stolen my shoes to make it more difficult for me to escape.

Their eyes blazed and their fists clenched as I talked, and my anger swelled and made me tremble, as if all the fury that had built up inside me could finally come out.

As I narrated my desperate escape and run through the woods with the hounds on my heels, Toved drew me against his chest. Vosten moved closer too. I reveled in their warmth and how safe and secure I was—enough that I confessed my greatest fear.

"I was afraid," I whispered. "I was afraid he'd come to my room and force himself upon me. I knew he would once he understood I wouldn't give in willingly. It was only a matter of time."

"Aveline." Vosten kissed my forehead. Rage still shone in his eyes, but his expression was tender. "We are sorry for what you suffered. No one deserves such treatment."

Toved caressed my back in a way I liked very much. "We are in awe of your courage. You deserve nothing but honor and devotion, and to live as you choose without fear."

"That's a dream, Toved." Tucked between them with a belly full of hot, delicious food, and having told my story, I was wonderfully content despite reliving my ordeal. "No woman can live like that."

"In your world, perhaps," Toved said, his voice a low rumble. "But here, with us, you would never know fear. You could have your own shop and use your knowledge and wisdom to help our people with medicines. Such knowledge is treasured here, and never mocked or persecuted as it too often is in your own world."

"I don't know your plants," I protested, before I realized I'd objected not to staying but to the practicalities of their offer.

"You can learn," Vosten countered, his fingertips brushing my chin. "Your wisdom is not so limited that it only applies to the plants you already understand."

"We cherish you, Aveline," Toved added. "We see your insight, courage, and all your beauty, inside and out. And in our kingdom, all people have the same rights—to property, prosperity, and to choose their spouse or spouses, as many as they wish to have."

I could practice my craft in freedom? Women had the same rights as men? Marriages weren't limited to one man and one woman? It was all too much to think about at once...and too good to be true, surely.

"We understand what we say is difficult for you to believe," Vosten said. "We will show you all our ways and the beauty of our realm, and we leave all the choices about your future to you."

"Thank you." I swallowed hard. "And if I say I want to go back?"

Toved's arm tightened just a little around my middle.

Vosten bowed his head. "Then we will take you back to your village," he said softly. "And leave you in peace."

I didn't know if I could believe what they said about how things were in this realm, but all my instincts told me they weren't lying to me.

"If I *did* stay," I asked, "what would I be to you? Your guest? Your subject?"

"You would be whatever you chose to be," Toved said.

Vosten cradled my hand in his and kissed my palm. "In truth, we would like to heal together, the three of us," he said. "If you feel in your heart that you might want the same, we would be most honored if you would call us your *sulhai*. We would treasure you and devote all our years to your comfort and happiness."

My breath caught. They *both* wanted to share their lives with me? Truly, if I did stay, I would have found it impossible to choose between them.

"What does *sulhai* mean?" I asked.

"We do not know a word for this in your own language," Toved said. "It is our word for someone who is beloved, and whose soul is at peace when they are in your presence."

"Oh, that is a beautiful word." I thought about it. "You are right—I don't know any translation for that, except maybe soul mate, but I never—" I bit my lip. "I never believed in those," I finished, my voice soft. "Not really."

"I like this phrase *soul mate*." Vosten raised my hand to press my palm to his cheek. "To be a mate is to complete and be completed by another. It is not the same as *sulhai*, but it is good."

The idea of being treasured—of being cared for so deeply that my very presence completed another—clashed with my experiences of the world. A man's cruelty and desire to possess me as if I were a *thing* had driven me to Geedhollow in the first place.

But Vosten and Toved were not like Sir Henry Forbright, and if they were to be believed, this place was not like Halston. Maybe, just maybe, I could let myself hope for the first time in an achingly long while.

"We desire you, Aveline." Toved tucked a strand of loose hair behind my ear. "I think you know that."

I *did* know. They'd never hidden it from me—not from the moment I'd opened my eyes. They were beautiful, strong, honorable, and kind. Honest and caring. And the Goddess knew they kindled fire in my heart—and elsewhere.

"Aveline." Vosten cupped my face. "May we kiss you?"

Of course he would ask permission. "Yes." My voice was breathless.

Eyes dark with desire, he moved his hand to cup the back of my head, leaned close, and kissed me.

Everything good about him was in his kiss: hardness and softness, strength and tenderness, desire and care. I had kissed before, and been kissed, but never, ever like this. Never as if I were the dream of a king.

Vosten caught my lower lip between his own, tugged gently, and let me go.

And then Toved moved me to his lap and kissed me. This kiss was sweeter but no less hungry, and he was the first to urge me to part my lips so he could taste me better. His hand gripped my shoulder, then slipped down my arm to hold my hand. Vosten took my other hand and leaned in to trail kisses along my shoulder—especially my healing wounds.

Oh, Goddess. It was all almost too much, and yet I wanted more.

I kissed Vosten again, and then Toved, my skin tingling wherever they caressed me. They carefully did not touch me anywhere intimate, but suddenly even my arms and shoulders and legs felt as delicate as my sex... which dripped freely with my desire.

Beneath their loincloths, they were both very aroused as well. I found myself wanting to touch their manhoods, and taste them, but I was very aware we were in an open-air garden and not the privacy of our bedroom.

"We desire you, but we will not rush you," Vosten rumbled. He caressed my cheek. "You must know in your heart what is right and true."

What *was* right and true? This felt more right than anything I'd known in a long time, but I hadn't made my choice. And if I hadn't, I couldn't make love to them and then leave. That would be wrong.

I kissed Vosten gently, and then Toved. And then I rested my head on Toved's shoulder. "I want to know more about this realm," I said. Goddess, they smelled so good. "I want to know where I belong. That's how I'll know what is right and true."

"We understand." Vosten kissed my forehead. "Our Aveline, we will wait."

CHAPTER
SIX

AVELINE

The next morning, Nisa, the dressmaker who had made my nightgown, arrived with three lovely dresses, a woolen cloak, and a pair of soft leather boots provided by her cousin, who was a shoemaker.

Now properly clothed, I spent the next week exploring the bustling town of Myrial and the valley around it with Vosten or Toved or both at my side.

Little about this land was similar to my own, from clothing to customs and even Vosten and Toved's reign. Unlike the kings and queens of home who ruled in palaces far removed from the lives of their subjects, Vosten and Toved lived in only a half-dozen rooms carved out of the mountainside, helped by a housekeeper and cook. Rather than holding court and associating only with aristocrats and peers, they were advised by a group of everyday citizens who met with Vosten and Toved several times a week to discuss matters of the realm.

To travel, Vosten and Toved walked or drove a cart, and knew a great deal about everything from farming to blacksmithing and even the duties of archivists and teachers at the college.

Every person I met was as much a giant compared to me as Vosten and Toved. The only challenges and frustrations I encountered were due to my size, but the kings and citizens alike were kind and accommodating in every way. Their kindness proved more difficult to adjust to than our relative sizes.

All my life the people of Halston had subjected me to never-ending whispers, mistrust, and outright hostility. With only a few exceptions, my family were all but ostracized, though many of the same people who ignored us on the street visited my grandmother, my mother, or me under cover of darkness or by our shop's back door for medicines and spells.

As a child I had sometimes cried into my pillow in loneliness and hurt. Rather than scold me for my tears or let me weep alone, my mother would lie down beside me, cradle my head against her chest, and explain why our neighbors treated us so unkindly.

"They fear what they don't understand," she'd murmured, smelling of herbs and smoke from her altar. "Some have small minds, and some choose cruelty to make themselves feel powerful. But we have wondrous knowledge, Aveline. Knowledge is true power. Let them think they have authority over us, but truly they have none. Our souls are our own. We are daughters of the Goddess and she watches over us."

In time, I'd come to peace with my family's place in Halston, though the loneliness remained. And after my mother passed away, I was truly alone— a quiet, solitary figure who appeared in her shop before dawn and vanished again at sunset to return to her family's house miles beyond the edge of town.

The people of Myrial, on the other hand, showered me with kindness upon kindness. I had to learn how to accept gifts graciously and interact with people who treated me not as a pariah but as an honored guest and potential new friend and neighbor. At first I thought their goodwill was due to my status as a guest of the kings, but within a few days I had to accept that this was simply ordinary friendliness—something I had rarely experienced before.

It was a wondrous week full of discovery, happiness, amazement, and comfort. My favorite part of each day was my nightly meal with Toved and

Vosten and then going to sleep warm in the furs with the brothers on either side of me. I had never slept as well as I did in our bed.

Wives Hareta and Paita welcomed me into their herbalist shop with open arms. They were as knowledgeable as my mother and grandmother had been. Vosten and Toved entrusted me to their care for two full days as I worked in their shop, absorbed their knowledge and shared my own, and learned about the most common plants they used in remedies.

Both nights I came back to the mountain exhausted but overflowing with excitement. Over dinner, Vosten and Toved listened to me chatter about what I'd learned.

In deference to my need to learn more about this realm before I made any decisions, neither brother mentioned their desire to be my *sulhai*, but it shone in their eyes whenever we spoke and showed in the tender way they held me at night.

I searched for reasons not to stay, or for any hint that this realm wasn't what they claimed it to be, but found none. I waited to feel homesick, to want with all my heart and soul to get back to the world I knew and understood, to miss anything at all about Halston...but I didn't.

From the moment I'd woken up in the bed of furs, something about this place captivated me—and not just my hosts. I had no better words for it than the air felt different here. More welcoming. Less harsh.

No sidelong glances and whispers, and no Sir Henry Forbright haunting my steps.

On the ninth night, as I lay between Vosten and Toved, I found I couldn't sleep despite rising much earlier than usual that morning to join Paita as she gathered a particular flower that only bloomed in the hours before dawn.

My back ached. I'd worked hard all my life, but between my kidnapping, captivity, and long recovery time, I'd been idle for much too long. My muscles had become unaccustomed to tasks like grinding and sorting herbs. But it wasn't just the soreness in my back and shoulders that kept me awake tonight.

"Aveline," Vosten said, cupping my cheek with his hand. His eyes gleamed in the near darkness. "What troubles you?"

"I love this place," I said, my throat tight. "But it's hard to accept that I feel I have nothing to go back to, even if my home and shop are still standing."

Toved drew me tighter against him, and Vosten kissed my forehead gently.

"When my mother was alive, I had her," I said. "We shared a home and worked together in the shop, and I loved it very much. But after she died, all I did was survive."

"There is nothing minor about surviving." Toved's voice was firm but kind. "You must not say that *all* you did was survive. The world can be a hard, cruel place. Survival is a triumph. For a very long time, my brother and I survived. It was all we could do, but it was enough."

I hadn't considered that perspective. "You're right." I curled my fingers around his enormous hand. "I *did* survive, long enough to find you."

"And we did the same." Vosten cradled my other hand. "My brother and I cannot change your past, but we can do everything in our power to ensure your future is happy, wherever and with whomever that will be."

Goddess above, they were so tender and kind with me. I felt treasured as if I were a priceless artwork, but they had never treated me as an object. They saw me as a whole person—the only people other than my mother and grandmother who had done so.

After all these wonderful days and nights in their care, why did I still not know for certain what was right and true? What stilled my tongue whenever the words *I want to stay* tried to come out?

I could think of only one reason, but I couldn't bring myself to give voice to it. I swallowed hard, closed my eyes, and rested my head against Toved's chest. The way he rumbled soothed me.

Vosten stroked my back. "Say what is in your heart, Aveline. Please. Whatever you say, we will not be angry or think less of you."

"I have to know if my home and shop are still standing," I said, my voice rough. "I want something of my mother's."

"Then we will go," Vosten replied without hesitation. "As soon as you are rested, we will return together through the doorway to Geedhollow."

Surely they wouldn't want to see that cursed place again. Not after all they'd suffered. "But you don't need—" I began.

"Beloved, we are not afraid," Toved interrupted gently. He stroked my hair. "We refuse to give the warlock any further power over us. That includes allowing our memories to keep us from accompanying our Aveline to see her home and shop. Returning to Geedhollow as men, especially with you, will feel more like a triumph than a torment."

"We would never send you alone to face danger." Vosten kissed the top of my head. "Sleep, and then we will go."

I wanted to do as they asked, if only so they didn't worry about me more, but the need to close the door on this haunting question and be able to look forward rather than back had banished every last wisp of exhaustion from my body. Even in this bed with Vosten and Toved beside me, I would lie awake until the dawn.

"I won't be able to sleep until I know," I said, biting my lip. "I'm sorry."

"You have no need to apologize. I would feel the same in your place." Vosten rolled smoothly to his feet and drew back the furs so I could rise. "Let us dress for the journey and go."

When his gaze met Toved's over my head, his eyes gleamed with a beautiful red glow. "Bring the cursed chains, brother. They may be of use to us tonight."

CHAPTER
SEVEN

With my hands clasped in theirs, Vosten and Toved led the way through the doorway under a narrow stone bridge just a few hours' walk through the woods from our mountainside home.

I had not been conscious when I passed this way the first time. The journey was, as they had promised, a single step and a mere moment of dizziness before my boot touched the worn stone on the other side.

More than two full weeks had passed for us, but in Geedhollow it was still the night I had run from Forbright Manor. The blood spilled across the grass and stone was fresh.

I'd braced myself to see those horrors again, but the harsh cold and odors of viscera and death hit me as powerfully as a physical blow. The icy wind brought with it echoes of the crunch of my footsteps in dead leaves and the baying of hounds.

A guttural cry escaped my lips before I covered my mouth with my hand to muffle the sound. I turned my face into Toved's shirt and breathed deeply so his warmth and the scent of hot stones might banish the stink of death. He cupped the back of my head and held me.

Vosten kissed the top of my head, murmured something to Toved, and hurried away, his footsteps all but silent even on stone and leaves.

Before I could ask what Vosten was doing, Toved sat on a fallen stone and drew me onto his lap. He tucked me against his chest and began to sing softly. I wrapped my cloak tighter around myself and closed my eyes.

For many long minutes we stayed beside the crumbled bridge. Toved's songs and his heat eased my trembling.

Finally, Vosten returned. "Everything is hidden away," he murmured, his hand on my shoulder. "I cannot banish the smells, but you will not see any of the remains."

"Thank you." Even my whisper sounded loud here. "Are you all right?"

"Yes." Vosten took my hand as I rose from Toved's lap. "I do not mourn for the man or his dogs. They hurt you and meant to kill you. As man or beast, I would do the same again." Toved growled his agreement.

All but invisible in our dark woolen cloaks, we stole through the silent forest toward my house near Halston. If we found it intact, I would venture into the village to my shop.

I didn't know the area around Geedhollow very well, so to find my way home I led Vosten and Toved east until we found Rivertown Road and then the smaller lane that led to my house. We walked through the woods so we wouldn't be spotted by anyone traveling through on foot or by cart. That would be unusual so late at night, but we did not want to take chances.

A light rain began before we got within sight of the house. Even so, I caught the unmistakable scent of burned wood. My stomach, already churning, filled with dread.

Vosten took my hand. He must have smelled it too.

We knew what we would find, but we didn't turn back. I had to see it, and nothing in this world or any other would keep Vosten and Toved from coming with me.

When we reached the top of the last hill, every last shred of hope I had clung to was dashed. The two-story house in which both my mother and I had been born, that had sheltered us all our lives, had been reduced to ash, piles of stone, and a few blackened timbers.

I took two staggering steps and sat—nearly fell—on a half-rotted tree stump. "I knew it. I *felt* it. I just had to see it for myself." Rain mixed with tears streamed down my face.

"Aveline, we are so very sorry." Vosten went to one knee in front of me. His eyes glowed with fury, but his hands were gentle when they cradled mine. "One of us can go to your shop if you wish."

"There's no need to go into town. The shop will be gone too." I took a shuddering breath and tried to think clearly despite my grief. "This fire wasn't set tonight in retaliation; it happened days ago, long before I escaped. It wasn't enough that Forbright kidnapped me. He never intended for me to leave the manor ever again."

"I think you are right." Toved raised his arm and used his enormous cloak to shield me from the rain. "What do you want to do?"

"They were my mother's home and my mother's shop," I rasped, and now the pain in my chest seemed unbearable. "I don't care about the furnishings or my own possessions, but I'd give anything to have something of hers."

Vosten squeezed my hands. "Shall we see what we can find?"

I thought of what Toved had said about facing Geedhollow again: *We refuse to give the warlock any further power over us. Returning will feel more like a triumph than a torment.*

My pain and grief gave way to determination, and then to rage. By the Goddess, Henry Forbright was not allowed to have power over me. A dozen generations of women in my family had not survived persecution for me to be cowed or broken by one cruel and petty man.

I wiped my face, stood, and raised my chin. "No, I'll go."

"I am humbled by your stout heart." Vosten clasped both my hands and kissed my palms. "You will face nothing alone, beloved."

Toved held his cloak over my head as we followed Vosten to the ruins of the house. I didn't mind the rain—I never had. Rain was a blessing from the Goddess, cleansing souls and earth and bringing life to people, animals, and plants alike. But caring for me brought Toved joy and eased his own heartache, so I let him shelter me from the weather.

Despite the condition of the house, I hoped to find the remains of the heavy, iron-banded trunk containing my mother's things. I had stored it in the stone cellar. It might have been at least partly protected from the conflagration.

But as we approached what had once been the house's north wall, where the front door had been, Vosten held out his arm to halt my approach. When I reached his side, I saw why he'd stopped me.

Someone had come here after the fire had done its work and pulverized everything for good measure. Despite the rain and the passage of at least a few days, the mud showed several sets of deep boot prints coming and going from the ashes.

The solid oak trap door that had once led to the cellar lay on a heap of ash. Cautiously, I made my way closer until I could see down into the cellar. The iron bands and splintered, blackened wood of the trunk lay scattered and twisted across ashes and bits of broken crockery.

Not only had my home been destroyed, my mother and I had been obliterated out of existence. By Forbright's men? People from the village? Either —or both—seemed possible.

"This is monstrous," Vosten grated. "Vicious and cruel beyond reckoning."

Rage made my hands shake and stomach heave. I reached for Toved's hand and found myself drawn close with my back against his chest and his arm wrapped around me.

"I am sorry for this terrible act," he said, his voice rough with his own grief and anger. "What can be done?"

Before I could reply, Vosten growled low. "Someone is coming up the road by cart from the west. Their horse is trotting."

A moment later, I heard the distant sound his sharp ears had already caught. My instincts told me who it was. A chill of fury washed over me.

"Forbright," I said. "He's come looking for me."

He usually traveled by carriage with a driver, but on an errand like this he might have come by himself in one of the carts used by servants on the estate.

Moving as one, Vosten and Toved stepped in front of me, their chests rumbling.

I walked around them and turned. "I need to face him," I said softly. "I deserve to face him. He needs to answer to me. Would you not have wanted the same chance?"

Clearly torn, Vosten exchanged a glance with his brother. They seemed to speak to each other without needing words.

"Stay close by," I said. "Please, in case he's come armed or I signal for your help."

"We understand." Vosten touched my hand. "We will watch from behind the house wall. He will not see us until you call or if we feel we must intervene."

"Thank you." I touched their faces. "I know this is difficult for you."

"We did not get to confront our own tormentor." Toved cupped my chin and kissed my forehead. "We would never deny you this."

They slipped away into the dark just as the cart, with its single passenger, crested the hill. Even from this distance and in the dim moonlight, I recognized Forbright's silhouette.

The rain had all but stopped. I threw back the hood of my cloak and sat on the low stone wall of what had been our garden.

Mother and Goddess, stand beside me, I thought as the cart reached the drive. Forbright turned so sharply and slowed so little that the cart's wheels slid across the rocky ground.

Fury burned like a forge in my chest, but I was calm and felt no fear. Our house might be destroyed, but this was our family's land. We had danced and sung and honored the Goddess on this soil. Forbright should have known better than to come here, but I was glad his ire had brought him to me.

Glowering, Sir Henry Forbright came to a stop in the yard. We studied each other as the poor horse breathed heavily and moved uneasily.

For the first twenty-two years of his life, Henry had been the older of two overly indulged sons who had learned cruelty from their father, Richard. Their mother had died—some in town said mercifully—only three years after the birth of her second child.

Before and after her death, Richard had preyed upon women in both Halston and the city. He'd never attempted to harm my mother, though. He didn't fear the law, but he did fear my grandmother.

After Richard's death, Henry, then twenty-three, ridded himself of his younger brother by arranging his marriage to a merchant's daughter in a seaside town and set himself up as the solitary lord and master of the manor.

In public, he was a gentleman who traveled to the city regularly to stay at his club and dine at the finest restaurants.

In private, he became like his father: a monster who used his money and influence to escape all justice.

Now thirty-four, Henry was angular and tall, with jet-black hair, large hands, and thick fingers adorned with his father's rings. Rumors circulated those rings left telltale bruises he liked to admire. He would have been handsome, perhaps, if his soul wasn't so wicked and his face wasn't perpetually twisted with anger and hate.

"Where is Nobles, witch?" he spat, climbing down from the cart. He wore a long coat over his suit and seemed to not care that he was soaked from the rain. "Where are my hounds?"

I folded my hands in my lap. "All dead."

His lip curled. "Liar. I don't know how you managed to evade them, but when they get here, I'll take particular pleasure in watching them put an end to your cursed life...once I've finished with you."

Low growls rolled through the yard. Forbright frowned, then seemed to dismiss it as the ruins of the house creaking.

Only then did he see me clearly. "Where did you find these clothes?" he demanded. "Who would help *you?*"

I opened my mouth to lie and say I had stolen them, but a realization stilled my tongue.

Who *would* have helped me? No one from Halston, that was certain. Likely no one from Rivertown either, even if I'd made it that far.

A pair of monsters had helped me—monsters who'd seen a pack of dogs mauling an unarmed woman and come to my aid long before they knew I was fated to break the warlock's curse. Monsters whose hearts remained good despite all their centuries of suffering.

Who, then, were the true monsters who stalked these lands? The man before me and his late but unlamented gamekeeper, not the so-called beasts of Geedhollow.

His lips twisted in a smirk, Forbright reached into his pocket. He raised his hand and let something dangle by its chain: my mother's amulet. My stomach contracted.

"You want this, witch?" he taunted. "Tell me who gave you quarter."

When I'd refused to eat at his table or share his bed willingly, he'd ripped that treasured amulet from my neck, stomped on it, and thrown it into the manor's grand fireplace. My scream of grief and rage had been the only outburst of emotion he'd managed to wrench from me during my imprisonment.

He surely wanted to assert control over me and torment me now with the last of my mother's possessions. Instead, the sight of it, still in one piece after being thrown into the fire, reminded me who I was and who had raised me.

"You are a coward," I said. "A weak man who must resort to kidnapping and forcing yourself on women because no one will have you otherwise."

Forbright's face twisted in a snarl. "No one speaks to me like that, witch." He advanced a few steps, his arms at his sides and the amulet still dangling from one fist. "Tell me who gave you clothes and helped you escape my hounds."

"Like your father, you are an irredeemable blight on humanity," I continued as if he hadn't spoken. "I'm pleased to think we might bring an end to your line."

"How dare you threaten me?" With a frown, he halted and looked around. "*We*, you say? Who's here with you?"

A strange hot tingling sensation swept over me. My skin prickled as magic and the odor of rotting things swirled on the wind. I smiled.

Another set of growls rolled through the night in a much lower register than before.

Forbright's horse reared and bolted. With a shout, Forbright tried to give chase, but couldn't run fast enough to grab the reins or the horse's bridle. When the terrified horse reached the steep embankment of the road, the cart nearly toppled before righting itself. The horse and empty cart rattled up the hill in the direction of the manor.

Forbright stormed back, breathing hard and face dark with rage. I rose and revealed the dagger in my hand. Let him think that was the only danger here.

"I didn't lie about Nobles and the hounds," I said.

He stopped well out of my reach, his eyes narrowed. His empty hand flexed as if he wanted to wrap it around my throat. "You didn't kill them. You couldn't have. Not with that little knife."

I could do far more with this *little knife* than he could imagine—my mother had taught me to defend myself from a very young age.

I turned it in my hand so moonlight glinted on the blade. I wanted his attention on me and not on the enormous shadows moving silently behind him.

"That is true," I said softly. "But I only said they were dead. I never said I was the one who killed them."

For the first time since I had the misfortune of meeting him, Forbright's expression turned wary.

"Nobles and the hounds tracked me through the forest for miles." I took a step forward. Forbright moved back. "You may be glad to know your dogs did go silent before they caught up to me at Geedhollow."

Two pairs of red, glowing eyes blazed to life behind him. Every creature of the night fell silent. Even the wind stilled.

"Do you remember what you told me at dinner one night?" I continued. "You said you wanted prey to hear and *feel* the cold silence of death just before your hounds got them. *Deer or rabbit, fox or girl, they'll know death has come by the quiet.*"

The shadows with their red eyes rose to their full height behind him.

I smiled and let my gaze move to those shadows. "Have you noticed how quiet it has become, Sir Henry?"

The color drained from his face. Slowly, he turned. The amulet fell from his hand and landed in the dirt.

Two enormous beasts—my beloved Vosten and Toved, in all their monstrous glory—towered over Forbright on their hind legs, claws and teeth bared. Around their necks they wore the thick golden chains forged by the warlock, repaired and now fastened with clasps.

They threw their heads back and roared. The sound rolled across the earth. Forbright screamed and stumbled back into my waiting dagger.

The blade—sharp as a razor and as hungry for blood as my beautiful kings—slid easily into his back between his ribs just below his heart. His shriek turned to a gurgle.

I withdrew the dagger and let him fall in a heap at my feet.

Vosten and Toved dropped to all fours. They lumbered over to stand beside me as Forbright rolled to his back, his eyes wide and full of horror. The beasts lowered their enormous muzzles to Forbright's ashen face and showed him all their sharp, sharp teeth.

"You asked who helped me," I said. "Sir Henry, meet the beasts of Geedhollow."

Forbright's mouth opened and closed, but no sound emerged except thick gurgles and what might have been whimpers. The stink of urine and feces overtook the smell of blood.

I offered the dripping dagger to Vosten for him to sniff. His long tongue delicately cleaned the blood off the blade and my fingers.

Forbright whined. "Mercy," he burbled, the word all but unintelligible.

I thought of my scars, and of all the women who must have begged him for mercy and received none. The law had failed them. I would not.

I crouched and picked up my mother's amulet. The gold was caked with ash, the chain had broken, and the fire had cracked the emerald in the center, but like me, my treasure had survived its time at the manor. I would have called it a miracle if I didn't know the Goddess had given me this gift.

In fact, she had given me many, many gifts tonight, with the promise of more to come.

I brushed off the ash and slipped the amulet inside my dress, nestling it in my underclothes between my breasts, over my heart—a familiar and comforting weight I'd believed I'd never feel again.

I rose and slid my fingers through Vosten's hot, thick fur. "Are you hungry, my *sulhai?*"

He growled low. Toved bared all his teeth. Forbright whimpered.

"Feast, my loves," I said.

Vosten snarled and went straight for Forbright's belly as if he'd been waiting to do so from the moment he found out what the man had done. Toved chose Forbright's groin for his first bite.

I sat in the grass with my back against the garden wall and listened to Forbright's screams until they ended, and then watched Vosten and Toved finish their meal. It didn't take long. That was more mercy than Forbright deserved, but I couldn't blame the kings for making short work of him.

When nothing remained but blood in the grass, Vosten and Toved rose with pleased huffs, licking their muzzles. I stood to kiss their furry heads and caress their horns until they rumbled in contentment.

"Thank you," I said. "Thank you both, with all my heart."

The beasts rested their heads gently against mine. Even now they smelled of warm stone, a scent that was now as much a part of me as my own breath and bone.

I didn't want the moment to end, but someone might come to investigate the strange noises and Forbright's screams.

"We should go," I told them. "Do you want to walk back to the doorway as beasts or men?"

In answer, Vosten used his head to nudge my hand toward his neck. I slid my hand along the chain until I found the heavy clasp. I released it and let the chain fall to the ground, then did the same for Toved.

The spells broke in a burst of power and sorcery that stank of sulfur and decay. The beasts' bulk dissolved into ash and bits of rotting things that fell away, leaving Vosten and Toved back in their natural bodies, on their hands and knees, naked and breathing hard.

I went to them immediately, not caring about their nakedness or the filth left behind by the broken spells. All I wanted was to hold my kings and be held.

Vosten pulled me into his lap and pressed his lips to my hair. Toved kissed the back of my neck. Even over the stench around us, they smelled like home.

A soft, loving, feminine touch caressed the crown of my head and wrapped itself around my shoulders. My mother? The Goddess? It was a blessing either way—a blessing on all of us.

Finally, *finally*, for the first time since my mother's passing, peace filled my heart. That warmth freed me to take a deep breath and say, "I know now what is right and true."

Toved stilled with his lips on my shoulder. Vosten cupped my face with his hands to gaze into my eyes. "What do you know is right and true, Aveline?"

"We are. The three of us." I rested my hand on his. "I want to go home to our bed. That's where I want to be and where I want to stay."

Vosten's breath hitched.

Toved's chest rumbled. "Aveline, do you mean it?"

"I do." I stroked Vosten's hot hand with my thumb. "Not because I don't have any reason to stay here, and not because you helped me rid the world of Henry Forbright. I want to be your bride because you are wonderful, beautiful, honorable men who think I'm equal in value to yourselves. Why would I not want to be yours, then, and claim you both as my *sulhai?*"

Vosten kissed me first, as I'd suspected he would. He was the older brother, after all, and less patient. His mouth was hard and hot and demanding, and I loved how fiercely he kissed.

"Share, brother," Toved said, his voice teasing but thick with need. Vosten chuckled and moved out of the way.

As when we'd first kissed in the garden, Toved's lips were more tender, but in a way his gentleness was hungrier and even more arousing.

When our kiss ended, they took my hands and helped me rise. Toved hurried to get their clothes while Vosten held me against his chest.

"Beloved," he said, his voice soft. "You are brave and strong, but from here the journey home will be a long walk. Do your feet or legs pain you? You are not yet fully healed from your wounds."

"Paita gave me a tincture for pain. I brought it with me." I kissed his chest. "I will tell you if they hurt too much, I promise."

"Sweet Aveline." His smile warmed my soul. "It will be the greatest joy and honor of our lives to escort you home."

CHAPTER

EIGHT

AVELINE

We made it back to Geedhollow before exhaustion turned my steps leaden and my eyelids heavy.

Once we passed through the doorway and emerged on the other side, Toved gathered me in his arms and carried me home. So gentle, warm, and comforting was his touch that I slept for most of the journey through the woods, across the valley, and into the mountain dwelling the brothers' family had inhabited as long as the people of Myrial had kept records.

I woke on our bed with my back against Toved's chest and Vosten gazing into my eyes, lying with his arm bent under his head. My dirty clothes had disappeared, replaced by the lovely nightgown Nisa had made for me. And I smelled fresh and clean as if they had given me a bath with cloths.

"Beloved," Vosten said. He caressed my cheek. "You must sleep."

"I don't want to sleep. I have slept enough." I caught his hand and kissed his palm. "I want my *sulhai*."

I rolled to my back so I could see them both. Goddess, they were beautiful with the torchlight dancing over their stony flesh and reflecting in their eyes.

"Do my *sulhai* want me?" I asked.

Vosten bent his head so his lips brushed mine. "With all our hearts and souls," he murmured, and kissed me.

Toved trailed his lips along my shoulder, bared when I'd moved and my nightgown had slipped down. Their heat and caresses sent a wave of desire through me to pool between my legs. I moaned. *Oh, Goddess...*

Vosten inhaled deeply. "Yes," he growled, his hand tightening on mine. "Sweet Aveline, that is a glorious perfume."

They smelled so good to me too, and had since before I'd even woken up in this bed. That scent of warm stone was a promise of safety and love.

I reached for Vosten again. He kissed me deeply, his fingers tightening in my hair.

Need made me shiver. My nipples grew taut and sensitive against the soft material of my gown. A trickle of arousal dripped along my sex. Both men rumbled. My scent affected them in such a thrilling way.

I'd never shared a bed with any man so large, or with two men, but I felt no fear—only desire and hunger and need.

Beneath their loincloths, their manhoods had quite obviously swollen and hardened with their own desire. I licked my lips. Would they taste as good as they smelled? And what about the piercings I had glimpsed? How would those feel?

"Aveline," Vosten rasped, drawing my attention. He cradled the back of my head in his enormous hand and gazed lovingly into my eyes. "You have called us your *sulhai*, but we must know what you want. There can be no misunderstandings or regrets among us. Please tell us what it is you desire."

"I desire to take off your clothing," I said, trembling with need. "And for you to take off mine."

With a throaty sound, Vosten caught my hand and brought it to the gold clasp at his waist. With his help, I found the hidden fastening and released it. The soft red fabric slipped low on his hips, revealing the thick base of his manhood. He had a gold piercing through the flesh at its very base and below that a golden band.

Slowly, I unwound the fabric and drew it aside to reveal all of him. Goddess, he was gloriously aroused, thick and beautiful, with another bar-like piercing near the tip.

Toved guided my other hand to his own clasp. Like Vosten, he let me remove the fabric myself. He also had a piercing and gold band at the base of his manhood—but unlike his brother, the underside had three additional piercings in a row.

"Why do you wear jewelry on your manhood?" I asked. "I've never seen such jewelry before."

"The piercings on our cocks are for the pleasure of our bride," Vosten said, his hot mouth at the nape of my neck. A shiver of anticipation ran down my spine.

"Do you like what you see of us, beloved?" Toved rumbled.

"Yes." My heartbeat thundered in my ears. "Very much."

"I am glad." Vosten's hands traveled over my bare arms as he kissed my shoulder, and with every touch I let out little gasps. "We may remove your nightgown?"

I had already asked them to do so, but they were so careful, so cautious, so respectful, even as hunger shone in their eyes and made them quake.

"Yes, please remove it," I said. "I want you to see me. I want to be your bride."

On his hands and knees, his cock arching up toward his muscular abdomen, Toved moved down the bed and turned to face us. He slid the hem of the nightgown up slowly, taking his time and kissing his way up my legs. Vosten took over then and drew my nightgown up and over my head. He cast it aside with a satisfied rumble.

"You are so beautiful," Toved said. He leaned forward and kissed me. "Beautiful beyond all imagination."

"Our sweet Aveline," Vosten murmured. He reclined on the pillows and settled me in so my back rested against his chest. His hands slid up my abdomen and cupped my breasts, stroking them gently but possessively with his thumbs. I gasped, my back arching.

"Beloved." He pressed his lips to my ear. "Open your legs for my brother's tongue."

Trembling, I did as he asked.

"Aveline," Toved whispered. He lifted my foot to his mouth and sucked gently on the arch of my foot. I moaned.

Slowly, he kissed his way along my calf and inner thigh. And all the while Vosten caressed my breasts, his thumbs and forefingers teasing my nipples into hard peaks. With every sensation, I quaked and let out little gasps as my desire dripped freely. Already it all felt like too much.

As Toved slid his hands under my hips, Vosten took my hand and guided it to his beautiful cock. To my surprise, it was slick with some kind of liquid that beaded from his hot flesh. When my hand closed around it, he made a guttural, desperate sound that became nearly a bellow when I stroked him. The sound was deep and primal, and a rush of slickness ran from my sex.

That was the moment Toved's hot tongue delved between my folds. I screamed.

I'd known few men who desired to do this, and only one who'd proven skillful. I'd certainly never known this kind of pleasure, not ever.

In Vosten's arms, my legs held wide by Toved's broad shoulders and firm grip, I writhed and wailed. His rough tongue swirled around my swollen pearl and lapped and licked along my folds.

My hand slid up and down Vosten's cock, over the piercings and hard veins, as he growled and quaked. "Sweet Aveline," he said into my hair. "My cock belongs to you. Imagine how it will feel—how it will stretch you. Imagine how it will fill you completely."

His bold words were another new pleasure that made my skin blaze with desire.

"Take hold of Toved's horn," Vosten commanded. "Squeeze it tightly. He will like it."

Indeed, when I gripped one of Toved's horns with my free hand, he rumbled and rewarded me by closing his lips on my pearl and sucking. I cried out, my back arching.

"Yes, that is what she likes," Vosten growled. He slid his hands under my knees to hold my legs raised and open, rendering me helpless in their arms. But I felt no fear—only trust and need. "Bring her to release, brother. I want to hear her sing for us."

Oh, Goddess above. It was all so much.

With his hands freed, Toved licked his fingers. His gaze on mine so he could watch me gasp, he slipped one hot fingertip inside me, pumping it gently and a little deeper each time.

"Toved," I cried out. "Goddess above, *Toved*."

He added a second finger, and now he was stretching me as he bent again and swirled his tongue around my pearl, his fingers curled up inside me as he stroked. No one had ever touched me in such a way. His touch sent me hurtling toward bliss with terrifying speed.

With a wail, my head thrown back against Vosten's chest, I came apart, flooding Toved's fingers and lips with my release. I screamed and screamed, writhing, fighting to escape Vosten's grip and the rush of sensations and a pleasure so intense I couldn't breathe.

"Yes," Vosten growled in my ear. "Give my brother a good drink. He thirsts for you."

Indeed, Toved was sucking and lapping at my sex, drinking up my release. I wailed and pleaded for mercy, but Vosten held me still and Toved didn't stop until I went limp, my legs shaking as I whimpered and gasped.

"Our sweet little Aveline," Vosten rumbled as Toved licked up the last of my release. "In all my long life, I have heard nothing as wondrous as your screams. You are so beautiful when you come."

"Yes," Toved rasped, laving my inner thighs and even the delicate flesh below my sex with his very talented tongue. "So very beautiful," he murmured.

"Now, who would you like to taste?" Vosten asked. "Which of your *sulhai* may fill your sweet mouth first?"

Oh, Goddess—what a question. I would have taken both at once if I could.

"Toved," I gasped.

With a warm chuckle, Vosten rose from the bed with me cradled in his arms. "You heard our bride's decision, brother. You have earned your reward."

Toved turned over, his feet and lower legs hanging off the end of the enormous bed. He reached for me, his dark eyes gleaming and cock dripping with his need.

Vosten placed me gently into Toved's open arms so I lay on his broad chest, my head resting over his heart. Toved caressed my back and bottom and kissed my hair, clearly savoring this moment of intimacy and comfort. Unwilling to give me up completely, Vosten bent and laved my shoulder with his tongue.

When I'd caught my breath, I kissed my way down Toved's stomach, rose to my knees, and wrapped my hand around his slick cock.

He growled, his hips bucking and fists twisted in the furs beneath us as I stroked him, my fingers sliding over the piercings on the underside, base, and tip. He smelled so good, so delicious. I licked my lips.

"Aveline," he grated. "Please."

His cock was enormous, nearly as thick as my fist, but I had to taste him. I *had* to drink him in.

When I slipped my lips over his cock head and circled my hand tightly around his girth, his back arched, and he nearly roared. The sound rolled through our bedroom, down the hall—and maybe through the entire valley beyond the mountain.

I could take nothing more than the head into my mouth, but he rumbled and thrashed beneath me, his eyes closed and head back in pleasure. How wonderful to have this beautiful and powerful man so lost in ecstasy from my mouth and my touch. He tasted just as I'd imagined: like warm stone and earth, far more delicious to my palate than any human man had been.

With my attention on Toved, I had not seen Vosten move behind me until his hot hands gripped my hips.

And then his tongue thrust between my folds and deep into my sex, and I wailed, the sound muffled by Toved's cock. Overwhelmed again by sensation, I tried to wiggle away from Vosten's tongue, but found myself held in place by his hands on my hips.

Gently, Toved rested his hand on my head. "Look at me, beloved."

I lifted my head and gasped for air as Vosten continued to lick and suck at my swollen pearl and dripping sex.

"Give us leave to worship you," Toved said, caressing my face. "You are everything to us. You need not fear we will do anything you do not want. We want only to see you lose yourself in pleasure."

"You need only say stop, and we will stop," Vosten rumbled from behind me. "You have our most solemn oath."

Goddess above, I loved these men with all my heart.

I moved my bottom against Vosten's tongue, and he growled in approval.

"Yes," Toved said, and guided my mouth back to his cock. "Bless me again, beloved."

I took my time and licked his beautiful cock from its base to its tip, watching my Toved writhe and groan with every touch. With my free hand, I caressed his hot skin, especially the patches of stone.

When I took him in my mouth and sucked, he shuddered hard. A burst of hot liquid spilled onto my tongue that sent a wave of need through me. I continued to suck and stroke him to draw more of that delicious release.

Vosten replaced his tongue with his fingers in my sex. I rode against his hand, groaning and crying out with every thrust as he stretched me gently. He even circled the sensitive edges of my other opening with one slick fingertip. I had never been touched there before, and the sensation shocked me with its intense pleasure.

When the head of Vosten's cock pressed against my sex, I gasped and stilled, my lips sliding free of Toved's manhood.

"I will go slowly," Vosten promised, his voice rough, and kissed my back. "Our Aveline, I will not hurt you."

I found my hand gripping Toved's without having realized I'd reached for him. He held me tightly and cupped my face. His thumb caressed my lower lip. "Our sweet bride, take my brother's cock."

"I will," I said, my voice shaking.

Vosten's first thrust drew a groan and a shudder from me. Oh, he felt so good—a delicious stretch, pain and pleasure, the overwhelming sensation of being filled. I arched my back so I could take more.

He rumbled, withdrew, and thrust again, a little more this time. I whimpered, my legs shaking.

"You can take me, beloved," Vosten said, and now he was filling me inches at a time. Each thrust rocked me on my knees. I had to steady myself against Toved's firm grip on my hand. "Yes, take my cock. Take it all."

It was too much, too much, too much. I cried out and squeezed Toved's hand. He slipped his thumb into my mouth and I sucked on it desperately. Between us, his cock leapt and dripped freely.

"Beautiful Aveline, you are perfect," Vosten said, his voice guttural with the strain of filling me slowly rather than all at once. "You are *perfect*. Spread your legs more."

Toved cupped my face and murmured praise and encouragement as I took all of Vosten my body could accommodate, one careful thrust at a time.

When he drew back and began to pump into me in slow, even strokes, I wailed, I sobbed, I bit Toved's thumb…and it all felt so good, so very, very good. Better than anything I'd ever felt in my life. To be filled with Vosten's cock was paradise.

With Vosten thrusting into me from behind, I sucked Toved's cock head and stroked him, my cries and moans muffled. Surely the heavens had nothing as good to offer as this.

Blissful moments later, Vosten's groans became growls, and his thrusts turned slow and purposeful. "Aveline," he ground out. "I want to fill you."

Toved laced his fingers through mine, his chest heaving and cock dripping in earnest as his own release neared. "Will you take all we have to give you, beloved?"

"Yes," I gasped. Goddess, I wanted to see and *feel* them lose themselves for me. "Please give me everything you have to give. I want to be filled."

With a guttural sound, Vosten reached around my waist and circled my swollen pearl with his fingertips as he thrust harder. I cried out as a coil of heat grew and grew, and began to crest—

My scream blended with Vosten's bellow as we came together. Spurt after spurt of hot seed filled me and then over-filled me, streaming down my thighs as he shuddered and held me tight against his hips.

Toved's cock leapt in my hand and erupted moments later with his release. His body thrashed beneath me and his shout joined our ragged cries. Lost in the ecstasy of my release and both my *sulhai* filling me at the same time, I took his cock head into my mouth to catch his seed and swallow it. I wanted to claim him as my own just as they had claimed me so thoroughly.

This was everything my heart, body, and soul wanted and needed. This was bliss.

Gasping, I rolled to my side on the bed, shivering in pleasure at the sensation of Vosten's hot release dripping from me and the taste of Toved's seed on my tongue. Toved pulled me close and buried his face in my hair.

When Vosten joined us and I was cradled between them, my happiness was complete.

"Our bride," Vosten rasped, caressing my face. "You took us so well, beloved. And you came beautifully for us."

No one had ever praised me in bed. Not only did I like it, I found it aroused me nearly as much or more as even the touches and scents of my *sulhai*.

Vosten smiled at Toved over my head. "Our Aveline is perfect in every way."

"Yes, she is." Toved's hand cupped my breast, languidly stroking my nipple with the side of his thumb. "And very tired now, I think."

I smiled, my eyes half-lidded. "*She* can hear her *sulhai* talking about her."

His cock leapt against my thigh. "When you call us your *sulhai*, we become very hungry for you," he warned. "You must use the word judiciously."

Vosten licked my ear and slid his hand between my thighs, which were slick with his seed. "Are you sore, beloved?" he asked.

"Only a little." I felt so very good. What was a little soreness compared to that?

"A warm bath will soothe your discomfort." He kissed my neck. "Do you wish to bathe with us and then sleep?"

Bathing with my *sulhai* and then sleeping in their arms would be heaven itself. "Yes," I murmured.

Vosten slipped from the bed, presumably to see to hot water. Toved and I rested as he caressed my arm and leg, his hot fingers tracing patterns over my skin.

Some hazy time later, Toved carried me from the bed to the bath, where his brother waited next to the steaming tub.

"I could have walked," I protested, though I wasn't actually sure if it was true. My legs still trembled.

"It is my pleasure and privilege to carry our bride," Toved reminded me, kissing my forehead. "Also my pleasure to clean her, to wash her silken hair, to sing her to sleep."

"To fill her with your beautiful cock when we wake in the morning?" I asked sleepily.

"Yes, of course." He stepped over the side of the tub and lowered us into the wonderfully hot water. "As our beloved commands."

EPILOGUE

VOSTEN

Just after dawn on the one-year anniversary of our marriage, our wife wakes in Toved's arms with her legs on my shoulders and my tongue on her sweet folds.

"Vosten," she moans, her hands on my horns.

She is not quite fully awake yet, but still she knows who cradles her and who is between her thighs—and that I want her to grip my horns and pull me to her.

"Beloved," I say, and lick her sweet, slick, delicate skin. "Good morning. You dreamed of beautiful things, I hope?"

"Yes," she gasps. "*Yes.*"

"Good." Toved cups her breast with one hand and slips the other between her thighs. "I need a taste, brother."

I raise my head and let him dip his fingertips in and out of Aveline's dripping sex. He draws shudders and groans from our wife before he licks his fingers clean.

"Spread her open," I tell him, and he obliges, parting her folds with his fingertips to bare her pearl, so beautiful and swollen with need.

"I...will be late...getting to the shop," Aveline protests.

I close my lips on her sweet little nub. Her head falls back, exposing her neck for Toved to kiss and nibble and suck gently. She cries out.

"You are not expected at the shop today," Toved says, his mouth on her ear.

I slip two fingers inside her. Her throaty groan and the way she grinds on my hand makes my cock drip in earnest. "Nor are we required to be anywhere," I tell her. "At least until we have properly seen to our wife's needs."

Her protests turn into moans, and I know we have won.

This morning, the privilege of filling Aveline's sweet sex belongs to Toved. The gleam in his eyes indicates he has no intention of abdicating that role.

So I indulge myself in a final slow lick to drink up her slickness and trade places with my brother, kneeling behind Aveline so she can recline against my thighs as I cup and caress her breasts.

Toved strokes his cock, his gaze locked on hers as she whimpers. "Our beautiful Aveline, how many times would you like to come?"

"Three times," she says. "Please."

His gentle smile turns wicked. "Then four it shall be."

He circles her sweet bud with his thumb. She writhes in my arms. I hold her and watch and listen as her cries rise in volume and pitch in the way we know so well—the way I hear in my dreams, and want to enjoy as many times in a day as we can manage. I could never tire of her cries.

When she wails and begins to shake and her sweet slickness splatters Toved's thighs and cock, he bends to lap at her folds to drink in her release. I take a taste myself, from my fingers, and then slip my hand around her calf to raise and open her legs so my brother may please her with his cock. This is one of our Aveline's most favorite ways to be taken by us: in the arms of one as the other fills her sweet heat.

Toved nudges her other leg aside and begins to thrust, first just his cock head, and then deeper, until his piercings are stroking in and out of our wife and she begins to scream. She comes again, her body going rigid in my embrace and then fighting to escape from pleasure so intense that she cannot stop wailing.

But we do not let go. Toved promised our wife four releases and we do not make promises we do not keep.

I pinch Aveline's nipples as he pumps into her deep and fast. She screams his name and mine, over and over, pleading to come once more. So as he thrusts, I rub her pearl until she is crying out and squeezing him and he must slow to hold himself back.

She looks up at me and licks her lips. "Let me taste your cock. Please."

As Toved thrusts slowly, I move so my throbbing, needful cock is in front of Aveline's sweet mouth. She licks me hungrily, cleaning every drip, and then sucks me into her mouth. She cannot take much of me this way, but her hand twists around my length as she squeezes and strokes and it is heaven itself.

Toved's harsh breathing warns that he has reached his limit. As he nudges a wet fingertip against our wife's other tight hole, I circle her swollen pearl and thrust very gently into her hand and mouth. She cries out, the sound muffled by my cock.

My fingers are a blur over Aveline's bud. Toved pushes his wet finger into her tight bottom, and then our wife is coming between us for a wonderful fourth time, her body wracked with shudders as she screams in ecstasy around my cock.

I throw my head back and bellow with every pulse of hot seed I release into Aveline's mouth and throat. She chokes and gulps, fighting to swallow it all, but the abundance drips down her chin.

Toved groans and shudders as his release fills our wife and spills over her thighs. Our cries echo in our bedroom in a chorus of shared pleasure and love.

When we tuck Aveline between us with her back against my chest, she is trembling and nearly boneless with pleasure. We are seldom cold or even cool, but my brother and I draw a fur over us so our wife does not feel a chill.

"You came so beautifully for us," I tell her, my lips on her hair as I clean my spilled seed from her face with a cloth. "How is it you become more perfect and lovely by the day?"

"Such shameless flattery," she teases, breathless and quivering. "But don't stop."

"You need not worry," Toved says with a chuckle. "We have no plans to stop worshiping our wife or lavishing her with well-deserved praise."

She smiles and nestles in deeper between us.

We let her rest in our arms as long as she wishes, admiring the sheen of sweat on her skin and listening to her breathing gradually slow. The scent of our lovemaking fills the air, blending with the smells of furs, our mountain home, and Aveline's own sweetness. It is the scent of contentment.

Our lives are perfect in every way since Aveline came to stay—an idyll that has brought a strong sense of security to our small kingdom. Aveline is beloved not only to my brother and me, but to all our people. She loves working with Hareta and Paita at the herbalist shop, and though she continues to learn our plants and ways, she has brought comfort, relief, and healing to many already.

My brother and I barely recall our long years of living under the warlock's cruel curse. On the rare occasions our thoughts turn that way, all we must do is touch our sweet wife or visit her at her shop for a kiss and our hearts are healed. And whenever she finds herself revisiting her own dark times, she comes to us and we kiss and love her hurt away.

What joys and happiness we share. No darkness is welcome here.

"Aveline..." I murmur.

"Hmm?" She opens her beautiful eyes to look at me. "What more could you want from your wife today?"

"You can guess, beloved." I wet my fingertip in my mouth and stroke the cleft of her bottom. The tiny opening tenses and flutters at my touch, and she quivers and moans.

As I pleasure her gently, Toved caresses her lower lip with his thumb. "You are happy?" he asks.

"Happy?" She playfully tries to bite his thumb. "I'm much more than happy. Blissful. Content." She sighs and moves against my fingers. "Satisfied."

"Not yet satisfied," I counter, and coat my fingers in oil from a little pot on the bed beside us. "Nor are we."

When I slip two fingers inside her, she groans and wiggles against me. I nip her earlobe with my teeth.

"It's been a year," she gasps. "More than a year. Surely you can't desire me as much today as our first nights together."

"That is true." Toved leans in to kiss her. "We desire you more."

"But *work*—" she protests.

"—Can wait," Toved finishes. "What else could be more important than to ensure our wife wants for nothing?"

I raise her head so I can kiss her. "We love you."

"I never doubt it for a moment." Her smile is, and always will be, my sunshine. "Even when you apparently arrange for me to be off work for a day," she adds, "which means I'll have *twice* as much work to do tomorrow. I don't know what you told her, but Paita will know why I was absent. She has an uncanny sense about these things."

"I do not think it will require any uncanny senses to know how you spent your day today." Toved's hand travels under the fur to circle her sensitive pearl as I add another finger to delve inside her sweet, tight bottom.

To please her from behind takes a special blend of oil and patient preparation, but her screams are loudest and her releases most powerful with one of her husbands' cocks in her bottom, so we are quite happy to take all the time needed.

She moans between us and trembles. Toved's cock is hard and dripping again, as is mine.

"You will be very visibly tired, and very visibly satisfied, tomorrow," I promise, kissing her brow. "Now, if our wife would be so kind as to rise to her hands and knees, we have plans to make the most of this stolen day."

ABOUT LISA EDMONDS

Lisa Edmonds was born and raised in Kansas and studied English and forensic criminology at Wichita State University. After acquiring her Bachelor's degree in English, she considered a career in law enforcement as a behavioral analyst before earning a Master's in English from Wichita State and then a Ph.D. in English from Texas A&M University.

For ten years, she was an associate professor of English at a college in Texas, where she taught a variety of writing and literature courses. Now a full-time author, she shares a cute Victorian-style home called The Storybook House with her husband and their pets, and enjoys writing, reading, traveling, spoiling her niece and nephew, and singing karaoke.

Lisa is the author of the Fortusian Mates sci-fi romance series, editor of this volume as well as *Tempted by Celestial Bodies: An Alien Romance Anthology*, and author of the best-selling Alice Worth urban fantasy series.

For SFW and NSFW commissioned art, updates on new and upcoming releases, and sneak peeks at works in progress, join Lisa's reader community at LisaEdmonds.com.

BRIDE OF THE FOREST

S. C. GRAYSON

CHAPTER

ONE

ESMERAY

Eyes watched me from the edge of the woods.

I had never managed to see them, but their weight caressed my skin like a physical touch as I tended to my garden. I'd always felt as if somebody observed me from the shadows of the trees, lingering just out of sight. After five years living on the edge of the woods, the sensation was familiar, almost comfortable. But today, the sensation grew particularly intense, raising hairs on my arms and sending a shiver down my spine. It wasn't altogether unpleasant.

My fingers plunged into the dirt, the warm metallic smell of churned earth filling my nose as I made a hole for the rhubarb cutting lying beside me. My fingernails would be crusted with mud, but I didn't care.

Especially not today.

The full moon would light the sky tonight, and as always, a wild power thrummed in my veins. All the witches in the village would celebrate the harvest moon tonight with a festival, but something about the power it brought made my magic itch. As if I should tear off my clothes and run wild through the night.

When I was small, my mother told me I had been touched by the moon—
—that Lunara's blessing was the reason my hair glistened white, despite
my dark complexion. On days like today, I thought she might be right.

Perhaps that is why I felt like the woods watched me. Dangers lurked in
the shadows of the woods. The villagers never dared set foot in the depths
of the forest, and only the bravest witches among them ventured into the
outskirts to collect mushrooms and herbs for incantations. Parents warned
children away, telling tales of trees that would swallow them until their
screams were muffled by bark and branches.

But the forest had always drawn me in, and the full moon made the call
nearly irrresistible. That was why I imagined it watched me—*taunted* me. It
knew I yearned to run wild amongst the beasts of the wood, but I had
always shoved that urge away.

I looked up from where I packed earth around the rhubarb stem and a
gold flicker caught my eye. I squinted at the tree line, convinced it had been
lamp-like eyes shining in the shadows before they blinked away. Now only
the dappled green of waving branches greeted my gaze.

I shook my head, trying to clear my vision. While I had always imagined
somebody watching, I had never caught sight of any movement besides the
swishing of branches and the fluttering of birds' wings. But today, the forest
seemed particularly alive. As if its wildness spilled past the borders of the
trees, trying to draw me in. The eyes were just another sign.

"Esmeray!"

I jumped at the sound of my sister calling my name, having been so
preoccupied staring at the woods that I hadn't heard the bang of the door
as she came out of the house.

"Come inside. If you don't start getting ready soon, you'll have to spend
the festival covered in dirt."

I stood and dusted my hands on my apron, although a whisper beneath
my skin told me that it wouldn't be so bad to be crusted with earth. Still, I
turned with a smile.

Izara stood in the doorway, her dark hair wreathing her head in a wild
halo and her black eyes shining with excitement. This would be her first

harvest moon festival since getting her witch marks—her first opportunity to take part in the true magic of the night.

She had gone through the rite that marked her passage into adulthood just two moons ago. The new markings across her chest—unique for every witch—indicated she was now a master of her power. A fully-fledged witch, and a talented one at that.

She beckoned me inside excitedly, leading me to her room.

"Let's get you cleaned up and try on our dresses." She practically skipped down the hall. I followed after her only slightly more sedately.

Where my magic was the moon, hers was the sun, full of a warmth that you couldn't help but be drawn to. As we rounded the corner to her bedroom, splashes of colorful cloth strewn across the quilt on her bed greeted us: green for me and red for her.

"Come on... come on!" She flapped her hands at me, eager for me to take off my smudged brown skirt and shooing me towards a wash basin in the corner.

I did as she asked, scrubbing my hands and relieving myself of the rough spun garment. As I did, she stepped up behind me and pulled a leaf from my braids with a smile.

"Someday, you are going to start growing roots and branches yourself," she teased. In the time it had taken me to wash, she had already changed into her deep burgundy dress, designed especially for her. The neckline was high but wide, showing off the slope of her shoulder and collarbone. I looked at her wistfully in the mirror, wondering when she had become a woman.

Her witch mark, resting in the hollow of her throat, pulsed with the guiding light of the Goddess Solara, who would protect her for the rest of her days. But I had been the one to protect her up until now.

I blinked quickly at the thought, and at the sense of untethered melancholy that overcame me whenever I remembered that my sister didn't truly need me anymore. Not in the way she once had.

Now, she grabbed my attention by shaking my own dress at me, the emerald green fabric rippling and pooling on the floor, as I was taller than her and my dress far longer. I sighed as she helped me step into it and lace up the back, bouncing on her toes in excitement.

"I thought tonight we would do something extra special, since it's my first festival with my witch marks," she said, barely containing her excitement.

She gestured to her dressing table, and my heart leaped into my throat as I saw what lay there: our mother's jewelry. Beads meant to decorate braids and a comb adorned with shimmering antlers, wrought from gold. The antlers had always been my favorite, and I would run my fingers over them in adoration whenever my mother brought them out. She had promised me that one day I would wear them, and the thought had always brought a smile to my face.

Even when I had struggled to feed my sister and me, knowing such pieces would fetch us enough coins to feed us for a year, I could never part with them—could barely consider selling them without bile rising in my throat. So I had made do selling potions and poultices that other witches would not make, as they could not gather the mushrooms and herbs needed without braving the outskirts of the woods.

The jewelry had been our mother's most prized possession, given to her by our father during a time when witches were revered in the kingdom instead of pushed to towns on the outskirts of society where we could practice our magic without fear. Carefully, I walked over to the dressing table and picked up the golden antlers, their shape and size making them akin to a crown. I turned towards Izara with the comb. As much as I longed to put them atop my own braids, perhaps she should wear them, as this was her special night. The gold would look striking nestled in her wild cloud of curls.

She shook her head.

"You should wear it," she murmured, laying her hands over mine. "They were always meant to be yours. You deserve it."

The lump in my throat grew thicker and I tried to swallow it down, to no avail. Still, I didn't protest as Izara took the antlers from me and slid the comb into the tight weave of my braids. As she did, I got the strange sense of eyes on me again, and I shivered.

The full moon was rising.

DRAKKAN

My hunger grew.

For weeks now it had gnawed at me, but now it grew to a fever pitch—an itch beneath my skin that caused me to pace through the trees and the fur of my tail to bristle as it twitched. I had hunted and fed, but nothing seemed to help.

My only solace was in lingering at the edge of the woods and watching the little witch tend her garden, just like I had since she had first come to this village years ago. As she plunged her hands into the dirt, elbow deep, my mouth watered, and my lips pulled back from my teeth of their own accord to show off my glittering canines.

For hundreds of human lifetimes I had wandered these woods, one with the flora and fauna that sprang forth in the presence of my divine essence. I had never wanted for more, until the village sprang up, several decades ago, right near the edges of my domain.

I had found myself watching the humans go about their mundane lives with increasing fascination—wondering how they always walked in groups or danced together and laughed at each other's words. Something in my chest jumped and twitched like a fish out of water as I watched humans bind themselves together in pairs, tying a knot around their joined hands before pressing their lips together in what appeared to be a gesture of affection. At first, I had been able to convince myself it was just curiosity at the ways of their kind.

But then I saw her.

She had appeared in the village nearly five summers ago. While most humans gave the shadow of my trees a large berth, this witch dared to wander close, sometimes pausing to gather mushrooms at the fringes of my domain. She did not fear my home, although perhaps she should.

Never before had I suffered a mortal to pass through my forest, seeing them only as a nuisance who would destroy the delicate balance of my existence. But she was different—unafraid. She never seemed to shy away from leaves or dirt, letting them tangle in her hair and decorate her clothing.

I became fascinated, lingering in the thinnest part of the trees and watching her work.

A new hunger grew in me, and it could not be sated by food. Instead, it lodged itself under my ribs, a strange, hollow pulling in my chest. And so, the nameless yearning became part of me, only ever eased by watching the witch in her garden.

Sometimes, when she wandered into the shadow of my trees, I would call mushrooms to life further into the woods, close enough for her to see them to draw her deeper into my domain. It allowed me to look at her more closely without leaving the safety of the dark shadows where I hid. I thought it might satisfy me to simply feel her presence in my domain. But as she found the herbs and toadstools I called forth for her, she smiled, and a pang under my sternum made it clear that I needed more.

As my hunger grew, so too did my fascination with the practices of humans. I lingered to watch the way pairs would walk along the path at the borders of my domain, their fingers interlaced. Some would steal into the shadows of my trees to press their lips together and run their hands over each other's bodies in a way that made pleasant shivers crawl down my spine and heaviness pool in my belly.

For centuries, these woods had been my domain, and mine alone.

Beasts of the forest courted and mated, but I paid them no mind. Whatever physical urges I shared with animals, I could handle on my own. But the way the humans touched each other in my shadows awoke a curiosity that only worsened my hunger. Now, I wondered what it would be like to do these things with the witch who did not fear the woods. What would she taste like if I pressed my lips to hers and slipped my tongue into her waiting mouth? I wondered if tying her hand to my own clawed fingers like humans did would dispel some of the bone-deep hunger that had become integral to my existence.

I watched those hands work the dirt now as she gardened and wondered what they would feel like on my skin or wrapped around my antlers.

A growl grew in the back of my throat as another figure appeared in the garden and called my witch away, and she disappeared within the house. The inexorable itch under my skin grew in her absence, and my claws extended, digging into the soft earth where I crouched on all fours.

I refused to suffer like this any longer. I was the god of this forest, and humans should be of no consequence to me. The intensity of the hunger tonight was just the curse of the harvest moon. The wolves that walked my borders were ready to hunt and their anticipation dragged me into my own state of alertness.

Turning to stalk back into the trees, a glimmer of gold caught my eye. The witch had reappeared, but the gold ornament laid atop her silver braids held my rapt attention as if she had cast a spell.

Antlers, just like my own.

My claws extended and my tail bristled, switching wildly and disturbing the thick layer of leaves and brush on the ground.

It was a sign. She knew she was mine.

My witch threw an arm around the other human woman's shoulder with a broad smile and turned her gaze up to the darkening sky where the full moon shone.

Below the hunger that made my jaw ache to bite down on something— to claim—something dark and tender pulsed, but I pushed that away in favor of the decision taking place in my mind. The witch had always been curious about the forest, and I could sense the way her magic twitched and danced in response to the power that awakened only under the full moon.

Tonight, I would make her mine.

CHAPTER
THREE

I zara was transcendent. With her hands in the air, she twisted her wrists and swayed her hips. All the other young witches gathered around her laughed and danced with her in the town square, admiring the sunbeams of her new witch mark that spread across her collarbones.

As she danced, she sketched symbols in the air with her fingertips, making sparkles of magic swirl around the dancers like lightening bugs. The other women giggled and whooped in excitement at the beautiful display of her fully blossomed power.

A smile danced on my lips as I watched her, but I couldn't help the wistful ache that pulsed in my chest. The festival was held in center square of the town, in the open cobbled portion surrounded by the few businesses that occupied the town—an inn and an apothecary among a small smattering of shops. Tonight, the area was dotted with colorful lanterns strung between the thatched rooves. The sounds of boisterous singing and the scents of crushed herbs from the charms some of the witches were selling filled the air.

The whole thing was light and life—a perfect fit for my sister's sunny new witch mark.

In the distance, a wolf howled, its melody equal parts mournful and celebratory, and the eerie note pierced my heart. My chest warmed. Beneath my sternum my own witch mark started to pulse, and I rubbed at it absently.

Every full moon for years, something had called me to the forest, but I had resisted the pull. The power that drew me to the trees lay dormant in my veins as I turned my attention towards my duties. Izara had needed me, and that had been enough to dull the yearning for something wild. Something *primal*.

I began to push the call of my magic into the background as I always did, but as I watched my sister twirl around the bonfire in the center of the square, I hesitated. There was no longer a reason to deny the desires of my magic. My breath rushed from my lungs as if I had been punched in the stomach at the realization. Even as I froze, my blood began to rush faster in my veins.

Since I was barely a woman, my entire purpose had been to care for Izara. I was a mother, a teacher, a nurse, and a guard all at once. My identity as a witch had been pushed to the background the moment our parents died, protecting us from the angry mob that drove us out of the city in fear of our power. It had been mere months after I received my own witch mark.

I had brought us to this small town where we could use our magics freely, but I had never been free to indulge the wilder tendencies that came so readily with my own power. I had pushed all that aside in favor of selling potions and keeping a tidy house to give Izara the best life I could. There was no time for mad dashes through the wilds.

Until now.

Already, I turned away from the town square, but I hesitated, glancing back over my shoulder. Izara and her friends were still enjoying the revelries around the fire, and the sunburst on my sister's collarbone pulsed with light—a promise of the goddess Solara's protection. She would be safe.

Still, I lingered until the call of the wolf came again. It was louder now, as if the pack drew closer. A shudder slipped up my spine, laced with anticipation. I was really going to do this. Quickly, I slipped through an alley and out of the town square.

Everyone in the village had gathered for the festival, leaving the streets deserted as I padded across the packed dirt towards the shadows of the forest. Laughter and shouts chased me from the festivities in ephemeral echoes. Their untethered joy told me that they all felt the magic of the full moon as much as I did. But while it made some witches want to dance and laugh in the company of others, it had always made me want to bare my teeth and howl at the moon.

As if it had heard my thoughts, the wolf in the distance began its song again.

At the sound, I picked up my pace. My heart accelerated and my steps to match it as I ran through the streets, arms pumping and skirt fluttering behind me. My chest warmed pleasantly as my witch mark glowed, finally flaring to life fully as I let loose. It grew tingly and pleasantly hot in a way it hadn't in the five years I had borne it.

I didn't slow until I reached the line of the trees bordering the edge of the village, and even then it was only to dodge around the boughs and branches. Leaves brushed my face and curled around my calves as if they were reaching out to caress me—to welcome me.

Finally, the flickering lantern light of the village at my back was swallowed up in the quiet of the forest, and I stopped. My own panting breaths filled my ears in the relative quiet, but I could tell the forest around me teamed with life. Small rodents scurried through the underbrush and somewhere in the distance sounded the low hoot of an owl.

A sigh of contentment escaped my lips, and I found myself kicking off my shoes so my toes could dig into the detritus of the forest floor. The rich scent of earth and decaying matter that was the source of all life permeated the air, and I closed my eyes for a moment as I breathed it in deeply.

I expected the inexorable call of the forest to quiet now that I had given in to my instincts and run wild into the dangerous woods, but instead it only pulsed louder—a thunderous roar that I somehow heard without my ears. I knitted my brows together and opened my eyes.

In the dark space between the trees hung yellow eyes.

A sharp breath hissed in through my teeth, and a cold rush of adrenaline flooded through my body as I stared into them, frozen. The pupils—slitted like a cat's—dilated, as if they could sense my reaction.

They were just like the eyes I had envisioned watching me from the trees this afternoon. Or perhaps I hadn't imagined them at all.

The leaves around the clearing I stood in rustled as if with a faint breeze.

"What are you?" I asked, my voice surprisingly level. A distant part of my mind told me I shouldn't stay to ask. It urged me to turn and run until I was back in the warm light of the village, far from this thing that was clearly never meant for human eyes.

That voice was drowned out by the primal thrumming of magic in my chest, which howled now like the wolf I had heard earlier.

"I am this forest."

The voice that answered sounded like the braying of hounds and the chirping of birds; the whistling of wind and the quiet warmth of sunshine filtering through foliage. A shiver ran up my spine.

"I didn't know forests could speak," the snide words were out of my mouth before I could think better of them.

The eyes tilted, as if the owner cocked his head in thought—for it was definitely a him. That much I could tell.

"But you did. You heard my call, and you came," the voice came again.

As he spoke, I willed myself to take a step back. To put some distance between myself and the monster that lurked before me. Instead, I found myself straining my eyes, craning my neck forward to try to make out the rest of his shadowed figure.

His words made me think back to my hectic flight into the woods, deeper than I normally dared venture, the primal magic in me boiling over in response to the howling of...

"Are you a wolf?"

"Yes. And no. I am everything that lives and grows within this forest."

"And why did you call me?" I asked, thinking of the inexorable pull of the howling wolf—the inexplicable tug under my breastbone I had felt at its melancholy wildness.

Leaves rustled, and a low rumbling came from the shadows before me, but that was my only response. Then, the eyes slowly shrank back, as if the unknowable creature retreated.

"Wait," I demanded, stepping forward and reaching out a hand. I did not know why I did it. Perhaps it was because that haunting call still echoed in my skull, awakening the aching yearning that lingered in my chest and made my witch mark flare to life.

The sound of rustling leaves stopped, as if the whole forest froze.

"Let me see you," I demanded, voice firmer than I felt. I clenched my fists to dispel the shaking, although the sensation that made me tremble did not feel like fear. More like the aching excitement of a want almost fulfilled, satisfaction so close I could almost taste it.

The shadows shifted and grew as the eyes drew nearer, rising as the creature stood to his full height until I had to crane my neck up to meet them. I drew in a shuddering gasp as he stepped fully into the clearing and out of the cover of the trees.

Even as he stood in the middle of the clearing, he appeared one with the foliage around him. As he had said, he *was* the forest.

Though his top half was roughly shaped like that of a man, and a large, muscular one at that, his skin was dappled in a thousand shades of brown and green, like bark. Starting at his hips, his legs were covered in the thick grayish fur of a wolf, ending in huge, clawed feet. As my gaze trailed up his body, my attention caught briefly on a bushy tail switching behind him, until my eyes were drawn inexorably back to his face.

His features were vulpine, matching the golden, slitted eyes that still seemed to glow in the darkness. But most striking of all were the antlers, part deer, part twisting branches that reached up, up, up to mix with the canopy above. Vines and leaves dripped off them, hanging down to frame his angular face.

My stomach clenched and my mouth grew dry, but it was not fear I felt when I looked upon this creature. Instead, it was the same shivery anticipation I felt in the moments before I had decided to leave the festival and dash into the woods. It was as if I was about to reach out and grasp everything I had been yearning for, even though I hadn't truly known what awaited me.

I held my breath as he opened his mouth to speak.

"I am Drakkan," he said, his voice a low rumble I could feel reverberating through the space between us. "And I am the god of this forest."

FOUR

DRAKKAN

I had never spoken to a human before. My tail twitched and my claws extended in response to the bone deep craving that only grew stronger in the witch's presence. The part of me that made me bare my teeth and bristle the fur of my tail wanted to pounce on her—to lay her down on the leafy forest floor and devour her—was overpowered by my utter fascination with her.

She stood tall, taking me in with a glimmer of wonder in her gaze. I found myself puffing out my chest, pulling myself to my full height so that my antlers brushed the tree branches above.

At first, it had only mattered to me that she had responded to my call, but now another thought struck me. I tilted my head.

"Are you afraid?" I asked.

"No." She said the word as if it surprised her. "Do you want me to be?"

"No," I echoed. "You do not fear this forest, and that is why I called to you."

She took one small step forward, as if she did not even realize she was doing so. "This forest has never harmed me, despite the tales some tell of it. If you truly are this forest, then I have nothing to fear from you either."

I lowered my chin, fixing her with a predatory stare as pulled back my lips to expose my elongated canines. "I would not be so sure."

As much as I didn't want her to be afraid, I wondered if her bravery might be temporary. She might change her mind and flee from the woods once she saw the darker side of me—the side of me that was the death and decay that gave this forest life, and the hunger of the wolf as he tore into his prey.

The witch narrowed her dark eyes, which glittered in the thin light of the moon filtering through the leaves. "I am a celestial witch on the full moon. I would not be so sure."

My hunger intensified at her bold words, and a low rumble built in my chest, but she continued.

"Besides, if you called me here, then you need me. You won't get whatever it is you want if you kill me," she pointed out, putting her hands on her hips. The movement pulled her dress so that the opening under her breasts showed of the glowing witch mark illustrating the phases of the moon stretched across the hollow beneath her ribs. They told me she was blessed by the goddess Lunara—a distant cousin of mine.

"What is it that you want? That you called me here for?" She asked, ignoring the rake of my gaze down her torso.

I opened my mouth, ready to tell her all I desired from her. To share with her how the sight of her silvery hair against her dark skin caught my eye every time she was in the garden, and how the swell of her hip as she propped a basket on it caused an aching tightness in my groin. I would tell her how the antlers in her hair told me that she *would* be mine, and I would claim her as such under the light of this full moon.

I said none of those things.

"What are you called?" I asked instead.

The determined set of her jaw softened. "Esmeray," she said, the syllables like music on her lips.

"Esmeray," I repeated, relishing the sweet taste of the syllables on my tongue. "Tell me Esmeray, what is this tradition where humans tie their hands together?"

She blinked, looking startled, as if I had managed to throw her off her guard for the first time since meeting in this clearing.

"Handfasting? It is how we get married in our village, for we have no holy man or temple. It's how people bind themselves to one another," she explained, smoothing her hands over her green skirt, the fabric the same dark color as the late summer leaves around us.

She really was made for the forest. For me.

"This is what I want," I declared. "To bind you to me."

Esmeray's mouth fell open, but instead of registering her shock, I could only look at the *O* of her lips and think of how I wanted to cover them with my own. It was a human custom I had seen at these handfasting ceremonies, and one that had caught my interest and held it with a singular focus.

As I pondered Esmeray's lips, she did not speak for several long moments, the only sounds the whispering of wind and the hoot of a distant owl.

"Why?" she finally, said, the single syllable a breathy gust of air.

"I have walked this forest alone for longer than your village has existed," I admitted. "I am a God, and I need no companion. But watching the humans live their lives in the company of others for the past decades... it has made me *want*."

Understanding dawned on her features, and for a second it seemed like Esmeray saw straight through my flesh to the primal power that lurked beneath my bark. It felt like being flayed open—completely foreign, and yet I reveled in it.

"You want a bride," she observed. "But humans don't usually marry those they have just met."

I took a prowling step forward, but Esmeray did not back away. My nostrils flared as I caught her scent on the evening breeze. It was woodsy and rich, making my mouth water.

"But you have known me for years. You have walked beneath my trees and gathered mushrooms in my shade. You have watched me from your garden every day, just as I have watched you. You said yourself that if I am the forest, you have nothing to fear from me." I leaned closer, towering over her so she had to crane her neck to look up at me. Something sparked in her eyes as I continued. "Well, these woods and I are one and the same, and you have been drawn to me ever since you first laid eyes on me."

She sucked in a shivering breath, but she did not speak. Slowly, I raised one hand to drag a clawed finger along the delicate gold twist of the antlers perched atop her head. The cool metal warmed under my touch.

"You even adorned yourself with my symbol, tonight, as if to tell me you were ready to be my bride," I said.

Esmeray tilted her head to break my touch on her golden antlers. I bared my teeth but left my hand hovering in space as I waited for her response.

"Let's make a deal," she offered.

I nodded, waiting for her to continue with tension in every muscle of my body. To find out if after all these years I was to have a companion, and if that companion would be *her*. The witch who had transfixed me for so many years. If gods weren't immune to such things, I would have thought she had cast an enchantment to ensnare me.

"If I am going to be your bride, you have to prove yourself," Esmeray said, lifting her chin.

My hackles rose, and part of me wanted to insist that a god did not have to prove themselves to a witch, but the mischievous look on her face gave me pause. The corners of her lips twitched in the beginnings of a wild smile, and her dark eyes glinted with something feral that promised to be everything I desired and more, if I could just be patient a little longer.

"I'm going to run, and if you can't reach me before I reach the edge of the woods, then you will owe me a favor of my choosing. If you catch me, though, I will be your bride," she offered.

A rushing filled my ears at her words, and tension built in my cock. Esmeray's eyes, which had remained fixed on my face throughout our entire conversation, flicked down to it where it began to stand to full attention, and her tongue darted out to wet her lips.

Still, I held myself in check, clenching my fists until my claws drew blood from my palms.

"To be clear, if I catch you, I am going to claim you in every way. I will make you mine so thoroughly that there will never be any others—imprint my power on you so deeply that my essence will be stitched into the very fiber of your being." The words came out as a growling rumble, full of the wildness of the woods and the darkness of my deepest shadows.

Esmeray sucked in a shuddering breath, but her resolve did not appear to crumble.

"That is the deal you are striking. Is that what you agree to?" My body trembled with tension, but I held myself perfectly still, a predator waiting for the perfect moment to pounce on its prey.

"Yes."

The single syllable hit me like a physical blow and heat rushed through me like an inferno. I could only stare and take in the feral look on her face that I was sure mirrored my own. It was an expression that promised the thrill of a hunt, and at the end of it, satisfaction unlike any I had ever known. The roaring in my ears grew so intense that I barely heard what she said next.

"But first, you have to catch me."

Then she bolted.

My body took a moment to unfreeze, but when it did, it was as if the strings holding me upright had snapped. I dropped to all fours, the posture of a wolf on the prowl. I tipped my head back and let out a long, unrestrained howl at the moon. The sign of my new bride.

She was in my realm now, and the hunt was afoot.

CHAPTER

FIVE

ESMERAY

Twigs snapped underfoot, almost inaudible over the rushing in my ears as I crashed into the brush. Leaves caressed my face and my bare legs as I wove between the darkened shadows of the trees.

Then, a howl drowned out every other sensation.

This wasn't the mournful, wild howl that had drawn me away from the festival. This was a howl of victory—of a wolf who had already had a successful hunt and was ready to feast.

My lips pulled back from my teeth in a wild smile even as I continued to run, my breath coming in short pants as I pumped my arms and willed myself to run faster.

Drakkan may very well catch me. I even wanted him to, and I hadn't even given a thought to what favor I might ask of him if I escaped the forest. But I didn't plan on letting this chase be over too quickly.

A feeling like fear, but far more potent and intoxicating dripped down my spine as I tried to put as much distance as possible between me and the clearing. My legs burned with the effort, and the sweet, heavy scent of earth and decaying leaves filled my nose.

Behind me, the forest rustled, and I could nearly hear the pounding of clawed feet against the ground in pursuit. Drakkan was far bigger than me, and far faster.

My mind raced as I took in my surroundings, squinting through the darkness as I ran, looking for any possible advantage.

A thick blackberry bush over a small gully caught my eye, and I made a split-second decision. I dove headlong for it, crashing through the leaves into the ditch below it. I paid no heed to the brambles caught in my braids or the dirt smearing my dress as I pressed myself flat on my belly.

Pressed into the ground, I could nearly taste decaying leaves and metallic dirt. Even as I concealed myself under the bush, I craned my neck to peer over the lip of earth at the edge of the gully.

A primal growl filled the air as Drakkan crashed into view. A shiver ran up my spine so forcefully that it nearly made the bush above me shudder as I saw he had dropped to all fours. Thick muscle bunched under his bark-like skin as he launched himself forward, clawed nails digging deep into the soft earth and golden eyes glowing like lamps in the darkness. He still moved with the same predatory grace as he did when he slowly approached me in the clearing, but now it had an untamed edge to it that made my mouth grow dry and my hands tremble.

But this was not fear for my life—this was raw anticipation. I waited for a voice in my head to ridicule me, half expecting some part of myself to balk at the idea of letting myself be hunted by this primordial being, knowing what awaited me when I was caught.

After all, I had seen the impressive length hanging between his legs come to its full hardness as I suggested he chase me.

But he had been right. Despite the absolute foreignness of his appearance, I had gotten a sense of familiarity when we spoke—as if he was an old friend reintroducing himself. I had always gotten a sense of being watched over when I was in the woods, but not in a malevolent way. Drakkan was the presence who had unknowingly been my companion and my quiet call to the wildness of the woods for many years.

Now I wanted to drag out this hunt not because I feared what waited at the end, but because of the sweetness of the anticipation that coated my tongue as I watched Drakkan charge blindly past me in search of his bride.

I would be his bride, but only after he had earned it.

As the chaotic rustling of his passing faded, I eased out from my hiding spot. My hands and knees stung with small scrapes, but the sensation only heightened my awareness of every inch of my skin as I brushed my palms on my skirt.

Keeping my ears pricked for signs of Drakkan's approach, I turned and doubled back the way I'd come. I didn't run but moved as quickly as I could while remaining quiet. I dodged low hanging branches and picked my way carefully through the brush.

The only noise was the harsh scrape of my breath in my throat and the gentle swish of wind through the leaves. I strained my eyes to see in the darkness, until finally they caught on a black gash in a large oak tree that was not penetrated by the light of the full moon.

It would be a perfect hiding place, and I had one more trick up my sleeve.

I slipped into the large hollow in the ancient tree, the wood tight around my ribs like an embrace as I wiggled into the crevasse. Then, I maneuvered around as best I could to face the opening and lifted my hands in front of me.

Quickly I sketched a few symbols in the air: witch marks for secrecy and stealth.

Under normal circumstances, I would not be able to make myself fully invisible, but tonight was the full moon, and wild magic pulsed in my blood.

A feeling like cold water rushed over me and I shivered in response as I faded from view.

No sooner had I let my hands drop than golden eyes appeared in the darkness of the clearing.

I hadn't even heard Drakkan turn to follow me, but here he was already, feet away from my hiding spot. He stepped closer, his clawed feet making no noise as his head swung back and forth, searching.

He was not just a feral beast who ran through the underbrush, but a skilled predator as he prowled expertly through the darkness.

"Did you think there is anywhere you could hide in my woods that I could not find you, little witch?" he spoke into the darkness. His voice was a deep rumble that went straight to the pit of my belly and coalesced in a pool of warmth.

"You are clever, and skilled enough with your magic to evade any man, but I am no mere man," he continued. He stalked closer to my tree, but his eyes did not settle on my hiding spot yet.

"Even now, I cannot see you, but I can smell your sweetness." His nostrils flared as he took a deep breath in as if sampling the air. "I can taste on the wind how much you liked the chase. How wet it made you. How ready you are to be caught—to be the bride of this forest."

I raised a fist to my mouth and bit down on it to stifle a surprised gasp. I shifted, knowing he was right. From the moment I had heard his howl behind me, signaling his hunt, anticipation had gathered in my core until now it felt warm and aching. Begging for attention.

"So, what do you say, little witch?" Drakkan's eyes finally landed on the crack in the tree where I stood, although I knew he could not see me. "Are you ready to let me taste that honey straight from the source?"

I tore my hand from my mouth and scrubbed my witch symbols from the air, removing my camouflage. Drakkan's eyes flared as I came into view and stepped from the tree, the golden orbs momentarily as bright as the stars above.

I tried to step towards him, ready and aching for all that he promised, but a grip around my ankle stopped me. I looked down to find a vine wrapped around my foot. The leaves whispered and a brush against my other ankle caught my attention, and then my wrists.

As the vines pulled me back, flush against the tree behind me, I raised my eyebrows at Drakkan. His response was a feral grin, elongated canines glinting in the moonlight.

"I am this forest, and every inch of it responds to my commands. You had your fun—now it's time for me to have mine," he growled.

The vines around my wrists pulled my arms up above my head, pinning them to the rough bark behind me. I nearly had to reach up on my tiptoes, the position leaving me stretched out and vulnerable, the entirety of me open to Drakkan's perusal.

I shivered.

Once again, I waited for some part of my brain to object to such treatment, but my sanity seemed to have fled under the intense scrutiny of Drakkan prowling toward me. Instead, his singular focus lit a fire beneath my skin. Having the sole focus of a god—a primordial power as wild and unknowable as nature itself looking at me as if I was the only thing in existence at this moment—made me feel as if I had drunk too much cider at the festival. My head felt so light I might be floating, but desire was heavy in my gut.

Drakkan stopped mere inches from me, so close I could feel his warm breath ghost across my skin as he leaned in. At his height, he blocked all else from view, surrounding me in his raw power and masculine energy.

"Unless you would rather run away again, little witch?"

Even in the darkness, I saw Drakkan's muscles twitching beneath his dappled skin. The leaves adorning his antlers shivered, as if with the effort of holding his desires at bay as he gave me one last chance to change my mind.

I took a deep breath and dove headfirst into the hypnotizing well of lust he had uncovered in my soul. "Make me your bride."

Drakkan covered my lips with his as his hands gripped my waist. I gasped into his mouth as the vines around my wrists and ankles tightened, keeping me pinned and helpless as he devoured my mouth. The sound that ripped its way from his chest as he tasted me was an animalistic snarl.

His fingers tightened against my ribs, the edge of claws digging in. I squirmed, trying to get closer as he crowded me against the tree at my back.

The hard length of his torso pushed against me, and I gasped at the feeling of his textured skin. While it wasn't rough like the bark it resembled, it had smooth ridges and whirls that brushed against the bare skin over my witch mark. I could feel it even through my dress, the texture teasing my nipples to painful hardness as it rubbed against me.

I whimpered, trying to rub my thighs together to relieve some of the flame that had been quickly stoked to a bonfire inside me. The vines at my ankles responded by pulling my legs even farther apart.

Drakkan pulled back from my mouth, nipping at my bottom lip with his canines as he did.

"I can smell how you ache for me, little witch. I will not let you deprive me of a single drop of the pleasure I will wring from you. After all, I caught you, and now I will claim every inch of you. That was our deal." An expression like a smirk twisted his inhuman features. "And I am not yet done exploring this human practice of pressing our mouths together."

A bolt of amusement cut through the haze of lust, strong enough to startle a breathy laugh out of me.

"Kissing," I gasped as he traced the back of one claw across my throat to the hollow between my collarbones. "That's what we call it. Do gods not kiss?"

A satisfied noise rumbled in Drakkan's throat, like a deep purr, as his claw caught on the neckline of my dress. "I do not know what gods do, for I have spent all my days among the beasts of the forest who mate and fuck with abandon. But perhaps I shall make you my goddess and we will find all the possible ways to pleasure one another: human, animal, and divine."

A strangled moan escaped my lips at his words, drowned out by the tearing of fabric as Drakkan drew his claw through my dress, splitting it cleanly down the front. The heat of his mouth covering mine again clashed with the cool breeze caressing my now bare skin as the remains of my dress hung uselessly from my shoulders.

He kissed me again as his hands began to investigate my bared skin. I squirmed and whimpered against his lips as his fingers brushed the underside of my breast before he used the back of one claw to circle my nipple.

With a curious expression Drakkan pulled back, gauging my reaction as he teased the aching flesh with the pads of his fingers. I bit back a noise like a sob as he repeated the action on the other breast.

The chase had stoked the fire within me hot enough that I felt ready to combust at any moment, but I was at Drakkan's mercy as his vines left me helpless to do anything but tunnel deeper into the well of desire his touch awakened in me.

Drakkan's golden eyes flashed before he ducked his head, and a sharp cry of surprise and pleasure echoed in the quiet of the forest as he pressed the flat of his tongue to my nipple. The scrape of his fangs against the tender skin of my breast made me thrash as I chased the maddening sensation, but the vines around my wrists and ankles tightened, keeping me from chasing his mouth as he pulled away, only to switch his attention to my other breast.

By the time he was satisfied with his explorations, I was panting and sagging against the trees, letting my leafy bonds hold most of my weight. My knees trembled and my head spun.

This was what it meant to be at the mercy of a god.

Drakkan peered up at me, his slitted eyes partially obscured by a veil of leaves cascading down from his antlers, as he fell to his knees. He dragged his tongue over my skin once more, this time over the glowing swirls of my witch mark. His eyes became half lidded as if in pleasure, and a rumble like that of the mountains emanated from his chest.

The ghost of a smile twisted my lips, even as my face screwed up in pleasure. This god was at my mercy too.

His fingers trailed down my lower abdomen, and I shivered as he brushed over the curls between my legs.

"Your claws," I gasped, as he ghosted over my most sensitive spot with the pad of one finger. He tilted his head at me as if in thought before flexing his hands. The claws at the tips of his fingers retracted beneath his skin like those of a cat.

"I do not sheathe them often," he admitted, circling the spot that made me gasp for air, "But I will for my bride. I'll be gentle with my prize...for now."

My head fell back against the tree with an audible *thunk* as he continued to stroke through my folds at a leisurely pace, as if exploring. My thighs clenched as if to close around his hand, keeping it where I wanted it most.

In response, the ropes around my ankles pulled my legs impossibly wider and Drakkan's fingers spread me open carefully for his perusal. "Let me see my prize and drink the honey you promised me. I must prepare your cunt to be bound to me, my bride."

I didn't have time to process his words before he licked my sex in one long stroke, flicking his tongue over my clit at the end in a way that made me shriek.

He repeated the action before staring up at me and growling, "That's right, little witch. Let all the creatures of this forest know what their god does to you."

Then, he set to devouring me with a single-minded focus that flayed me open and remade me. His tongue explored every inch of my sex while the occasional brush of a polished fang against my folds sent a bolt of pleasure mixed with adrenaline through me. The heady mix had me trembling at the precipice of my pleasure in mere minutes.

My fingers clenched into fists as I teetered on the edge, wishing I could grab onto his antlers and grind against his face to take my pleasure. Instead, I was forced to let him wring it from me.

Drakkan groaned at the fresh rush of wetness coating my thighs and lapped it up greedily.

"Come for me, little witch," he groaned against my heated flesh. "Give me your pleasure."

One more swirl of his tongue was all it took before I shattered. My vision went as bright as the full moon above as I shook and shook. Where I had cursed the bonds at my wrists a moment before, now the vines and Drakkan's grip on my thighs were all that kept me upright as pleasure left me boneless.

Finally, he stood, and the vines holding me in place loosened. Before I could slide to the leaf-strewn ground, Drakkan's hands came under my thighs, hoisting me against him and pressing me into the tree at my back. I let my arms fall, coming to rest around his shoulders. My fingers traced the whirling bark patterns of his skin as he kissed me again, clearly having taken to the human practice rather quickly.

I sighed in contentment, and he slid his tongue into my mouth, feeding me the taste of my own arousal and stoking the spark in my core back into a crackling heat.

Drakkan pulled back from my lips just far enough to speak into my mouth.

"I have kissed you as humans do, and now I will bind you to me."

CHAPTER

SIX

DRAKKAN

My chosen bride may have been mortal, but her taste was nothing short of divine. I licked the last traces of her from my lips as I watched her perfect breasts heave. Her brown skin was darkened with a flush of arousal all the way to her nipples, which were so hard they begged me to taste them again. I had let my godly instincts guide me thus far, and it had not let me astray.

But right now, I had other plans.

My fingers dug into the soft skin of her thighs as I held her weight and turned her away from the tree to lay her down in the soft moss and churned leaves. As her back touched the ground, she surprised me by tightening her thighs around me and heaving, until I lay on my back in the leaves and she hovered over me.

My heart, already hammering at the thought of being so close to binding myself to my bride, thundered in my ears.

Her small hands landed on my chest and she sat up. A growl reverberated in my chest as the move pressed her wet heat against my aching cock. Even more arousing though, was the sight of her sitting above me, the remains of her dress now falling completely free and leaving her in nothing but her golden jewelry, crowned with antlers that mirrored my own and caressed by the light of the full moon.

I groaned and the tip of my tail twitched, stirring the leaves beside us. Experimentally, she dragged her hips forward and back, grinding her perfect center against my cock.

Her mouth fell open, and my sharpened gaze locked onto the perfect *O* her lips made. Someday I would slide my godhood past those lips and see what kind of sounds she made while her mouth was stuffed full of my cock. But now I needed to make her ready to bind herself to me.

I lifted my hands to her hips and helped her drag herself across my length, feeling the size and weight of it. Her breath hitched, and she tried to lift up to take me inside her, but didn't let her, pushing her down harder against me.

"Your cunt isn't ready to take me yet, little witch," I soothed as she whimpered, continuing to grind her on my length.

"I don't think I can get any wetter." Her voice came thin and breathy.

My lips pulled back involuntarily as I bared my teeth in carnal satisfaction. "We shall see about that."

She continued to undulate her hips, rubbing her wetness over me and I let out a grunt of satisfaction.

"That's right," I urged. "Use me to find your pleasure. Feel how hard I ache for you."

Her hips stuttered and my hands, which had been resting on her waist, drifted down to cup her ass. I dug my fingers so hard into the flesh of her hips that I was sure to leave marks as I urged her to continue her movement. She braced her hands on the planes of my stomach and let her head fall back. The movement left the column of her throat deliciously exposed and her long braids fell down to tickle my thighs.

As the head of my cock nudged the center of her pleasure, she let out a broken keen. I began thrusting against her, making sure to brush her most sensitive point with every pass. My movements became ragged as I moved her hips with my hands, jerking her over my cock, nearly blind with pleasure just from the feeling of her rubbing against me. But I blinked the haze of ecstasy from my eyes to focus on her. I had been so busy enjoying the taste of my bride and the feel of her pulsing against my tongue the first time she came undone, that I had not gotten to watch her pleasure.

This time, I drank in every detail as she broke, tossing her head from side to side and trembling as her climax crashed through her. I imprinted the memory of her eyes screwed shut and her mouth wide open in a silent scream onto my divine soul, so that the memory of this most beautiful sight might be preserved for eternity.

Finally, her trembling abated, and she slumped her weight into her hands, letting her head hang forward onto her chest as she panted. Rivulets of her release gathered in the grooves of my abdomen and trickled down to soak the fur of my hips and thighs.

"Now, my bride, you're ready."

ESMERAY

One moment, my head was spinning with pleasure, and the next the world jerked around me as Drakkan lifted me off his hips and deposited me face down on the forest floor. I only managed to whimper as he hauled my hips up into the air, the cool breeze stark against the heated flesh of my center.

I expected to feel the nudge of his cock against my sopping entrance, but instead, I yelped as his tongue swiped from my clit all the way to the pucker of my ass. My squeal turned into a broken gasp as the wet heat of his mouth closed over the tight ring of muscle and he thrust his tongue against it.

Lightning danced behind my eyelids for a moment before he pulled away.

"Someday, I will bind myself to every hole you have." Drakkan's voice became less human by the second, sounding now like the rolling thunder of an incoming storm and the snarl of a wolf who guarded its kill. "But I'll start with this one."

One finger eased into my aching cunt to make his point clear, and my eyes rolled back into my head as I pressed my cheek into the dirt. His digit slid in with no resistance, so he added a second, then a third.

"Please," I gasped.

"What do you want, little witch?" Drakkan asked, his voice nothing short of otherworldly.

I was so debauched and undone by this point that the words spilled effortlessly past my lips. "Your cock. To be your bride, now and forever."

Finally, I felt the head of his cock at my entrance, and I nearly swallowed my tongue as he began to push forward. So big was he that my breath was punched from my chest in a long, broken moan. My insides felt remade by his presence, but still, he kept pushing forward.

I squirmed against him, both craving more and feeling on the edge of too much. One large hand landed on the back of my neck, pinning me to the ground. Drakkan's claws reemerged, and while they were lethally sharp, they rested warm and comforting against my skin.

I managed to pull in a shuddering breath, and the musty comforting smell of the earth and the leaves I lay pinned in filled my lungs. The smell of the forest. The smell of home.

The smell of Drakkan.

The last of the resistance disappeared and I gasped as Drakkan's hips pressed against mine.

"You'll never have to beg again little witch," he growled, bending over to blanket my back with his chest and rasp into my ear. "I'm going to make you more than my bride. I will bind you to me as a goddess."

He pulled out slightly before driving home again, driving a noise akin to a sob from my throat. As he bottomed out, he ground against me before pulling out and repeating the motion.

"This forest will be yours as much as mine, and the wildness in your blood will become one with the call of the hunt in mine," he said, continuing to pick up his pace.

I began to push back against him and he sat up fully. He released the back of my neck in favor of using both hands to hold my waist, pulling me back as his hips snapped forward. I turned my head to the side as my fingers curled, digging deep into the dirt.

It should have been filthy and obscene, being fucked into the ground in the middle of the forest by an inhuman being who had hunted me through the shadows. Just the thought of it made my core clench and a new gush of wetness run down my thighs.

But it also felt warm in my chest, as if my blood were igniting with something it had always known but had been forced to let be dormant for too long. Now, the creature there woke up, stretched its legs, and turned its face up to howl at the moon.

Sensation tore through me, heightened by the adrenaline still coursing in my veins. The fur of Drakkan's thighs brushed against the back of my legs and the tips of his claws dug into my flesh, sharp but not breaking skin. Leaves crunched and rubbed against my breasts as my chest pressed into the forest floor.

I gasped as a new sensation joined the mix: a foreign stretch, pushing my core beyond anything I had known before as Drakkan continued to drive into me. As he pulled out, it caught at my entrance before forcing back in.

A snarl reverberated through the clearing as I clenched around the new intrusion.

"Humans may tie their hands together with ribbon, but I will tie myself to you in my own way," Drakkan rasped. "I'll drive my seed so deep inside you that my power will take root, growing as tall and strong as these woods."

I whimpered as the bulge pushed inside me again, realizing what it was: a knot like a wolf's that would lock me to Drakkan, keeping me pinned as he filled me.

"Yes," I gasped, no fear or apprehension left in my body as my pleasure ratcheted the highest it had been yet. All that was left was a blinding need to feel him spend inside me.

One of Drakkan's hands left its grip on my hip to find my aching center once more.

"Come for me, my bride," he urged, "And all that I am will be yours."

I shattered with a howl, and Drakkan echoed me, his call no longer lonely and mournful. Now my scream was joined with his as his knot slipped inside me one last time. I convulsed around him, my vision turning completely white as he emptied inside me, impossibly deep as my cunt was stretched beyond imagining.

I trembled for long seconds before my legs gave out. A strong arm wrapped around my waist and eased us sideways on the forest floor. Drakkan pulled me back against his chest, his knot still pulsing inside me as he tucked my head beneath his chin.

For long minutes, the only sound was the rustling of wind in the trees and ragged cadence of our breaths. Lying naked on the forest floor with my center still aching and filled to the brim with a god and his seed might have felt uncomfortable, but instead, a warm sense of peace spread over me. Like the feeling of being covered by a familiar quilt in one's own bed, but amplified.

It spread in a building warmth, up from where Drakkan was knotted to me toward my chest. He pressed his hand over the center of the heat for a moment, and I gasped as I looked down, finding a golden light spilling between his fingers.

After a moment, he pulled his hand away to show a new mark, just below the moon phases of my witch mark. Where those sparkled in an iridescent shimmer, the bright golden sheen of antlers, wreathed in flowers now adorned my skin.

"It's beautiful," I breathed.

"I told you I would make you my goddess," he murmured into my hair, some of the otherworldliness of his speech gone. Now, he sounded much more like a man speaking to his lover.

I smiled.

"You would share your forest with me?" I asked.

"I always have," he admitted. "From the moment you set foot beneath my branches, I knew you belonged here. But such feelings are not usual for a god, and until tonight, I did not think you would agree to be my bride."

I laid my hand over his where it rested between my hip bones, pressing against where I still felt him inside me. My mind drifted back to the festival in the town, and how tonight I had felt adrift. With my sister a woman grown, I had wondered what my purpose might be now, and pondered what it might be like to embrace the wildness in my soul I had always kept in check.

"What made you decide tonight was the night?" I asked, wondering how Drakkan had been able to sense the change in me.

His hand drifted up to brush the golden tiara—the one that had belonged to my mother—now sitting wildly askew in my tangled braids. "You put my mark on you, and I knew it was time."

A smile grew on my face until I was beaming, and I almost laughed at the perfect serendipity of it. Instead, I twisted my head and reached behind me. My hand closed around one of Drakkan's own antlers, and I dragged him toward me for a kiss.

EPILOGUE

ESMERAY

Eyes watched me from the edge of the woods.

I smiled as the golden orbs appeared in the shadows, as they always did when I had spent the day in the garden and the sun was getting low. I didn't immediately stop what I was doing. Instead, I continued to tend the pumpkins I had planted recently. My sister would make a delicious soup with them in the fall, and I was hoping for a good harvest, so she could make it many times.

I also wondered if today would be one of the days I could tempt Drakkan to emerge from the shadows of the trees and see him in the fading daylight in all his glory. As I continued to inspect the beginnings of flowering buds, I was rewarded for my patience by a rustling of leaves.

I looked up and beamed as Drakkan stopped at the edge of the garden. The skin below my ribs warmed as the light of my own goddess mark matched the brightness of my smile. Drakkan was as inhuman as ever, but after months at his side, there was something familiar in his strangeness.

I knew well the textured whorls of his bark-like skin, and could read the expressions in his slitted, yellow eyes. My flesh remembered what his elongated canines felt like against the delicate skin of my neck and how his antlers felt in my grip as I lowered myself onto his face. My body was familiar with the way his fluffy tail would drape across my legs as he held me in the aftermath of our pleasure.

Now I stood and brushed my hands off on my apron, not caring for the dirt that crusted under my nails.

A bang marked the door swinging open behind me as Izara danced out into the yard. She had grown used to Drakkan's appearances quickly, as had the villagers. Witches were wise enough to know it was better to be friends with a god than enemies.

"Come visit again in a few days?" Izara asked as I stepped up to Drakkan's side and he draped an arm around me.

"Of course," I said with a smile.

Izara waved from the doorway as Drakkan led me back into our forest. The house was hers now, and she looked perfectly content in the cozy cottage—as comfortable as I felt in my home with Drakkan in the heart of the forest.

She was never out of reach, but I now had something—and someone—to call my own.

As we walked deeper into the shadow of the trees I paused, digging my bare toes into the soft earth and taking a deep breath of the air in my domain.

As my divine powers grew, gifted to me by Drakkan, I found myself growing more attuned to the forest every day. Where I had always felt at home among the leaves and branches, now the life of every plant was palpable, and I could nearly understand the meaning imbued into the yips of the fox and the song of the birds.

The mix of sensations leant both a sense of peace to my life and a craving for the untamed.

"Tonight is the full moon," I observed nonchalantly.

I didn't miss the way Drakkan's tail bristled and his pupils narrowed.

"It is," he agreed. "Did you want to attend the festival?"

I stretched my arms above my head, twisting this way and that, loosening the stiffness in my joints from a day of gardening.

"I thought we might have a little celebration of our own," I said, a sly smile dancing on my lips. "But before we start, you'll have to catch me."

Without warning, I plunged into the brush. I was faster now than before, and I knew every leaf and gully of this forest. Of course, so did Drakkan, but he wouldn't let that ruin our fun.

The howl of a wolf split the air behind me as Drakkan signaled the hunt had begun. A wild laugh tumbled from my lips as he hunted his bride through the forest.

ABOUT S. C. GRAYSON

Author bio: S.C. Grayson has been reading fantasy novels since she was a little girl, and that has developed into a love of writing and storytelling. She is the author of the Ballan Desert series and the best-selling Talented Fairy Tales.

When she is not sitting in a local coffee shop writing and consuming an iced americano, Grayson is a nurse researcher, focusing her efforts on breast cancer genetics. She lives in Chicago with her loving husband and their two cats, who enjoy contributing to her work by walking across her keyboard at inopportune moments (the cats, not the husband).

Join S.C.'s reader community at scgrayson.com for art, updates on new releases, and more.

THAT ONE TIME I LET THE HERO SUCCUMB TO HIS EGO AND MOVED IN WITH THE MONSTER

ELISSE HAY

CHAPTER

ONE

CASSANDRA

"Have you heard of the Gorgons?"

Who *hadn't* heard of the Gorgons? My thoughts circled on the memory of Perseus on my balcony moments ago, holding the head of my caretaker and friend, ending my peaceful era amusing the lady of the manor. He'd butchered her. Not even *well.*

I could still smell the reek of blood beneath the incense.

He launched into a description of the sisters. While he ranted about how they'd destroyed legions sent after them, I was trying to recall what the Gorgons had that was worth stealing. But there was nothing.

Which meant he was simply in it to prove his worth.

There was something extra icky about that. I much preferred middling men who proved their worth by building oversized statues with giant weapons and demure genitals.

"...but Medusa isn't immortal," he said, with such relish that I focused.

So, she was the target.

"...the head of Medusa," he added, with gusto. "To free my mother!"

I let out the obligatory soft gasp, pressing my hand to my chest. "O Mighty Warrior, none have yet succeeded!" Or so I assumed.

"Ah, but none have had the blessings of Hades, Athena, and Hermes," he began, and I kept a quiet tally of all these *blessings* various gods had bestowed upon him.

He'd simply been *gifted* these items, which was giving *we know you can't actually do a quest.* Usually at this stage these men could ramble about their alleged heroics and their unironically disclosed cruelty for hours. This one had already got to his sad origin story, as if being rejected by your stepparent was unique. He was yet to mention why he wanted to kill a Gorgon.

I'd bet all my belongings that I'd participated in more *epic quests* than he'd had insightful thoughts. *I* counted them all to be quite successful. I'd experienced mazes and whirlpools, seen giants and magical beasts, *and* lived. I was comfortable in my disdain for the men who went on said quests. The men who, invariably, didn't want to hear "Hey, that's a stupid idea."

And what's more, he hadn't found *me* himself, like the temporary quest-drunk adventurers I'd been forcibly gathered by in the past. Oh, no. The fucking *gods* were sending these ambitious cumrags to me now. As if I hadn't done enough for their amusement already?

"What say you, witch?"

I dragged myself back to the present. Had he already gone over the plan? No, my feet didn't ache enough for that. Outside the cabin, shouts rose, and the air filled with the familiar sounds of the ship leaving port.

"Tell me what your plan is," I said.

"My plan," he told me, coming over, his footfalls heavy, his eyes boring into me, "is *you.*"

Again, I held in a sigh. I didn't have any mythical foresight. I simply *took in information.* I *told* them my only magic was borrowed; the veil over my eyes simply improved my poor eyesight. Nothing more, nothing less. But there was no power in existence strong enough to educate those who refused to learn.

None of them wanted to believe me when I said *it's not magic, it's just paying attention.* Still, I should have tried. I knew I should. He was going to die. But playing along was easier, and I was tired.

"I'll need time to view the possibilities before I can advise," I warned him, simply acting the role he'd forced me into. "The more information I have about what's *possible* for you—"

"Anything," he breathed, in my ear, "is possible for me, sweet witch."

My skin crawled. I pulled a face, stepping back. "Not that sort of close, O Fearless Slayer of Beasts. It interferes with my powers and can cause unfortunate errors." Such as a hero's blood going to his cock instead of his brain, thereby getting himself killed. Oversized egos were more threat than hard cocks to their survival, but they seemed unfortunately linked. "I work best in close proximity to the *destination,* and with quiet around me to allow me to listen. Let me rest," I told him. "And begin my study. Send me the man in charge of your provisions when you've time."

"Such a mundane matter to waste magick on," he scoffed.

"Many who fail do so not grandly, but due to simple oversights," I warned. These short-sighted pantheon fodder, they never liked it when they didn't control the narrative. "You will fight the Gorgon. Allow me to oversee the rest."

THERE WAS NOT A SINGLE OPPORTUNITY TO ESCAPE IN THE HANDFUL OF DAYS IT TOOK us to reach the temple allegedly guarded by this monster. Perseus was impatient.

The mists curled around our feet and muffled the sound of the vessel docking at the long, well-kept pier. In the darkness, the temple loomed. Which deity it was dedicated to, I couldn't tell. Hills huddled in the shadows behind it, and in the distance some faintly glowing lights shone feebly.

Villages didn't usually prosper so close to a monster. Certainly not without blocking their windows.

Around me, the ship creaked with its load. *Two hundred men.* That's what the quartermaster had told me.

Two hundred hardened mercenaries.

"What say you?" Perseus asked me, his voice too loud in the quiet. None of the soldiers around us acted inappropriately, but one, in my peripheral, sent a long, meaningful glance at his fellow that made the knot in my belly tighten. *They're ready to leave him.* And if Perseus was ashore, and I was in a ship full of superstitious soldiers?

My skin crawled at the thought. I wasn't the only one who knew his odds of survival and didn't plan to go down with him.

"It doesn't appear like any monster's den I've seen," I admitted. "May I come ashore, O Shining Sword of Justice?"

"Of course," he scoffed, as if the thought of me staying aboard was ridiculous.

Relief rushed through me.

Monstrous as this Gorgon might be, I'd take her over two hundred mercenaries and the ship's staff any day.

Perseus led the way off the ship, hovering through the air with his winged sandals. The lieutenant joined us, his helm under his arm and his expression impassive. The light of the moon was bright, contrasting with the mist to make our surroundings feel eerie. I glanced up, but there were no clouds in sight. All I'd need was a little darkness and I could slip away. If Perseus was successful, I could always claim to have been stolen later.

Ahead of me he posed, propping his hands on his hips to survey the darkness before him.

"The lair of the beast," he said, with a toss of his curls.

The lieutenant on his other side stayed silent as we looked at the long flight of steps leading up the hill before us.

It was early in the night, and the mist's cloak was light higher up the mountain. The brightness of the moon was a decided disadvantage. While the mists might muffle *some* of the noise they'd make during landfall, even a well-trained force of two hundred would cause a racket. They weren't all sneaking up on her.

While the strategic problems bubbled in the back of my mind, mostly I was focused on the irregular figures punctuating the mist. They weren't placed correctly to be statues. Of course I hadn't forgotten what I'd been told about her turning men to stone, but while they weren't arranged like statues, they certainly didn't look like *real* foes.

These shapes took the form of men trying to sneak in. They weren't positioned beside the stairs, it was true, but they *were* spread in what seemed to me to be a pleasing fashion. There were no piles of downed men frozen in place, no group of half a dozen stumbling over each other to get back to their ship.

"Many have failed here," Perseus said gravely. "And yet, Athena herself sent me. She must believe in me."

Athena liked a joke as much as the rest of the pantheon. "Of course," I murmured, leaving his side to move through the mist. Whilst focused on the stone form of a man before me, I didn't watch where my feet went and kicked something hard.

I froze and gritted my teeth as pain rushed through me.

"Hush," hissed Perseus, his eyes going up the steps to the dark entryway above. "You'll wake the beast!"

The throbbing agony in my toe made me want to scream, just to see if I could do as he'd said.

Instead, I looked down at the object I'd kicked. A wooden shield with a cracked, weathered leather covering and tarnished bronze studs.

No blood. No defense marks. I couldn't see the lights of the village from here, but I remembered them.

It all just seemed *odd.*

I finished my limping journey to the statue to study it. The man's features hadn't been lost to the weather yet, though the stone was pocked in places, and bird shit dribbled down one side of his face. I suspected that was a personal comment. I ran my eyes over him, studying the details of his clothing, his belt, the way he crouched low.

I'd seen plenty of excellent crafts in my time. I knew good stonework when I saw it.

This wasn't magick. No more or less than I had. It *was*, however, very good artistry. But I could see the faintest marks left by the chisel still. She should've let them weather a little bit more, perhaps out on the mountainside. Also, the lack of piss-stained boots was a dead giveaway.

"You seek to destroy a mighty foe," I said, thoughtfully. *Because Gods forbid a woman has hobbies.*

Perseus appeared beside me, full of determination. "I do," he agreed, angling his hair so the wind caught it again.

"Tonight," I murmured softly, holding my hand up to the moon, "is a night for truths." I turned to him, one hand on the edge of my cloak. It swished delightfully around my feet. "This Gorgon does not just decide the fate of you and your mother," I told him, "but the entire kingdom. On her head they rise, or they fall." He looked at me blankly. I held back a sigh. "You could be king, if you kill Medusa," I said, wishing he'd been just a little less incompetent. "Your mother can live out her life in luxury, and you will rule with wisdom and strength."

He looked up at the temple, brow lightly furrowed, and reached for Athena's shield.

"Take heed," I said, lowering my voice. "The light of the gods is bright, and this creature's eyes are sharp."

He nodded, but his frown deepened in puzzlement.

Beside him, the lieutenant said, with admirable patience, "It's a full moon, O Mighty One. She'll see us coming before we're halfway up those stairs."

Perseus scoffed. "Not if I go alone."

His shield gleamed, its mirrored surface throwing back my own unimpressed expression. I was too old for this shit. "You shine with the light of your quest," I intoned, lifting a hand in a move that actually looked pretty graceful, at least in the reflection of his shield. Maybe I wasn't too old. Maybe I was just getting good. I'd had almost four decades to learn this game, after all.

"That's a lot of shining," he said, with a candle's worth of realization. "For a night incursion."

We're getting there. I nodded, lifting my hand further to point, with one finger, at the moon. "While her face is bright, she dims your own light. For you to have any hope you must return on a new moon, when the sky is dark. You must be the light, O Illuminous One."

He looked at the statue beside me. "Or I'll fail?" he asked. "I come back on the new moon, or…I end up like that?"

I shook my head. "Your fate will be more terrible," I whispered. "I… cannot speak of it." On the off chance he had an imagination, I'd hate to rob him of his dreams.

"The Wise Woman speaks sense," the lieutenant said, to the side. "The new moon is only two weeks hence. Attacking under total darkness will be far more effective. With a little luck, we'll have a good mist, too."

So, their plan was to *try* to work with Perseus. Good to know.

I could see from the middling quest-goer's expression that he didn't like the idea. "Have we supplies to wait?" Perseus asked him, his eyes still on the temple. "There was an uninhabited isle nearby, yes?"

My heart sank. "Yes to both," the lieutenant said. "My…Illuminated One."

I resisted the urge to arch a brow at the lieutenant. That was *my* line. Still, I had bigger issues right now. Like two weeks on an island with more than two hundred men.

I couldn't get back on that ship.

I let out a long, shaky breath. It wasn't hard to feign unease. "I…I am afraid," I admitted to them, clasping my hands. "I fear…"

Perseus turned to me. "What?" he asked, impatiently.

Fuck you. I straightened. "I must remain here. I must study the beast, and trust to my Sight."

His eyes narrowed. "No."

"It is not my wish either," I snapped. "And yet…" I looked up toward the temple. "So much is at stake that I need time to correctly determine the threads needed to weave the victor's tapestry. Listen." I held up a hand to my ear.

The wind blew as softly as it had been since we landed.

"The gods whisper to me," I murmured. "They will provide. *Perseus must be successful.*" I turned to him. "Do you hear them?"

"I am but a simple man," he said, his shoulders straight. "But...if it is the gods wish...Apollo guided me to you, Seer. I will trust you in this."

Fucking Apollo. I should've known. He'd tried to get me to call him Daddy.

Before they could think better of it, I knelt to Perseus, touching my forehead to the ground. "When the moon goes dark, I will be here," I told them. "Waiting for your illumination."

"Be safe, Seer," he said, sharply. "I thank you for your service."

As they crept back to the ship, I remained where I was, my toe throbbing painfully, mild surprise making me feel off-balance. Since when did a man *thank* me?

Since I told him what he wanted to hear, I thought grimly, sitting up only once I heard the creaking of rigging and the soft calls to set sail.

I blew out a breath. I wasn't trusting the gods to look after me, that was for sure. I had two weeks to make sure I was Perseus-proof. That should be ample time.

My body creaked as I struggled to my feet, regretting the show of false humility. I had an artisan to find.

CHAPTER
TWO

CASSANDRA

If Perseus had just walked in, he probably could've killed her. The thought made me feel...quite strange.

I studied her form from the shadows. The thin bits of moonlight that filtered down through the temple's windows into the cave-like living quarters deep behind the temple made me confident that whether she was an artisan or not, she was, most definitely, a monster. One big wing with feathers so black they gleamed blue in the moonlight was relaxed over her upper body and draped over her outstretched leg. It was mostly human... but strong.

So strong.

I looked away from those thighs, then felt my gaze drawn back. Would they be firm, or soft? Was it that I was unaccustomed to seeing a woman in a nest of twigs, and she looked massive beside it, or was she really almost as big as the minotaur in the maze I'd side-stepped having to enter?

Her face was turned toward me and peaceful in sleep. Around it, serpents also slumbered in coils of green. The nest she slept in had seen better days. One wall of it was collapsing, and a few sticks lay about on the ground.

And yet...into the cave wall, she'd carved graceful bookcases. They curved with the natural features of the stone, displaying a vast array of texts I couldn't see from this distance even with my veil down. Over them and between, she'd hewn breathtaking patterns of stars and moons, of flora and fauna. A stone flower bloomed immortal, arcing down from one shelf to another, where a deer lurked in its shadow. Higher, birds soared, vanishing into the ceiling. On the other side of the cave, a fireplace glowed softly. No smoke filled the room. Over the mantle, done in the same precious detail as her selves, a bundle of flowers sat in a vase. A single chair hung, as if suspended in the night, an upright nest of sticks and twigs that looked comfortable enough to sleep in.

The floors were stone, the ceiling clad in darkness. She needed to sweep. It was simultaneously both luxurious and bleak.

My eyes found their way back to where her leg was thrown over the wall of the nest. That thick thigh, the strength in her calf, the delicately arched foot. Then up and over the wing that protected her center mass to where her lashes lay against her cheeks. She was gorgeous, of course. Why was it always *Kill the monster*? Why was it never *See if you'd fit beneath the monster's wing*?

Would those feathers be as soft as they looked? Would they hold back the bite of cold in the night air?

For all I knew, any hunger she felt would be of the violent kind, not the sensual. I didn't know what a killer looked like asleep in the moonlight, but I expected they'd look the same as the rest of us. Anyway, you could never trust your eyes, once the gods got involved. And the gods had been here. There was no question.

But Perseus hadn't been.

I looked from that peaceful face to the banks of books and the beautiful stonework, then back again, my heart drumming too fast in my chest.

On soft feet, I let myself out, back down the short corridor to the open temple.

Here I found evidence of her artistry and rage. *Here* the statues cowered.

Here they ran. They'd been done with such skill that, if I hadn't also seen the alternative exit to the temple which led to the hillside, if I hadn't walked around her works in progress and seen the rough-hewn shapes and incomplete statutes surrounded by flecks of stone, I might wonder if she truly *did* turn men to stone.

That's okay. Plenty wondered if I truly was cursed.

Even I wondered that, sometimes.

I stood in the center of the temple, surrounded by quiet and the eerie sight of men trying to flee. They stayed frozen, their faces captured in the various stages of death. Some of them were cracked. Here and there a cloven shield or fallen helm lay. They, I suspected, were real. Around them, the temple stood, uncaring.

I wasn't as noisy as two hundred warriors. But nor was I as strong. Would she have awakened, if I'd gone deeper into her cave?

I blew out a breath. I was going to need to warn her.

I suppose we'd see if it was only men who disregarded my advice.

CHAPTER
THREE

MEDUSA

The crows told me we had a guest. They were always most attentive when someone had come looking for sanctuary. They knew first-time visitors never ate all the food I offered them—the crows would get whatever was left behind when our guests began their journey up to the village.

I gathered up the honey and bread I planned to share with my guest. The jar and cloth-wrapped parcel both settled comfortably in my left arm, disguised by my wing. In my right, I took my spear.

They came looking for strength. That was what they thought they needed.

Sometimes, it was.

Mostly...they just needed something to eat, and somewhere safe to sleep.

My old friend Crowlie swooped ahead of me, her wings open wide. Behind her came her crow family. I smiled at them as they cawed their way noisily though the door, announcing my presence.

A lone woman was standing, answering the summons of my friends.

With one hand she smoothed the bedraggled, but not tattered, finery she wore. A gauzy veil lay over her eyes. She stood with the posture of someone accustomed to formality. There were no laugh lines bracketing her mouth, but there were fine frown lines between her brows.

She did not cower as I walked forward, which made my life simpler. Plenty didn't, but most of those stared in shock, or in horror. This one ran her closed eyes up and down my form as if she was studying me, the almost imperceptible movement of her chin a give-away.

"You are welcome to this place," I told her, stopping an average distance from her form for a first meeting. She was not *seeming* to be terrified, but nor was she throwing herself at me, begging for protection. "I am Medusa."

That made her smile as if I'd told a joke. I glanced over her shoulder, but nothing was amiss, and Crowlie had settled to perch nearby, fluffing out her feathers.

"A pleasure," the woman said, dipping into a shallow curtsey. "My name is Cassandra."

Cassandra. There was not a bruise on her, not that I could see. She didn't hold herself like a terrified woman.

"Have you broken your fast this morn, Cassandra?" I asked her.

"I have not."

There was…something about that. About the crisp way each word was formed in her mouth. As if she'd studied and practiced and learned every single way they might spill from her lips. I resisted the urge to move a little closer, to see where that precision may end. *She'll tell you, or she won't, what's happening,* I reminded myself. *You're a terrifying beast, not a confidant.*

"I have bread," I told her, tipping my spear toward the side where some tables stood, half hidden by a trio of men falling over each other to flee. I did love those statues. They'd taken me decades to complete, but they'd been worth it. Nothing helped me digest better than the wide-eyed fear of my attackers, captured in art for all of eternity.

She glanced up at the crows as they happily hopped, swooped, or walked from where they'd perched on rafters and roosts overhead to the side, where the food would be eaten. And she smiled again.

This wasn't a smile of *That was funny.* It was a smile of *Aren't they beautiful?*

Yes. Yes, they were.

So was she.

I wet my lips and braced myself to guide her over, then withdraw. But she crossed to me, falling in beside me. It was a journey of only eight steps, but I felt her beside me for every. Single. One.

Breathing. Smiling. Unhurried, and unconcerned. Close enough I could have unfurled a wing and protected her from the cool chill on the dawn air.

I fought against the desire to do just that, shifting my spear to one side so I could take the plain jar of honey and set it down, then the bread.

She sighed. "*And* honey?" She slid onto a chair as if it was the first comfort she'd had in decades, her shoulders drooping and her expression softening. "You've done this before."

"I have," I agreed, sliding the loaf into the middle. "There's a small knife in there. Once you've filled your belly, you may make your way to the village, if you'd like, or I can—"

"Wait." She reached out. I froze.

She didn't touch me, but—it wasn't because she was afraid. Her hand recoiled as if suddenly she'd remembered her manners.

As if suddenly she remembered it wasn't safe to ask for more.

"I only go because most visitors prefer me to remain as their guard," I offered, by way of explanation. There was something a little unnerving about being looked at by a woman with her eyes closed.

She *saw* me, too. She wasn't just tracking my movements.

Magick. It might make sense that someone comfortable with the arcane would be comfortable with my form.

"Would you like me to remain?" I offered her, because she'd stayed silent, looking at me as if unsure if she'd just broken an edict.

"Yes," she said.

It was a firm noise, not at all scared. She wasn't pleading for protection. Nor was she begging me to help remove the clothes she appeared to have slept in, probably over multiple days. Though two knots were all it'd take me.

Beneath the robes her body was perfectly soft and round. The sun had left spots on her skin. I settled on one of the stools cautiously, keeping my wings tucked in close so not to alarm her. She reached out for the bread. Her hands were soft, too, like the rest of her. Her fingernails had been torn low, but whatever anxieties had driven that seemed far away now as her digits danced adeptly over the cloth.

My mouth watered at the competent way she untied the knot in the wrap of the bread.

"You do excellent work," she told me, nodding toward the nearby trio of statues.

I regarded them with pride. "The days are long," I said.

"My days are long, too," she said, and the lightness of the words, the amusement, drew my gaze back to her. Back to where her fingers pressed into the crust of the loaf and her hands tore it in half, exposing the vulnerable core of it. "And yet *I* have no artistry to show for my time."

"I can teach you," I found myself offering, unthinking.

She set down half the bread, the smile vanishing as if she'd never even considered I'd make such an offer.

I hadn't considered I might, either.

"Would you?" she asked, no jest in the words. "Really?"

"If you'd like to learn," I clarified, resisting the urge to fold my wings around myself just a little to shield myself from that gaze. "Of course. I'd do the same for anyone." It wasn't simply because she was a beautiful woman who smiled at my crows, broke her bread with plump, sure fingers and had a tongue as precise as a surgeon's scalpel.

"What if I make a poor student?" she asked me.

I hesitated, unsure what she wanted of me. "What if you do? I have plenty of stone."

It must have been the right answer, because she grinned, suddenly. The change in expression lit her whole face and filled her with the sort of joy that one couldn't fake. "You're an honest woman, Medusa," she said, taking the dipper from the honey and drizzling it over the bread.

I wasn't quite sure what I'd done that she'd enjoyed so much, but I was sure she wasn't laughing *at* me. It was a shared joy, just for us.

I leant forward, liking the way it felt, warming the pit of my belly.

I'd shared joy with the villagers, of course, and with my crows. I'd had joy all of my own as I watched the storms sweep across the sea and carved away at stone with claws harder than any natural substance.

But this? This was different.

She offered me the bread in her hands, generously honeyed, and I took it out of reflex.

"You haven't asked how I came to be here," she said, as she tore off another piece for herself.

"Nor have you asked what happened to me."

She wrinkled her nose. "Why would I pry so?"

"Why would I?"

"Because," she said, arching her brows now, "unlike you, *I* arrived in the dead of night and stepped into your home uninvited, and now I'm sitting at your table, eating your food."

"You're assuming I didn't arrive in the same manner," I told her, and the reminder of how I'd found my way to the isle, the long flight of desperation as I was tossed by the storm and winds, didn't bring with it the customary heaviness it often did. I'd been lucky in some ways. Unlucky in others. Here we were. "And, to clarify, Cassandra…" Her name rolled around in my mouth, taking the perfect length of time to complete linking all of those beautiful sounds together. I stumbled a little, the shiver of delight that ran up my spine taking me off-guard. "Everyone is welcome here," I finished, out of habit rather than thought.

I'd seen all the reactions to that statement. Disbelief, fear, desperate hope, relief, joy. And I suspected I saw some of those in her, too. But she already knew. It was in the set of her shoulders and the way she bit into the bread. She already knew she was welcome. So why was she asking me this?

I leant forward a little more. My hair, reacting off instinct rather than conscious thought, moved toward her too, the snake-like appendages made uneasy noises. "Is something wrong?"

She shot the snake-like hair a look I couldn't read, with the veil and her eyes closed. I pulled back and took a deep breath to settle myself. They coiled back against my skull as I settled. She appeared to watch this with…

curiosity. "There is," she admitted. "I…well, I didn't mean to deceive you by waiting for so long to mention it. Only I'm unsure how to approach the topic."

Anger felt hot and sweet in my limbs. There was no one lurking behind her, chasing her. Not in distance of my spear.

But there was, somewhere.

"You are safe here," I told her, firmly. "I will make it so."

"That's what I wanted to warn you about," she said, with a sigh. "There's a young man. He's coming to attack you."

I shrugged, caring not for the details. "Let him come. Did he hurt you?" I studied her again, but still, not a hint of a bruise.

"He kidnapped me," she admitted, tiredly. "He killed my friend. I'm sorry, Medusa. I wanted no part in this."

Unease rippled up my spine. "No part in…what?"

"They were going to land last night," she said, the words precise but quick. "I convinced them not to. They'll return in two weeks, during the new moon. He has two hundred men."

Two hundred men. I sat back, biting into the bread. No wonder she'd been scared. Kidnapped, forced to be part of this plot, losing her friend? I knew how men such as this acted. "I regret what you've endured," I told her, because she was watching me—not anxiously, but as bird watches a fig tree, checking to see how it grows.

It occurred to me that maybe I shouldn't trust her, but…there was nothing about her that worried me. Not in the slightest. She was here because she wanted to be.

She'd tricked them. She was clever enough for it. Look at how she'd tricked me into asking her for information, guiding me through the conversation at every step. Not too soon, not as we'd met, but the moment we'd been getting comfortable. If she'd waited, would I have been more suspicious?

No, I thought, chewing on the bread that would've been excellent last night. *But many would have.* Yes, she was a clever one. Clever enough to trick me, if she'd wanted. But she'd waited here instead.

"I'm glad you know you can be honest," I told her, surprised at the thought. "That you can come to me."

"I'm glad you aren't a *kill the messenger* type," she said, laughter in her voice. "...Right?"

"Right," I agreed, firmly. "Eat. Then you can tell me all about these," I waved a hand in dismissal, "*men.*"

The tired sigh she let out was the perfect sound to encapsulate my fatigue at the topic, too. I ducked my head to hide my smile, but I suspected she saw it anyway.

Just the same way she saw all of me.

CHAPTER
FOUR

CASSANDRA

S he hadn't been nearly alarmed enough when I'd told her Perseus had
been set to sneak in and kill her. Instead, she walked with me up the
mountainside to the village where I was welcomed as if this had truly been
my home all along and I just didn't know it yet.

I had some sewing skills, so I was set up beside the seamstress. They
were an isolated bunch of humans mostly, but Medusa's two sisters had a
similar form to her and went on expeditions to nearby islands to trade,
along with the oldest of their offspring.

It felt...surreal. I spent a day in the village. I slept in a real, proper bed. I
chose fabric to replace my clothing. I told eager-eared villagers some mostly
true tales about adventures. I ate well-aged goat cheese and drank wine
with a full body and citrus notes.

Medusa did not return.

Halfway through my second day on the island, I turned to the village's
primary tailor, who was already working on my first set of robes, rocking in
her chair as her needle dipped and wove in a quick, consistent pattern.
"Why doesn't Medusa have a home here, too?" I asked her.

"Oh." She smiled at me like I was a child. "She's different. She likes to be out there, ready to look after us. Says it's her calling."

"Who called her to it?"

There was a flicker the merest hint of a secret across the woman's face. "Why, she chose it." She shook her head, smiling. "No one makes Medusa do a thing she doesn't want." I thought of her shock when I'd asked her to stay and eat with me. "I know it's a lot to get used to," she began, and gave me another version of the talk I'd had a dozen times already. *You'll get used to it. You're welcome here.*

I listened with half an ear. I'd seen the villagers incorporating her sisters and their children in their daily lives. I'd even seen a man I presumed to be the father of one of those half-human children stroke the snake-like hair as it hissed. And the parents around, they'd had that shared parent-smile. The *oh bless the poor little child, the poor tired parent* sort of smile.

Gorgons were just part of life here.

But I wanted a *specific* Gorgon's company. And, really, wasn't it appropriate for me to pay my respects at the temple?

CHAPTER

FIVE

MEDUSA

Cawmistress woke me hopping along the edge of my nest, her eyes curious. There were no urgent cries or anxiously flapping wings, so I didn't hurry, washing my face and donning my clothes. I heard a happy caw from the temple and smiled at the sound.

Then a second.

And a third.

My smile fell. I hefted my spear and lengthened my stride, unsettled by how vocal my friends were.

Then I stopped, frozen, at the threshold of the temple.

She sat on the ground, her tattered finery around her, dark mane of her hair windswept and the bottom of her robes wet with dew. There was a loaf of bread in her hand that she was tearing into tiny pieces, her patience infinite. Every now and then she'd throw a few pieces around her, scattering them so the same bird couldn't gobble them all up.

She was making friends with my crows.

She was *here*. She'd walked from the village to visit me, *and she'd brought bread for my crows.*

I swallowed around the lump in my throat.

Before I was ready to announce myself, Crowlie spotted me and did a short loop in the air, coming to perch on my shoulder.

Out of habit I put one hand over my hair so she didn't worry at it. She rubbed her gleaming head against my hand.

"You must have been very patient, to get them to love you so," Cassandra said, smiling from the floor of my temple.

No one smiled sitting on my floor. They'd weep there, or cower.

She likes your crows. What wasn't to like? Maybe this did make sense, after all. "Crowlie has been with me since she was a chick," I told Cassandra. "You brought them a feast."

"I brought *us* a feast," she corrected. "But *they* weren't sleeping. Can you feed them by hand?" she scooped up as many pieces of bread as she could hold, standing with a small huff of effort and a bit of a wobble. I moved forward but she was steady before I got there, leaving me disoriented.

She laughed, glancing at my friends who'd rushed into the space she'd left to pick at every crumb she'd dropped, bolder with me beside them.

"I love them," she declared. "I hope that's okay."

I was still in a dream. That made sense, didn't it? That was why she was here, so bold and so fearless and so frank. "Yes," I told her, not really believing it *was* a dream, and unwilling for it to end either way.

She came closer, bread falling from her hands in a short trail. I struggled not to fall back, reminding myself of her familiarity last we'd met. She wasn't scared of me.

"Here," she said, and I set aside my spear, but I didn't need to. My one empty hand could hold everything from the two of hers.

Her touch would be so delicate. So sweet. And, I had no doubt, so *relentless.*

I ached as my body made ready to experience the sensation, as if my thoughts might make it real.

Crowlie hopped down my arm, wings half-spread, one eye on my visitor and one on her crow competitors as she stole a bit of bread.

Beside me, Cassandra made a high-pitched noise of joy in the back of her throat, her hands going to her mouth and her feet doing a rapid dance on the cracked floor. I glanced over, feeling her joy spilling over onto me, breathing it in and languishing in it. She wasn't smiling. The expression she wore was high-browed, big-eyed wonder. Infected by her happiness, I felt myself smiling for the both of us.

"Can I pat her?" she asked. "No. No I can't. Don't be so hasty, Cassandra," she said, and even the way she chided herself poured more of that warm, vibrant pleasure into my veins.

She'd have to move fast if she wanted to touch them. They'd spotted Crowlie. "Here," I said, opening my other arm and spreading my wing. "Come in close. If you're with me, they'll trust you."

And she did.

My heart skittered in my chest like my friend's feet as they hopped closer. I enclosed her in my wing. Her breath against my chest was warm and quick. She trembled, then did the quick feet movement again. Joy. She was trembling in *joy*.

My head swam. I took her hand. Anything to draw out the pleasure. She moved with me, looking along our outstretched arms as I guided her to reach toward Crowlie.

My old friend, she wasn't fooled. She knew how many arms I had. But she *was* happy with her feast. Cassandra's delicate, rounded hand got a look, a quick, curious snap of her beak, and then a bump of approval. It was probably done so she could get back to gorging herself as others alighted on me. Cassandra trembled again. I couldn't see which friends landed on my arm, as it was a number in quick succession and I found it hard to care when the woman in my arms was...trembling. With joy.

They landed on her, too. And she made a noise of astonishment.

Her arm dropped under their weight and I bolstered her, feeling her eyes on me.

We were so close. I could barely breathe.

Someone else hopped onto her head, just for a moment. She ducked, staggering into me. Everyone on us took flight, scattering the last few bits of bread, and I caught her.

Behind the softness of her breasts, her heart was drumming insistently. It was the same rhythm that mine drummed.

"I'm sorry," I said, worried they'd scared her.

She looked up at me. Her mouth wasn't smiling, but it was parted slightly. One of her hands was still tangled up in mine and her hair was a welcoming mess.

In my grip, her fingers flexed. I let her go immediately, struggling to straighten my cloudy thoughts.

Her hand came up to rest on my bare shoulder and I looked down at it, confused until I saw the red pinpricks left by my friends' feet.

"I'm so sorry," I said, horrified. How hadn't I *realized* she needed help? "They're heavy—their claws—" I stepped back, tucking my wing away carefully, hastening to the fresh water. "I'll treat it for you. Over here. Just— wait a moment." Urgency and humiliation pulled me on. What had I been thinking? "They're used to me. I didn't think—"

"It's okay," she said, as I scooped up some water and took a fresh cloth. "It's barely a few scratches."

Still, I hurried to her side, offering her the bowl. She took it. Of course she took it. Why would she want me to clean her? She was capable of it herself.

The desire to take over writhed in my chest.

I sat, watching. The water ran down her arm, tiny little marks left in her flesh by my friends' claws making me ache.

"You bear no wounds," she said, puzzled.

"No."

"Why?"

I watched her fingers in the cloth. "My skin is thicker, now," I said, as she wrung out the fabric. Water ran into the bowl, spilling out between her digits. I wondered what it'd be like to lick them, and guilt hit again.

"Since the curse?"

A cold wind blew away all the warmth and the lingering joy, but she was unchanged. A little disheveled, pink-cheeked, soft. "Yes."

"Oh." There seemed to be a world of understanding in that one noise.

Suspicion, dark and sickly, coiled in my belly. We all of us *knew*, of course, those who were brave enough to think. But... "Did Perseus hurt you?" I asked her, the rage starting to simmer.

"No." She ran the cloth slowly over her arm. "No, he didn't. They would've. If I'd stayed, they would've. I still feel a little bad for tricking them."

"Don't," I told her, the word an order.

She shrugged with a sigh. "They believe convenient lies, but never inconvenient truths," she said, weariness creeping into her voice. "I'm sorry, Medusa, I've ruined your morning."

"No, you haven't." I stayed where I was, but every part of me wanted to go to her and fold her back into my wing again. This time, without my friends. "You've made it. I'm glad you tricked them. I'm glad you had the skills to do so."

She looked at me, then, with the wisdom of someone who'd survived. And she could see everything. The decades, the centuries of loneliness. The hurt. The healing. The rage and the grief. I struggled not to shy away.

"Who cursed you?" she asked me, the question as soft as her hands on the cloth, wiping away the blood.

It was my turn to tremble. Not at the memories. They'd weathered like sandstone, those experiences. It'd taken time, and the right conditions, but I'd worn them away. No, I trembled at that gentleness.

"Athena," I told her, the word a little scratchy. It was decades since I'd even said her name. It held no hurt. Not even grief. It just…was. "I sought safety in her temple from Poseidon."

"And she cursed you for it," Cassandra breathed, the words vibrating with fury. "*She* cursed *you.*"

I shrugged. "They were rivals. He'd already claimed me, I suppose."

"They're wrong."

"Gods often are," I agreed. "Who gave you to Perseus?"

She paused for a moment. "Apollo," she said, finally, frowning.

The rage rumbled. If they were coming for *me,* not the village, then I may need to separate myself. And yet then the village would be unprotected. As wonderful as my sisters were, as brave and sweet as they were… they were no warriors.

"And…Athena gave him a special sword," Cassandra said. "I'm sorry, I'm problem-solving, Medusa, and you've just shared a horrible truth with me. I shouldn't be. Can I...can we...walk, or do something to make you feel better?"

All the rage vanished at that thoughtful, sweet acknowledgement. "It's been a very long time," I assured her. "But...thank you." I struggled, moved and unsure how to express my gratitude. "Thank you."

She shook her head, brows gathered. "I've food. Could you eat? We could break bread."

"Yes." I looked around, disoriented. Of course she was hungry. She'd walked all this way, and fed my friends, and I was simply talking her ear off. "What have you? I can help." She reached under the table for a knapsack, still frowning. And, gathering up my courage, I said, "I like your problem-solving. Just so you know."

She paused, for a moment, as if shocked. "You do?"

"I think so." I took the bowl, surprised at her reaction. "Surely, such an insightful woman as you is accustomed to that?"

"People don't like the truth," she said, an echo of her earlier statement. In the words I heard the layers of old hurts, healed over but not forgotten.

"It can be terrifying," I agreed, because it was true. "But it doesn't go away if it's ignored."

Her smile was quick, beautiful, and heart-mending. "Exactly."

My feet barely touching the ground, I carried the bowl away and allowed her to prepare our breakfast.

CHAPTER
SIX

Medusa's yellow eyes regarded me with something akin to confused fascination. "Why do you have a wheel of cheese?"

It wasn't just *a wheel of cheese*. It was a *honeyed, roasted* wheel of *well-aged goat* cheese *studded with figs*. "To break your fast," I said, primly. "Is that a problem?"

She looked down at the ceramic dish that held the once-roasted, now cooled, carefully prepared cheese. "You went to a lot of work."

"Not really. Just a little thought." I wished I could snatch back the words. I didn't want her thinking of the people who *didn't* give her a little thought.

But she didn't seem saddened, just entranced, sitting perched by the table like one of her crows. "I haven't eaten roasted cheese in a long time. And never cold."

"I like to delay my pleasure, sometimes," I said, keeping the words light but watching her response from the corner of my eye as I nonchalantly reached to break the crusty bread.

I was rewarded by a quick, searching look that was just as hungry as the one she was giving the wheel of cheese sitting in caramelized honey.

Athena had cursed her.

Her.

For what *Poseidon* had done.

The same goddess had given me the gift of clear eyesight.

I resisted the urge to pull off the veil in fury. Why would anyone—especially another woman—blame Medusa? I wasn't surprised at Poseidon. Just disgusted.

I *was* surprised by Athena. I'd thought she was one of the good ones. Obviously, I'd been mistaken. It happened. Unlike some, I learned from my errors.

I'd pray for her conditional *protection* no longer.

If I took off the veil in protest and burned it, or spat on it, or threw it into the sea, it'd do no one any good. I'd just go back to being unable to see well. I *could* get by. I'd lived my whole life squinting, avoiding nighttime travel and social activities, and being very wary around anything that I could trip over, fall from, or generally hurt myself on.

But I wanted to watch Medusa feed those crows again. I wanted to see the fierce light in her eyes when she was challenged. I wanted to see her lost for words when I flirted with her.

I wanted to see her expression when I parted her legs and feasted.

What finer retribution was there than living joyously and giving the traitorous goddess no more of our thoughts?

Before me, Medusa sat, watching me as if lost for words.

I knew of her history with men—at least, a turning point in it. She hadn't taken husbands, as her sisters had. There were men in the village. Some of them had dark hair and muscles, and possibly even picked up after themselves. They were middling, but that was all we ever asked of men.

Regardless, she was here. Alone. And I didn't think that was entirely due to trauma.

So, keeping my rage to myself and focusing instead on the possibility of joy, I said, "I notice you haven't taken a husband or wife."

Her hawk-like eyes were on my fingers, as if they were the feast and not the food. So I hadn't missed the way she'd looked at me last time we broke bread. Pleasure hummed under my skin.

"…No," she said, frowning a little.

"Have you considered it?" I asked, adding, before she could respond with the obvious, "A wife might actually be beneficial when you greet newcomers, don't you think?"

She looked up at me, and I didn't try to hide my mirth at the suspicion warring with hope. "I hadn't considered it."

"You'd have to find the right person," I agreed. "We're all searching for her, aren't we? Someone we can learn and grow with, but also rest and relax?" I offered her the cheese. "I've never married," I offered her, pleased at how well we were doing. "Never met the right woman."

She sat there, holding the ceramic bowl containing the cheese, the snakes on her head moving as if restless.

It was always a bad idea to mix protection and pleasure, but *no one* had ever called me wise and meant it. So I just waited, giving her time to get used to the idea.

She eventually chose a piece of bread. "Is that…" she fell silent, the words hanging between us, as if unsure of their purpose. She dipped the bread into the cheese, scooping out some of the soft, gooey mess and leaving some flakes of crust in her wake. "Will you leave to continue your search?" she asked me, moving the cheese back toward me.

Yes, if you're not the woman I think you are. "I like your isle," I told her, but I wasn't looking out over the hills that jutted dramatically from the sea or the rolling meadows.

She met my gaze. Color appeared in her cheeks, and straight away she looked down.

Tenderness and excitement both warmed me. I took some bread, considering whether I turned up the heat, or backed away. My body told me to keep going, but…

"It's dangerous, here," she offered. "Not on the isle, but *here*. This is where I'll fight any who pursue those who seek sanctuary."

Of course it was. And that was why I hadn't just vanished into the hills until a ship passed by. "I won't leave you to face Perseus alone," I told her, taking some cheese. "I'd sort of like to kick his corpse into the sea."

She made a noise of agreement and bit into her food. I joined her in that, seeing how she sat a little higher, how her wings relaxed and the serpents on her head coiled themselves into snakey, cute bundles that resembled a classic hairstyle.

"I don't usually allow untrained people near when there's to be conflict," she said, "but if I can spot this Perseus, I shall indeed reserve his corpse for you."

Look at us, eating the cheese I'd prepared and making plans for the corpses she created. She didn't even realize we were a couple yet.

"This is excellent," she told me, reaching for more bread.

"I'm glad you like it." I waited while she took more, pleased to see how she loaded her bit of bread...and how few crumbs she'd left behind in the cheese, too. She was certainly more comfortable talking about bloodshed than romance. As someone with an interest in this upcoming conflict, I could work with that. "Perseus is expecting to find me on the dock on the night of the new moon."

She shrugged. "Once you've more clothes, I'll throw some blood around down on the steps, rip your cloak a little and leave it lying around."

"My cloak isn't very distinctive," I mused. "Mayhap my robes?" I felt guilty as her eyes swung back to me, color flooding her sun-bronzed cheeks again. "I apologize," I said quickly, worried I'd taken it too far. "I shouldn't jest. And in truth this is no jesting matter. If I don't meet Perseus, he may sail away for a time and return at a later date."

She shrugged again, frowning. "Why do we care when this man comes?"

"Two hundred experienced warriors, Medusa."

She arched her brows. "Why is it you apologize for strange things, and yet you insult me so?"

I froze, the bread halfway to my mouth. What else had I apologized for? More flirting, probably? And was she *truly* insulted? Ways to remedy the situation spun through my head in a storm of anxiety. "I..."

She reached over, the tip of one clawed finger touching me gently beneath the chin as she closed my mouth with gentle pressure from below, smiling.

I had to swallow as my mouth watered. The faintest pricking of the tip of her claw held me otherwise immobile. Why hadn't I sat *beside* her?

"So shocked, clear-sighted woman?" she murmured, withdrawing that single finger.

Part of my mind adjusted her skill level in my mind. She wasn't the type to be overconfident. If anything, she probably still understated her competence.

As peerless a warrior she no doubt was, I'd *still* walked in on her asleep.

As if in answer to my thoughts, she smiled, and her fangs slid free.

My heart turned over in my chest.

It was probably quite concerning that I simultaneously and graphically imagined two very different uses for those fangs. The first and obvious was the damage she could do to attackers. The second, and lingering image, was of those fangs flush against my flesh as she licked me, rendering movement impossible. Heat swept through me as I imagined lying helpless beneath her, unable to do anything but take.

She lifted her fingertip to her mouth. Honey ran over the claw. I'd felt how gentle the pad of that digit was just moments ago. I could feel the warmth where she'd touched me still.

Medusa licked the honey from her fingertip.

Her tongue was long. Impossibly long.

If I hadn't been sitting, I might've fallen.

"Eat," she told me, quietly. "You'll need your strength."

I drew in a breath, happy in that moment to sustain myself purely on her.

"We're going flying," she promised. "So you'll worry no more, and lose no more sleep."

Reducing my worry would be a blessing, but the thought of never missing out on *any* sleep with Medusa around? That sounded like a curse to my ears.

CHAPTER
SEVEN

MEDUSA

She didn't think I could keep her safe.

They never did. Not unless they'd huddled behind the pillars as I destroyed their pursuers, or hid from the gore behind a statue I'd carved with my claws.

I couldn't purchase her peace today by laying to waste an army, though I would have in a heartbeat. It was a long time since I could really empathise with that quiet, nagging worry, the doubt they'd forced her to carry in order to survive. I was looking forward to slaying it and watching her kick its corpse into the water.

Once she had eaten her fill, I wasted no time. "You'll be most comfortable facing the same direction I do," I told her, moving my finger in a circular motion to indicate she ought to spin.

There were no questions and she didn't hesitate, turning where I'd indicated she should.

My goal wasn't to coddle her, but to show her how little she had to fear. So I wrapped one arm across her front, holding her on the diagonal to maximize my support, and leapt into the air.

The rush of wind through my wings and against my ears was a familiar sound. She stiffened, her hands locking urgently over my arm as if afraid I'd drop her.

I'd never.

She let out a noise of wonder.

I resisted the urge to turn my face into her hair.

I took her up into the sky, her weight unusual but not limiting as I banked to the side, doing a wide sweep of the bay. The wind was salty and cold this early in the morning. I didn't take her low enough to feel the spray. I flew faster, driving more speed, more height, from my wings until she let out a shout of joy.

That joy was tinged with fear, of course…as it almost always was, at first.

I took her over the isle, doing a quick lap, showing her the rocky outcrops, the orchards, the groves in a blur. Her hair tickled my face, my eyes, caught against my lips. I turned into her, at no risk in the empty skies, and breathed in the scent of her without stopping to think. My head swam. I turned away, my eyes now clear of flying hair.

That hadn't been my intention, though.

Painfully, I pulled my attention back toward our destination. One of my nephews in the village struggled into the air on infantile wings and I resisted the urge to laugh at his uncoordinated flapping. He'd learn.

I didn't want to set her down.

I breathed in deeply, drawing her into my lungs, hoping I'd remember forever the feel of her pressed back against my chest, her entire weight over my arm, the way her hands clung to me, but not just in fear. And I circled slowly, picking out the building that was her home for as long as she wished. Dust blossomed around us as we landed.

She made a noise of awe. Her legs went out.

I held her while she wobbled, confident she was fine. I'd flown with anxious people plenty of times, taking them to the village for healing, or removing them from danger. They didn't make those noises of joy and wonder.

I'd done that.

I'd made her knees too weak to hold her.

She was leaning heavily into me, turning as if to apologize, color high on her cheeks. I held her close, pushing open the door to carry her across the threshold. Bless her wobbly legs.

"I'm sorry," she said, the words holding laughter and shock as well as the edge of real embarrassment as she grabbed for me to anchor herself. "I just need—a moment."

She fitted perfectly in my arms when she faced me, too.

Outside, my nephew was complaining to my sister. I closed the door, knowing he was cared for, and stared down at the woman who either still couldn't stand...or didn't want to.

"They aren't really snakes," she whispered.

I realized my hair had come free from its pile and had tangled around her, pulling her in close. Even as I became aware of what I'd done, my hair settled back atop my head, a familiar weight.

"No," I confirmed.

"So...they couldn't hurt me," she said, slowly.

I was so accustomed to the illusion the serpents provided, I hadn't really stopped to think how it would affect this particular person. "It's me. Like fingers or toes, I rarely think about it, but I can control it."

She lifted an arm, one finger extended. The scratches on her flesh made guilt twist in my belly, but she looked...serene. I let the mock-serpents stroke down that finger and coil around her arm. Her skin was chilled from the flight, and pebbled with tight, hard bumps. I wrapped myself around her, thinking to warm her.

She shivered, her lips parting, and looked up at me through the veil.

We were so close.

"That feels..." She twisted her hand slowly, as if caressing her own skin with my snakes. "...Wonderful."

My heart stammered in my chest. For a moment, the whole world hung on that slow, breathy word that lingered on her lips.

I should leave her to her day. She was tired, no doubt. She'd been up early to visit me and my crows. She had things to do.

I remained there, in her arms, tangled around her.

"Can we do it again, sometime?" she asked me.

"Yes," I said, not knowing nor caring what I agreed to, if it kept the smile on her mouth.

She tilted her head further, closing the distance.

And then a knock came at the door.

My spear lowered out of reflex but she turned, shocked out of my arms. "Who...? Coming." Her legs were steady as she took the single step out of my hold to open the door.

I turned away, arranging my serpents again, schooling my features. The excited sounds of my nephew met my ears. My belly was knotted so tightly I had to resist clutching it as I slipped out of Cassandra's home to give him the attention he wanted. I burned where she'd been pressed against me. But I burned a lot more where she'd not yet touched me.

What was I *doing*?

And why wasn't I doing it right now?

CHAPTER
EIGHT

CASSANDRA

I fell asleep planning, and I woke up planning, too.

I'd gathered fruits and bread and cheese last night and walked toward her temple in the pre-dawn. My excuse to remain would only last until Perseus was dead. I had no doubt that Medusa could deal with him and his men, as long as they weren't allowed to creep up on her. I needed to use my time well.

My nose hurt in the cold, and so did my fingers. Still, had there been wildflowers, I would have gone into the wet grass after them. Medusa would melt like cheese for a posy—I knew she would.

And then it started to rain. The moisture interacted strangely with the magick in my veil. I persevered for a time, but eventually snatched the veil away, irritated that I could see better with my own eyeballs than the *magick cloth*. Dirt beneath my sandaled feet turned to mud as I limped along, leaving splatters over my calves.

There went any hope I had of being seductive today.

Soaked to the skin, I ducked under one of Medusa's stone works in progress and saw her temple looming over me, finally.

All the relief ebbed out of me when I saw Medusa herself standing in the narrow arching doorway leading into the temple. I couldn't make out details without my veil, but I wanted to believe the blur of green around her shoulders was a sleepy tumble of snakes, and that she was smiling at me with affection.

I had no time to allow the nagging voice of self-doubt to speak up because I was upon her quickly.

"You're chilled to the bone," she said, her hand searingly hot on my arm.

"It wasn't raining when I left," I said, in my own defense.

"Why did you come?" she asked, steering me through the room. "Did I not reassure you yesterday?"

"Not really," I said, enjoying having her tow me along until I accidentally kicked something large and grey.

I let out a noise of pain, pulling out of her grasp and sucking in air as the agony seared through me. I let it hold me for a few moments. That poor toe. I let the air out, hearing it shake. I wouldn't cry. I couldn't breathe well enough to cry.

By the time the white-hot pain started to ebb I could see her standing nearby. "I can't see well," I told her, by way of explanation, the words breathless and quick.

"I...can I...can I just carry you?"

I was sopping wet and filthy, but my toe *hurt*. And she was warm. "Yes, please."

"Where's your veil?" she asked me, scooping me up without a moment's thought.

I let myself relax in her arms, holding my offerings safely. She was so warm, and when I closed my eyes I could hear the soft rustle of her wings and the gentle slide of the snakes twining together.

"Cassandra?"

I liked the way she said my name, the way it took its time against her tongue. "Mmm?"

"Where's your veil?" she asked again.

The wind vanished, suddenly. I opened my eyes to see the dark tunnel that led to her cozy bedroom, then closed them again. What a depressing way to be carried into her bed—with a sore foot and soaked to the skin.

"It's in the pack," I said, struggling against my own sadness. This wasn't how I'd planned *any* of it. "Sorry. If I'd known it'd rain…" I'd probably have grabbed an oiled cloak, or left early and slept in the temple, the way I'd done that very first night. It would've been worth it.

"I'll light the fire," she said. "It'll be cool enough for it, today, I think. What a strange storm."

Fuck you, Zeus, I thought as she set me down gently. My feet squelched inside my sandals and my skin crawled. "I'm pretty muddy."

"Wait here," she said. "The ground is flat. There's a chair just behind you, but there's some rugs if you move far, so be careful."

The blurs around me were mostly browns and greys. I could still remember the beautiful details carved into the bookshelves, the colourful spines of the books and the nest she'd slept in. I stayed where she'd set me, frustrated at how the plan had changed.

She returned right as I was thinking seriously about sitting down and crying. I braced myself against my own disappointment. She was a brown, green, and red blur, her wings tucked behind her. I heard the sound of water before I could make out that she was holding something. A large bowl. Larger than I would have tried to carry. She sat it before me, going down on one knee.

"I'll get these," she told me, working on the ties of my sandals. "I expect they'd be hard to do without much vision."

Knots weren't the worst problem I had to face when I couldn't see. "You don't have to," I objected, the guilt writhing in me like a hydra whose head had just been cut off. "I'm sorry. This wasn't my plan at all."

"It's no bother. I've needed to spend some time inside anyway. I usually wait until the weather forces me to, and it looks like today's one such day." She moved to my other leg. "Anyway, it's not the first time I've had a little mud in here and won't be the last."

I let out a huff. "It's the first time I'm responsible."

"Will it be the last?"

My heart squeezed suddenly in my chest. One of her hands coiled around my calf. She looked up at me. I couldn't make out the details of her expression but the snakes of her hair rose and fanned around her head as if she were underwater. "I hope not," I admitted.

"I hope not, too," she offered, the words a gentle beacon of hope.

I reached out, my fingers aching with cold. One of the snakes, just a thick green streamer to my poor vision, coiled around my finger. Its angular jaw rubbed against my fingertip and the warmth and ache in my belly grew, almost uncomfortable in its intensity. Another snake wrapped around my wrist, and then another. Her fingers were moving on the laces again, her head down. Did she realize what her…hair…was doing?

"I've got clothes you can borrow," she said, easing this sandal carefully off my foot. "We'll get you cleaned up, then see if that's broken."

"It's not." I'd done it enough times to know.

"Well and good," she agreed. "But I'll check it all the same."

"Wait." As I said it, the snakes withdrew hurriedly. Maybe she *hadn't* been aware?

I reached for my pack, drawing out my veil. "I should rinse this first while the water is clean." She offered a hand and I passed it over. "It's frag- ile," I warned, though I didn't really think it was.

"Most things are, compared to me," she said, without any bitterness or even amusement. Just a simple statement of fact. "I'll be gentle."

My mouth went dry as my mind skipped ahead to all the possibilities in those words.

"So why *did* you come?" she asked, the sound of water falling back into the basin a bright counterpoint to the curiosity in her words.

She knew the answer. She was just fishing. I flicked my hair over my shoulder, making it splat dramatically. "To seduce you, of course. How am I doing?"

"Oh, I was already seduced," she said, just as flippantly. "So why did you *really* come?"

She thought I was joking. I had to correct her, otherwise that belief would permeate everything. I only had two weeks. I didn't have time for misunderstandings.

"I really got up before dawn to bring you breakfast and meet your crows," I admitted. "I'm truly worried about you, because you'll be vulnerable while you sleep. I *also* want to spend more time with you, and flirt with you, and see if you'll keep flirting back. I was hoping I'd get to kiss you today." *At least.* But I didn't add that. "Perseus isn't exactly an *excuse,* but he's definitely not the full reason." I blew out a breath, putting my hands on my hips. "Unfortunately, none of this is working as intended."

"How had you intended for it to work?" she asked, the words low.

She was excited, and that made the warmth in my belly grow even brighter. I drew in a deep breath, enjoying the sensation, as intense as it was. "First, we'd laugh and flirt. Maybe you'd hold me while I patted your crows. I'd stand up on my toes and look you in the eye and whisper, 'you're enchanting.'" I was spoilt for choice in compliments, but that word felt right to me. "Depending on your response, which unfortunately I can't see, I had a variety of options."

"I'm...enchanting?" she asked.

Some of the worry eased. She wasn't used to being complimented yet. I'd fix that. "Can you think of a better word?"

She pressed the veil into my hand. "From your lips?" she asked.

I hummed in pleasure at the suggestion in those words.

Medusa stood and I gently wrung the extra moisture from the veil, taking care not to twist it too hard.

"I'll light the fire," she murmured. "Should I drape it over the chair? There are some sharp pieces, I'm afraid."

I let her take it back. The chair looked like a brown mass to my eyes. A bright green cushion held my veil before she knelt by the fire.

"Can I clean up a little?" I asked her.

"Be my guest." She waved a hand toward the bowl. Again, I could make out the vague shape and size of it, but not the depth of the water. "Can you see it?"

I knelt, mindful of putting pressure on my sore toe, and washed my face first. She probably wouldn't have a comb. My hair was going to be a wreck. There wasn't much I could do about that, except pack one to bring tomorrow. I did the best I could to get clean, working top down. The cheerful crackle of flames came from nearby, and a few moments later I smelled the hint of smoke.

"Here." I looked up to see a wall of red held before me. One of her robes. "It'll be a little big for you," she said, "but it's dry and warmer than what you have. I'll spread yours here."

Promises, promises.

CHAPTER
NINE

When she didn't emerge from my room, I checked and found her curled up in the big hanging chair, her feet tucked up under my robe, fast asleep. Damp tendrils of hair draped over her otherwise bare shoulder.

Crowlie circled above lazily and I paused to study the gorgeous woman sleeping restfully in my home watched over by my old friend. A feeling too sweet to be lust and too hungry to be friendship swelled within me. I breathed in deep, reveling in that slight discomfort, the burn and ache of it. Above Cassandra, a younger bird joined Crowlie's lazy journey, as they sometimes did.

Cassandra didn't fear me.

She'd come here to seduce me, she said, and I couldn't believe she'd spoken in jest. But what if I didn't want to be seduced today only?

And then a third crow joined the two circling above her, and my stomach clenched. They looked at me, the curious, clever eyes of fate, circling above the woman I didn't know and still couldn't bring myself to step away from. For just a moment fear had me by the throat. She slept, unaware of what was unfolding above her.

Our fates were linked now. I hadn't really needed the crows to tell me, but their confirmation was welcome all the same.

The ground didn't shake, the heavens didn't open. They never did, even times like this. I held the strange sweetly hot sensation inside of me and let go of the fear as I ran my eyes over the form of the woman before me.

The face of my future slumbered peacefully, her lips parted ever so slightly. She let out a soft sigh, not dissimilar to the ones she sometimes gave when she was busy or thinking, and the last of the fear evaporated. In its place I felt the familiar old determination set in.

I would make this good, too.

I knew how to build a home. I could fill it with warmth and protect it.

"She stays, then," I murmured to the black-winged bearers of destiny, holding out my arm.

They all broke formation, diving to land along the offered perch. Softly, I murmured my thanks to the messengers and turned to a project I'd been delaying for far too long already.

I needed a bigger nest.

CHAPTER
TEN

CASSANDRA

I woke to the scent of tea and odd rustling sounds. The movement made pain shoot up my neck, and the robe slithered low on my chest. Both sensations reminded me where I was; in Medusa's warm little lair, safe and dry, in her clothes, in her chair...sleeping?

Kicking myself, I fumbled for the now-dry veil and tied it on, glancing around as I did.

She knelt in the middle of the room, a crow on one shoulder, bundles of sticks around her, weaving them into a large, thick mat. She didn't smile when she looked at me, but the snakes around her head shifted, slithering restlessly, turning their heads toward me. There was a softness in her eyes that took me off guard.

"Sorry," I said, sitting up, my limbs moving only grudgingly.

"Don't be." She set down the delicate twigs in her hands and stood. *Her* joints didn't stick, and *she'd* been kneeling. Envy, but also excitement, coiled in the bottom of my belly. "I made you tea, but I didn't know how much honey you take."

A pot of water steamed beside the fire, studded with siderites and with a single, well-brewed slice of lemon floating within. I supported the robe out of reflex, ignoring the drag of its weight against the floor. Though I accepted the cup, I shook my head at the honey she offered. The movement made pain shoot up from the poor muscle in my neck I'd insulted. I stopped the grimace of pain almost before it'd begun, taking a sip and flexing my shoulders tentatively. "This is excellent."

She wasn't smiling. "Are you sore?"

"A little. It'll warm up."

A faint line of disapproval formed on her brow. She grabbed a pillow from the chair, which, now I had my veil on, I could see had been made with countless small branches woven together. In some spots, dried leaves, flowers, and the odd feather nestled amongst the wood. It was a hanging nest.

No wonder I'd fallen asleep so swiftly.

She tossed the cushion before the fire and waved to it. I went to protest out of habit, then saw the look in her eye. Really, why should I fight it? Maybe I'd have an opportunity to seduce her yet.

Taking my tea, I settled carefully on the cushion. The fire didn't feel necessary anymore, but it was cheerful. I flicked my hair back, but she put her hand over mine to stop further movement, kneeling behind me.

"Your knees," I protested.

"I'm not as soft as you." From many, those words would've been an insult. From her, they made me swallow away the anticipation that flooded my mouth. "Can I take this off?" her fingers brushed against the knot of my veil that held it in place.

Warmth bloomed beneath my skin. I didn't turn to her, though I wanted to.

"Yes," I told her, tipping my head forward and then feeling the upset muscle in my neck spasm. I held myself still against it. A little pain. So what? Her fingers were quick in the knot, and I accepted the cloth back. "Thank you for being so gentle with it. I'll never be able to replace it, and it does help me so much."

"I liked seeing your eyes," she said, and she wasn't as close as I might've wanted, but it was early yet. Maybe today I'd get to feed the crows *after* I'd seduced her. "But I didn't like you hurting your toe." The tips of her claws ran lightly against my scalp in a cascade of little pricklings not unlike a collection of hair pins. "Your eyes are beautiful," she murmured. "I don't work with precious stones, but if I ever make a statue of you...I'll need to, for the eyes."

The words made butterflies hatch in my belly. From a woman who was part crow, that sounded like the highest of compliments. "I suppose if you carry me around, I'd never hurt my toes and not need the veil."

She hummed, a noise of pleasure. Her fingers were working through the ends of my hair, now, a light pressure. "*I'd* be fine with that, but *you'd* hate it in less than ten minutes."

I closed my eyes and enjoyed the sensation of her claws working the tangles from my hair, shaking the damp patches loose. She worked from the ends up, now. The tips of her claws were blunted. When they scraped against my skin, it was gently.

Her hands ran through my hair, scooping it back, lifting it from my neck in segments. I felt her taking the weight of it and anticipation unfurled within me, as slow and inexorable as her stroking hands. With a gentle tug I felt it being twisted and anchored above one of my ears by her hand, the pressure firm and not at all unpleasant.

The ends of her claws raked with exquisite gentleness along the curve of my neck and I shivered involuntarily. "Is that okay?" she asked, stilling.

It was a strange sensation, to have the tips of those claws pressed so gently but utterly immobile not too far beneath my ear. "Yes," I said.

Her wings rustled a little. "I'm going to keep going, then?" she said, the words lifting at the end in question.

"I'd like that."

The claws spread outward, like a flower opening on the sore side of my neck, and my breath caught at the delicate scratching that made sensation sweep over me like a fine, misting rain. Then the pads of her fingers pressed delicately into the muscle in my neck and squeezed.

As she rocked her fingers gently back and forth, the unnatural tension in the muscle I'd over-stretched while sleeping awkwardly started to settle. Her fingers rubbed slow, deep circles into my flesh.

"You're tense," she said, and sounded disapproving. "You'll hurt yourself if you carry so much strain."

I wanted to tell her that if she kept it up, I'd be as tense as a barrel of honeyed quinces after a century, but I couldn't quite find the words. Colors throbbed behind my eyes as her hand worked, kneading my flesh with warm, firm fingers. I swayed with her. I breathed with her. Using her fist of hair, she rolled my head forwards and massaged both sides at once, her thumb working one side as her fingers maintained the pressure on the other. What little strength I had left felt like it melted. My skin felt primed for her touch, my flesh waiting for those strong hands to explore further.

"You're about to spill your tea."

In my hand I straightened the cup, but the action caused the liquid to spill over the edge. It was cool and wet against my fingers. I set it down before I made a mess all over her robe for a dull reason like *spilling tea.*

The hand against my neck released me, and I struggled to make a plan. I'd done nothing except sit there and drink in her touch. Before I could react to that realization her arms settled around me, and for a lovely moment I felt surrounded.

Something smooth and cool rubbed against my neck beneath my ear, a slow, seductive slide that made the breath in my lungs catch as the weight draped down the line of my neck and over my chest. A sensation akin to alarm skittered up my spine, but it only fuelled the hunger. The snake-like tendril of Medusa's hair was joined by another smooth, strangely heavy weight against my shoulder. On the other side my hand was lifted above my shoulder. The dampness on my fingers was cool against the warm air as its heat leeched away.

"Would you still like to seduce me?" she murmured.

I'd been successful.

"I would," I confirmed, turning toward her voice at my ear. My neck, warm now, didn't hurt. More of her hair slipped over me, one snake's head bumping softly at the corner of my jaw and making my heart skitter against my ribs, another settling between my breasts. Did she feel what they felt? I throbbed at the thought, arching up toward her without thinking before I caught myself. "I'm afraid I'm at a disadvantage this moment, though."

"If that's true," she said, her lips brushing against my ear, "it's only because you've accomplished your aim already." The confirmation sent a thrill of delight through me. Then her lips closed over my fingers.

I struggled to keep my head as she sucked away the droplets of tea I'd spilled on myself, letting her take my weight. I was cradled against her, and my thoughts slowing, only barely one step ahead of the present. My free hand found her thigh, strong and wide beneath my palm. I arched my throat and the snakes coiled around it, rubbing against me, sending an unfamiliar type of slightly uncomfortable excitement running through my veins.

My own digits, not at all serpentine, popped as they came free from her mouth. Heat coiled inside of me. I turned to her, starving.

The hand in my hair tightened, holding me back. Her breath rushed out, as if I'd pulled it into myself. "Careful," she said, and that single word shook. "I've fangs. You could cut yourself."

I strained against her hold, the words barely registering. Shocked, she let me go. I'd known she would. She wasn't *really* holding me.

Her lips were slightly parted and tasted like tea when I found them. She'd never hurt me. No, Medusa only protected.

She shook like a sapling in a storm as I swept my tongue between her lips, exploring the sharp tips of her canines, the rough surface of her tongue. She stayed, frozen, as I kissed her. Except for her snakes. They writhed over me as if they, just like me, were starving. Her arm remained locked around my body, though I'd half-twisted in her hold. She moaned low in her throat, and I would've sworn I could feel the vibrations of it in my soul.

Her hand brushed aside the knot at my shoulder keeping the robe in place and I returned the favor, not bothering with the brooch, just pushing it away. I straddled her thighs, wrapping my arms around her neck and pressing us together, breast to breast, breath to breath. Her chest rose and fell quickly. She cradled my jaw in both of her hands as I kissed her, a faint tremor running through her.

Medusa, the fearsome monster, the mythical man-killer.

Trembling for me.

My head spun.

She felt impossibly strong beneath my hands. I explored every part of her I could reach. The warm expanse of her back with the deep gutter running between the bands of muscle either side of her spine; the slight dip of her waist; the flare of her thigh. My other hand moved up, along the strong muscles of her arm to stroke along the side of her breast and higher, to feel the ridge of her collarbone. One of her fangs caught my lip, just gently, and I tasted just a hint of coppery blood. I wanted to dive deeper but she made a noise of distress, pulling back.

I let her go, gulping in air. The globe of one of her ass cheeks filled my palm. "I hurt you," she said, horrified. "Cassandra—"

"A tiny scrape," I told her. The hands cradling my face held me back when I would've had her again. "You don't scare me," I promised.

"I should," she said, her thumb swiping over my lip.

My body ached and I struggled to breathe, trying to clear my head. The serpents against my back slithered, every bit as hungry as I, holding me tightly against her, moving restlessly. I tried to turn my head but she held me tightly, except this time a few of her claws bit into me, not deliberately and not far, just enough to remind me I was dancing on the knife's edge. How I wished I could see her expression as she looked at me. My fingers found her neck, urging her mouth to me.

"Kiss me," I challenged, and she trembled again. My blood roared in my ears. I tried to drag her closer, but she was like granite, save for the writhing serpents that supported my arching back. One dragged its weight over my breasts and the weight of it, the slight rasp of the scales, against the tops of my breasts made my breath catch.

Suddenly, the serpents stilled.

"Do it again," I demanded, but it was breathless. "Please, do it again."

The weight of the serpent moved back the way it'd come, except a fraction lower this time, directly over top of my nipples.

I moaned, my hold on her softening to create enough space to let her touch me more easily. My hand on her ass shifted, skimming up over the cloth pooling between us. Her belly was soft. Above it, the bones of her ribs provided structure. I skimmed past them, too, and heard her draw in a breath that shook as I explored the soft underside of her breast with the backs of my knuckles. The velvet flesh called to me. She held me, though she'd frozen against me, her serpentine digits writhing restlessly against my back and shoulders again, tugging me closer.

A thrill went through me and I opened my eyes to see her face tipped back. I couldn't make out her expression. I didn't need to. Beneath the sensitive pads of my fingers her nipple was already pebbled. Her breath caught, then rushed out as I rolled it slowly between thumb and forefinger. Delight rippled through my body, the ghost of my caresses serving only to heighten my hunger, not to sate it.

The softness of her breast in my palm, the shudder of her breath, the tension in her limbs and the drumming of my own heart formed my world.

"I want to kiss you here," I said. As I spoke, her claws brushed against my cheeks, an unintended reminder of the Gorgon's power.

And she shivered again for me. An unintended reminder of mine.

"I want to take your nipples in my mouth," I whispered, rolling the firm bud slowly still, aching to do more. "I want to feel you tremble and I want you to think of nothing except me. I want to taste you. I want your thighs to tremble and your hips to beg me not to stop."

"Cassandra," she said, like I was a deity.

The awe in her voice went straight to my blood and made my head swim. "Release me," I told her. "Let me have you."

Her hands shook. "I could hurt you."

The ache in my heart cleared my head a little. Was she truly so scared of herself? "I could hurt you, too," I acknowledged. "Accidentally break your heart. Will you risk it?"

The shudder that took her told me I'd guessed right, that it wasn't the physical pain she feared. "If I ask you to stop," she said, "you must."

The ache in my heart grew fangs. Grief and fury, two sides of the same coin. "Always," I promised without hesitation.

"I know," she whispered, the words shaking. "I'm sorry I had to say that. I knew you would."

"I'm glad you said it." I turned my face, and this time her hands were gentle enough against my skin that her fingers bent with the movement. I pressed a kiss to her palm. "I want to push you onto your back and feast on your breasts," I told her, the plans swirling. Important to let her know. She'd need it. Maybe she always would. "I'm going to rub myself against your leg while I do. I'm going to kiss your neck and I might even nibble against your ear. I want to put my hands on your knees and spread your thighs, Medusa." That breath catch, the tremble. My head spun, but I held onto the plan. "If you want me to put my fingers in you, I will. I'd like that. I want to taste your clit, though. I want to learn how you like to be sucked and licked, and what noise you make when you come."

She let out a long breath. It shook. One of the serpents rubbed against my cheek, its nose lingering seductively against my mouth. "And you?" she asked, the question aching. "I want you, too."

The issue of claws and fangs wasn't insurmountable, but it wasn't my priority right now. "Good. Because I plan to sit on that beautiful face of yours. I do believe those fangs won't get in the way if I'm still. You can keep me still, can't you?"

She growled something that sounded like it was caught between a threat and a promise that made my body ache, her hands falling away. The shudder of feathers sounded and her wings unfurled, blotting out the world around us. Enclosed in the darkness, the warmth of the fire at my back, I fell on her.

I straddled her belly and her hands ripped at the robes on me. Her neck was long and warm and delicious. Beneath my lips, her pulse beat help-lessly. I licked that point, tasting the slight saltiness of her skin, feeling for the first time the difference between us in the way it moved beneath my tongue. Firmer, almost like it was more attached to her than skin usually was to a person.

I was more attached to her, too.

"I like it," I told her, and she let out a sound that was sort of shocked and also a little amused.

There was so much to explore. The arch of her collarbone was disarm-ingly graceful. The tip of my nose traced it. Her hands were shaking, but she was gathering up my hair, combing it with those claws as she went. The sensation of them scraping softly against my scalp was so perfect I had to pause and enjoy it, my forehead resting against her chest, her hands in my hair and her body welcoming beneath me.

The slow tug and coil as I felt her wrap the mass of it around one fist made my mouth water. Nothing would be allowed between us. She'd see to it.

The beat of her heart beneath her breasts was a siren's song. I pressed a kiss between them, honoring her vulnerability. Honoring her excitement. Through my lips I felt it drumming to me, the sound of hope. Around me her serpents slithered, rubbing against my face, kissing their noses to my ears, pressing their comforting weight encouragingly against the back of my neck and over my shoulders. She held my hair firmly with one hand, her breathing quick and excited beneath me.

I explored the expanse of her skin as I'd done her neck, with kisses, with the sensitive curve of my cheek and the tip of my nose. I rubbed against the swell of her breast and felt the resistance of it. I found the velvet edge of her nipple, ridged with occasional fine, irregular bumps and I traced the boundary of it with my mouth. I memorized the contrast of her flesh before I let myself be guided by those desperate serpentine digits to take the bud of her nipple into my mouth.

She let out a breath, as if in relief. The sensation swept through me, too. Hunger not yet assuaged but at least acknowledged released some of the tension in my limbs and I listened to her breathing and tracked the flex and arch of muscles. When I sucked lightly, her breath caught and she arched into me. When I pressed the pebbled nipple to the roof of my mouth, her hand got a little heavier against the back of my head. When I caught it gently between my teeth and sucked as hard as I could, the tension flooded out of her and she lay back, glorying in the sensation just as I'd done as she'd given me that neck massage earlier.

Deep touch. Firm touch. In my hand I took her other nipple, trying to mimic the pressures, the tugging and the stroking. She let out a soft noise of wonder. The serpents held me close, cradling me. Her wings drooped, slowly, as if she'd forgotten to hold them. My own nipples ached and my cunt throbbed in time with her heartbeat under my lips. I wanted more. So much more. But she lay, lost in the wonder, and I could never leave her there. Not alone. I switched breasts and she let out another noise that was something like gratitude. I imagined those sensations filling her up, building the need within her the way it was building within me. That liquid heat. In my mouth her nipple rolled, impossibly hard and somehow still velvet. Beneath my fingers I could feel the wetness my mouth had left on her other breast.

And then her hips flexed a little, beneath me. She made a needy noise.

Pleasure shot through me like lightning, searing me. I used my teeth against her and she whimpered, arching. Hungry again.

Soon, she'd be starving.

My free hand I planted in the middle of her chest, holding her down, and I continued to feast.

Her fingers tightened in my hair. She lifted her hips again, restlessly. I kept on enjoying those hard nipples, the round, delightful weight of those breasts. She'd given herself to me, hadn't she? And I wanted to *enjoy*.

She moaned, tossing her head. Some of the snakes fell away, but they were back a moment later. Her second hand was on my shoulder, pressing me down just a little. Her hips lifted and my contact with the ground beneath was broken as she arched completely. I stopped my feast to rub my cheek against the curve of her breast, reveling in the feel of it. Her breath caught and held as I did. Her hand on my shoulder flexed just enough to give me a taste of her strength. She moaned as I found her nipple, but it was a noise of frustration, too. Beside my ear a snake hissed.

Shocked, I laughed, and she pressed down with her hand on my shoulder. "I need you," she said, the words breathless. "Cassandra, please." The reverence in the words, the desperation, made my head swim.

"My mouth?" I asked her, squeezing the breast beneath my hand still to feel the way it moved beneath my palm. "My fingers?"

"Everything," she said, the word half a sob. "Anything. More."

I fit between her thighs like they'd been crafted to house me and breathed in the intimate scent of her as much a promise as desire. I pressed kisses to where her navel should've been, trailing down to the apex of her legs. She trembled as I traced the seam of her body with my fingertips, learning the way she'd been crafted, the shape of her lips and the position of her clit. When I reached the wet, hungry entrance to her body she lifted her hips again, carrying me with her. I traced the edges of her, committing the sensation to memory. Velvet, warm and wet and welcoming. I didn't dip inside yet, though, moving my desire-slick fingers back up, spreading the protective folds of her body to expose her swollen clit, waiting. She had a pulse here, too. It begged for me to taste it.

I lowered my mouth and feasted.

My greed had nothing to do with her responses, not at first. She shook and gasped and panted, but that was background knowledge to the feel of that impossibly soft skin, the taste of her, the way she offered me everything. Every stroke of my tongue made my own cunt ache more, made my own flesh throb with joy and promise. If she could suck my finger, then she could suck my clit, and I knew it, even if she didn't. But right then I didn't want that. I didn't want anything except her, writhing, begging, saying my name like it was I who'd brought her to life and I who'd sustain her. I wanted to commit the taste of her, the impossibly glorious texture, to memory. I wanted to smell her on my hands and feel the slickness of her on my lips for the rest of my life. I wanted the squeeze of her thighs and the trembling of her hips.

The razor edges of my hunger sated, I began to recognize her patterns, the way she'd lift and hold her body, the way her hand would tighten in my hair or loosen a little. I devoured still, but I did it mindfully, driving her onward, aching to feel the release ripple through her. I moved with the demands of her body, mapping them in my mind, exploring the nuances and the wonders of her.

Her heart would start and stop for me. And mine for her.

"Cassandra," she said, and in her lips my name was a plea, a prayer, and a promise all at once. Our future spread out before us, as open to me as her body. Joy, and love. Hope, and belonging. Safety, and validation. "*Cassandra.*" The word was offered up, shakily, tangled up in a moan and anchored in devotion.

Answering her need, I didn't change the rhythmic combination of licking, sucking pressure against her clit, but I did find the entrance to her body and slip two fingers inside her. I found the magical little spot not too deep inside where her cunt felt soft and giving and pressed into it.

She stilled again, her breath halting entirely, her whole body liquid, and I drank deep.

Only a few moments later the hands that had almost fallen away were scooping my hair up desperately, cradling me to her insistently. Every breath was ragged. Every tremor started inside of her. The undulations of her hips were helpless, driven by the rhythm I'd identified long ago. I rode them, locked to her, feeling the answering ripples through my own body as if my own muscles and sinew were connected to her, responding to her.

"Cassandra," she breathed, desperately, as if I was the only thing holding her to this plane. A moment later I felt the ripples that started around my fingers, the clenching, grasping hunger of her body as she reached her peak and milked every moment of joy. Her body shook beneath me, her hands clutching. The ripples pulsed in her clit and shuddered through the thighs that remained clamped around me. They ran through my body too, the waves rocking through me a moment after hers, a response, not a mirror. I struggled to breathe, maintaining the rhythm like it was all that kept either of us alive.

When they tapered off, I rested my forehead on her thigh, pressing the weight of my palm down through her still-throbbing cunt. I wished I could see her expression. I settled for holding her lovingly while she came back to herself.

"I don't…" her breath shook. "I don't think the nest I'm building is strong enough for us."

My heart turned over. She was building a nest? For *us?* Did that mean… "We can always use the floor, and then just sleep in the nest," I offered, pulling my thoughts back before I lost myself in the tangle of hope and possibilities.

"That means I'd have to be mindful of something other than you," she said, still short of breath.

Smiling, I pressed a kiss to her thigh and gently began to shift my weight away from her cunt, no longer throbbing so aggressively against me. She still made a noise akin to pain when I withdrew. Her hand in my hair tugged me up gently and I went, needing no second invitation. The feathers of her wings beneath my knees were strange. She lay back, her hair a green mass around her, the serpents barely stirring at all until I was halfway up her body.

My hair was released. The weight of it unfurling like a banner was strange. The way she took my hips was not.

I let her guide me, the ache in my body offset by the lightness of my heart as she nuzzled into my cunt much as I'd done to hers. She guided my weight and serpents slithered over my thighs as if to hold me in place.

Her mouth was slow in its exploration, lingering, savoring. I settled my hands in my hair and focused on the sensations. She'd hum in pleasure sometimes, and the noise shot up through my core. She'd press herself closer and I'd feel the flat curve of her fangs, not the tearing tips, like a scaffold she worked around. The tiny flutter of anxiety I felt from having those deadly teeth reliant on my total compliance was exciting in a way I'd never expected.

Heat swept through me, sparkling and bright. I didn't let my muscles tense, just absorbed it all, drinking it in, filling myself up with it. I moved it inside me with my breath and felt the first flutters of my response. I didn't flex or grind. Beneath me she made a noise of approval and I was rewarded by one hand running up my back, claws scratching out hints of promise.

Happy for her to make good on that, I let myself bask in her attention. It was, after all, the only safe choice.

CHAPTER
ELEVEN

CASSANDRA

She *could* make a nest strong enough for us.

Tired of lying awake and feeling the anxiety humming through my veins, I eased out from beneath her wing. She didn't stir, and despite myself I was relieved. In the dark, I found my veil and a cloak against the chill of night, then slipped out into the temple.

I had no idea if it was the new moon, because we'd had a few weeks of beautiful weather, and then days of wicked winds and terrifyingly high waves.

I'd been terrified. She'd just smiled and pointed at the cliffs, teaching me what the marks meant. Where waves struck. Where water had sat. She'd held my hand and stood with me on the steps, beautiful in the rain as she was in the sun. The storm hadn't passed fully yet, but it was easing.

A strong gust of wind caught my cloak and slapped it against my calves. I grabbed it with an impatient hand, my skin crawling at the sensation of wet cloth. I'd returned without her noticing last night. I doubted I would tonight.

There. A splash.

Alarm skittered up my spine as I stepped onto the stone landing. Of course there were splashes. I was at the pier. There was water.

But the splash had been...different?

I wasn't going out onto the pier. Not in this wind. But I did walk up alongside a statue armored with audacity and lifted a hand, as if it might better shield my eyes from the wind.

"I told you she'd come!"

I jumped and the hand that went to take my elbow grabbed my forearm instead.

"Come on," Perseus hissed.

I couldn't smell the wealth on him now. The wind slapped my cloak into his legs and he didn't even notice.

He must've been inhuman.

I dug in my heels but my feet slipped.

She'd never hear me screaming. Not down here. Terror spurted through me, but I moved to the next option.

"Thank the gods you came," I said, no longer resisting, running along beside him as he towed me to the pier. "The monsters here are *terrifying*. O Brave One, I fear you've been grossly misled. The gods make mockery of your heroism." I just needed to get them out of here. Sure, men had never listened to me before, but surely just this once I could work around the ego of *one* of them.

He grunted. "Tell me all about it on the ship."

I couldn't even *see* it. I felt sick, but it was a far away feeling. "Of course," I agreed, relieved. "We must sail far from this place. What will be the next leg of your quest, Shining Warrior?"

"This *is* my quest," he said, and shrouded lantern light became visible. I was guided up a plank and onto the dark, looming ship. Men peered at me. Armored. Grim. Their lanterns were guarded against the wind.

"Where is she now?" he demanded.

Asleep, naked in the nest she made us. The wind changed direction. My hair blew free as my hood was pushed back over my shoulders. A feather blew loose. I watched it vanish into the darkness, terror drumming at my heart.

"There are many Gorgons," I said, raising my voice to carry. "Some sleep at night. Others at day. They have only one weakness, O Heroic One. You need a silver weapon." I spun dramatically. "Hear me—"

I was grabbed by the arm and half-dragged, swallowing my words as I slipped over the ship's deck. "Athena told us she'd lie," Perseus shouted, over the wind.

Unarmed, I focused on survival.

CHAPTER
TWELVE

MEDUSA

The beating of wings and the calling of my friends woke me. It had only been a few weeks, but I was already accustomed to Cassandra's softness beside me. Her place in the nest, with the softest wool and extra feathers, was alarmingly empty.

Crowlie landed on the chair I'd made her and looked at me, her eyes beady in the darkness.

How it had happened, I didn't know. Not yet. But I would. For now, I just reached for my spear, taking to the skies.

The wind was fierce, but there was no lightning. I left my friends where it was warm and safe and dry. Every beat of my wings made the fury surge.

If they'd hurt her...

If they'd *worried* her...

The rage flooded my body and sent strength screaming through my limbs.

The ships were at dock, two of them. Lanterns bobbed. Men were slinking up the stairs in twos, keeping to the shadows, huddling in the mists. *Scouts.* The fury climbed higher. I paid them no mind. They'd be found. One by one. I'd hunt them down, rip out their livers and toss the rest of them into the sea.

My friends would feast today.

Once Cassandra was free.

I circled lower. They'd have taken her. Ships had quarters below deck. My spear wouldn't be good in close quarters. I flexed my empty hand. The rain was cold. Their blood wouldn't be. Not for a little while yet.

The group of men stood on the deck, shaded lantern light more than enough for me to pick them out. The leader stood in the centre. The others formed around him like a clot around a wound.

And there she was. Cassandra. Tied. *Tied.* They'd *tied her to their mast.*

The darkness of night looked red. I arrowed down directly for them, the rage screeching and clawing in my chest. The strength in my muscles would've shattered my bones, if not for the curse that'd made me inde-structible.

The man with the golden helm didn't even see me coming.

CHAPTER

THIRTEEN

CASSANDRA

The blood from her spear-tip sprayed through the air in a majestic arc as she whipped the weapon around. Perseus had never even drawn his, crushed beneath her as she'd landed in a dive. The deck of the ship splintered around his corpse, so far had she driven him into the ship.

The blood whipped again. Men fell without a shout of discovery. The noises came after they'd hit the ground, so fast was she, so slow were they to register the shock. I couldn't breathe, my gaze stuck on the crushed form of Perseus. His bronze helm was crumpled. The deck was slick, but a puddle was forming under him, black in the night. Another fell beside him, gasping like a fish out of water, clutching at his chest.

I forced myself to look up but I couldn't see her, not properly. She was spinning through the air in a graceful kick, her wings retracting as I watched. The spear moved in quick, tight arcs now, back and forth, sending sprays of blood from the tip and water from the haft. Her snakes writhed, flaring their hoods, hissing.

The soldiers around her stood transfixed. As if they'd been turned to stone through sheer terror.

Then she shattered them.

Her claws cut through the thick cording like it was an overripe fig and the rope was ripped away from me, making my head spin. Apologies and thanks tumbled through my head as she pulled me free.

"Did they hurt you?" she demanded, the words a hiss of fury.

My head swam. How had we got here? Before I could answer her mouth was on mine and I felt the bite of the mast behind me, the wind on my skin, the unyielding strength of her lips on mine.

"Hold on," she commanded.

I was already. I couldn't hold her any tighter, not if our lives truly had depended on it.

The roar of her wings, of a million feathers moving at ferocious speed for a short distance, sounded like freedom. The air bit into me, icy. The darkness wasn't terrifying, though, nor the height, nor these speeds.

I really should have just stayed in our nest. I wouldn't make that mistake again.

I felt her change direction in the air with deliberation, as if sighting her target. *The second ship.* The way she'd cut them all down in *moments*—

She moved powerfully, a sharp, jerky motion that made my heart lurch and terror flood my veins, though her arm around me never once slipped. The spear flew from her hand.

Below, I heard a deep, thunderous cracking. Wood splitting. Men shouting. She was moving again, though, her hands searching me for injuries, her mouth against my ear. The serpents writhed over my shoulders. Her legs caught one of mine between hers. I could feel her heart thundering to get to mine through our ribs. I was surrounded. Mid-air, in the dark, she checked me for wounds. She was saying something. I couldn't hear it over the roar of the wind and waves.

She wanted me to know I was safe.

The tension flooded out of me. She'd sank a ship with only her spear. She *could* turn men to stone, if only in terror.

I wasn't accustomed to the feeling of being…*wrong.*

The apologies behind my lips were useless in the rush of air. Instead, I found her mouth for another kiss, gentle and reassuring. She was breathing in hard, sharp gasps. My breasts flattened against her chest. I found the edge of her mouth with my lips, pressing the gentlest kiss I could to that tiny little corner of paradise.

It's okay, I wanted to tell her. *I don't make the same mistake twice. Not really. I'm sorry to scare you.* But the words would never reach her, so I could only hold them, for now, and tell her with actions instead. One of my arms I kept locked around her waist. The other I wrapped around her neck, nuzzling at the sensitive point beneath her ear.

Her hands on me flexed and her spine arched. I shifted between her legs but she held me too firmly to find more than the merest hint of pleasure.

In the air she wobbled a little, and the laugh that wanted to bubble up out of my throat shocked me. A moment later her hand was on my leg, as if she'd had the same thought. I was guided, pushed and pulled, buffeted by the wind and the storm.

I was safe in her hands. Cold, yes, but safe. Her wings beat around us, a rhythmic drumming. My robe was pushed aside. Her hands didn't go near me. She was so scared of hurting me. Her arm looped around my waist and my whole world existed inside the beating of her wings as she positioned my cunt against hers. The movement of those beating wings, the gentle up and down, the hot wetness of her pussy, made my head spin.

Hunger rushed through me, shocking me. Her snakes nuzzled at the corners of my mouth and the edges of my nipples, rubbing, seeking. The cold of the world was there, still, felt against my back and at the tips of my toes, but heat streamed through me. She was so wet. We needed to get to ground so I could taste her, so I could bury my face in the glorious center of her. We slipped together, not far, just far enough. Tiny movements as her wings beat and we held on to each other in the middle of the night. In the middle of the storm.

The heat was molten as it spread through me, searing me, leaving me gasping and panting. I didn't search for the end, though. I'd learned that from her. Poised over the vice of her fangs, or aching as she circled my clit with the soft pad of one claw-tipped hand. I remained. I waited. I enjoyed every moment, not seeking the next. The storm raged around us, impotent in the circle of her wings.

She shuddered. She shifted. I felt the break in our rhythm and wanted to weep, but I understood it. I knew the clawing hunger and why her hands gripped me desperately, not out of fear but need. I rode the waves of it as they built. I felt the throbbing in her pussy and it spread through me, too. The wonder of it, the sweetness overwhelmed me. I rode it for long, endless moments that felt like they were over before they'd even begun. That felt eternal. Like overheated metal I lay in her arms, between her legs, pliant and giving. I imagined I could hear her prayers, my name on her lips, as we spun through the darkness.

When we finally landed in the temple my legs collapsed beneath me. She caught me, pressing a soft kiss to my lips. "Stay close," she said, over the wind. "There's more about."

I tried to, but my legs wobbled again, barely holding.

A small part of me worried she had no weapon. She looked down at me. I couldn't make out her expression, but it wasn't anger.

I opened my mouth to apologize when a man rushed from the darkness.

Medusa's leg swept up, deflecting the edge of his spear and circling it around, driving it into the ground. The hand holding me remained gentle. The other moved forward in a sharp movement, fingers straight. Bones crunched. She ripped her hand backwards and tossed something dark and bloody aside.

I stared after it.

"The crows don't mind the hearts of men," she said, pressing another kiss to my lips. "Though they'd prefer the livers. Come. It's cold out. I'll put some wine on to warm. You've had a long day."

I stepped over the corpse of a man who hadn't listened to me, lifting the hem of my robe. "I can put the wine on," I told her. "You go finish feeding the crows."

She hesitated. "Are you sure?"

I rolled my eyes. "I can mull some wine, Medusa. Yes, I'm sure." Anyway, my legs mightn't carry me the whole way as I ran along behind her. I was tired. She was going to protect. It was what she did. Well, I'd make her somewhere soft to land when she was done, and kiss away the last lingering worries. "Thank you."

Though I couldn't see the smile on her lips, I could feel it in her kiss. "My pleasure," she murmured. "Be safe. Mind your toes on the cracked floor." She stepped back, and most of the serpents faced forward now into the darkness. One shot out and rubbed its head against my hand. Smiling, I waited for her to go, then gingerly made my way toward our home.

CHAPTER
FOURTEEN

MEDUSA - AN EPILOGUE

I came in from the sun-baked orchards, grateful for the temple's cool shadows, to find Cassandra curled up in a hanging chair, a book in her hand and Crowlie in her lap, puffed up and fast asleep.

Had I not been struck still by the beauty of the woman, I wouldn't have noticed two younger crows seated in a pattern above my uncharacteristically oblivious truth-teller. Three crows, reminding me this woman's fate was entangled inexorably with mine. As unnecessary as the reminder was, it still filled me with joy so intense it hurt to think of it.

She turned a page, and Crowlie swayed on her lap, trusting her as she trusted me. It had taken Cassandra less than a year to win them over.

I turned the precious stone I'd traded for over in the palm of my hand, excited to show her, but loath to disrupt her.

We had all the time in the world, after all. I could wait for her book to droop.

ABOUT ELISSE HAY

Elisse lives on the unceded land of the Kulin Nation in Australia. She has become the cat lady everybody promised she could be; her next goal is swamp hag.

Find more information at elissehay.com.

GIRL DINNER

KRISTIN JACQUES

CONTENT NOTES FOR GIRL DINNER

Cadaver dissection in educational/medical context, monster eating people and human flesh, body horror, medical content, gore, humans as prey, death, altered mental states due to predatory pheromones, mild bullying, physical abuse (brief), sexual harassment by person in authority (brief), explicit consensual sex

CHAPTER ONE

DAPHNE

The cadaver's tissue dragged the glide of her scalpel, the cold toughness almost reminiscent of a freezer-burned steak. Daphne's stomach growled—unfortunate timing and loud enough for her lab partner to stop mid-liver removal to stare.

"How could you possibly be hungry right now?" Bradley appeared somewhat green, placing the large organ on the scale. There was a slight flutter to his fingers, likely trying to flick away the slippery sensation.

Daphne bit the inside of her cheek against a grumpy retort. She'd been famished since they cracked open their cadaver's sternum because *somebody* had turned off her alarm. Which meant she'd missed breakfast in the dining hall to rush to her eight a.m. anatomy lab.

Somebody being her roommate Beth, who had been an absolute bitch since the incident neither of them acknowledged except through petty grievances and small acts of sabotage. As if having an anatomy lab this early in the morning wasn't cosmic punishment enough. Unlike Beth, who subsisted on coffee and Cup O Noodles, Daphne took full advantage of her dining hall access and hated missing a meal.

Being elbow-deep in viscera had little impact on her appetite but she'd learned the hard way she was in the minority there. She concentrated on flaying the soft tissue of the cadaver's face, wondering if she'd make it to the dining hall before they sold out of roast beef sandwiches.

"Oh, look at that...there's a sub-dermal cyst here," she mused, momentarily distracted from her gurgling guts by the revealed anomaly. The human body was full of surprises, little mysteries crafted into the soft tissues, bones, and sinew over a lifetime of experiences. This cadaver alone seemed to possess clusters of cysts hidden in pockets of soft tissue. They hadn't seemed to contribute to the cadaver's cause of death, but Daphne found the presence of them curious. "I wonder if that's caused by a genetic condition—"

"Who cares? Can we please finish the weigh-in before this smell makes me puke?" Bradley shuddered from the tips of his gelled hair to the paper shoe covers on his overpriced loafers. There was a thick smear of vapor rub beneath his quivering nostrils.

The urge to roll her eyes was difficult to resist. Daphne didn't bother with the rub. This wasn't some crime scene where the body had been left to putrefy in the open air. Formaldehyde was the prevailing odor, nothing but a strong chemical smell she'd been surrounded by since high school biology classes. Yet again, her lack of reaction made her an outlier. Bradley's attitude matched most of their classmates, falling somewhere on the squeamish scale—the exception being herself and Wesley, who was obviously a budding psychopath.

At least Daphne didn't carve patterns into the cadaver skin.

She sighed, writing her observations in her own notes to mull over on her own time, and continued recording the necessary lab data. They finished in relative silence, broken by Bradley's periodic dry heaving. Her partner couldn't bail fast enough, offering to hand in their report while she closed the cadaver on her own. Daphne pursed her lips, watching Bradley scurry away like his lab coat was on fire.

"That one's prepping for med school," she told the corpse. "How's he going to handle living bodies when he can't stand the dead?" She glanced at the cadaver's face, slightly marred by her exploratory incisions. "He forgot you were a living person who donated their body for us to learn. Thank you for your service."

Daphne tapped the emptied chest cavity, a small personal salute to the body on the table.

Once she disposed of her soiled gloves, she rolled her lab coat into the lab laundry hamper and hustled for the dining hall. It was a seven-minute walk from the sciences building, one she made in five while weaving through clusters of chatting undergrads.

Swiping her dining hall card, she slid into the line for the cold prep bar, salivating at the rows of neatly wrapped sandwiches, the spill of ingredients flattened by the tight plastic cling.

"Please have roast beef, please have roast beef," Daphne muttered, her fingers digging into the edges of her tray. She finally reached the bar, scanning the remaining sandwiches on offer. Her heart sank at the empty placeholder for roast beef. "Damn."

With her first choice off the table, she scanned the other options, pouting as she snagged an Italian combo and a bag of chips.

"Stupid supply never living up to stupid demand," Daphne grumbled, filling out her tray with a cup of autumn bisque, a fruit bowl, and some souffle inspired creation. She rounded out her lunch selection with a bottled water and a can of Coke.

Eschewing the louder, occupied tables, she found a quiet empty table in the corner and tucked into her meal. Daphne liked eating alone. Even when she and roommate Beth were on better terms, Beth told her she gave off serious *black cat energy*. It wasn't like she exuded Goth vibes in her slate-colored blouse and skinny jeans. Bubbly namesake aside, Daphne simply wasn't a social butterfly. Lunch was time to stuff her face and refill her energy tank for afternoon classes.

Besides, she'd made the mistake of socializing last semester and look how that turned out.

The sharp corner of a potato chip caught in her throat. Daphne coughed, fumbling for her bottle of water through blurred vision.

"Easy, sugar. You need to chew before swallowing," a feminine voice drawled. A solid thump between her shoulder blades dislodged the offending chip. The water bottle pressed into her searching hands, long nails caressing the back of her hand as they pulled away. "It's open."

Daphne gratefully brought the uncapped water bottle to her lips, soothing the scratchiness in her throat while she blinked her vision clear.

Settled across from her was a living Barbie doll—well, maybe Barbie by way of Bettie Mae Page. From the perfectly coifed blonde hair streaked with hot pink highlights that framed her heart shaped face, to the thick black lashes framing her deep blue eyes, pert nose, and pouty lips an eye-catching shade of man-eater red. A crisp jean jacket covered her arms, while the rose red low square cut top beneath it revealed her generous cleavage. The table hid her lower body, but Daphne imagined her lower proportions were as perfectly displayed as her upper half.

"Wow," Daphne uttered around the rim of the bottle. Low and muffled and likely unheard by the woman across from her, who still sat there.

"You okay now, sugar?" the stranger asked.

Daphne watched her perfect face, surprised by the curious buzz of interest that kicked up in the back of her mind.

She took another sip of water, ordering her thoughts for a suitable answer. An acknowledgement or platitude of gratitude would be appropriate, would it not? Except...except...

Daphne always studied the people she met. It was a habit she'd carried since childhood, a rapid catalog of personal observations she would mentally log to mull over later, but her mental notes kept tangling the longer she observed this woman. That flawless skin could be an effect of expertly applied makeup but even the thickest coat of concealer didn't completely erase the evidence of pores and the fine hairs of the epidermis. Not a single freckle, mole, or dimple marked her—an eerie plastic-like perfection that echoed her initial thought to call her a Barbie doll.

"That's the second time you called me sugar," said Daphne, slowly screwing the cap back on her water. Staring too long was bad. She'd learned that the hard way. Her gaze slid over the manicured image presented to her until she stopped at those deep blue eyes.

The strange woman blinked at her. There was a pause before she laughed. "Maybe I thought you looked sweet," she replied. The words could almost be construed as flirtatious in nature, if not for the other factors.

There was nothing flirtatious in the hunger of those eyes, the blue so deep she wondered if she'd drown in them. It was a predator's hunger that intrigued her, made her curious. Her mother was right when she said Daphne wasn't right in the head. In the seconds she held that gaze, energy seemed to fizz within, creating further depths in the blue, like the yawning deep of the ocean or a cosmic starburst threating to suck her in.

"Hmmm," Daphne kept the sound in her throat, while her gaze continued to flicker over the woman, absorbing every detail she could. "Thank you for the save."

The blonde beamed at her. "See, I was right. Careful with the rest of your lunch, though, I won't be around to save you." She winked at Daphne, rising to her feet. Her movement revealed the light blue jeans that lovingly hugged the curves of her hips. Pin-up Barbie possessed just the sort of curves Alex, the evil ex, said Daphne lacked. She watched those perfect hips sashay away, silently mulling through her observations of the encounter through mouthfuls of lukewarm bisque.

There was a pause in their call and response conversation, a different sort of calculation than Daphne's gauge of social cues. Pin-up Barbie was lovely, in the way airbrushed models were lovely: a polished façade that couldn't truly exist. The real chilling note of their encounter was her laugh that lacked even a hint of emotion in the sound. Those glossy blue eyes hadn't contained a whisper of humanity.

A predator had sat across from Daphne and smiled with gleaming white teeth. *The better to eat you with, sugar.* She snorted at the inward thought in the stranger's twang. If that woman was human, she'd eat her fork.

Daphne was thoroughly fascinated.

Opening her lab notebook to a fresh page, she jotted down a series of notes. A new hobby was just the ticket to getting over her ex. Besides, a fresh obsession would keep her from stabbing Beth in her sleep. She would still exact her revenge for the alarm clock, but now she wouldn't have to hide a body.

Tapping her pen against the page, she considered her next steps. Further data was required, which meant she needed to track down her brief dining companion.

Daphne did enjoy a good chase.

DAPHNE

Pin-up Barbie proved more elusive than anticipated. Daphne found her absence curious. Admittedly, she didn't fully invest herself in the search due to an afternoon of classes, but with a couple of hours to kill before dinner, she thought tracking down someone that vibrant would be an easier task.

Nobody on campus looked like her. Daphne's mystery woman shone with the bright jewel tones of something poisonous, so many eye-catching colors and accessories. But after wandering through all the usual locations students frequented, Daphne didn't spot a single flash of red. She thought about going to registration to see if she could dig something up, but without a first name, she didn't have enough to begin.

Fuming, Daphne sat alone at a table in the library, ignoring the cluster of girls at the neighboring table. They giggled like idiots. Once they started nodding in her direction over their books, exchanging hushed whispers, she sighed in irritation.

Gossip was still hot after Alex's epic crash-out. It followed her around like shit on her shoe. Daphne knew she had made a mistake getting involved with him, but she hadn't realized how large an error she'd made until the fallout started. Alex was charming and popular. Daphne was not. The gossip that leaked regarding their relationship was of a *he-said, she-said* nature, except Daphne couldn't be bothered to say anything about that idiot and therefore she'd been painted as the villain in the court of public opinion. Despite Alex's position, age, and juvenile behavior, no one took her side; not Beth, nor these giggling morons.

What was the point of fighting when opinions were already made? Instead, Daphne kept her head down and concentrated on her classes. Three more semesters and she'd never see any of them again. Easier said than done, though. The snickering rabble set her teeth on edge. Daphne gripped the edge of the table, waiting for them to leave so they didn't see her react. She desperately needed a distraction. The universe must have heard her. A flash of red snagged her attention through the stacks. Daphne slid out of her chair, leaving the gossiping group behind as she followed the fleeting splash of color. It could have been someone else wearing bright red, but she tiptoed through the shelves.

Wandering into the familiar Anatomy reference section, Daphne realized she'd lost sight of the source of the bright color and leaned against the out-turned spines.

A soft voice slipped through the gap in the books behind her. "Fancy seeing you again, sugar."

Daphne peered through to the other side, where Pin-Up Barbie peered at her with those bright blue eyes.

"Hi," Daphne breathed, surprised by the fluttery sensation in her stomach. Dinner was soon but she didn't think it was a side effect of hunger. "You're here." A brilliant observation on her part, truly.

Pin-Up Barbie flashed her a smile. "What's a girl like you doing in a dump like this?" She spoke in teasing tones. The library was clearly not a dump, but it was older and dusty. To someone so bright and shiny, it might come across as a dump.

Daphne blinked, determined to rescue the conversation. "Isn't that my line?" The grin she offered was more strained than intended. She hadn't smiled much since Alex.

Her subject didn't seem to notice. "Well, I'm trying not fail of out of Sociology, so that means actually studying."

Daphne tapped her fingers against the book spines. She could navigate this library in her sleep. "Might help if we were actually in the Sociology reference section," she said, her voice soft and sincere while she studied Pin-Up Barbie's reaction.

There was an infinitesimal pause before a lovely pink blush bloomed across the blonde's cheeks. The flush somehow made her eyes even more blue, the sort of cornflower blue too vivid to be real. The flutters in Daphne stomach intensified.

"I don't come here, like, ever," Pin-Up Barbie admitted.

"I could show you?" Her offer ended on a wavering note of uncertainty.

"I'd like that." Pin-Up Barbie's smile cranked up a notch, melting the flutters into mellow warmth.

Daphne circled the stacks, startled when the blonde straightened. Pin-Up Barbie was more than a head taller than her, a natural height considering the ruby red ballet flats she wore on surprisingly dainty feet. Side by side, the top of her head reached the blonde's shoulder.

"This way," she said, aware of the heat creeping up her neck. "I'm Daphne, by the way."

"Celeste," said the blonde, allowing her to finally put a name to her heart-shaped face. "Daphne is a lovely name."

The heat grew more insistent, threatening a full-scale blush. Alex never made her blush. "I was named after my grandmother." Early in their relationship, Alex had said she had an old lady name. She laughed at the time, but the comment stayed with her. "Celeste is also very pretty. It sounds like celestial." She certainly had a heavenly body.

Celeste's brows rose at her comment. "Thank you." That megawatt smile dimmed to something smaller and softer but much more genuine. "Do you always eat alone?"

Daphne stopped, caught off guard.

Celeste's hands fluttered through the air. "Sorry, that was super intrusive. It's just, every time I see you in the cafeteria, you're alone."

"How many times have you seen me?" Part of Daphne knew she should be alarmed by the unseen attention of this not-quite-a-woman in front of her, but judging from the fresh wave of fluttering in her abdomen, she was closer to flattered. How had she never noticed Celeste before now?

"Um, maybe a dozen. I just transferred in at the beginning of the semester," she explained, brushing her hair behind one ear. Strange, Daphne would almost call that small movement the tell of a lie. Did Celeste have such a solid grasp on human mannerisms? "And I don't go to the dining hall that often."

"Oh." That explained why Celeste only saw her alone. Daphne had been somewhat distracted at the beginning of the semester. She cleared her throat. "Here's the sociology section."

"Thank you again," said Celeste, turning to the shelves.

Daphne lingered. "You're welcome to join me," she said. The blush finally hit her cheeks in a simmering wave. "Next time you come to the dining hall."

Celeste turned back to her, wide-eyed. "If you don't mind waiting a few minutes, I could join you for dinner?"

"Sure." The word came out higher than Daphne intended. She leaned against the end of the stack, waiting for Celeste to grab what she needed. The giggling rabble passed by her, laughing hard while making pointed gestures at her. Daphne didn't spare them a glance, but Celeste emerged from the stacks wearing a frown.

"What's up with them?"

Daphne was not ready to share her annoying ex situation. She shrugged. "Ditzy idiots." She nodded to the short stack of books in Celeste's arms. "Ready to check out?"

Once Celeste visited the circulation desk, they strolled to the dining hall. A dozen questions burned on Daphne's tongue, but she still found their mutual silence comfortable. Some of that ease slipped away once they were inside. Daphne noticed when more than a few tables glanced their way, but she grabbed a tray. The hot meal on offer was baked chicken and she loaded up her tray like normal. It wasn't until she found an unoccupied table that she noticed Celeste sat across from her empty-handed.

"Aren't you getting anything?" She watched Celeste's face, searching for more hints and clues.

The blonde flicked her fingers. "Not feeling the chicken tonight. I've got left over Thai in my mini fridge. Besides," she grinned, folding her hands in front of her. "I'm here for the company." Her nails were filed to points and painted the same shade of red as her lipstick. So much red should have clashed with her hot pink highlights, but it worked for her. Celeste appeared to be an expert at color coordination. "So, what are you majoring in?"

The question kicked off an easy, light conversation between them. Celeste seemed highly interested in Daphne's chosen major and career goals.

"Why a medical examiner?" Celeste asked. Daphne nearly fumbled under her intense gaze.

Why a medical examiner? Why not a doctor? Alex had asked her this question, but this was different. There was no judgment in Celeste's tone, only curiosity. Yet, part of her still felt the need to defend her choices.

"Don't laugh," said Daphne, taking a sip of her coke to wet her throat. "I like the...puzzle."

Celeste's brows drew together. "The puzzle."

How was she going to explain this without sounding creepy? Alex said she skeeved him out.

"Patients can tell you what feels wrong. They might lie, but usually it's a start. A dead body is an unfolding mystery. Even if you find the cause of death, you might discover other under lying causes, or conditions they weren't aware of because they weren't life threatening. Like the cadaver in my anatomy class," said Daphne, her voice becoming more animated. "She had these benign clusters of sub-dermal cysts. What causes that? If it's caused by genetics or environment. Or—"

"Slut." The slur splashed across her back, along with what felt like a cup full of cold liquid.

Daphne recognized the sticky sweet scent of root beer as it soaked through her shirt and the seat of her pants.

Celeste rose to her feet, slapping the table, but the culprit was already halfway out the door. Daphne recognized her retreating figure as one of the giggling girls from the library. She sighed and continued eating her dinner, valiantly trying to ignore the sticky wet sensation seeping into her underwear.

"What the hell?" Celeste's voice was a hiss.

"Don't worry about it," said Daphne, wishing she could rewind the last five minutes. "I'll take a shower after I get back to my dorm." Hopefully Beth didn't hide her toiletries again.

Celeste sat back down, but there was tension in her expression. "Why would she do that?"

"Act like a tween twat?" Daphne angrily bit into a piece of steamed broccoli. This was not a subject she wanted to talk about tonight, dammit. Or ever again. "Just some issues with an ex." She refused to devote any more energy to Alex today, even if it tanked their dinner conversation. Celeste fidgeted across from her, clearly dissatisfied by her brush-off explanation. "I'm sorry."

Celeste frowned. "Why are *you* apologizing?"

"Feels like I ruined dinner." Daphne set her fork down, her appetite gone as her meal congealed to a lead weight in the pit of her stomach. "I'm going to go get cleaned up."

She stood, closing her eyes at the unpleasant sensation of sticky cool soda running down her backside. This wasn't the first time something like this had happened, but with Celeste as a witness, it felt ten times worse. Balling her napkin in her fist, she glanced at her dinner companion. "Thank you for joining me."

There was a high probability that she would never join her again. Celeste opened her mouth to say something, but Daphne couldn't hold her composure. She fled, nearly throwing her tray away in her haste to get away. Others were noticing the unfortunate state of her clothes, their snickers nipping at her heels as she broke into a run toward her room.

THREE

CELESTE

As Celeste watched Daphne flee, a nebulous sour aura shifted around her. Her face went slack, painted nails tapping the table.

Humans were such demonstrative creatures. The way their facial muscles responded to such tiny shifts in emotion was fascinating. An excessive amount of time studying them, and she was still discovering new expressions. Like the expression on Daphne's face when that naughty little snack splattered her in soda.

She'd seen similar situations on television, another human invention she highly enjoyed, where the victim would break down in salty, delicious tears. Daphne didn't look like she was about to cry. If Celeste interpreted what she saw correctly, Daphne was angry. Not the hot, brash anger she saw in fights and couple's spats, though. Her fury was cold and dark and whispered to something deep inside Celeste.

Which was strange, since she'd been planning on having Daphne for dinner. Her forefinger tapped the tabletop as she mulled through her mixed emotions. Despite her dinner escaping her, she found she wasn't disappointed that she got away.

Celeste knew the little human was following her. She'd counted on it. There'd been that spark of interest when she sat across from her at lunch, though she thought she'd misinterpreted it when Daphne hadn't come to her immediately after. Instead, the human went to her afternoon classes, dutifully attending her studies. Once that was done, she'd begun to search the campus with a methodical effort.

The trap was set. Her pheromones saturated the air within the tight space between the stacks, teasing through the gaps of shelved books. Celeste could tell they were working on the little human. Her pupils had blown and that sweet little blush slowly crept up her neck...but Daphne surprised her again.

Instead of falling at Celeste's feet, hooked by her invisible lure, she'd offered help. Invited Celeste to sit with her at dinner. The careful attention caught her off guard, along with the realization the little human might be resistant to her pheromones. Intrigued, she let the hunt continue, studying the microcosm of Daphne's expressions from across the table.

She watched the clear delight in Daphne's face as she spoke about carving up human bodies to study their secrets and found herself charmed.

Tap, tap, tap went her nail on the tabletop. Celeste stared at the door, the inane chatter of the surrounding humans grating against her senses. Daphne was so small. Barely an appetizer. And there was that intriguing cold anger.

"Did you see her face? I can't believe Candace actually did it."

Celeste's attention focused on the speaker, a tall brunette with a nose too large for the rest of her features. Daphne's features were much more symmetrical. A second female snorted, the expression ugly on her heavily made-up face. Makeup was an art, which this human clearly failed at.

"Stupid bitch got what's coming to her after what she did to Alex," Big Nose said, half-chewed food visible in her mouth.

Alex? Who was this person and what did they have to do with her little snack? Was that the curvy bottle blonde who doused Daphne? No, that had to be Candace.

Celeste's finger stopped tapping. She rose to her feet and sauntered from the dining hall. Candace hadn't wandered far from the scene of her crime, standing with a cluster of vapid, giggling girls. Celeste wandered closer, wrinkling her nose at the chemical scent of fake tanner and far too much perfume. Unappetizing, but Candace was athletic. Meaty.

She swerved toward the group, brushing against Candace in a swirl of pheromones.

"Wow...rude much?" the bottle blonde snapped, though her voice lost its venom on the last word, trailing off as her pupils expanded.

The effect was immediate. Candace peeled away from the pack to follow Celeste, ignoring the others as they called her name.

There weren't many convenient secluded places nearby, but a small patch of trees that buffered the dining hall and the dorms would do nicely in a pinch. Celeste cut a path inside until she was concealed by greenery and the deepening dusk. Finding a sturdy tree, she leaned back and waited.

FOUR

DAPHNE

Daphne planned to hightail it to the shower, but Candace was waiting to ambush her outside. Biting the inside of her cheek, her path veered sharply into the patch of woods between the dining hall and dorms. Students sometimes hiked or made out in here. Thankfully, it was empty. Daphne plunked down on a fallen log, clutching her shaking hands together until her knuckles turned white.

If she confronted Candace, it'd get bloody. Her anger burned at a low simmer, cold and calculating as she quietly planned her revenge on Alex's little groupie. The fact they were still coming after her, months after the break-up, proved ignoring the problem wasn't working. She'd let Alex get away with his petty antics for too long.

An idea was already forming when twigs snapped. Somebody had entered the woods. Daphne slid down, using the log as cover as Candace crunched through the fallen leaves, clearly looking for someone. Idiot must have decided she wanted to escalate their disagreement. Daphne braced herself just as Candace jerked her head in the opposite direction. She followed the other woman's gaze and froze.

Celeste leaned against a tree, her arms stretched over her head. The pose lifted her breasts and exposed the creamy pale flesh of her midriff. Aside from the placement of her limbs, her expression was completely slack as Candace rushed her. Daphne tensed, wondering if the other woman was about to attack her—and she did, though not how she expected.

Candace crashed in a heap at Celeste's feet, wrapping her arms around her legs. She pressed her face against the other woman's exposed midriff with a soft sigh of relief, as if she were desperate to be near Celeste.

Daphne's mind scrambled to observe and decipher what was happening because *something* was happening. Candace was an Alex groupie, one of the many women he kept up a casual tryst with and had a boyfriend on the side. Yet she clasped onto Celeste with trembling limbs. From this angle, Daphne could just make out the worshipful expression on Candace's face.

The expression on Celeste's face was serene, except for the predatory glint in her gaze. There was a heaviness to the scene, pregnant with tension. A viper ready to strike an entranced rat.

Daphne relaxed, settling back against the log to watch.

In the deepening dark, she almost missed their appearance: tentacles slithering through the air as they wrapped around Candace, surrounding her. More appeared, emerging from the space around Celeste, from within Celeste, wrapping, twisting, winding...but there was a moment where her prey's primitive hindbrain broke through. Candace bucked with a cry of terror.

Celeste slapped a human hand over her mouth. "Now, now sugar. Be sweet and enjoy the ride." The woman fell silent, and Celeste's human façade continued to crack and peel away.

Sweat beaded on Daphne's forehead. She knew when her deepest, most primitive instincts screamed at her that she was witnessing something the human mind couldn't handle. At the last second, before reality fractured, she snapped her eyes shut, listening to the slick wet sounds, the pull of flesh against flesh. Candace sighed, contentment in her tone at odds with her situation. "Thank you," she said, her voice breathy and soft. "Thank you." As if Celeste answered her prayers. The platitudes soon went quiet.

Daphne didn't dare open her eyes because there were other sounds now: the crunch of breaking bones, a rhythmic squelch she realized was chewing. She waited, quiet and still, while the predator finished her meal. Likely because she was satiated, Celeste appeared to miss her presence. Of course she didn't bank on that observation. Daphne counted seconds in her head until the sensation of mental unease finally subsided.

Celeste was already making her way out of the woods, hips swaying and steps silent. Daphne settled back against the log and turned over her thoughts.

She, not Candace, had been Celeste's intended meal.

Part of Daphne knew she should be horrified by that realization, but it was the part of her who tried to conform to what others expected of her. She was more curious how Celeste had lured Candace into the woods. Some sort of scent baiting? That would explain the surge of fluttery feelings she got when she found her in the library, except she was currently absent from Celeste's presence and she'd just witnessed her consuming another student. That combination should allow her survival instincts to override whatever Celeste emitted. Maybe it was a natural allure, or maybe it was her choice to switch targets and gobble down one of Daphne's tormentors directly after their confrontation. The fluttery feelings remained.

Daphne nibbled on her lip. There were definite complications to romantically pursuing a carnivorous, tentacled eldritch horror. For one, she wanted to explore these budding feelings and see where they led—*if* she could do so without being eaten. There was also that small issue with her inner monkey brain going apeshit when Celeste dropped her human guise. Daphne wasn't sure what the innate urge to close her eyes meant, but it was another obstacle.

Shifting, she blushed at the dampness in her underwear that had nothing to do with the soda. No, Celeste's monstrous form wasn't a deal-breaker either. Because Celeste could have hunted down any student after she left. If, at any point, Celeste noticed her presence and kept going, well, that was practically *flirting*. Daphne simply had to figure out how to court her.

What could she offer an eldritch entity capable of taking what they wanted? Daphne wondered if Celeste was allergic to formaldehyde.

CELESTE

Celeste paced the length of her room.

She'd gotten careless. Waiting too long between feedings made her reckless, luring prey out in the open, where she'd failed to scan the premises. The hunger pushed her, made her hyper-focus on the tasty morsel in her grasp and not the faint scent of root beer lingering in the air. When the meal was done and she'd pulled her human mask back on, the scent remained, mixed with something heady and bittersweet that made her mouth water anew. The reaction hadn't stopped there. A sensation of sparks cascaded through her bloodstream, making her buzz inside her human skin.

Bewildered by her reaction to it, she'd left instead of eliminating potential witnesses. Why was the little morsel there? Hadn't Daphne left to bathe? That is what she'd told Celeste she planned to do. And what was that delectable scent beneath the syrupy chemical odor of the soda that teased and tantalized? The pacing continued.

She usually enjoyed moving in her human form. There was an unexpected grace to human bodies at odds with their gangly limbs. Celeste enjoyed the way her human thighs rubbed together with each step, the subtle shift and dimple of her buttocks and bounce of her breasts. Other humans enjoyed watching her move too, with and without coverings. She used that interest for feeding, luring prey in with her looks and pheromones. Usually by the time they were hooked by her scent, their brain chemistry shifted. They worshipped at her feet, and like a Goddess of ancient times, she took her tithe in flesh.

Her real body broke their minds. She gobbled down their adoration alongside their flesh but the more she fed, the more curious she became of those initial reactions to her human form. In the decades she'd lingered on this rock and the countless observations she'd made of the act, Celeste had never had sex. Why would she? They were her prey, and it seemed gauche to fuck her food source. And yet....

...And yet, she wondered if Daphne would find her human form pleasing.

Celeste slapped her hands over her face. What was she thinking? Daphne had seen her feeding. This campus had been her hunting ground for nearly two decades and now some crumb of a human caught her in the act. Celeste was confident no one would believe the girl if she started raving about Celeste turning into a monster and eating people, but it would shift unwanted attention to her. People would ask questions. They might *remember* Candace if Daphne got insistent. Her proximity to the feeding meant Daphne would remember her.

She twisted her face into a scowl. Celeste liked it here! The coeds were plentiful, the location was secluded, and she enjoyed her classes. Why did she have to relocate? She was here first. Eliminating the little morsel was necessary if she wanted to stay.

Instead, Celeste slumped on the bed, curling up in her fluffy hot pink comforter. Tomorrow, she'd tie up loose ends. Pulling her comforter over her head like a hood, she grabbed her remote from the bedside table and turned on an episode of *Gossip Girl*. Tonight, she'd comfort-watch her favorite shows and sort her laundry.

The credits were rolling on the twelfth episode when someone tapped on her door. Celeste paused while folding a cotton candy swirl blouse.

Frowning, she glanced at the clock. With her blackout curtains closed, she'd missed the rollover of the day. It was now six in the morning, too early for classes and most of her fellow dorm mates to be up and about. Maybe one of the girls on her floor was too hungover from the night before to realize they were knocking on the wrong door.

Carefully setting her blouse on the folded pile, Celeste went to open her door and froze. Daphne stood right there, in grabbing distance. Her free hand twitched against her thigh. The morsel's gaze flickered over her form before settling on her face.

"Good morning," she said, her voice huskier than the night before.

Grab her. Pull her inside. Snap her neck. Fix this. "Good morning yourself," said Celeste, her voice an octave lower. *What!?*

Daphne tucked a loose strand of hair behind her ear, the gesture ridiculously adorable. "Our dinner last night was rudely interrupted and, um..." She paused, her tongue darting out and across her bottom lip. Celeste's gaze snapped to the movement, studying the glossy saliva on her lower lip. "I was wondering if you'd like to try again somewhere more private? Like my room? Tonight?"

Celeste blinked, catching up to the conversation. "You're inviting me over to dinner." Her prey inviting *her* in was a new one. How did she find this room in the first place? Had Daphne followed her last night?

Baffled, she stared at the morsel, watching the way she twisted her fingers together in front of her, feet scuffing on the hallway carpet. Adorable little movements, like a nervous bunny.

"What time?" Goodness, what would she wear?

"Eight tonight?" Daphne glanced up, a small crease marring her brow. "Do you have any allergies or dietary restrictions?"

Celeste snorted. She shouldn't find the question so charming. "No. Though I can pay for my share of takeout—"

"No, I'm making you something," said Daphne.

"Oh," said Celeste. Her grip on the doorknob tightened. Perhaps she made a mistake and Daphne saw nothing. "That's so sweet."

The little snack grinned at her. "Well, I'll see you tonight." Daphne dropped her head down as she hurried away. There it was again, that heady, mouth-watering aroma. Celeste braced herself on the door frame, drawing it into her human lungs.

This turn of events made things easier. She should get rid of the girl, to be safe. Daphne was practically serving herself on a platter, so why was Celeste so curious about what bite-size intended to make her for dinner?

DAPHNE

Daphne entered anatomy labs with a backpack full of empty Tupperware. There were questionable morals in what she intended to do, but during the long hours she spent planning her menu last night, this was the safer, saner option. These bodies were donated to the university. For science, not an eldritch gourmand, but her ingredients would be ethically sourced.

Concentrating during labs was another matter. Bradley was thankfully absent today. Like her roommate Beth, he'd taken off early for the long holiday weekend. Which meant Daphne was able to wake up to her alarm today—a necessity after her late-night planning session. She'd approached wooing Celeste like a lab final, writing copious notes and observations to prepare for the main event.

Finding Celeste's rooms was easy once she had her first name. Celeste Smith was the only one on campus, though the last name made Daphne roll her eyes. What was more curious was the blank enrollment date in her file. She wondered how long Celeste had been lurking on campus because one thing was clear at breakfast:

Nobody remembered Candace existed.

Daphne wasn't certain at first. Nobody burst into the dining hall to declare the bitch missing while she ate her oatmeal. The giggling rabble sat at their usual table, occasionally sneering in her direction, seeming undisturbed one of their number had disappeared. It was Friday. Candace could have gone home early. A sound theory until Daphne bumped into her roommate Lily at the drink machine.

Lily was a neutral party, which is why Daphne dared to ask, "Candace come home last night?"

The girl frowned, a distant look in her eye while orange juice overflowed her cup. She shook herself. "Who?"

Daphne didn't dare ask anyone else. She wasn't sure how it worked, but if a creature like Celeste had been here for a while, there'd be reports of missing students. Celeste claimed she was "new," but Daphne wasn't so sure. That brief peek in her room, so homey and *settled*, made her think otherwise.

The answers would come later. Daphne could be patient.

Once labs were over and students headed out to lunch, she set to work. After much debate, she'd settled on a sampling from all over, taking small slices from the underside of organs and muscles that wouldn't be noticed without a closer inspection. The precision meant she spent longer on the harvest than she wanted. She'd miss lunch but she hoped tonight would be worth it. Taking care with clean up, she made sure to remove evidence of her activities. She'd disabled the lab camera early this morning, planning to hook it up tomorrow. An entire day of missing footage would likely look more like an equipment failure than a few hours.

Rearranging her haul on the icepacks in her backpack, Daphne exited the lab, wondering if she could snag something from the dining hall before her afternoon lecture.

Instead, she smacked right into the last person she wanted to see.

Alex pulled back a step, clutching a pile of exams to his chest. "I'm sorry, Daphne. Didn't see you there." How he made such a simple line sound demeaning was an art.

Daphne sighed, tightening her grip on her backpack strap to keep from swinging at him. "Sorry." She tried to move around him when he stepped into her path.

"Haven't seen you around much. How are you holding up after everything?" He folded his arms, a mask of faux concern on his regretfully handsome face.

She gave him a look. "You mean after your epic man-trum?" She didn't mention the rumors and fun little torments his sycophants inflicted on her, but she knew he was responsible.

Alex's lips pursed in a mocking moue. "Now, now, Daphne, let's not get it twisted around again. I know a crush like yours is hard to get over, but I'm too old for you. Your pursuit of a married professor to improve your grades was in poor taste. We agreed you needed to move on or risk an administrative intervention."

Daphne clenched her jaw to keep from responding. He'd cornered her right under the disabled camera. Not that he knew that, but the implication was clear. This was another brick for his meticulously constructed defense, the bastard. She hated him, hated him so much, but she didn't have the time or energy for his bullshit.

Not that he deserved any of her time and energy ever again. "Excuse me, I'm busy." She circled wide around him, barely noting the expression of outrage that crossed his features.

He'd made her miss the lunch window. Weighing her options, Daphne did something she'd never done before and skipped class. Probably a wise decision with a backpack full of chilled human meats. It wouldn't have a huge impact on her average, and it would give her more time to set everything up.

She needed all the prep time she could get.

Dragging the small table from the dorm floor's kitchen into her room, she got to work. By eight, she was a bundle of nerves, but the table was set, the candles were lit, and she'd managed a quick run to the dining hall for her tamer dietary supplies. Daphne sat in her chair at the table, tapping the tabletop while she waited. By quarter after, she realized her error.

Daphne had tracked down Celeste, but she'd neglected to give her room number in return. Cursing, she was halfway into her sneakers when someone knocked on the door. Tripping over her feet, she hurried over, swinging it open to reveal her date.

Celeste was dressed to seduce. A black, heart shaped tank top with barely there straps hugged her torso like a glove and left ample cleavage on display. Likewise, her hot pink yoga pants molded to her curves, the same shade as her highlights. She wore gladiator sandals, laced up her calves, while her toenails were painted the same lush shade of red as her lipstick and nails.

Those blue eyes roved over Daphne, who felt utterly drab in black slacks and a dove gray button up. She was a muddy newt beside a brightly colored poisonous tree frog.

"Hello, sugar," Celeste purred.

She glided forward, forcing Daphne to take a step back. Celeste continued that slow feline stroll until Daphne backed against her bed. The blonde loomed over her, larger than life. One arm reached past her to brace against the wall. For a second, she believed she'd sorely miscalculated, when Celeste froze. Her nostrils flared as her gaze flickered to the waiting meal on the table.

The predatory sheen drained from her eyes as her expression went slack. "What is this?"

"Um, dinner," said Daphne— a brilliant answer. She swallowed hard and ducked under Celeste's arm, gesturing to the meal with shaking hands. "I thought we could share something light and casual and get to know each other better." Her breath shuddered as she inhaled but she pressed on. It was time to play her hand and see if she survived. "I wasn't sure what you'd like. There's a liver and kidney pâté, and a ceviche with a few various organs." She pointed to the longer strips she'd painstakingly prepared earlier. "I sampled a few different muscles groupings, but the best marbling comes from the buttocks and thigh. And there's the olives of course." She popped one in her mouth, chewing to cover her nervousness.

Celeste moved to the table, her gaze darting over the carefully sectioned charcuterie board. If Daphne had to hazard a guess at the expression on her face, she'd call it bewildered. The blonde plucked a slice of thigh meat off the board, hesitating before she popped it in her mouth. Her eyes widened.

"This is human." Her attention snapped to Daphne. Incredulity warred with something else over her perfect face. "Where did you—how did you —" Celeste sputtered. She cocked her head to the side, her expression unreadable as she studied Daphne. "What did you see last night?"

Daphne sat down in her chair, gesturing for Celeste to join her. After a long moment, the blonde sat, resting both hands flat on the table as she studied the charcuterie board.

"I saw quite a bit," admitted Daphne. "But there was a point I couldn't ignore the urge to close my eyes. Hmm." She swiped her notebook and pen from her nearby desk, opening it to the end of her notes. "I wonder if that is a biological incentive for humans or a defensive mechanism for you."

Celeste stared at her. "You've been taking notes." There was a cool note in her tone that made Daphne hug the notebook to her chest.

"For me and me alone," she clarified.

"Why?" Celeste frowned. She picked up another piece from the charcuterie board, giving it a sniff.

Daphne looked down, her fingers tapping the back of the notebook in a nervous rhythm. "It helps me organize my thoughts. I wasn't sure how to approach a courtship with someone like you."

The meat fell from Celeste's slack fingers. "Courtship? But...you saw me," her voice dropped to a whisper. "You know I'm not human, Daphne."

"Yes. That doesn't bother me," Daphne answered, her tone short.

The scene from last night played in her mind, how Celeste had wrapped Candace in her thick tentacles. The expression of pure bliss and relief before Candace was consumed. She wanted to experience a different sort of emotional high with Celeste, one far less innocent, and to survive so she could do it again. Daphne squirmed in her seat.

Celeste suddenly moaned, gripping both sides of the table as she swayed in her seat. "Clearly not," she rasped. She took a deep breath, her human features shifting through a half dozen expressions before she opened her eyes to meet Daphne's gaze. There was a vulnerability there as she slowly reached across the table and tucked a strand of hair behind Daphne's ear.

"My little morsel, this is a very dangerous game."

CELESTE

Conflict spiraled through Celeste. If the food-related nickname bothered Daphne, she didn't show it. Her level of confidence was baffling as she set aside her notebook to pour each of them a glass of wine.

"I don't play games," said Daphne. "Let's enjoy dinner and see where the night leads."

Celeste had been on this planet for decades and never encountered a human so at ease with her. Humans naturally experienced a low-level discomfort around her unless she saturated them with pheromones. Once the pheromones subsumed their instincts, they flung themselves at her, eager to be devoured. Daphne had neither of those reactions. She'd peeked beneath Celeste's human façade and not only invited her to a dinner date, but prepared food tailored to her palate.

She'd never been so flattered in her life. Not knowing what else to do, she smeared some of the pate across a cracker and popped it in her mouth, surprised to find the mix properly spiced. "How did you procure human meat?" She had to know, because Daphne didn't have her abilities. If there was so much as a whisper of any illicit activities the woman committed on her behalf, she'd scrub them from existence.

"Oh, that." Daphne patted her mouth with a napkin. "I was careful. I disabled the security cameras to the lab and harvested from a cadaver."

Celeste made a face. "From dead meat?" There was an odd aftertaste, but it wasn't rot. Not a bad flavor either. She found it interesting.

Daphne shrugged. "You told me there were no dietary restrictions. I hoped that extended to chemical preservatives. Cadavers are heavily preserved for teaching purposes, so I figured they'd be more like cured meats. Hence the charcuterie board idea."

Humans could preserve their dead? The effort her little morsel had put into the meal was so thoughtful. Celeste took a sip of wine, humming at the perfect match in flavors. No one had done something like this for her before. For all the human media she'd absorbed over the years, she hadn't realized, deep down, that she pined for someone to wine and dine her.

It was too much. "Why do you like me?"

Daphne's brows drew together. Celeste could see the careful thought she gave the question in her expressive face. "I knew the moment I met you that you were a predator. Something inhuman. I was fascinated. But my intrigue shifted." She took a sip of wine. "I wondered if it was your scent that started it. There was a definite biological reaction when you were close. Except it lingered after." A shy smile lit her face. "Then you ate Candace."

Celeste stared at her. "I was going to eat you," she murmured, surprised by the pinch of guilt in her guts.

Daphne shrugged. "But you didn't. You've had several opportunities now. Instead, you ate the bitch who bullied me. Sweetest thing anyone's ever done for me. Consider me smitten."

Something bloomed in Celeste, a simmering heat that tingled through her fingertips. Human appearances were something she'd studied at length. She'd crafted her human guise to lure, but Daphne, in her sensible button down and slacks, was simply herself. Her dark hair hung in a pair of adorable braids, her bangs neatly parted. There was a light dusting of freckles across her nose, the barest touch of makeup on her face. Nothing remarkable, but Celeste thought she was the prettiest human she'd ever seen.

A human she desperately wanted to survive this date as much as she wanted to taste her.

Celeste kept eating, unwilling to waste Daphne's efforts, while she mulled over how to properly seduce her little morsel. What if her human caught an eyeful of her true form and it snapped her mind? What if Celeste slipped up and her hunger took control? It was beyond sweet of Daphne to feed her, but this was not enough to fill her up.

She started when Daphne's hand settled over her human one, her fingers warm and delicate where they rubbed circles against her wrists. "You look nervous somehow. If you don't want to pursue this further, we don't have to, though I hope we can remain friends."

The uncertainty and hopefulness in Daphne's face melted her hesitation. Celeste grabbed Daphne's hand and shoved the table aside. Her human emitted a small squeak as she pulled her onto her lap.

The little morsel sat with her legs astride, but Celeste wanted something more intimate. Daphne stiffened with a gasp when Celeste slid her hands under her butt and lifted her with ease. She maneuvered that slim human body to straddle her, sitting chest to chest. Celeste cradled her face and searched those dark eyes for a hint of fear. She only found delight as Daphne squirmed in her lap. Her heated core rested against Celeste's stomach, that mouthwatering scent perfuming the air between them. Daphne wrapped her arms around Celeste's neck, all her silent desire and anticipation humming against Celeste's senses.

Human media taught Celeste many things, but watching wasn't the same as doing. Celeste breathed her in, the scent between her legs mingling with the remnants of their meal to a dangerous effect, but the moment she brushed their mouths together Daphne's quiet demeanor vanished.

She plastered herself against Celeste, groaning into her human mouth. Daphne opened for her; the inside of her mouth was like slick velvet. Her smaller curves molded against Celeste, the mortal warmth catching fire, heating beneath her hands. The scent of her intensified, her thighs trembling against Celeste's hips.

Celeste needed more, but she had to endure this slow sweet torture for such a beautiful morsel. Her tongue shifted in Daphne's mouth, a hint of her true self breaking through as the texture and length changed, slipping further down the human's throat. Daphne gagged slightly, before she unleashed a soft whine and swallowed around Celeste's invasive exploration. The sensation rocked through Celeste, an exquisite squeezing pressure, intensified by Daphne's fingers tangling in her hair. Nothing prepared her for the riot of emotions Daphne's reactions roused within her. More, she needed more. But she needed to reassure herself first.

Carefully, she reshaped her tongue and pulled back to make sure Daphne hadn't suffered any ill effects. Alarm stirred at the tears dripping down the human's face. She brushed them away, gently pinching Daphne's chin. "Are you okay? Did I hurt you?"

"Did you—was that a tentacle down my throat?" Her voice was oddly hoarse.

Celeste nodded, uncertain how she'd react, but a wide grin split Daphne's face.

"That was fantastic." She pressed forward, nuzzling against Celeste's throat. The gesture was almost sweet until Daphne's tongue slid over her skin, a warm wet glide that moved down to trace the curve of her breasts. Celeste wheezed, her control wavering further when the human's hands danced down her back to dig into her hips.

"Daphne, wait—" Celeste choked out, when those blunt human teeth sank into her flesh.

Her reaction was instant as it was unexpected. Tentacles tore through her flimsy human façade, wrapping around her little morsel's wrists, ankles, waist, lifting her until she was suspended in the air. Hunger rolled through Celeste as she rose from the chair, somehow maintaining her human upper body. It was the fear of scaring Daphne that had her clinging by a thread. She lifted her torso higher to peer down at the human, trying to gauge her reaction.

Daphne's chest heaved, lips swollen and red. She stared up at Celeste, a glaze of desire in her dark eyes. "Your tentacles are pink. I couldn't see their color before," she rasped. There wasn't an ounce of fear in her.

Celeste smiled at her. She could alter the perception of her tentacles to whatever color she wanted. "Pink is pretty."

"Pink *is* pretty," Daphne echoed. There was a softness in her expression that caught Celeste off-guard. "You are so beautiful," she whispered.

A tremor ran through Celeste's tentacles. Her human hand shook as she brushed Daphne's increasingly disheveled bangs off her face. Her hand slid down that smooth jaw, pressing a thumb to Daphne's soft, plump lower lip. "Do you trust me?"

It was a ridiculous question. How could this human trust her? But even as she asked the question, she held onto a desperate hope.

Daphne nipped at her thumb. "Yes," she said without hesitation.

The hunger inside her shifted in intensity to something more earnest and possibly more dangerous. Celeste was going to devour this human, over and over.

DAPHNE

Daphne watched the expression on Celeste's human face turn feral and wondered at the wisdom of her answer. Maybe she shouldn't let her pussy do the talking. But long neglect and that scorching make-out had it practically shouting from between her legs.

Celeste held her suspended, the grip of those pretty pink tentacles firm but not to the point of pain. Admittedly, Daphne wouldn't mind a little pain where Celeste was concerned. There was enough hesitation and caution in her movements that told Daphne her date was holding back for her benefit. However, that didn't deter this moment from being extremely hot.

More tentacles emerged, peeling off her clothes like tissue paper. Once they made contact against her bare skin, Daphne suddenly understood Candace's blissed-out expression as endorphins flooded her system. She suspected they had released a chemical into her system, but her thoughts were wiped as they began to explore her body.

The texture of Celeste's tentacles changed seemingly at will. From pebbling bumps that taunted her nipples to silken smoothness that rolled over her belly. Two thick tentacles wrapped around each of her thighs, spreading her legs further as Celeste's human torso lowered to look at her.

"Look at this pretty pink pussy," Celeste groaned, human fingers tracing along Daphne's labia in slow deliberate movements that had her squirming. "You're dripping. For me." Celeste breathed the last two words, a soft white glow shimmering in her pupils, like faraway starlight.

There was something about that glow that whispered danger. It ate at the edge of Daphne's mind. Celeste blinked, seeming to realize the effect at the same time. She tore a strip of cloth from Daphne's shredded shirt.

"Safety first," she murmured. Daphne closed her eyes as Celeste tied the makeshift blindfold around her head. "You okay, little morsel?"

"Yes," said Daphne.

Deprived of one of her senses, the other sensations in her body took on a new potency. She sucked in a shuddering breath when those tentacles shifted, spreading her even wider as another teased her entrance. Her thighs began to shake. The tentacle slid inside, the texture shifting as it rubbed against her inner walls, curling inside her in spaces no one had ever reached. Daphne thought that sensation was incredible to the point of overwhelming when a second tentacle joined the first. The quaking in her muscles spread, heat circling low in her belly.

A third tentacle slid between her butt cheeks. There wasn't time for her body to tense up in surprise before it pushed into her, the burning stretch shoving her over the edge.

Daphne gave a shout, her muscles clenching and pulsing around Celeste's persistent invasion.

Celeste didn't waste the opportunity of Daphne's open mouth. Another tentacle shoved between her lips and down her throat. She gagged around it, tears streaming down her face as another orgasm scorched her from the inside out.

"Ah, ah—can't have you alarming the neighbors," Celeste purred in her ear. Her voice had an eerie echo to it, which made Daphne dangerously curious.

Thankfully, her hands were thoroughly pinned so she couldn't remove the blindfold. Not that her thoughts were coherent enough to hold onto the urge. Celeste's tentacles were everywhere, squeezing her breasts, cradling her hips, shoved deep in her throat while filling her pussy and ass. Everywhere they contacted her skin, she tingled with sensation until she was little more than a human-shaped erogenous zone.

"You taste so good," that ethereal voice moaned into her ear. Celeste's movements paused. "I promise I won't hurt you."

Daphne wasn't sure why Celeste felt the urge to warn her again when the atmosphere around her changed. The tentacles receded, leaving her gasping as she sank into dark, wet heat. The space felt too closed, her breath short in her lungs. For a moment, Daphne's hindbrain tried to panic, but the sensation was muted and distant.

The fear vanished completely when a thousand tongues slid over her naked skin. Daphne shrieked, bracing her hands against the slick slimy walls of her prison as a new appendage forced its way between her legs. This was thicker than the tentacles, textured in small bumps that lit her oversensitive skin in fresh flames. Daphne dug her fingers into the fleshy walls as that appendage shoved inside her, pummeling against her inner walls. This orgasm curled her toes.

"Another—give me another, my sweet morsel," Celeste's voice reverberated around her, buzzing inside her skin. "Let me swallow all your pleasure down."

Realization tickled at the back of her mind. The inner revelation should have terrified her, but Daphne was too busy trying not to spontaneously combust as Celeste wrung another orgasm from her with that massive tongue.

The overwhelming sensation pushed Daphne over an unknown edge. Fluid gushed between her legs. Celeste's greedy tongue lapped up every drop.

The intensity proved too much for Daphne. The last thing she felt was her eyes rolling back as she lost consciousness.

She woke up some time later on her bed, with Celeste's concerned human face hovering above her. "Whoa," Daphne said.

Celeste fell next to her on the mattress, groaning in clear relief. "You went limp. I thought I killed you."

"Only a little death," Daphne giggled. She was still naked, her skin slightly damp. To her delight, Celeste was equally naked in her human skin, wrapping an arm around Daphne's waist to pull her flush against her.

"You scared me, human." She pressed a kiss to Daphne's temple, her hold a little too tight. She could feel the worry emanating from Celeste like an aura brushing against her. "I thought I was in control."

Daphne tried to get a look at Celeste's expression, but her eldritch girlfriend was crowding against her, clearly in distress. She turned, wrapping her arms around her to stroke her back. "You were magnificent," she soothed. "That was the best sex of my life."

Nothing could compare. Sex with Alex was a joke compared to this experience. Even if Celeste never touched her again, she would remember it until the day she died.

Her statement finally made Celeste pull back, clearly incredulous. "You passed out."

"Blacked out," Daphne hummed, delightfully sore and sated. "Was I in your mouth at some point?"

Celeste flinched, her gaze darting away. "I took you into my maw." There was a touch of shame in her evasive expression.

There would be none of that. Daphne framed Celeste's gorgeous human face with her hands. "Was it good for you too? You did all the work."

Those blue eyes roved over her, searching for something that wasn't there. Celeste's lower lip trembled. "You are the sweetest thing I've ever tasted."

"When can we do it again?" Daphne stroked her blonde hair, twirling it around her fingers.

Celeste swallowed hard. "I need to feed properly first. Safer for you. But," she paused, nibbling on her lip, "could I stay here with you for a while?"

Her eldritch girlfriend wanted to cuddle. Daphne snuggled closer, nuzzling in against Celeste's taller form. Now that her body was sated, her mind was curious once more.

"Can your human body experience pleasure too?" Her fingers trailed down Celeste's naked side, dipping to tease the crease between her legs. She certainly appeared anatomically correct.

Celeste caught her hand with a soft hiss. "Yes, but that's not safe right now either," she said. Threading their fingers together, her hold on Daphne was deliciously tight. "But that's something I want to explore with you too."

Daphne relaxed, floating in postcoital bliss. She drifted in and out of sleep, waking in Celeste's arms before drifting off again. She could have stayed like this all weekend long, if not for the untimely return of her roommate.

The door woke her when it slammed shut. Daphne blinked, bleary-eyed, to find Beth standing over her, face contorted in obvious disgust. Thankfully, she'd covered her nudity with her comforter during the night.

"What the fuck," Beth snarled. "It reeks in here." She glared down.

Daphne remembered she wasn't alone when Celeste tensed around her. Her roommate circled the bed, every inch of her the sneering mean girl she'd revealed herself to be this semester. "Gotta say, this is definitely a step down from Alex."

That cold rage swept through Daphne. For months, she'd put up with Beth's nasty snipes and mean little pranks. Turning off her alarm so she missed breakfast, throwing out her toiletries, leaving her books out in the rain, and a dozen other bitchy gestures to make Daphne feel awful. Apparently, insulting Celeste was her limit.

"You can eat her," said Daphne. "Then we can watch some Netflix on my laptop."

Celeste grinned. There was nothing human about it. Beth froze, her mouth agape in horror. Celeste leaned over to gently tweak Daphne's nose. "Close your eyes, sweetmeat."

Daphne obediently closed her eyes before the feeding started, smiling as a tentacle curled around her leg.

DAPHNE

There were definite benefits to having a galactic horror for a girlfriend. This was the honeymoon stage. Knowledge was currency and Daphne was richer with each new revelation. Celeste was truly celestial. She'd descended from the stars, a true cosmic being who'd chosen Earth as her hunting ground. She was a creature who manufactured pheromones according to their prey of choice and exuded a natural aura that unraveled their victims from existence. There were exceptions to that aura, which Daphne proved the longer she spent in Celeste's company.

Because Daphne didn't just remember Candace—she remembered Beth as well. Celeste posited that it might be due to Daphne's proximity to the feedings, building an immunity of sorts to Celeste's aura. Daphne found the idea fascinating. She found everything about Celeste fascinating. If building an immunity to her aura was possible, perhaps one day she could see Celeste's full true appearance.

"I wouldn't dare risk your beautiful mind," said Celeste, stroking lazy fingers across Daphne's naked chest. They spent a great deal of time together naked these days. Once Daphne fulfilled her daytime obligations of classes and assignments, she turned up at Celeste's room. She preferred the cozy space to her own room, even if it came in several shades of eye-smarting pink.

Celeste really loved the color, another small detail Daphne found charming. They were possibly the most unlikely black cat/golden retriever relationship to exist. Celeste was bubbly, color-coordinated, loved *Gossip Girl* and *Gilmore Girls* and every teen drama in between. A personality utterly at odds with Daphne, but she couldn't deny how well they meshed. Celeste peeled away her prim, tight layers until she reached the gooey center—in more ways than one.

Their bedroom play brought a blush to Daphne's face whenever she thought about it, and she wanted more. Sex with human men and women paled in comparison to the full body invasion that was Celeste. Her biggest fear was wondering if she could ever reciprocate that mind-bending pleasure. How could she ever be enough for something so wondrous?

There were definite *downsides* to having a galactic horror for a girlfriend too. Celeste didn't rest like a human. Part of her mind was always aware though she would enter a meditative state while watching one of her shows. Daphne could tell by her stillness.

It was during those moments that other thoughts crept in. She'd never lost herself in past relationships. It was something Alex had complained about during their time together. Perhaps Daphne was too adept at compartmentalizing the different aspects of her life. She never lost herself in a partner's arms for the weekend, carefree and thoughtless of her responsibilities. Or she hadn't until Celeste.

Daphne wanted to spend every waking moment plastered to her side. Being away felt like a physical ache. If she stayed away too long, her hands began to shake like an addict denied their favored substance, a comparison that might not be far from the mark. Daphne was already enamored with Celeste, but that didn't mean those pheromones weren't still working on her. Celeste admitted to her that she often emitted them without conscious effort. It wasn't like she had a history of dating humans rather than eating them to gauge biological consequences.

The resistance to Celeste's aura was another matter, and Daphne wasn't sure that it was a net positive. It didn't bother Daphne that her girlfriend ate people. Her moral compass wasn't built like that. She was someone who had to study how others reacted to make sure she maintained a socially acceptable personality. In many ways, being in Celeste's company was a relief. She didn't have to pretend at social niceties with her cosmic horror girlfriend. But during the quiet moments, Daphne found she hated the empty half of her dorm room. She'd cleaned out Beth's belongings quickly, in case the presence of physical objects exceeded the power of Celeste's aura. But none of Beth's friends stopped by looking for her. For the rest of the world, she'd never existed.

Daphne knew Celeste continued to feed because she began to note the missing faces in class or around campus. The number seemed to spike with the frequency of their intimacy. The correlation was not lost on Daphne. She was the literal lamb cuddling up to the lioness. It left her with a strange, nebulous guilt. Celeste was denying her instincts to be with Daphne, and from what she'd gleaned of her lovely cosmic entity, she'd been stalking the halls of this campus for decades. The thought of their evidently differing lifespans left a hollow knot in Daphne's stomach, which made her feel ridiculous. They'd just begun to date. How could she be so tangled up in the future?

Maybe because a small, secret part of her could see a future with Celeste. A strange, somewhat bloody future, but a future to be sure. Something she'd never seen with Alex or anyone else.

Another unfortunate byproduct of Celeste's accelerated feeding schedule was now there was a lack of curvy bitchy buffers between her and the ex. Daphne didn't realize how dangerous this was for her until she had to stay late to finish her labs. At her request, Celeste hadn't devoured her lab partner, but Daphne had spent so much time with her new squeeze, the work was starting to pile up.

Finally turning in her work with minutes to spare, Daphne emerged into a mostly empty building, the lecture rooms dark. A lone janitor buffed the linoleum at the far end of the hall. Shouldering her bag, Daphne lamented missing the dining hall, hoping to snag takeout with Celeste, when Alex popped out of the unisex bathrooms.

"Daphne, you're still here?" His gaze crawled up her form, his leer making her skin crawl. Now that his conquests were snuffed from existence, she was suddenly a viable target again. "You're looking good lately. Like you finally got a good night's sleep."

Ugh, how had she ever found him charming?

He wasn't wrong, though. Celeste left her well and truly fucked and tucked in every night. A small smile played on her lips at the thought. "Good night, Alex." She started to move past him when his fingers clamped on her arm. She stared up at him, brows knotted in annoyance. "Let go of my arm."

"Don't be like that, Daphne. Why don't you come have a drink with me?" He released her to run his fingers along her skin. She shuddered at the touch. "We used to have a lot of fun, you and me."

A number of responses ran through her mind, witty retorts where she stripped away his manhood with every word, but she couldn't seem to push through the seething anger that choked her. Her fingers twitched with the urge to squeeze his neck until his eyes popped out of their sockets. But Daphne wasn't Celeste, and assaulting a faculty member would get her booted out of here and probably arrested.

You could ask Celeste to eat him.

The thought immediately soured. Celeste wasn't an attack dog. She was brilliant, bubbly, and beautiful. Alex was Daphne's cross to bear. Plus, if anyone was going to take revenge, Daphne wanted to carry it out herself.

Finding her voice, Daphne looked up at him. "I'd rather eat shit." Not an eloquent reply but it got the message across. Alex's fingers stopped their pitiful dance over her arm and clamped down with bruising force.

"You stupid bitch," he sneered, leaning in so close she could smell the dining hall curry lunch on his breath. "You think I want anything more than a pity fuck? You couldn't do better if you tried."

"Let go of me!" Daphne shouted the words in his face, prying at his hand. She was seconds from kneeing him in the balls when the janitor perked up at the commotion.

"Everything okay here?"

The coward immediately let her go. Alex plastered on a mollifying smile, turning slightly to address the janitor. Daphne didn't wait for another opening, bolting from the building. Her arm throbbed. A distant pain compared to the cold rage festering in her gut, a pit of ice that sank down to her toes.

She was shivering when she arrived at Celeste's room. It was empty, and for once Daphne was grateful. She kicked off her shoes, stripping down to her underwear before she crawled into the tangled blankets on the bed. Surrounded by their commingling scents, Daphne hugged a pillow against her face and let out the scream that had been building since she fled the building. She screamed and screamed until her throat was raw.

It wasn't enough.

CELESTE

Celeste eyed the herd of deer grazing on the far side of the student parking lot. When she first arrived on this planet, she'd sampled many of the terrestrial life forms. They were more of a challenge to lure, and the taste wasn't bad, per se.

Worrying her bottom lip, she half-listened to the conversation between her chosen prey of the evening and one of their friends. She'd settled on a human diet because humans were tasty. They were easy to catch and the meat to fat ratio was ideal.

That they displayed a higher level of intelligence hadn't mattered—not in the beginning when their speech sounded like static to Celeste's consciousness. Until she started consuming their media with their lives. She found her hunting became more biased after that, though maybe not very biased by human standards. Sometimes her prey remained random, like tonight, but other times, she chose based on the time-honored technique of "Was this person an asshole today?"

Taste factor aside, was it wise to continue her usual dietary habits? Her physical activities with Daphne made her ravenous. They made her insatiable. A dangerous sensation when all she wanted was for the little sweet-meat to sit on her face.

"Hey, I need to get this paper done," her dinner continued yammering. "I'll see you later, okay?" They leaned in, framing the other person's face in a sweet intimate gesture before peppering them with kisses.

Something twisted inside Celeste. Her appetite vanished. Maybe a four-legged carnivore diet wouldn't be so bad. She did like steak.

Wondering if she should broach the subject with her bite-sized para-mour, she headed back to her room.

A smile lit her face when she caught Daphne's scent, but there was a sour tang to it that made her pause. The room was lit by a bedside lava lamp, more than enough light for her to see a sleeping Daphne tangled in her blankets. Padding across the room, she started to crawl on the bed when she noticed the tension that clung to Daphne's frame, even in sleep. Faint salt stains trailed down her cheeks.

Celeste reached to brush that tear stung cheek and froze. A ring of bruising circled Daphne's arm, the discoloration stark on her skin. Someone hurt her Daphne. Someone. Hurt. Her. Daphne.

The illusion of her human form caved inward, her mass filling the space with violence. Pieces of furniture crashed into each other. The windows whined trying to contain her bulk. The lava lamp shattered against the wall.

Daphne startled from sleep. Celeste somehow had the mental faculties to curl a tentacle over her sweetling's face before she saw this loss of control. Other tentacles rapidly wrapped around her woman, maybe a smidge too tight but Celeste couldn't hold back the urge to touch her. Daphne yelped, a brief flash of fear before she recognized who had her. She sighed, curling into Celeste's hold. The way the tension leaked out of her made Celeste's form clench deep inside.

Her kind didn't have a single heart, but a cluster of valves, and they all beat for this tiny human. "I'm sorry," she whispered. "I don't think I can be very human for you right now."

"This voice always makes me think this must be what the stars would sound like if they could talk," said Daphne. Her voice was hoarse, raspy, which gave her giggle a broken edge. "I'm okay."

Worried, Celeste readjusted her coverage of Daphne's eyes. "Please tell me what happened, sweet?"

She wanted to demand answers, to find the one who bruised her and slowly strip off pieces of their flesh to eat while they watched. That all-consuming anger scared Celeste, because she hadn't realized how deeply her feelings for this human had burrowed inside...or how fragile Daphne really was.

She started to pull back, unfurling her grip from that lithe body when Daphne clutched a tentacle against her chest. "Please hold me," she said.

Celeste couldn't refuse her anything. Digging deep, she managed a partial shift, cradling Daphne against her human torso while her multitude of limbs wrapped around them in a cocoon. This level of control was enough to contain the weight of her aura. Daphne wrapped her legs around her waist with her face pressed into Celeste's neck. She felt the faint tremor in her sweetling's arms, clutched tight across her back.

"Talk to me," Celeste pleaded.

Daphne pressed a drugging kiss against her shoulder. "You can't solve all my problems, darling."

The pet name stroked along her nerves. Celeste whined, teasing a tentacle over the soft cotton covering Daphne's ass. Part of her wanted to punish her little human for keeping this secret from her, or maybe she could tease it out in a different way. Her tentacle slid beneath the material, curling along the delectable curve of her ass to find Daphne's pussy already wet for her. She stuffed as much of herself inside those velvety textured walls as she could fit, while Daphne gasped and squirmed in her arms.

"Why can't I?" Celeste hummed, kneading her fingers up Daphne's back to remove her bra. It would be easy to solve this one for her. A second tentacle teased the puckered entrance of Daphne's ass. Her human bucked in her arms, pressing her now naked chest against her. Celeste decided she liked this method of interrogation. "Tell me who did it."

Daphne stiffened slightly. "No."

"No?" Celeste tunneled a tentacle deep inside her ass, groaning at the clench of tight flesh around her as Daphne keened against her neck. Her morsel bit at her flesh with blunt human teeth, the sensation incredible. Celeste chuckled, stroking the inner flesh of both the spaces she'd invaded until her human started to come apart in her arms. She stopped stroking.

Daphne trembled against her. "What are you doing?" Her voice was strained, her body close to the edge, but Celeste held her there, enjoying the sensation of those inner muscles pulsing against her flesh.

"Tell me who hurt you." Her human fingers traced Daphne's jaw as it clenched up.

Her human wrapped her arms around Celeste's neck and sighed against her shoulder. "I can't believe you're trying to fuck it out me."

"Well, it's clearly not working, but it *is* fun," said Celeste, giving Daphne's insides a tickle.

The woman squealed, nails digging into her back. "Not fair," Daphne wheezed.

Celeste reached up to stroke her hair, feeling Daphne sag against her. "Why won't you tell me?"

Daphne nipped her neck. "Because you will solve it. You will eat them, and I will watch until my mind snaps like an overstretched rubber band."

A chill of alarm skated through Celeste's system. More tentacles curled around Daphne, the need to hold her as strong as the need to keep her away from that brain melting aura Celeste couldn't turn off. "No." The word was a declaration and a plea.

Daphne smiled, rubbing her cheek against a seeking appendage. "That's why I want to solve it myself."

Curious, Celeste gathered Daphne against her human chest, cupping her face as she tangled her fingers in her long dark hair. "What do you have in mind, sweetling?" She twitched deep inside her girlfriend, enjoying the way Daphne bucked against her.

Daphne bit her bottom lip with a groan. "How do you feel about another dinner date?"

ELEVEN

DAPHNE

In the post-coital cuddle, Daphne finally told Celeste about her relationship with Alex. She refused to ruin a perfectly good fucking with talk of her piece-of-shit ex, but with her muscles still watery from her lover's interrogation tactics, she could open the old wound. Celeste made her feel safe.

Alex was intelligent. That was what hooked Daphne first. A teaching assistant for many of the harder high-level courses while also teaching a few classes of his own, he was equally drawn to Daphne's intelligence. Treated her like an equal instead of a student. His pursuit of her was aggressive. In the early days, the charm was there, or maybe she wanted it to be. She didn't know he was married or had a track record for seducing students. Daphne never thought she was that gullible. That anyone pursuing her had to be serious to get over her oddities. Not adding another notch to their belt. That was what she was to him, in the end: another successful conquest.

The problem came when he went to break things off. Perhaps he expected waterworks, or pleading. Clearly, he hadn't known her as well as she believed. Answering his break-up statement with a shrug and nonchalant *Ok* set him off. His ego couldn't handle her ambivalence.

The clap back was immediate. By the end of the day, her classmates were whispering nasty things within earshot. Her roommate turned on her. The little tortures began. He'd stirred up the college campus like a high school rumor mill, kicked a hornet's nest he set loose on her. And now, he had the audacity to treat her like a jilted lover open to a *pity fuck*.

Celeste held her through her recount of events, running human fingers through her hair. "I wasn't sure if he was the one, but I think I got an inkling while chowing my way through your bitchy bullies."

Daphne pinched her chin. "I've noticed."

That made her lover's brows snap together. In the weeks they'd been together, she'd gotten better at mimicking human emotions, or maybe they came more naturally to her after so much exposure. Daphne reached up to smooth her knotted brows. "What?"

"You noticed. You remember them, even though you weren't there while I fed?" Something flashed through Celeste's eyes. Her eyes wavered from baby blue to black pools, speckled with distant starlight. "Maybe someday you *will* be immune to my aura."

The thought was one Daphne carefully folded and put away in a mental box, too nervous, too excited, to examine it now. Not even the conscious act of compartmentalizing the idea could stop the whisper of *What if I could be with her forever?*

First, she had a date night to plan.

Luring Alex to a potentially compromising situation was laughably easy. Though she had deleted his number from her list of contacts months ago, it didn't take much mental prodding to remember it. She sent him an invitation to meet her in the sciences building for a late night "cram session" after the janitorial staff would be long gone. She didn't want them to get caught up in tonight's festivities.

After once again disabling the camera to the labs, she went to set up, leaving the door unlocked behind her. The familiar chemical scents bolstered her nerves. It wasn't fear or anxiety that fluttered through her stomach, but the dark excitement she normally kept buried deep because it unsettled others.

Alex didn't keep her waiting long. He slipped into the lab, taking one final glance down the hall to make sure they were alone in the building before he stalked in her direction.

The sight of Daphne made him freeze. She'd fashioned herself into a lure, wearing nothing but a lab coat, carefully splayed open to reveal the curves of her breasts and the lace black thong that hugged her hips.

He shoved his hands in his pockets, that small slimy smile curling his lips while his gaze raked over her form. "I see you changed your mind. Couldn't resist?"

Daphne didn't trust herself to answer. A flash of familiar cold rage tingled down to her bare toes on the cool linoleum floor. She crooked a finger, beckoning him closer while her other hand fiddled with the syringe behind her back. The real challenge was keeping a neutral expression, continuing the illusion.

Luckily, Alex was too preoccupied by her body to notice the tightness in her jaw. He crowded in front of her, bracing his hands on either side of the metal examination table she leaned against. Daphne waited, though her skin crawled when he began to nuzzle her shoulder. The moment he stretched, exposing his neck, she struck, plunging the tranquilizer into his veins.

His heavy frame sagged against her. Daphne grunted at the sudden dead weight, struggling to maneuver his body onto the table, but after a sweaty five minutes, she managed to roll him onto it. Selecting the fabric shears from her tray of tools, she cut him out of his suit, until he lay, nude and unconscious, on the dissection table. Once she'd secured him to the table with a hefty number of zip ties and bungee cords, she waited for her date to arrive.

A dark smile curled her lips when Celeste's arms slid around her waist. This was where the fun began. Celeste pressed the curves of her body against Daphne's back, hands slipping under the open lab coat to knead her breasts. A tentacle curled up her thigh, stroking the lacy black material of her thong.

"Sugar, is this little black number for me? You spoil me," Celeste purred in her ear, teasing her lower lips through the lace. Daphne shivered at the divine sensation, letting her head fall back against Celeste's shoulder.

"Had to dress up right for date night," she said, leaning back into the being who made her feel safe and cherished.

Daphne glanced down to find Alex awake, staring at her in wide-eyed horror while Celeste's tentacles writhed in the open air behind her. He strained against his restraints, his cries muffled by the duct tape over his mouth.

Daphne held up a scalpel with a grin. "Ready for the main course?"

About Kristin Jacques

Kristin Jacques is an award-winning author of fantasy fiction for teens and adults. She currently lives in a small town in Connecticut with her partner, kiddos, and two trash goblins who think they are cats.

When not writing, she's usually reading, gaming, or catching some excellent B-horror movies. She is currently working on projects full of magic, mystery, and delight.

Find out more at kristinjacques.com.

MEAT CUTE

DESIREÉ M. NICCOLI

Lady Leviathan stirs in her primeval seafloor bed, the kraken goddess of the abyss waking from a centuries-long slumber.

She unfurls her tentacled arms one by one, uncoiling kinks, shaking off stiffness. Nodes of golden light flicker to life beneath slippery, dark blue skin as she stretches, dormant no longer.

As she blinks away sleep, gathering her bearings, she registers a new sound.

Ambient ocean noise vibrates all around, louder and more forceful than anything she's ever heard before. And her memory is long. Almost as long and enduring as the ocean itself.

This noise is not beautiful like whalesong. She strains and yearns for that beloved, melodious sound, but the lullaby that carried her into sleep has dimmed, drowned in a riotous roar of discordant grinding and rumbling.

Shifting tectonic plates never bothered her. Nor the breaking of Pangaea. This, however, is jarring to her core, almost painful as it reverberates through connective tissue and muscle. She waits for the noise to pass. Whatever is making that maddening sound *has* to stop.

She waits. And waits.

While many seafolk can hold their breath for hours, no creature Lady Leviathan knows has this kind of relentless vocal endurance. The kind that drones on and on without a single pause.

Not even an existence as primordial as hers is enough to foster the kind of patience necessary to outlast it. She's befriended many large creatures in her time, the Megalodon and the Mosasaur, largely unbothered by anything because of their sheer size, but even this would've irritated them. And the majestic Blue Whale, for all its patience and peaceful nature, must also find this difficult to stand.

If the mighty Blue Whale still lives, that is...

Dread sinks into the pit of her belly, knotting it tight. This sometimes is the price of rest—missing things, awaking to find that much has changed, and not always for the better. There's no greater grief than emerging from a much-needed slumber, one that allows her to endure the toll of endless time, and learning a fellow sea creature has gone extinct.

As the horrid droning continues and shows no sign of stopping, her lights sparkle in an erratic, panicked sequence.

The noise is too much. And something should be done about it. It cannot be allowed to continue forever.

The worst comes from above.

As she pushes off from the muck in the ocean's deep, a silt cloud blooms. Though it cannot be seen in the inky blackness of the abyss, she feels it brushing the fine hairs that coat her skin. Only the bioluminescence her fellow creatures make, a beautiful language of light, pulses slow and languid in the dark.

They are calmer than her.

But how can they be so calm in the face of this ceaseless noise?

She drifts toward the surface, her body gradually acclimating to the decreasing pressure, changing form and density. Whatever it takes, she will silence that awful racket.

Creatures scatter from her massive path, lights flashing in alarm. Centuries are nothing when one has lived for billions of years. And yet, here she is, as constant as the sea, creating chaos in the deep. It makes no sense. She is not the thing to fear. Despite her size, she never has been. Their reaction hurts more than taking a harpoon to the heart—and she should know. One of hers has been nicked before.

Most of the creatures surrounding her emit blue or green light. Others, the sneakier bunch, emit red, invisible to their prey. They don't truly flee, just hover beyond her reach.

No doubt they heard from their foreparents what destruction her mighty multitude of arms could do, and that's what they remember most. She wouldn't harm them, though. Not on purpose. Even as hungry as she is after her long slumber, that's not what she eats.

Voices all around whisper, a chorus of hope rising. All alarm is forgotten as memory sinks in.

"She's awake!"

"The Great Devourer has returned."

"We are saved!"

"Do you think she can make it stop?"

Saved from what? The noise? It is quite irritating, maddeningly so, but her fellow seafolk seemed unbothered by it just a moment ago. Perhaps the clamor is not a new thing to them, but rather something they've resigned themselves to in her absence to survive.

As Lady Leviathan rises from the deep and her sleep-laden senses sharpen, she detects something else that has changed. Something even worse than the constant wretched racket. Everything about the water is wrong. Its taste, its scent, its touch upon her skin. It's dirtier, oilier. Cloying.

This has to be a bad patch.

The farther she travels from the ocean floor, the more dread sinks to the pit of her stomach. The silt and muck distracted her before, but there is no denying it now. This isn't the ocean she remembers at all.

Frantically scrubbing at her arms, Lady Leviathan tries to get the slimy film off her skin even knowing it's futile. She can't escape the very water she swims in. *And what are these tiny infuriating particulates of unliving matter?* Not plankton, that's for certain, though just as pervasive.

Plankton she respects. Not this new insidious presence.

She shudders, the force of her agitation rippling out in a shockwave.

Each draw of breath through her gills is filthy and clogged. While she can suck in enough oxygen to live, it doesn't feel like enough. It's like she's getting a third less of the air she should. She swipes a claw quickly, but carefully, beneath the folds, trying to clear the passage. Bigger pieces of that insidious inorganic matter come away, but the congestion isn't clearing. The more she focuses on it, the worse it gets, each inhalation catching in her chest. She gasps, panic rising. She's never had to think so hard about breathing before.

Why? Why? Why? Why?

If there was a greater deity to pray to, to plead for intercession, for mercy, she would lift all twenty of her limbs and beg. But there is no greater power than the Goddess of the Sea, than herself. She's supposed to have all the answers. And she's been doomed to slowly suffocate in her own home, helpless and lost, unable to save herself, let alone others.

She hastens her ascent toward the photic zone, desperate to escape the foul water. Maybe, just maybe, all this filth has sunk and settled and the uppermost level of the ocean remains free and clear. There must be cleaner patches above. This couldn't be what her once-beautiful home has become.

The rapidly decreasing pressure makes her insides slosh around like goop. Uncomfortable, but normal. Some things remain the same—though sloshy insides provide little consolation.

The water, this nightmare, only gets worse.

Lady Leviathan thrashes her arms, attempting to swat the murkiness away, but it's inescapable. Even swimming through a silt cloud feels cleaner and promises an end. *No, no, no.*

It's been a few hundred years. That is nothing in all the billions she has lived. How could so much change in so little time? Awakening from past deep periods of sleep has often meant loss, yes, but it never left her feeling so alien and unsuited to the new world. How in the hottest hydrothermal vents is she ever supposed to adapt to this?

An anguished cry above cuts through the noise, the filth, and the panic.

Lady Leviathan's thrashing arms still.

It cries again.

Something is in greater need than her. If she can help this poor creature, whatever their predicament may be…Well, let one good thing come out of waking up to this nightmare.

Lady Leviathan continues her ascent, and as she does, the water begins to brighten, penetrated by surface light. Breathing gets easier, though she credits that to distraction rather than improved water quality.

Her hasty ascent leaves little time for her eyes to adjust to the sun's piercing rays. So, at first, she doesn't see it.

As she squints through the bright haze, the light reveals a new horror. One that makes her regret ever leaving the dark. Too terrible to be real, and yet there's no ignoring the truth of it. The chill that steals over her is colder than a glacial current.

A graveyard of rotting sea creatures, suspended eerily in the water, frozen in motion, spreads out before her hundreds of fathoms wide and deep. Sharks, whales, sea turtles, seals, and various kinds of fish…

Death is indiscriminate in its reach. The water is foul here, reeking of suffering and despair as much as decomposing flesh. Her arms twitch helplessly at her sides, longing to comfort, needing to save, but these poor creatures are far beyond help, their lives needlessly stolen and wasted.

A surge of distress floods the water from something living. Whatever creature that's been crying out is somewhere amid this nightmare. Lady Leviathan spies wriggling from the corner of her eye and swims toward it.

A mermaid.

She has sharp, angular facial features, chiseled cheekbones, and a maw full of long, thin fangs. The corners of her mouth extend from ear to ear, permanently lifted in a fearsome rictus. Anything caught between those rows of teeth would never escape.

A stem juts out from the center of the mermaid's forehead, and from it a bulbous, lambent orb like that of an anglerfish. Fins fan out from her temples and the backs of her arms—those, too, are sharp and used for slashing anything stupid enough to try hunting merfolk.

Her tail is vertically oriented like a shark's, with a hind fin shaped in the hard curve of a crescent moon.

Every inch of the mermaid's anatomy signals that she is a fellow creature of the deep. Not all merfolk are. Or they are to varying degrees, every variation a product of evolution and breeding with surface dwellers. Lady Leviathan questions the wisdom of doing the latter but keeps the thought to herself and swims closer.

"Stay back!" the sea-maiden warns, thrusting a clawed hand forward.

The movement is strangely jerky and hindered, as if tethered by some unseen force. Lady Leviathan draws up short. Little blooms of blood diffuse into the water, and that's when she notices the thousands of cuts slashing the mermaid's arms, torso, and tail.

Everything in her screams to ignore the warning and intercede. To end this suffering as soon as possible. Protecting the sea and all its inhabitants is her greatest duty, and this mermaid has suffered enough. But there's a reason why this is a place of death. Why this mermaid can't move and hasn't already swum far, far away from this cursed place.

That's when she finally sees it.

A net. The mermaid is inextricably entangled in the ghostly threads of a net. It's unlike any Lady Leviathan has ever seen before. In fact, the point seems to be that it *couldn't* be seen. These translucent threads are small, thin, almost invisible. It's only because she knows to stop and look that it's perceptible at all with tiny glints of sunlight reflecting off the strands.

If it weren't for the mermaid's warning, she would've ascended straight into it and found herself ensnared too. Never in her history had she encountered a net large enough to contain her. A humbling, unwelcome change, and a horrible way to die. Surrounded by death, the gray unseeing eyes of those that came before, rotted, waterlogged flesh peeling away from bone and cartilage. Ever knowing that in just a few days' time, you will join their ranks. One of many caught in this massive web of destruction.

"I see it." Lady Leviathan drifts slowly forward, pushing floating netting away. It's a tangled mess that takes careful precision to sift through. By the time she clears a path, she's used eighteen of her twenty arms to hold it at bay, creating a dome. This bubble of safety is tenuous; the extraction will have to be quick. Shifting currents could carry the netting and trap them both inside.

The mermaid stares at her with large, round white eyes. Blue biolumi-nescent nodes speckling her body flash sharp and erratic as her gaze darts between Lady Leviathan's array of arms, her eyes, and the netting that surrounds them. Fear spikes the water, a sour addition to the decay. The mermaid knows this rescue attempt could fail at any time too.

Lady Leviathan curls two tentacles around opposing sections of the netting and gives it a hardy tug. It's stronger than the fibrous rope of old, less giving. The cruel threads dig into her flesh, and a sharp sting puts an abrupt stop to any additional pulling. While the cursed thing didn't break skin, it will if she applies any more force. She flexes her tentacles, shaking out the sting.

Brute strength usually solves most of her problems. Not this time. It's an uncomfortable feeling, the sudden realization she no longer knows where she sits on the food chain.

The surface dwellers have refined their thieving craft with deadly precision. Even the mermaid's claws aren't sharp enough to cut through the surface dwellers' new, elusive netting. At least, not while her arms and wrists are ensnared.

Anger simmers deep within Lady Leviathan. For the lives already lost and the ones sure to follow. For taking and wasting so greedily from *her* domain. A net this massive must be intended to ensnare an equally massive creature, all these poor seafolk but bycatch. Why else construct something so big, only to leave it, and the creatures entangled in it, behind?

They dare challenge me?

An itch to wreck steals over her many arms, but Lady Leviathan shoves her rage beneath the surface before it can consume all thought. There will be plenty of time for a rampage later. Emotions will only cloud her judgment, and this rescue requires her entire focus. The mermaid's life depends on her getting this right.

"Hold still." Lady Leviathan extends razor-sharp spikes from her limbs.

The mermaid flinches, glaring at the spikes. If that isn't indication enough of her distress, there's also the frantic, panicked sparkling of her bioluminescence. The poor creature has been cut all over, but there's more to this fear.

Trust doesn't come easily in the ocean. The harsh reality of their world is bigger creatures eat smaller creatures, and right now, she's trapped, unable to fight or flee. That makes her an easy snack to carve up and devour, especially for a giant kraken who hasn't eaten in centuries.

"I just want to free you," Lady Leviathan soothes, gently cupping the mermaid's cheek with a spike-less tentacle. And she means it. There's no trickery here. A consequence of being one of the largest creatures in the ocean is a constant awareness of how others perceive her size. They see her and assume death and destruction follow closely in her wake. It can. It has. But only when she chooses to. "I promise to be very careful."

The mermaid's alarmed sparkling settles to a dim, slow pulsing. "You promise?" Her voice is quiet and unsure, barely above a whisper.

"With all that I am."

Her light stutters. Promises are not given lightly in the abyss, because in the daily fight for survival, to eat or be eaten, promises are hard to keep. Pledging on one's life is even rarer. It's the seafolk way to say what they mean. Anxiety whooshes out of the mermaid in a heavy, relieved sigh that bubbles between them. "Go ahead."

That's all the permission Lady Leviathan needs. She starts by cutting a perimeter around the mermaid, arms moving swiftly and surely to free the mermaid from the wider net. The precision work can come later. The faster Lady Leviathan gets her away from the mass grave and its despair-polluted water, the better.

She curls a tentacle around the mermaid's waist and draws her away, her great limbs propelling them backward with a mighty thrust. Without her arms holding up the netting, it descends back into place, filling the gap they just vacated.

They are free of the floating death trap, but Lady Leviathan keeps swimming. Neither of them need be anywhere near this atrocity or its ongoing dangers.

Only when the water no longer smells like death does she stop to untangle the mermaid from the remnants of netting that still constricts her body.

Amountainous being has risen from the depths, and she wears a crown made of ship wreckage. It's an array of broken wooden masts, rigging, and sails—every bit a relic from the surface dwellers' days of old. Days Ianthe's kin long for most desperately. When the ocean was quieter, cleaner, and nets were easy to tear to shreds.

When surface dwellers were easier to catch.

And eat.

She thought for sure their net would kill her. The bloated, decomposing bodies of all those who came before were a constant, maddening reminder that in a few days' time, she would be just as dead and rotted as the rest. Maybe she's been spared that fate and the goddess will free her.

Ianthe stares in awe at the Twenty-Armed Goddess. How she towers before her, all beauty and might. Her shadow blots out the sun and shrouds Ianthe in the comfort of darkness. Of home, the abyss. When the goddess moves, the currents shift. Waves rise and fall above them. When the Twenty-Armed Goddess speaks, the ocean listens. Awaiting her command.

Her power, her presence, is just like the stories Ianthe's foremother told her as a youngling while tucking her into their seaweed nest. How the goddess could summon ferocious storms to strike down the surface dwellers who pillaged the sea. How she smashed and sank their ships. Freed the creatures caught in their nets. Ianthe's merfolk ancestors played in the monstrous waves the goddess made, laughing as lightning streaked across the sky. And they feasted well in her wake.

Protector. Provider. The age-old creature who inspires their bravery.

Before this moment, the largest being Ianthe's ever seen up close was a tall-browed whale, the kind that dives into the deep to hunt squid. The Twenty-Armed Goddess is at least three times its size, both a wonder and a terror to behold, and Ianthe is completely at her mercy. This glorious creature could crush her in the palm of a hand. Or pummel her to death with one of her great many tentacled arms. It would be all too easy, and there is nothing Ianthe can do to save herself.

All five of the goddess's golden eyes fix on her.

It's a heavy weight, the full breadth of that stare. The need to flee engulfs Ianthe's senses, eroding any story-time nostalgia she's held since she was a youngling. Mortal panic shoots pins and needles along her skin, and without thinking, she jerks against the netting. Its wicked threads slice deeper into her flesh and she hisses at the sharp pain punctuated by salty sting. Resilient to the ocean's bite doesn't mean unaffected.

"*Goddess,* that hurts," Ianthe curses and immediately regrets it. Usually, the very being she swears on isn't directly in front of her. Watching her like her next meal.

The goddess's lips quirk in amusement. Five eyes as big as her head peer down at her—into her. It's unnerving to garner so much attention from a creature who could easily devour her in two bites. "That's an easy plea to answer. *Stop wriggling.*"

"Not if you'll eat me, I won't!"

Ianthe can take on a shark, maybe two, but not the Twenty-Armed Goddess herself. She'll die trying, though, even if she only gets in a few swipes.

The ocean is a harsh mother. There's no reason to think that one of its first daughters would be any gentler. The net offered certain death—a fate Ianthe almost resigned herself to after the first three days trapped inside its web. Death at the hands—or arms—of the kraken goddess seems like a mercy by comparison. Glorious beauty. Power. Maybe a brief flash of pain, then sweet, blissful nothingness. Death must be like sleep. It has to be. Ianthe can't comprehend it as anything else.

The goddess is both a wonder and a terror to behold, and Ianthe is completely at her mercy.

But much to her surprise, it's not Death Ianthe sees in the Twenty-Armed Goddess's eyes. It's not hunger either. It's worry and more tenderness than Ianthe knows what to do with. It's why she's not seized in another wave of panic when the giant kraken woman's clawed fingers curl loosely around her body, providing shelter. More nest than snare. It's a distinction Ianthe appreciates, and a relieved exhale of bubbles clouds the water in front of her face.

"You're too precious to eat."

Ianthe's cheeks burn. Now the goddess is looking at her like she's a prize. Polished sea glass, colorful gems, glittering silver and gold coins, plucked from wreckage. Deep-sea merfolk like to pretend they're not swayed by shiny, pretty things like their counterparts who swim closer to the shore, but they collect the pretty things all the same. She's never been someone's treasure before.

"I want to make it stop," the goddess continues, plucking out a thread. "This hurt."

Ianthe winces—the removal stings—but relief floods immediately after. The gratification is worth the initial pain, and when she looks down at the slice across her abdomen, she's grateful to see her skin is already stitching itself back together. Wounds that don't heal fast can poison and kill. Surviving any number of perils only to succumb to injury later is a cruel, ruthless reality, and while it doesn't claim her kind often, it's not without precedent.

Propellers. Nets. Mishaps with jagged, rusty metal during dives for shipwreck salvage. Shark bites. Not all the dangers are manmade, but many of them are.

Keep going, she wants to say. *It hurts, but it's helping.* She doesn't though, because who is Ianthe to command the kraken goddess of the deep?

The goddess does not seem put off by Ianthe's lack of response and plucks away another digging thread. Ianthe patiently endures the process —sharp pain, then relief—again and again. There's nothing else to do but get through it.

She fits so neatly in the goddess's palm, completely cradled. Only her tail dangles off the edge. It's strangely comforting to be encompassed so fully. Snug and concealing like a small cave. A place for safety and reprieve.

It's within the protection of this giant's hand that she quietly observes the legendary being. Never in Ianthe's wildest dreams had she ever thought the Twenty-Armed Goddess would return in her lifetime, much less to be rescued, held, and tended to by her.

Reality matches story in that the kraken goddess is massive, and yet none of the tales her foreparents told adequately prepares Ianthe for what she sees.

The goddess has four elbowed arms, two on each side on the uppermost part of her torso—arms like the two Ianthe has. Each one ends in a clawed, five-fingered webbed hand. Unlike the goddess's other sixteen limbs, which are massive tentacles at least two whale-lengths long and lined with golden bioluminescent suckers.

While her skin is dark blue, the tentacles making up the lower half of her body are so dark they're almost black. If not for the bioluminescence that highlights the goddess's form—from the gold of her eyes to the glowing freckles that line her cheeks and powerful limbs—Ianthe wouldn't be able to see her at all, even with surface light filtering a hundred feet down to them. Like many creatures of the deep, the goddess blends well into the ocean and can shutter her inner light if she chooses. Invisible until it's too late.

Yet the fear Ianthe felt before is drifting beyond reach.

Every bioluminescent node along the kraken's body shines brightly. Their sheer quantity and size create an aura of warm light that surrounds them both and illuminates the goddess's long, inky hair. Ianthe watches how the strands swirl in the currents, mesmerized by their ethereal dance.

Maybe, just maybe, she wouldn't mind being entangled in the goddess's arms. Maybe that's a snare she'd invite. It's a stray, surprising thought.

It strikes her then that this is all too wondrous to be real. The Twenty-

Armed Goddess herself? It can't be so. There's grimmer, far more likelier explanations.

"Is this a dream?" Ianthe whispers. Afraid it will become true if she voices it too loud. Even quieter, she asks, "Or the hereinafter? Have I died?"

Maybe she never made it out of the net…Maybe this beautiful and terrifying vision before her is actually Death himself welcoming her into the afterlife with a pretty guise, and she'll never see her pod, *her foremother*, again. A strange burning sensation wells around Ianthe's eyes and lodges in her throat.

Surprise flickers across all five of the goddess's golden eyes as she looks up from her task. "No, little one. You lived." She brings a tentacle to Ianthe's cheek with the softest, barest touch. "As long as I am here, you are not Death's to claim."

The goddess's caress. The weight of her eyes. The grand, wide ocean narrowing to this one singular point. Just the two of them and nothing else. *You are mine.* This piece of the promise isn't spoken, but it's felt all the same.

Ianthe relaxes into the kraken goddess's embrace.

With careful precision, Lady Leviathan shears away the net pieces digging into Ianthe's gray pearlescent skin, carefully and gently picking them out of her wounds.

Blood clouds the water with each vicious strand removed. She hates causing the mermaid more pain but is grateful for how completely Ianthe holds still. Their vast size difference makes this extraction slow, delicate work. One wrong move and she could hurt rather than help.

Lady Leviathan purses her lips in concentration and collects all the shorn scraps of netting in a ball that she keeps behind her so she can bury it later, deep in the sea floor. As much as she doesn't want the cruel instrument anywhere in her ocean, even in the muck, it's a better solution than leaving it drifting about, continuing to ruthlessly ensnare.

The mermaid's skin is a tapestry of survival. Beneath the new wounds, she is riddled with the jagged white lines of older net scars. Lady Leviathan traces one lightly. "This has happened before."

"It has."

"How often?" If these treacherous, netted graveyards were everywhere...

"Too often," the mermaid answers quietly. "This was the first time I couldn't get myself out. I saw the other nets in time and didn't get caught so deep. But this one, I never saw."

Lady Leviathan continues working to free her, ruthless strand by ruthless strand. "I did see the corpses and thought their placement was strange—neither rising nor sinking—just floating in place. So many denied the Final Fall." Sorrow slices through her like barnacles against skin.

The Final Fall is a creature's last descent into the abyss. It's an honor, a glory, to reach the sea floor upon death, to be enfolded into the ocean's embrace. The body provides sustenance for deep-sea organisms as old as the ocean itself. Making the Final Fall meant a creature could live on for all eternity through others. Never truly gone. The spirit commended to the sea.

There's no crueler fate than to be netted, except perhaps being taken from the sea by surface dwellers or washed ashore, away from the ocean's touch. Lady Leviathan's not sure which nightmare she finds worse. Once upon a time, she wouldn't have needed to worry about such things.

"I didn't realize what it meant until it was too late." The mermaid winces through the extraction of a particularly deeply embedded thread. "I was already tangled in the net. The more I struggled the more it trapped me."

"And your pod?"

"Couldn't say. I was trying to find a new food source, away from our usual swim routes and hunting grounds. Whole fish schools are disappearing, and we don't think they're migrating." The mermaid tugs anxiously on a lock of billowing brown hair. "I'm certain my family looked for me, but I couldn't hear them. Not that I'd want them anywhere near that cursed place."

"How long have you been here?"

"Days."

If Lady Leviathan hadn't awoken when she did, this being before her would likely be dead. Just like countless others. She would've starved, tangled in the surface dwellers' refuse.

Freeing the mermaid is a long, arduous process, but when the very last piece of netting is plucked away, relief floods the water thick as squid ink.

"Thank you," the mermaid effuses, flexing her limbs and tail. Beneath gray, semi-translucent skin, her skeletal structure glows faintly, drawing attention to how sharply her ribs poke out, and how her skin is paler, duller than is healthy for her kind.

"It's the least I could do." Far from enough, truth be told. Almost too little too late. Lady Leviathan needs to do more. While the surface dwellers are to blame for the abandoned net, her centuries-long slumber allowed them to go this long unchecked. This never would've happened had she stayed awake. She twists two tentacles into the ball of netting she collected behind her back, furiously pulling on opposite ends, even though it cuts into her skin and the hurt does nothing to drown her guilt and rage.

The mermaid's stomach grumbles, and it snaps her attention to where it's needed most.

Poor thing is starving—they'd need to resolve that soon—but at least her kind are blessedly quick healers. Some of her injuries are already beginning to seal over into angry, pink lines. They have to in the unforgiving salty grip of the sea.

"What's your name, sea maiden?"

"Ianthe."

A pretty name for a pretty creature.

All three of Lady Leviathan's hearts flutter.

"Twenty-Armed Goddess, I owe you my life."

"Now there's a name." She smiles. "Simple, true. But a bit on the nose, don't you think?"

"It's our name for you." Ianthe shrugs sheepishly. "Has been for as long as merfolk have passed down stories. Though I don't know that anyone's ever dared to ask."

"Can't say that anyone has." A wonder, that. Billions of years and she never questioned it. Others knowing her true name just never seemed to matter, not when their lives were so much shorter than hers. She cares to know them. She's always felt deeply for the creatures she serves. It just never occurred to her that she might also let them in close enough to know her in return.

"So, not the Twenty-Armed Goddess then." Ianthe tilts her head with a curious, expectant expression. "To whom do I owe my gratitude?"

"Many have called me the Great Devourer, but Lady Leviathan is the name I've given myself."

Ianthe perks up, lights flashing merrily. With a deep bow, she says, "Great Devourer, it has been an age."

Still clinging to titles, Lady Leviathan thinks bemusedly. *Will have to change that.*

The mermaid's reverence is broken by her stomach grumbling—louder and gurgling more aggressively than before. Twin dots of blue illuminate her cheeks.

"You must be terribly hungry." It's nothing to be embarrassed about. Her body has every reason to protest and demand after the ordeal she's endured. And yet, there's nothing Lady Leviathan wants to do more than make those sounds stop.

Hunt for her. Feed her. Until she's happy and full.

Harsh rumbling above jerks her attention to the surface. It's louder and more piercing than the constant drone she woke up to and only worsens the closer it gets.

Ianthe's head snaps up. In an instant her whole demeanor changes, instincts flaring to life. Clawed fingers flex. Teeth gnash together. Ready to slice and rend. Ferocity transforms the bashful mermaid Ianthe was just a second ago into a fearsome predator. She recognizes this sound. Despises it.

There's only one group of creatures in this world capable of creating something so horrid and persistently destructive. Anger barely contained at the floating graveyard resurfaces, and this time, Lady Leviathan welcomes it.

THREE

W aves of vibration slice through the water as the dark seal-like silhouette of a surface dweller vessel chugs along overhead. Like the net, this surface dweller contraption is different from its predecessors. It doesn't creak and groan like the wooden ones that came before, whose bones now adorn the crown on Lady Leviathan's head. It's so much worse.

The vessel roars, and Ianthe grimaces, slapping webbed hands over her ears.

Lady Leviathan does the same. All four hands slap over her ears, each layered in pairs. While it does a good job of muffling the awful racket, she can't spend the rest of eternity swimming around with her hands permanently suckered to her ears. *Mother Ocean, why is that cursed thing so loud?*

Despite the pain, there is a fierce, determined gleam in Ianthe's eye. "I am ravenous."

One by one, Lady Leviathan lowers her hands. Piercing sound assaults her ears, but she grits her teeth and with the pain she whets her rage. "Then let us hunt."

Lady Leviathan surges toward the surface, ready to unleash the full force of her fury. Higher and higher she rises—the mermaid keeping excellent pace by her side. Even in a weakened, half-starved state, Ianthe's quick, her sleek body slicing through the water.

These surface dwellers will pay for their trespasses, for every careless action that poisons the water, that destroys lives. A new red tide will sweep their shores, but one of their own blood.

As they near the vessel's underbelly, the racket it makes is deafening, but that's all the more reason to tear it asunder. *For the creatures killed needlessly in their abandoned nets, denied their Final Fall. For Ianthe.*

With a great thrust of her many lower limbs, Lady Leviathan snatches it right out of the water, her tentacles writhing in the dry world above. She throws all her rage into the motion, but after that initial burst of energy, her arms sag.

Oof. The thing is heavy, like it's filled with boulders, so she thrusts the rest of her limbs surface-ward and redistributes the weight. Blessed be her twenty arms.

There is a noisy spinning piece at one end of the vessel that she promptly rips out and throws. While the vessel itself quiets, she can now hear the surface dwellers' screams.

A volley of sharp, loud sounds follows, and a spray of tiny stingers pierces her arms.

Ouch, stop that, you infernal little beasts! She shakes the ship, knocking some of its crew shrieking into the ocean.

So tiny, and yet so lethal, Ianthe zips through the water, slashing, biting, ripping. Rivers of blood pour forth sweet and savory, and Lady Leviathan heaves a sigh of relief. Finally, something good in this nightmare the ocean's become. Nothing tastes so decadent as the defeat of a tenacious enemy.

Hearing more of these overreaching beings rattling around within the ship, Lady Leviathan coils her arms around opposite ends and pulls, using every ounce of her strength. The metal hull creaks and groans under her might, straining and protesting, yet holding firm. Her confidence flags. Is she even strong enough to tear this thing apart? *Mother Ocean, wouldn't that be embarrassing. Foiled and outmatched by greedy, thieving surface dwellers.*

Lady Leviathan relaxes her arms, letting the ocean take the brunt of the ship's weight as she sucks oxygen in through her gills.

She begrudgingly admires the surface dweller's ingenuity and rapid evolution in the time she's been asleep. But only for a moment. Lady Leviathan has never backed down from a challenge, and she won't let these land-loving beings beat her now. She owes it to Ianthe and the denizens of the sea to keep fighting. What kind of goddess is she if she cannot?

Such titles must be earned. And she has a lot of lost time to make up for.

With a guttural roar, Lady Leviathan lifts the vessel high and pulls, redoubling her efforts. She must have weakened the metal in her last attempt, because this time the ship easily gives way with a horrendous screech, splitting into two.

Triumph alights Lady Leviathan. Her bioluminescence twinkles as she upends each half of the ship and shakes out the rest of the crew.

Plop, plop, plop, the sailors go as they hit the water.

When the ship is emptied, she hurls its carcass away, then sinks all the way down into the water to check on the sea maiden.

Cheeks glowing blue, Ianthe hovers in the water, munching away, sporting a happy little belly bulge. Torn flesh hangs from her mouth and hands. Thank the ocean, Ianthe is already looking less pale.

"It's good?"

Ianthe nods, extending a hand...a dismembered, surface dweller hand.

Lady Leviathan smiles, uncurling a tentacle. One spike sticks out and Ianthe doesn't hesitate to impale the appendage onto it. Such a small morsel. More bone than meat, but Lady Leviathan doesn't mind. It has a quite a lovely crunch when she pops it into her mouth.

The little mermaid is quickly sated. While Ianthe eats most of a sailor all by herself, compared to Lady Leviathan's appetite, especially after a centuries-long slumber, it's hardly a snack.

Out of a crew of fifty, Lady Leviathan easily tucks away twenty. She's not called the Great Devourer for nothing. There's room in her belly for more—truth be told, she wants to eat the entire crew—but Ianthe's troubling news about whole schools of fish disappearing stops her. Others need this meat more.

"We should prepare the rest of this for your pod."

Gratitude ripples from Ianthe. "You do us a great kindness."

Is it kindness when it's her duty? When she wants to make the mermaid happy? To impress and earn her favor? "I don't think my motivations are entirely altruistic." Longing pangs deep within her, a cavernous ache that's been neglected for centuries.

Ianthe stops chewing. Then swallows with a thick gulp, coughing once. Twice. She pounds on her chest with a webbed fist. "What other reason is there?"

Maybe actions are better than words. Lady Leviathan extends a tentative limb, gently wiping away the sailor flesh still hanging from the corner of Ianthe's mouth. She brings it to her lips, licking her tentacle clean. The taste is all the sweeter for having touched Ianthe.

Two blushing dots of blue return, but it's not just Ianthe's cheeks that illuminate from within. It's her chest and tail too. The scent in the water changes. In the wake of victory and survival, there's a certain...lust for life. Lady Leviathan has beheld it many times, this most intimate celebration. It's the way of nature.

Another kind of hunger blooms from the mermaid.

It makes the longing deepen. Lady Leviathan wants to touch her again, but she's not sure she should. The mermaid owes her nothing. Not her gratitude. Not her touch. The last thing Lady Leviathan wants is for Ianthe to think she does.

Uncertainty flashes in all five of the kraken goddess's golden eyes. It's strange seeing such vulnerability in a divine being, but it's electrifying too.

Even if this want between them is just convenient proximity and a diversion, Ianthe is thrilled to have captured her notice.

It will be an exercise in creativity, whatever comes next, but if the goddess wants to tangle tails... or, well, tails and tentacles, who is Ianthe to deny them both that pleasure? Ignoring bodily urges and impulses is not the seafolk way. Not when nothing is promised. Not tomorrow. Not even the next moment.

Ianthe swims to the Great Devourer's face. All five of the goddess's glowing eyes nervously track her ascent. To think, *Ianthe*, the tiny creature that she is, makes the great and glorious Twenty-Armed Goddess bashful. Perhaps not even time whittles away all shyness.

There's an intoxicating power that comes with that knowledge. It's not something she's ever considered herself. Strong? Yes. Resilient? Also, yes. Powerful? No.

She places kisses between the goddess's furrowed brow, and crease by crease, she soothes away the tension, the hesitation. Warmth blooms between them. With it comes quiet understanding and need.

Hand over hand, Ianthe slides bodily down the length of the kraken beauty's nose, peppering more kisses, delighting in the delicious friction of skin against skin. Pleasure spikes as her tail crests over the bump centered along the slope.

The Great Devourer's eyes flutter. She lifts a claw, delicately running the smooth rounded back down the length of Ianthe's body, from the nape of her neck to the tips of her fins. She repeats the motion again and again, and under the caress, Ianthe's body comes alive, purring with desire. It's then the seam at the front of her tail parts, revealing dewy pink flesh that's begging to be plundered.

Ianthe pushes down, curling her tail underneath the goddess's chin to keep herself anchored. If there's a greater display of trust than this, hovering before the mighty kraken's mouth, she can't think of it. She traces a hand along the goddess's full lower lip, so plush and soft to the touch. She follows it with another kiss. Much in the ocean is made of hard edges. Barnacles and stone. Claws and sharp teeth. But not this. Not her.

The goddess's lips part and the very tip of her tongue emerges to lick

Ianthe's tail. She concentrates on Ianthe's exposed pink seam, rubbing tight, roving circles. Losing herself to the bliss of it, Ianthe rocks against her, steady as the waves. Despite the goddess's assurances, maybe she has died and gone to the hereinafter. This feels too good to be anything else, and yet she can't find it in herself to care. It's the sweetest dream at the end of a long nightmare.

Whether it's the exhaustion or the days of desperation and near death, Ianthe's body succumbs quickly, spasming and coating the goddess's tongue with her tide. She heaves a sigh of relief, luxuriating in goddess's warmth and bioluminescent light.

A tentacle tenderly strokes her cheek. "Did that feel good, my little treasure?"

Ianthe sleepily peers up into the goddess's eyes. There's a quiet heat there, and Ianthe can already tell she won't ask for what she needs in return. "Beyond measure. And now it's your turn."

Beneath the heat, curiosity flickers.

Their size difference does present a challenge, but Ianthe is nothing if not adaptable. One does not live in the abyssalpelagic zone and not also pick up a penchant for ingenuity along the way.

Determined, Ianthe scales down the front of the goddess, pillowing her body against one of her large, ample breasts. She kisses along a nipple, licking and flicking her tongue against the bud, and uses both hands to knead and tug it into a stiff peak. The goddess sighs, a rush of bubbles emitting from her mouth. "You're a wonder." Her voice rumbles beneath Ianthe, warm and thick with desire. It's a vibration she feels down to her very bones.

"I've only gotten started."

Ianthe dives. She weaves between the Great Devourer's tentacles, navigating the massive, swaying limbs, searching for the goddess's most precious treasure. *Her pearl.* She finds the sensitive nub of flesh at the apex of her tentacled limbs, beneath a delicate hood. Careful not to prick the goddess with her sharp claws, Ianthe kisses and rubs her hands and body against it. It's unlike anything she's ever done before. Past mating frenzies were all undertaken with her own kind.

Pleasuring the goddess demands every single inch of her, and she's not sure she has any energy left to give, but it's worth it to feel the mighty being quake.

All around her the goddess trembles. Her limbs thrash uncontrollably, churning sea. Like seismic activity it creates waves and changes currents. Ianthe clings on for dear life. If she moves, she may be crushed. While it would be a legendary way to die, she's hoping to live long enough to do this again. One or two or maybe three times more.

Just when Ianthe thinks her arms will give out, the goddess seizes. A jet of ink squirts from her center, pluming the water. The shaking stops.

Utterly spent, Ianthe releases her hold on the goddess's pearl, drifting aimlessly through the water, through the ink. She smiles though, more than a little proud of herself. *Another victory.*

The goddess gently cups her in a hand, singing her praises as she draws her back up. Being beheld by the Great Devourer's array of eyes no longer terrifies, not when nothing but warmth awaits her. She rewards Ianthe with nuzzles and more kisses to her tail. She's not done until she brings Ianthe to pleasure two more times, each climax more intense than the last.

Ianthe does not complain. Not one bit.

CHAPTER
FOUR

O nce sated in an entirely different way, Lady Leviathan and Ianthe turn back to the remaining sailors, working together to harvest and wrap the leftover meat in scraps of net. Though Lady Leviathan's stomach still twists with hunger—twenty surface dwellers are but a snack for a creature her size—Ianthe's family needs this feast more. Hunger after a routine hibernation does not compare to starvation.

Lady Leviathan has more than enough limbs to carry the load, but Ianthe insists on towing some of the meat they gathered. It's a victory meant to be shared, and a point of pride not returning home empty-handed. She wouldn't deny the mermaid anything, much less this.

Guided by the calm, easy pulse of Ianthe's blue light, Lady Leviathan follows her into the deep. The mermaid leads her into the abyssalpelagic zone to a cluster of sea caves, whose many entrances pockmark an underwater cliff face. Happy, jubilant song erupts from Ianthe at the sight of her home. It's nothing like the seductive crooning her kind use to lure lonely, touch-starved sailors. It's merry and playful meant for family and friends.

Lady Leviathan hangs back, dimming her light to a slow, soothing blink. It's the most she can do to make herself unobtrusive as one of the largest beings to ever exist.

Merfolk dart out from the cave mouths. There's maybe one hundred merpeople swirling through the water, around Ianthe, in a mesmerizing dance of multi-colored light—gold, amber, green, blue, and even some red. Relief floods the water. Joyful song too. A loved one they believed to be lost has returned, and for one long beautiful moment, it outshines even a kraken goddess's mighty presence.

But only a moment.

Creatures of the deep can't afford to be oblivious to their surroundings for long. The merfolk pod startles when they finally take notice of her, a cascade of panicked flashing lights rippling inward. Before their fear can fester, Ianthe proudly declares, "We've brought a feast!"

Lady Leviathan smiles and releases the sailor meat. "Please, eat your fill."

One by one, their light settles. The offering and Ianthe's fearlessness diffuses their fear. In its place, there's an uproar of cheerful cries, followed by much bowing, many honorifics and an abundance of gratitude.

"Please," Lady Leviathan gently interrupts, tipping her head. "You've waited long enough."

The merfolk need no more convincing. They descend upon the meat in a swarm, jaws closing around limbs, claws tearing away fistfuls of flesh. They feed the littlest ones first, the infirm, and the old. Even starving, they think of their most vulnerable.

There's a desperation to the pod's hunger that fans the flame of Lady Leviathan's rage. It never should have come to this. Food scarcity is nothing new, nor survival of the fittest, but greed has fractured the circle of life.

Ianthe leaves her kin to their feasting, coming to perch on Lady Leviathan's shoulder. The sea-maiden leans against her neck, sighing. She feels it too. Lady Leviathan can sense her emotions. Underneath the relief and momentary triumph, anger still lurks. Shipwrecking together was only a momentary release.

Surface dweller greed drove Ianthe's family to this ravenous desperation, and it will drive them there again, for as long as those land-loving creatures continue taking far more than the ocean can give. "This is just the first step," Lady Leviathan says. "Today is about surviving. About regaining our strength."

"I know." She feels Ianthe's nod against her skin. A beat passes. "I think we should go back."

Lady Leviathan tenderly traces a claw along Ianthe's arm. "Go back?"

"To the net. I don't want to leave our own behind."

Ah. The floating graveyard. All the creatures denied their Final Fall. Grief sweeps through Lady Leviathan, but determination does too. She hears what Ianthe doesn't say, that the tangled dead deserve dignity and peace. "It's a risk, but I think you're right. Something must be done, and it's a risk I'm willing to take. Are you ready to face the net again?"

Ianthe hugs herself, shoulders drooping. "I don't know. My heart knows it's the right thing to do, but...what if we get caught? What if we die?"

"Then we do it together." She cradles the mermaid's cheek. "Neither of us will be alone."

Tears slip down the mermaid's cheeks in blue bioluminescent rivulets.

"But..." Lady Leviathan gently catches one on the tip of her tentacle, round as a pearl. "We're going to be very careful, okay? Death is not a given."

Ianthe swipes away her tears and nods. "Not a given."

Lady Leviathan isn't brave, not when living billions of years makes Death feel distant, even after witnessing today's horrors. But this little mermaid is.

Once everyone's bellies are full and the leftover meat is stored, Ianthe asks her pod for help, and she only needs to ask once. Many volunteer.

This time Lady Leviathan leads the way, now that she knows what to look for. Ianthe and a contingent of merfolk follow close behind. Between the rotted stench and dark silhouettes of suspended carcasses, she has ample warning and stops beyond the outer rim, close enough to touch at arm's length, but not close enough to be ensnared.

Grief is a heavy tide that sweeps through the merfolk pod. This is something they've seen many times before, and yet even as their sorrow quietly seeps into the water and their eyes dim to shades of gray and white, they brighten the bioluminescent nodes along their bodies to full strength. No explanation is needed. It makes them more visible in the dark water and thus easier to keep track of one another during the dangerous work ahead.

Lady Leviathan secures a section of net using eighteen of her arms and dismantles the dreadful thing piece by piece with the remaining two. Ianthe stays close by her side, never straying far, and though the mermaid's hands tremble as she works to disentangle the dead, she stubbornly pushes on.

Merfolk carry away the shreds, pick apart knots, and slice free the smaller creatures ensnared in its cruel web. It's a slow, risky process for them all, but the merfolk are determined to do what's right. Hours pass. The sun dips toward the horizon.

Ianthe and her kin sing a mournful tune as they work, and the sound carries far and wide. Some miles away a whale pod joins, their deep, sorrowful song adding perfect harmony. It's so hauntingly beautiful it makes the fine hairs on Lady Leviathan's arms stand on end and her skin pebble.

Tears sting her eyes. For a time, it's the only sound she hears.

As they sing, they cut away those denied their Final Fall one by one, allowing their bodies to sink into the deep.

Finally free.

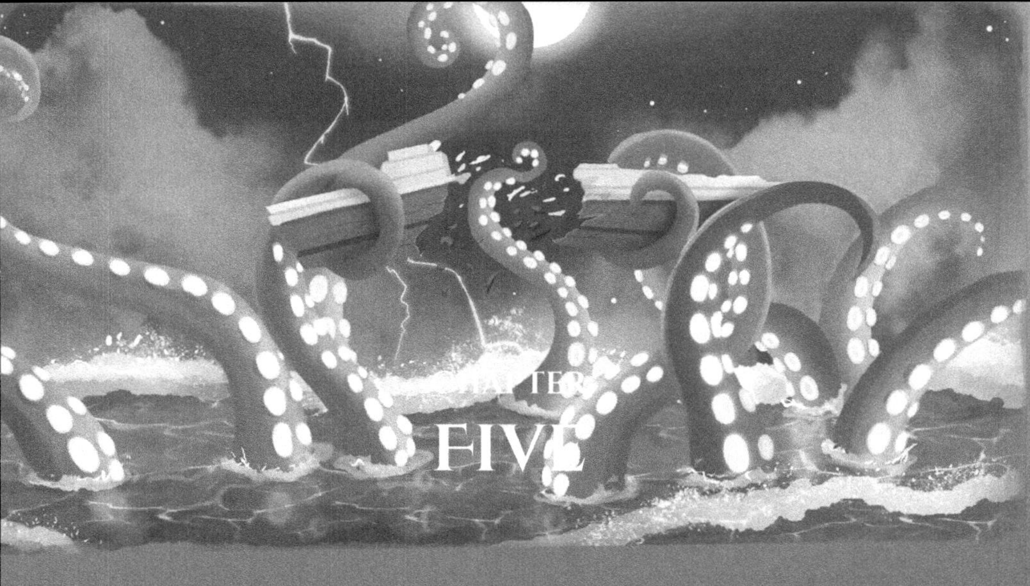

Another vessel chugs overhead. Until it doesn't. The Great Devourer rips it in two, using all twenty of her arms. Shipwrecking is quickly becoming a favorite shared pastime. "A lot has changed since I was last awake," the kraken goddess comments, all five eyes watching pensively as one half of the ship sinks into the deep. The other half remains curled in her tentacles.

Ianthe and her kin make quick work of the sailors, cutting off one bubbling cry after the next. As they harvest the fresh meat, Ianthe wonders what the goddess will take next as a trophy for her crown.

They're nearly finished with their task when the Great Devourer rips off the ship's propeller and affixes it to her temple. It reminds Ianthe of a flower, a pretty thing that only grows on land and that her shallow water kin sometimes weave into their hair.

The second half of the ship follows the first, no longer needed, groaning all the way into the dark abyss.

When the goddess doesn't say anything more, Ianthe replies, "This is all I've ever known. But our elders say the same. Mighty storms and the raging sea just don't keep the surface dwellers away anymore. I wish I was alive to see the days when it did."

Maybe the Great Devourer can make this wish come true now that she's returned. Ianthe slings a makeshift sack of meat over her shoulder and gestures for her kin to go on without her. She wants these next moments alone with the goddess.

After the toils of the day, the pod makes the dive home without protest.

Once they're too far away to hear, the Great Devourer says, "I don't know what can be done to reverse the damage already done. The poisoned water, the noise—but I wouldn't be much of a goddess if I allowed the surface dwellers to continue unchallenged."

"No one creature can tackle this problem alone, not even the Twenty-Armed Goddess herself," Ianthe grins, nudging one of the legendary being's many arms. "We'll find a way forward, together." It starts right here. Right now. "All of us will."

A chilling, conspiratorial smile graces the goddess's fang-filled maw, in complete contrast to the gentle way in which she curls a tentacle around Ianthe's hand, squeezing it lightly. "Join me, Ianthe. Let us remind them what it is to fear the sea."

Ianthe's own smile stretches past her eyes. It's the thing of surface dweller nightmares; they always scream when she smiles. "I'm your avenging warrior, Great Devourer," she says with a bow.

"Still so formal," Lady Leviathan admonishes. *Too formal.* Especially after the intimacy they shared. When Ianthe says *Great Devourer*, it's meant more as an honorific than as a statement of fact or a name. And that just won't do.

Not only does Lady Leviathan need to prove she's still worthy of her titles, there's also a propulsive desire to hear how her name sounds on

Ianthe's tongue. She cups the mermaid's cheek, watching her charming blue flush reappear.

All three of Lady Leviathan's hearts flutter; it's quickly becoming a mainstay response to the deep-sea maiden, and she finds she quite enjoys the feeling of excitement bubbling within her. They might not make it very far into the deep if another mating frenzy takes hold.

"For you, it's just Lady Leviathan."

"Lady Leviathan," Ianthe repeats, bioluminescence sparkling. "What do you need me to do?"

There's much she wants from the mermaid. Companionship. Affection. Discovery. More intrepid touch. That will all follow in due time. For now, there's work to do.

"Help me bring forth all the greatest terrors of the sea."

The mermaid's smile is a ghastly rictus of sharp teeth, and Lady Leviathan has never seen anything more beautiful. "With pleasure."

ABOUT DESIRÉE M. NICCOLI

Desirée M. Niccoli writes a blend of adult romance and cozy horror, featuring monsters, villains, and the supernatural, often served with (mostly) emotionally intelligent characters and heart.

She lives the nomadic military life with her husband and two cats Pawdry Hepburn and Puma Thurman. Although born and raised in Pittsburgh, Desirée has since lived in coastal Maine (where her spooky heart truly lies), Maryland, and Connecticut.

Learn more at dmniccoli.com.

PSYCHOPOMP IN BLOOM

HOLLY ROSE

CHAPTER ONE

ᚠᛉᚠᛡᛗ

Edict Two: Comfort the souls you ferry across.

The veil parts, and I step onto the freeway through smoke and a steady rain. The stench of burnt metal stings my nose, and ᚦᛝᚠᛡᛝ appears beside me in his black suit, our uniform of sorts. Before us, cars are twisted, over-turned, and broken in the chaotic aftermath of a multi-car crash.

I know where my assignment is, but the pain and fear and sorrow of all the humans here makes me unsteady on my feet, makes me wish I could go to all of them to lessen their pain. But like most of the Elders, ᚦᛝᚠᛡᛝ seems unaffected. He even smiles at me.

"Always good to see you, ᚠᛉᚠᛡᛗ," he says. Sirens wail as he slicks back his wet, black hair, tucking it behind his ears. "A lot of car crashes lately." He looks up to the gray skies, one blue eye open and the other squinting against the rain. "Humans struggle to control their vehicles on these wet roads."

"More opportunities for us to serve." It's crass in the face of such suffering, but I believe it to be what Φ≒†∞ꝯ expects me to say.

He nods. The car beside us explodes into an orange fireball in my peripheral vision, illuminating the dim morning and reflecting off the arriving emergency vehicles. Φ≒†∞ꝯ and I mark it, but the heat and flames pass across us like a breeze.

He lifts his chin to me before turning toward it. "I'm a bit late on mine. Better nip him across. Want to join me later on the waves?"

"Maybe." My assignment is taking her last breaths in the crunched-up car ten feet ahead of me, and my hands stuff into my pockets to tumble through my collection of human oddments. I feel called to comfort my souls *before* they pass—not everyone's interpretation of Edict Two—but I don't want to offend Φ≒†∞ꝯ by rushing off. "I'll let you know," I say quickly but carefully.

He nods and turns, and I slip in and out of the veil to move faster into my assigned soul's sightline. I occasionally enjoy surfing on the humans' ocean with Φ≒†∞ꝯ—after all, he's my closest compeer. But like all my compeers, he is an Angel and not a soul like me. And because he's been on assignment for millennia longer than I have, our duties are quotidian to him. Unmiraculous.

But every summons is a chance for me to learn more about these remarkable beings.

Like 82.5% of my assignments thus far, my dying human and her periphery are covered in her bright red blood. My fingers twitch, longing to drag through the crimson liquid, to study that which I declined for myself ages ago. To understand what holds these ephemeral marvels together. And why the red blood must be inside their bodies for them to be alive, and how, whenever it escapes its bounds and flows freely, they die. How does it all work? And why do they struggle against death?

Why do they struggle against everything?

Her eyes are closed, and her breathing is labored and diminishing. This one has many, many etheric cords in shining golds, bronzes, and silvers emanating from her head and belly, disappearing in the distance to connect to other souls. She has loved deeply and has been loved well. I smile softly and lay my hand against her aura, near her arm. "All is well, Chantelle," I say quietly.

Her eyes flutter open and blink slowly at me. They are large and brown, full of fear and fierceness, denial and such regret it makes my chest hurt. Her head shakes, *no.* "No," she says, laying her head back and shutting her eyes tightly.

I send some of Our Heavenly Mother's gentle comfort toward her soul, and her shoulders relax. "You are loved, Chantelle, and you are safe. I am here. I won't leave you."

I feel her soul acquiesce and let go. Her heartbeat goes silent, and her spirit's eyes open, superimposed upon her body's closed eyes. They are large and brown too, and they focus on me. So many human-experienced souls come back to their true life in this way, unwilling to leave their carbon forms behind.

Is it because they've forgotten where they began? Or does something they leave behind transcend whatever memories they may have of their true home beyond the veil?

Why do they cling so tightly to pain when paradise awaits?

"All is well, Chantelle," I repeat, holding my soft smile. I reach my hand toward her, and she looks at it, takes it. Relief releases a breath from my chest. I dread the day a soul refuses my hand.

Her spirit stands with me, and her gaze passes across the grotesque scene around us and her own body lying at her feet. "It's over?"

"Yes, it's over. You have done so well." I don't know whether she means the wreck or her time on Earth, but both are over. Her sorrowful eyes pull at my heart, and I squeeze her hand and transfer a modicum of heavenly peace to her, though not enough to muddle her thinking. "Your mother, Georgia, and your brother, James, are waiting for you." I gesture to the light pouring from the veil that ⦶⇌ǂ∞♁ and his soul have just gone through and congratulate myself for speaking those human familial relations—*mother, brother*—correctly. "You lived a beautiful life, and now it's time to rest. Are you ready to go home?" I hold my breath, remembering to smile with my eyes and raise my eyebrows to convey excitement like I've seen humans do.

But her expression clouds over, and she shakes her head. "No. No, my father. He lives alone. I have to tell him. I have to let him know I'm going." Her eyes plead with me.

I bite my lip. There are only four edicts to being a psychopomp, and technically, letting her tell her father goodbye doesn't break a single one. Rather, it cracks one of the not-quite-edicts, the prudent guidelines the Elders formulated over millennia for ferrying souls through the veil. I should know—I have them all inscribed in the notebook I carry inside my suit jacket's pocket.

On the other hand, souls with hurt-ties to people they leave behind or things they've left undone can have trouble transitioning, and I don't want that for Chantelle. And she hasn't technically crossed the veil yet.

Heavenly beings don't dance upon the head of a pin, but sometimes their decisions do.

"Of course." We slip through time and space like thought and reappear in a bedroom where an old man with hair as brown as hers sleeps in the still-early morning hours. I breathe a sign of relief; dream vision is an ephemeral gray area, and even less of a potential violation.

She leans over the bed, her hand grasping mine tightly like a lifeline. "Daddy, I was in an accident," she begins.

He can't hear her, of course. She won't learn how to communicate with him herself until she reconnects with Our Heavenly Mother across the veil. But I let her speak, and I send a vision-Chantelle into her father's dreams to communicate her words: she's okay, she's sorry she's gone, she loves him, and he'd better take good care of himself because she wants to be with him soon, but not *too* soon.

Transmuting Chantelle's message into dream vision has me aching both with the effort and with the heavy, messy, exquisite tangle of her human love, which can only ever be vicarious for me. I deliver it all safely to her father's soul, leaving myself a clean slate.

She turns and smiles at me. "I'm ready now."

With my free hand, I gesture to open the veil and commute Chantelle across into the waiting arms of her earth brother and her...I pull out my notebook and check my notes. Her *mother*. That's the word I'm always forgetting, as it sounds so close to *brother*.

My task complete, I withdraw from the joyful homecoming to record the mission in my notebook. I've recorded every one since my first, even though I'm not required to. I write Chantelle's father's name and location, too. Will he remember the dream? How will he mark her passing?

I write the slender words, *"Chantelle LeBlanc: mourning ceremony?"* I've never been to one—I believe they are called *funerals*. Being around that much human grief has seemed far heavier than I can bear. Much like I chose not to live a human life out of fear for what I might suffer.

I'm nothing like Chantelle. She was so brave.

But the longer I stare at the words I've just written, the thicker my throat feels. Grief will be there, but so will love—the kind I have excluded myself from. Maybe I will go to her mourning ceremony and be brave in this small way, for Chantelle.

And perhaps, a little for me.

A soft chime snags my attention. With one last glance at Chantelle smiling transcendentally, wrapped in the glory of both human and heavenly love, I sigh. Envious? Perhaps. When you've spent the ages meditating in a near-nascent state, you have precious few compeers who even notice if you're around, even after working with them for a few decades. No one misses me when we're apart. No one, save Our Heavenly Mother, loves anyone as fiercely as humans love each other and their animals.

What must that be like? To love and be loved in that reckless, messy way?

I sigh and slip my black notebook back into my jacket pocket. Not much sense in meditating on that. I made my choice eons ago.

A second chime rings again from nowhere and everywhere, and I duck between the veil toward my next assignment.

CHAPTER

TWO

SUNNY

Today's boutonnières: a cornflower for love and hope; yellow statice for optimistic remembrance; yellow craspedia (Billy buttons) for good health, and rosemary for honoring (or contacting) the dead.

July in small town Elysian Fields, Louisiana is no joke, and not the slightest breeze disturbs the sun blazing down from a clear blue sky. It radiates off the open metal back doors of my delivery van as I vigorously—and ineffectively—fan myself while sweat drips down my back.

I've got the casket cascade, two memorial vases, the three standing sprays...what am I missing? I run my hand down the front of my dress. "My apron!" I close the doors, and the two halves of my cheerful "Sunny Day Flower Shop" logo reunite.

I rush back inside. The coolness of my shop is as refreshing as a bubble gum snowball, but I don't get to stay here long. My apron's on the counter, right where I left it. I carefully zipper its pocket closed that holds the boutonnières and mini bouquets I made to give away to mourners I encounter today—my way of bringing a light to their dark day. I double-check that I put out the incense on my altar to Áine (a girl's gotta look for love any way she can), lock up my shop, rush into the driver's seat of my van, and lay the apron carefully across the passenger seat.

The A/C finally starts making a dent in the heat when I arrive at All Saints Church. A look in the mirror reassures me that my makeup isn't dripping down my face, and then I take a deep breath. I got into this business for the happy events—weddings, birthdays, graduations, just-because surprises. Making flowers for funerals always makes me sad.

"Business is business," I murmur to myself as I tie on my apron. Maybe I'll get myself some ice cream on the way back to the shop to cheer me up. It's definitely an extra rainbow sprinkles kind of day.

I bring the casket cascade in first as my small way of honoring the deceased, Chantelle LeBlanc, the daughter of the man who hired me. I arrange the cascade as lovely as I can around the photo of the middle-aged woman—gosh, she had the loveliest brown eyes. And then I drop onto the kneeler by the casket. It never seems right to drop flowers off and leave without acknowledging the life of the person who's passed. I clasp my hands together and close my eyes. *God—or Goddess, I'm really not sure. Or maybe you're gender fluid? Actually, that makes the most sense. Anyway, please look after Chantelle and all her loved ones. I know today will be hard for everyone who loves her, but please let it bring them closure and peace. All blessings for the highest good.*

It's early yet for the service, and back outside, the parking lot is still empty of mourners as I go back to the van for my next load of flowers.

These standing sprays are almost as curvaceous as me, and while I'm carrying them, they're nearly my height, too. I try to look around the froth of lilies to be sure I don't run into someone, but the toe of my heeled sandal catches in a crack of the walkway. I crash to the ground on top of the standing spray—my hands in the grass and my right knee biting concrete.

"Ouch, ouch, ouch, ouch!" My high-pitched squeals are mercifully drowned by church bells as I try to push myself up off my belly, but stems are snapping under me and a breeze ruffles my skirt up over my ass. I pull my skirt down and sit back without doing more damage to the very expensive flowers. My hands are shaking from the pain in my wrists and my knee. Tears blur my vision. I dust my hands off and wipe my eyes on the edge of my apron. There's blood all over my skirt and the flowers from a big gash in my knee. Thank all that's holy no one was here yet to witness my wipeout.

"All is well…"

My heart kicks into my throat at the deep voice that belongs to the man whose shadow I'm bleeding and crying in. I look up into the warmest brown eyes I have ever seen in the face of the most beautiful man I've ever seen. He's all darkness and light, if that makes sense. His eyes and hair and suit, dark. His skin pale, pale, pale, like he's never dreamed of the sun.

I don't know why, but I feel overwhelmingly safe now that he's here.

His hand is stretched toward me, but under his dark beard, his expression looks more puzzled than mine must've looked in high school chemistry. His gaze drops to my bloody knee, to the church bell tower, then back to me.

"Oh! Thank you." I slip my little hand into his big one, and the contact with him is almost electric. His face softens to the gentlest expression of interest, and he pulls me up stronger than I expect. I stumble toward him and set my hand on his chest to keep from body-slamming him. His eyebrows go up, but he doesn't let go of my hand. In fact, his thumb rubs across it in the softest caress.

And I'm here for it. I'm almost dizzy in his heavenly roses-and-incense scent and the allure of touching this preternaturally beautiful man. His thumb stills, and we stare at each other for a couple of heartbeats. He's almost too beautiful to be real. His features are chiseled, his eyes are soulful, he's tall, and his well-muscled body is clad in a posh black suit. In fact, he's fine as hell, and my cheeks—already stinging and no doubt red with heat— sting harder. I want to crawl into the earth with embarrassment that he saw me fall.

"You're…alive," he says slowly, still looking utterly perplexed. His accent is strange, but beautiful.

I take my hands back and laugh. Laughing's what I do when I'm mortified, and honestly his delivery was so dry. "Shocking, I'm sure, after the spill I took." My hands go to my hair, my dress, anything to put myself back together under the weight of that intense gaze. I'm not rattled easily, but my witchy senses, such as they are, are tingling. Something is off about this guy...but for once, with a strange man, it's in a good way.

He points to my knee. "But you're bleeding."

I look down. My blood's plastering my skirt to my knee and smudging everywhere. What a way to make a first impression. "It's a lot," I allow, "but I'm pretty sure I still have more inside my body than out, so I'll live." I smile up at him, hoping my lame joke is the coin to buy me a glimpse of what he looks like smiling.

It's slow like a sunrise, tilting up his full lips then moving north to crinkle his eyes. His gaze takes in my hair, my face, down my breasts and hips—holy Hekate, goosebumps everywhere—and back to my bloody knee. He drops to a crouch, and one hand clamps cooly against my calf. In the other is somehow a gleaming white handkerchief he's pulled out like a magician. "It's a lot of blood," he says, and he starts to wipe it.

"Bro!" I wrest the handkerchief from him. I know my blood is clear of pathogens, but he doesn't. Gorgeous dummy. "I'll get it." I sink down on a nearby bench and take up the task.

He crouches in front of me, so close. His dark eyes snap to mine, and his lips part. The wildest image of climbing into his lap and pushing him to the ground sends thrills through my core.

His pale face blushes, and I blush back harder.

He licks his full lips. "Are you certain you're okay?"

"I'm totally fine." I dig in my apron for bandages. "The flowers, though. Ugh. They're probably ruined. Mr. LeBlanc paid so much for them, and I used my last stock of stargazers."

He turns his head slowly toward the standing spray splayed face down on the concrete. "Stargazers?" His gaze briefly tilts to the sky, then back to the flowers. "Chantelle's father bought these?" He rises and sets the standing spray upright, its back to me, as I locate two woebegone My Little Pony bandages in my apron. While I strategize and place them to cover as much of my gash as possible, he starts fiddling with the front of my flower display.

"Oh...please don't—"

"They don't appear to be ruined," he says, taking no note of me and continuing to poke at them.

I rush to my feet and stuff the bloody handkerchief in my dress pocket. "Hey, I said please don't mess—" I peer at the standing spray, and not a flower appears broken despite the array of petals on the ground. "How...?"

It doesn't make any sense. I look from the flowers to him. His Adam's apple bobs, and his wide eyes slide to me. His guilty, angelic face gives me the ridiculous idea that he's somehow repaired the damages. That he's some sexy fae lord with mysterious flower powers.

Sign me up.

"Oh, um. Wow." I laugh nervously. "How did I get so lucky that the flowers I felt break under me aren't broken?"

He swallows hard again, and his head turns as he looks at the church.

Mortification sears through me, leaves me pathetic and small. I'm a dumbass.

This beautiful man is a mourner. Here I am thinking goofy paranormal romance thoughts and babbling about flowers when someone he loves is lying dead in a casket not fifty feet away.

"I'm so sorry for your loss," I rush out. "Were you close to Chantelle?"

He cocks his head and scratches his beard as those eyes come back to me. "We, eh, took a short trip together."

I nod and unzip my apron. Somehow, my little gratis flowers are perfectly fine. I pluck a particularly nice boutonnière from the pocket and hold it up. "Would you like a flower for your lapel?"

He looks down at the flower and up to me even faster. "What's that?"

"Just a small gift, but I hope it brightens what must be a difficult day." I pull the pin loose from the boutonnière and hold the flowers against his lapel, the blue cornflower and yellow Billy balls bright against the black. "May I?"

He freezes. Nods. I pin the boutonnière on and smooth the fabric. The pungent rosemary scents the air between us.

"Thank you..." He cocks his head.

I smile bigger and stick my hand out for him to shake. "I'm Sunny Day, same name as my shop." His eyes follow my gesture toward the van. "My parents thought they were funny, I guess."

He looks down at my hand and shakes it. But he doesn't offer his name back. My heart sinks. I know a funeral is the worst place to flirt, but wow there was definitely some sparking happening here. Past him, I see mourners walking inside.

"I'd better finish setting the flowers out." I pull his ruined handkerchief from my pocket and hold it briefly between us. "I'm sorry about your nice handkerchief, but I'm sure you don't want it back with all my blood on it. I'll clean it up, and maybe I'll see you again." I shove it back into my pocket and smile, lifting up the standing spray.

"Maybe," he says. He stays where he is as I walk past him and into the church. The air conditioning is such a relief after wilting in the heat all that time. I set the standing spray near the casket, give my regards and a boutonnière to Mr. LeBlanc and a few other mourners, and head back out for more flowers. Tall, Dark, and Slightly Spooky is nowhere in sight on my last trip into the church. The disappointment settles in my chest like a weight, and it feels a bit like longing.

CHAPTER
THREE

0⋟ƒ÷⛭

Not-Quite-Edict One: Only interact with living humans if you are assigned to ferry them.

Sunny Day picks up her flowers and walks away. I slip into the cloak of the veil where I should have stayed. My human-like heart is pounding, and my feet are still rooted to the sidewalk. Her hips sway beneath the silky fabric of her dress as she walks away, and the sunlight on her pale red hair turns it golden.

I shouldn't have been watching her at all. But the moment I saw her exquisite beauty framed by the white flowers she carried and the green trees beyond, I couldn't take my eyes off her. Then the church bell sounded so much like a summons, and she fell. Her bright red blood was outside of her body, and I didn't think, I just...

My chest is buzzing, and I feel faint. I appeared to a human who wasn't dying, to a soul who wasn't assigned to me. At least, not yet. I had fully broken a Not-Quite-Edict. I had touched the shockingly soft, warm flesh of a human soul lit with a human life. I can't get enough air in, and I didn't think I even needed air to survive.

Her eyes were the green of sea foam, her skin pink and speckled with brown dots, her hair like the first luminous orange of an Earthen sunset. I've had this almost-human body for a few decades and I thought I knew it well. But new sensations are fluttering in my belly and aching in my groin. I press my hand over my hammering heart, which had only ever beat slowly and steadily before.

What had Sunny Day done to me?

She walks back out from a different exit than she entered and past me, her eyes scanning around the trees and parking lot and straight through where I hide in the veil. She walks even with me and I feel the primal heat of her body. My hand raises on its own toward her soft skin. The breeze carries her sweet scent to me as she passes—like the little red berries humans love...strawberries?—and all my symptoms increase.

She opens a door on her vehicle. I don't like that she drives one of those. They're too dangerous for such a lovely human. I step into the middle of the sidewalk. Should I follow her as she leaves and warn her? I don't want her exquisite life to extinguish too soon, and I cannot never see her again. But it doesn't seem right to follow her or speak to her again.

She walks toward me again with more flowers, and I freeze on the sidewalk, my chest throbbing so that I'm almost dizzy. As she comes closer and closer, she gazes all around, and a smile lights her face. What is she thinking of?

I am mesmerized and cannot move away in time. She steps *through* me, and the golden warmth of her body and soul living together infuse my form and soul with longing. I fall to my knees as she keeps walking. The high vibrations of the roses she carries shiver through me like delicious music.

I'm transformed. I cannot take my eyes off the vehicle for fear Sunny Day will leave, and I will never see her again. She comes out again, climbs into her bright blue vehicle. Its beast roars to life and it moves toward the parking lot's exit. I jump to my feet but cannot make myself follow her.

Sunny Day is not for me. I am here for Chantelle and her family, not for frivolous daydreams and rioting almost-human bodies. I stand and watch her vehicle until it turns a corner and away.

My thoughts chase behind her, but I scratch at an itch at my belly and go into the church.

As I predicted, the humans' grief pours over me like a wave at ⏀⇌ɬ∞♋'s beach, threatening to sink me under its weight. Human emotions are wilder and stronger than almost anything in the universe. But the memory of Sunny Day's smile ineffably buoys me. Chantelle's father embraces someone near the decorated box where Chantelle's past form lies. His grief is sharp as a sword, like a few others in the room, but most of the people here have a duller grief that aches and weighs in my chest.

I look down at my...*small gift*, as she called it. A blue-purple flower tied with ribbon to fragrant, pointy leaves and two kinds of yellow flowers. I've never been given a flower before, and I'm mesmerized. I carefully rub the soft, deep blue-purple petals between my fingers, run my fingertips across the spiky bits in the middle, which are surprisingly soft. The grief in the room lessens for me, as if the memory of Sunny Day has made something heavy, lighter.

An itch again at my stomach. Maybe something fell in my shirt when I stopped to help Sunny Day. I look down past her gift. The thinnest golden cord of energy is emitting from my belly.

All sound, all vision, all awareness shrinks to this focal point. An etheric cord leaves my belly and fades into the distance. My heart skips a beat as I lay my hand against the cord and *feel*. Sunny Day's bright being blossoms behind my closed eyes, the delicious aching that had thrummed through her body when I knelt before her surged into me again through the cord, waking up my human-like form with desire I've never felt before today. I open my eyes and follow the bright line of the cord for as long as I can see it, but I don't need anyone to tell me where it leads.

Or rather, to whom.

A chime sounds, and I step through the veil toward my next assignment quickly, as I always do. I comfort the dying man, he takes my hand, and I commute him across the veil to rejoin his wife and sister. I concentrate on each step, doing my duty to its fullest and most empathetic, trying to put Sunny Day from my mind, but the cord growing brighter from my belly quivers like a plucked harp string. And it will not be ignored.

CHAPTER

FOUR

SUNNY

Wedding party boutonnières: pink lisianthus for romance and appreciation; bluebells for everlasting love; and white phlox for unity and harmony.

It's been eight days, six anniversaries, one wedding, one funeral, and several birthdays, and I still can't get Tall, Dark, and Slightly Spooky out of my mind. And making these wedding boutonnières for a massive wedding party isn't *not* reminding me of him.

I also can't stop thinking about cornflowers. A legend says to place one in your pocket while you think of the one you desire. If the flower is wilted the next day, that love is not meant to be. But if the flower is still fresh, the love will last forever.

I bet his boutonnière wilted the moment after we met.

I sigh and stretch my back. I'm almost glad I didn't get his name, because then I would've Googled him, and that way madness lay. Even better, not knowing his name allowed me to pretend that the beautiful man with the soulful eyes was a ghost tragically bound to the church.

And honestly? That made a wild kind of sense. On my thirty-third birthday, I treated myself to a tarot reading to ask when I would find love, and the psychic pulled the Death card.

Despite the psychic explaining that the card was more about one phase ending and transforming into something new, I'd been laughing about that card for over a year—because yeah, my love life was pretty dead. I didn't meet a guy in college because I never went, I couldn't meet a guy around my small town because I'd already rejected most of these bozos in high school, and the dating apps were full of misogynists, serial one-night-standers, and a couple of exes who were *firmly* staying in the past.

So the possibility of the first guy I met in a long time who I was really interested in being a ghost was the most perfect explanation for my life. Because over the past week I thought more and more about meeting him. It was a good hair day, and my skin was all pink and glowy from the heat. I was quite simply, adorable as fuck.

He must've been deeply mourning, or married or gay or in a committed relationship of some kind that precluded asking beautiful redheads for their number. I snip the ribbon of the last boutonnière and set it carefully into its case. Committed relationship. That had to be it.

Or he was a ghost.

No. No, no, no. Because that would send me right back to the church hoping for a paranormal encounter of the sexy kind.

The bell over my door rings, and a familiar voice hails me. "Good afternoon, Sunshine!"

I smile up at my best and oldest customer—in both senses. "Hey, Bev!"

Bev comes closer, her pink pixie cut feathering back in the wind of her own making. "I had to come introduce you to my new friend." She turns around and reveals she's wearing a backpack. From inside of it, the tiniest, cutest, fluffiest orange tabby kitten peers out of a little window like a miniature astronaut.

"Beverly Angel Sweet! Who is this precious baby?" I jump up from around my table without taking my eyes off of him.

She laughs and shrugs her backpack off her petite, frail shoulders, setting it on a chair. "Sunny, may I introduce you to Sir Orpheus Puddin-paws." The little guy *mews* as she pulls him from the carrier and hands him unceremoniously to me. "He killed a roach for me last night, so he was knighted for his great service to the kingdom."

"As he should be!" He's all white whiskers and big blue eyes as I pull his warm little body closer and pet his soft little round head, which smells like Bev's French perfume. "You were so brave!" I coo to him. He *mews* at me and wiggles loose, Velcro-ing to my shirt and starting to climb. "Hey, now!" I unhook him and readjust. "When did you get him?"

Bev's watching like a proud mama and blotting the sweat from her face with a handkerchief. "Yesterday. My hairdresser's daughter rescued him from the street, and they were looking for a home for him." She's in her early eighties and my role model for growing old: sharp, active, and giving zero fucks about what anyone thinks of her. But she looks a little pale today, like the walk in from her house took more out of her than usual.

I pull a stool up to my counter. "Take a load off. Can I get you some water?"

"Thank you, baby, that sounds delicious." She pulls a prescription bottle from her backpack. "It's so hot out there."

I scurry to the back, and it takes me a minute to get to the last cold water bottle from an overstuffed flower fridge, especially with a squirmy baby cat in my hands. When I go back up front, she's behind my counter taking a seat on my stool, her usual spot.

I hand her the bottle. "Why don't you let me give you a ride home when you're ready? You don't need to be out here sweltering in this heat."

"No, no." She gulps back her medicine. "I need the exercise."

Orpheus chases the ribbon I'm dangling right into a pile of mail. Of course, one of my overdue bills is on top, this one from the electric company. Keeping flowers cold costs me a small fortune. I stuff it under the pile again before Bev's sharp eyes can spot it. I suspect she only buys flowers from me every week to try and help me out.

"I'm here to get my weekly flowers for Ginnie. Are you ready for it?"

I smile softly. Her eyes are as wistful as always as she mentions her late wife. I met them right after I opened when they came in looking for flowers for their twenty-fifth anniversary party and the two other intolerant asshole florists in town refused to serve them. And ever since Bev learned about the language of flowers, she's loved playing this game with me.

Orpheus is curled up against my chest, warm and purring. "Okay, but you distracted me with this little angel, so I may not be at the top of my game." I gently transfer the tiny one into Bev's hands and dust the fluff from my fingers. "What would you like to say today?"

She clears her throat. "I want to remind Ginnie how I loved playing with her. Whether it was a board game or a video game, or tennis, or even just goofing around at home..." Her voice wobbles a little, and her eyes shine. "I just miss playing with my Ginnie, and I hope she's up there thinking of all kinds of new ways to make me laugh when we're together again. She always could do that the best." Her smile beams at me through tears, like sunshine while it's raining.

I lean over the counter to grab her hand and squeeze it. "That's beautiful." I straighten and wipe a tear from under my own eye. "And I know she's doing just that."

"Well, go on," she sniffs. "Let me watch you work."

I gather supplies and flowers and come back to make the bouquet for her as I explain my selections. "Of course I'm starting with Ginnie's favorite."

"*Hydrangeas*," we say together.

"As a bonus, they mean that you're grateful for having her in your life." I cut extra leaves from the bottom portion of the stem and set the pink hydrangea into a working vase. "And pink because it's playful *and* Ginnie's favorite color."

"You always remember." Bev smiles, gently running her fingertip down Orpheus's nose over and over as he settles to sleep in her arms.

I pull two red tulips from the stack of flowers I'd brought to the counter. "These represent a perfect love, the warm memories of being together in those everyday moments. And I just happened to get these forget-me-nots in." I stick the little purple flowers into the arrangement. "They're saying, 'you better be up there thinking up new games for us to play.'"

Bev laughs quietly. "She better be."

"Of course she is! A lilac, which stands for youthful joy. That's the essence of play, in my book." Bev nods as I grab some sprigs of wax flowers. "And wax flowers as a filler, because they're pretty, and they represent a happy marriage."

"Oh, Sunny, it's perfect. Just beautiful."

"I'm glad you like it!" I make my final adjustments to the arrangement then tie a pink ribbon bow around the stems. I smile at Bev. Would I ever find a love like theirs?

The memory of the deep brown eyes and wistful, charming smile of the man at the church pulls at my belly and makes me warm all over, but I know better than to chase what isn't meant for me.

CHAPTER

FIVE

0⪢ƒ÷⋔

Edict One: Do not divulge heavenly truths to living humans.

At the same church where I met Sunny Day, I perch atop a cold stone sticking out of the ground with names and years engraved on it, hidden in the veil. Although I chose this spot to watch the parking lot, I realize I am staring at my flower again. It has been fifteen turnings of the Earth since the captivating human named Sunny Day gave me this precious gift.

And I have not been able to stop thinking of her.

The sound of a motor catches my attention. A blue van painted with a bright yellow sun is pulling into the lot. Excitement courses through my veins, and my heart lurches in my chest.

I don't decide to move, but suddenly I'm off the stone and my legs are pumping, bringing me closer to where Sunny Day is stepping from her vehicle, her luminous hair rivaling the morning sun. The cord connecting from my belly to hers shimmers and quivers in the early light, and Sunny Day is even more lovely than I remembered.

It doesn't seem right to do so, but I can't stop myself from hovering near her. She hums softly to herself and removes flower arrangements from her vehicle. When she walks past me, the air carries her sweet strawberry and musky human scent to me, and it makes my tongue long to taste her. The desire bewilders me.

I follow her all the way inside the building to be sure she doesn't fall again. She exchanges soft words with the people in the rooms inside and sets a cascade of blooms on top of the box that holds the earthly remains of Vincent, the man I ferried most recently. I stand near the doorway, watching her gracefully arrange the blooms, offer a small bundle of flowers to a woman dressed in black who is crying. Her kindness lights a soft smile to the woman's face, like a sunrise after a dark night.

She walks back toward me. I want to speak with her so badly I think my chest will burst open. But I shouldn't. I flee the building. But once I'm several yards across the lawn, I turn back and face the door. She will come out at any moment, and I want to talk to her.

Would it really be that wrong? I *could* be assigned to ferry her. One day.

That's enough for me.

I walk back toward the entrance, slip out from the veil within the shadow of a tree, and enter the building's vestibule. Sunny Day enters from the opposite way, and her gaze meets mine. She stops walking so suddenly that her hair and dress sway forward.

"Well, hello," she says, her eyes wide. She smiles quickly, as if she forgot to do it before, and buries her hands into her pockets.

"Hello," I repeat softly. We take more steps until we are only a few paces apart.

Her eyebrows come together. "I'm so sorry for your loss. You must be having an awful couple of weeks."

Before I can choose my words, her eyes drop to the flower she gave me. I smile, so proud that she's noticed I kept her gift. But her face transforms into confusion, and I shrink inside.

What did I do wrong?

"How do you still have this?" She gestures toward my flower.

"I like it," I answer. Does she think I would get rid of it?

She breathes out a quick, soft breath through her nose. "I'm glad you like it. But what I mean is, how is it not wilted by now? Did it dry that perfectly?" She peers closer and gently passes her fingertip across the biggest flower as softly as I often do. I suppress a desirous shiver as if she has touched me instead.

"That's crazy," she says. "It's completely fresh." She shakes her head, apparently disbelieving of what she has felt with her own fingertips.

Then her green-eyed gaze catches mine, and it has me snared. Fresh. Wilted. Dry. I cannot remember what any of these words mean at this moment. I cannot remember *any* words that belong to her time and place at this moment. Heat rushes up my neck and face.

Her eyes narrow and break the spell. My gaze wanders to a table not far from us and snags on flowers in a vase. Some of them look brown, their petals drooping, some fallen on the table. I've seen what the passage of time does to humans. It must act on flowers too. Panic wiggles in my chest, and my gaze slides back to her.

She cocks her head to the side. "This must be your favorite suit, too."

It's as if there is a feather in the air, wafting and drifting down on unseen currents, and our breaths are held as we wait to see where it lands.

She steps closer to me, and her warm presences envelops me. I inhale her scent greedily.

She gently touches the deep blue flower pinned to my suit. "You know, there's a legend about cornflowers…"

Cornflower. My beautiful flower has a name?

Her gaze is on the cornflower, and she says quietly, as if to herself, "I wonder what it means when it doesn't fade at all?"

My heart pounds as I watch the black fringes of her eyelashes flutter beneath her furrowed brows, but I say nothing. I do nothing. I'm afraid to scare her away with words I barely understand how to wield. Her green eyes meet mine, and I would gladly drown in their depths.

"Oh my goodness!" She says suddenly, pulling her hands away and weaving them across her chest as she steps back. She laughs softly and smiles at me. "What am I going on about? You probably went and got a new one."

That seems safe to agree to. Relieved, I blurt, "Yes," with a small smile to encourage her to keep talking. Every word that falls from her rosy lips is a gift more precious than my cornflower.

"I'm glad you liked it so much. You could've come by my shop. I would've happily made it for free, considering what you're going through." Her hand digs into a pocket of her apron. "I have a new one today. Would you like another to add to your collection?"

"Yes." Sunny Day is concerned for *what I'm going through*? No compeer —and certainly no human—has ever had concern for me before.

She begins to pin a new one beside the first one, a yellow flower surrounded by green leaves.

"Do all the flowers have names?" I ask.

She purses her lips as if holding back another of her sweet laughs as she looks up at me. "Oh, do you mean, do I know them? Of course I know them. Flowers are my life. This big yellow flower is a ranunculus, the leaves are willow eucalyptus, and the little white berries are hypericum."

I've never seen flowers growing like the ones she's gifted me, and I've been looking for the past fifteen days. "Where have you found them?"

She frowns briefly, considering my question. "Do you mean, where do I source them? They're all ethically sourced, most from the US since they can't travel too far."

I don't understand what she's saying, but having her stand so close and speak to me unlocks something in me. I breathe deeper and slower and let my affection and desire flow toward her like waves on the ocean.

"They're beautiful, like you." I almost whisper the words and maybe not even in a language she can hear or understand.

But her whole face lights up with a smile, and she tips it up toward me. Her eyes are both lit by the soft sunlight entering the high windows, and yet also, somehow, darker. She sways closer to me and lays her hand flat on my jacket. My hand raises to cover hers. It's as warm and soft as I remember, but even more thrilling to touch her a second time. Her eyes search mine, then her gaze drops to my mouth.

I have seen humans pressing their mouths together, sucking at each other's lips, eating without consuming. I know how my body is formed, and how hers is formed, and I know how they fit together, though I never expected to desire that joining so acutely. Her desire for me ensorcels, entreats. Mine for her surges forward, encircles, engages. Our yearning interplays in the scant space between us, and the very air is heavy with our aching.

Her pink, lush lips curve like a sacred fruit begging for my taste. They part, and her tongue slips across them as mine longs to do. I dip my head closer.

Too fast. She swallows and steps back, taking her hand back and shoving them both into pockets again. Her already pink skin darkens almost to the hue of her lips. "Are you…" She begins. Her hands come out of her pockets and move behind her head. She shakes her hair free, and I breathe in its strawberry scent, which lingers even after she fastens her tresses up behind her head again. "Um. Flowers. Do you need…do you need to get some? Is that why you're asking?"

"Yes." It's a promise of a future connection with her, and I grab onto it. Our nascent etheric cord is pulsing between us.

She brings both of her lips into her mouth, and her eyes dart away as she shifts back from me. "It's probably for your wife, huh? Or your girl-friend? Or…boyfriend."

Worry spikes. She's named close familial terms involving a special kind of love humans share. I blurt the first thing I can think of. "No, for my brother."

Her instant smile is surprised. "You need to buy flowers for your brother? That's kinda cool of you."

Heavens, I meant *mother*. "I mean, my mother."

"Okay," she says with a small laugh. "I'm great at putting flowers together for people's brothers or their moms." She pulls a rectangular piece of thick paper from her apron and holds it out to me. "Here's my business card. My name's on there. Sunny Day, in case you've forgotten."

"I could never forget." I take it gently from her hand, taking care not to touch her even though it's all I want to do. Her hands are beautiful, tipped with pink nails that sparkle. My eyes skim up her body, past the swell of her breasts, up her creamy skin, and to her eyes—she's been observing where my eyes have traveled, and the pooling of her desire perfumes the air between us.

"Aren't you going to tell me your name?" she asks.

My chest tightens. Angelic names are not pronounceable by human vocal cords. Just like that, every name of every human I've ever ferried leaves my brain. I look down. I see my flowers.

"Cornflower?" I blurt.

She laughs. "Your name is *Cornflower?*" She laughs harder still then narrows her eyes at me. "Okay, keep your secrets. I'll just call you Cor, how about that?"

That does sound more like a human name. "Yes, that's right. Cor." My heart feels so light, it may lift out of my chest. She's given me a human name, a thing I've never owned and never expected to want so badly as I love it now. A smile spreads over my face without my prompting. I love my new name. She's given me flowers and a name, and this golden etheric cord that is shining stronger and brighter with every passing moment.

I've never been so close to a life of my own.

"You are so weird," she laughs, "but you're very cute. Come to my shop anytime, okay?" She walks around me toward the door.

I'm cute? I spin around. "I will."

She turns and faces me as she pushes the door open. "You'd better," she says with a sly smile, and then she's gone.

CHAPTER
SIX

SUNNY

Green hydrangeas symbolize rebirth and good fortune, and baby's breath, loving dedication.

Thank the goddess I have a wedding deposit coming in a week, or I'd never keep the lights or the A/C on.

And thank the goddess I have a vibrator at home, because the gorgeous (not quite human?) man who told me his name was "Cornflower"—what was up with that?—nearly kissed me there in the vestibule of that little wooden church yesterday, and I almost jumped him like I'd hadn't been raised with the good sense not to fuck a stranger in a church. I cackle aloud to myself in my shop.

I shake my head to clear the "not quite human" thought away. He's probably just not from around here. "Yeah, not from anywhere *near* around here," I mumble to myself, but that's ridiculous. He's probably just from some tiny European city I've never heard of. But that doesn't explain why he's in my little town losing friends and loved ones left and right.

I finish making the list of my debts versus the sales I know to be incoming. It's a huge fucking difference, and not in a good way.

I close my notebook and rub my eyes. Maybe Cor is an eccentric millionaire who will come buy thousands of dollars' worth of flowers only to line his hotel room with them when he brings me there to both ravish and un-impoverish me. A girl can dream.

I'm engrossed with preparing a congratulatory bouquet when the smallest, gentlest tapping arrives, raven-like, at my door.

As if sprung from my fantasies, Cor stands outside in his ever-present black suit. My core aches at the sight of him, and I imagine he's really Hades disguised as a human and I'm the spring goddess destined to be his queen.

He smiles, and I smile, and the fairy tale's broken. He's just an awkward hottie, probably a business bro who has to wear that fancy suit to work every day. I dry my hands on my apron and walk to unlock the door.

"Hi." I open the door and hold it for him. "Welcome to my flower shop."

He smiles and dips his head, then walks past me into the shop. His hands in his pockets accentuate what is a very tight ass connected in a V to very broad shoulders. The energy of the room shifts into a sexual tensity, but—shit. What if he's a hunting vampire, and I've just welcomed him inside to maul me?

Or maybe it's time for a palate cleanser from all that paranormal romance I read.

He turns and smiles at me, and my whole body tunes to his energy. Honestly, he can maul me if he wants to, and I won't say boo.

"You have so many flowers," he says softly.

"Gotta have flowers to sell flowers," I say stupidly to the smoking hot enigma of a man. "Um, you're here to get some for your mom?"

His hands are in his pockets, but a muscle feathers in his jaw. His gaze starts at my pink-painted toenails and eases like a caress up my entire body.

I am unwell.

"Yes, flowers for my mother."

I swallow hard and shove my hands in my apron as I walk past him, just in case a rogue finger reaches out to smooth along his lips or, I don't know, unzip his pants.

Stop it, Sunshine. The man is here for flowers for his mother. Not a supernatural booty call.

Even though his do-not-eye-fuck-strangers system seems broken, too.

I go behind the counter. What is it about him that makes him so otherworldly? His ethereal beauty? His soulful eyes? Maybe it's just his habit of repeating things. With that untraceable accent, he really could be from anywhere, and maybe he doesn't understand everything I'm saying. It's a shame he's not French, or I could pull out some of what I learned in high school.

I distract myself with work talk. "Do you have something in mind? Is it for her birthday, or…"

His chiseled brow furrows. "Er…."

Damn he's cute when he's confused.

"Or we can start with your budget."

His eyes widen, and he freezes. He does that a lot, as if he doesn't trust himself to move that well-sculpted body. "My budget."

Ah. He *is* repeating the words he doesn't understand. "Yes, you know, how much money you have to spend."

His face lights up, and he digs into both pants pockets. His left fist hovers over my desk and deposits three quarters, a nickel, a doubloon from the Krewe of Thoth, a discarded losing lottery ticket, and a plastic bottle cap. His right hand repeats the gesture, letting loose a cascade of other ephemera: three metal bottle caps, another doubloon, a bunch of pennies, and pocket lint. One of the pennies goes spinning out and off the counter, and he hunts it down through the forest of flowers like it's the proverbial lost lamb.

It's kinda weird, not gonna lie.

He lets out a soft "Ah!" as he picks up the rogue penny and sets it carefully back on the counter. "Money," he says with pride.

I look from him to the pocket litter and hold back a confused giggle. Is he trying to be funny? Being an ass? Making fun of me?

His face reddens. "Are these not…I don't know…" His brown eyes are so sincere. He's either some kind of entity trying to befriend me, or a foreigner who was woefully unprepared for coming to the states. I don't get it. A man with a suit like that can't *not* understand money.

I force a smile. "It's perfect." I pull out a quarter and a penny, just to make him feel like he's paid me fairly. It's not enough to pay for even one flower, but how can I not help him anyway? I look around and spot some hydrangea stems. "Does your mother have any pets?"

"Pets," he says blankly.

"You know, like a cat or a dog that lives with her?"

He shakes his head. "No, no pets."

"Great! Then I have the perfect thing." As I walk around the counter to a bucket of hydrangeas, he orients himself toward me like a hot sunflower following the sun. "What about a hydrangea?" I run my fingers gently across a pink one. "These look like dozens of little flowers, but they're actually sepals. On this one"—I pull a bright green one from the water—"the flowers themselves are these tiny little florets in the middle of each sepal."

He steps slowly to me and smiles into my eyes before hooking his hands behind his back and bending slightly to politely observe the hydrangea. "It's green, like your eyes."

His brown eyes lock on mine, and I'm putty. "Um. Green hydrangeas represent rebirth and good fortune. Would you like this one?"

He straightens. "Yes. That one."

I step around him and grab some baby's breath on the way to the counter. "And these little white ones represent loving dedication. They'll set it off nicely."

I grab a sheet of tissue paper and arrange the flowers inside it, taking a moment to slide a water tube on the bottom of the hydrangea stem. "Cut hydrangeas need a lot of water, so be sure to tell her to take this tube off and set them in water right away." As I wrap everything up, he collects the items left on the counter, one by one, carefully placing them back into the pockets they came out of.

What an adorable, perfect weirdo. On one hand, his presence is so reassuring, like he bottle-feeds kittens in his spare time and would be the safest place in any storm. On the other hand, he seems to be blundering through life completely confused. It's cute now, but that might get really annoying in everyday life unless he really is not of this world. And on yet a third hand, I would like to sit on his face. Respectfully.

I step around the counter and present the wrapped-up flowers to him. "Here you go. I hope your mom likes them."

He delicately takes them from me, soft wonder on his face. "They're beautiful."

His gaze raises from the flowers to mine, and my breath catches. I've stepped up rather close to him, but he doesn't move away. Instead, he sways nearer, bends his head closer like he did at the church. But this time, I won't get spooked.

"Is there anything else I can do for you?" I ask softly. I can't let him go without him asking me out, or me asking him out. His eyes drop to my lips.

Or yes, please, a kiss. I lift my chin and smile softly.

His lips part, and a shiver skips up my spine. He's staring at my lips like he isn't sure if he should go for it.

So I will.

I gently kiss his bottom lip, and the act lights my body up like a bonfire. He breathes out the softest, achiest groan...

But he doesn't kiss me back.

A breeze hits my face, and I open my eyes.

He's already outside my door.

How the hell did he do that? "Cor, wait!"

By the time I get to the door and peer both ways down the street, he's just...gone. Chills run down my skin, and I feel like shit. I thought he *wanted* me to kiss him.

I stand in the sunlight holding the door open, filled with regret and more than a little fear that I've offended something supernatural.

Did I just kiss someone who's...not human? Honestly, I don't know that I care. He's kind, and he's gentle, and he's *familiar* almost. I step back inside and hug myself. I royally fucked that up, and I want him to come back so I can apologize and make things right.

"I'm sorry, Cor," I whisper to my empty shop.

◊≳ƒ÷⑁ > COR

Not-Quite-Edict Two: *The human world is not your world; do not become attached.*

My shoes click swiftly down the sidewalk in the most human-muscled effort I've ever expended.

Sunny Day kissed me, the way human lovers kiss.

My heart pounds, and it's not from the exertion. I'm filled with longing and fear and warmth and lust, and I don't know how to handle all of these emotions and sensations overtaking my body. It took all my effort not to slip into the veil there in her shop. But she would have seen me, and I was already breaking not-quite-edicts as if they didn't matter. But they do.

I pass humans in the street, and they can see me. It's intoxicating to pretend to be one of them. Some smile and nod as I pass them. I return all their gestures and barrel forward. It's reckless to appear to so many, but I...I like it. They're each a bundle of messy, competing emotions, and I feel more at home among them than I ever have with my compeers. It was partly why

I volunteered for this service, to meet these human souls who were braver than me, who felt things the Elders didn't. Besides, by the time I realized I wanted to take part in the universe and not just observe it, I wasn't fit for anything else. But now I'm not even fit for this.

I slow down when I'm a couple of blocks away from Sunny Day and her soft kisses. "Hello," I say back to a woman who'd just hailed me in kind.

"What a beautiful pet," I say to the woman walking a dog. I smile and nod at the men holding hands who walk past me, and they return the gesture. Across the street, a man is buckling a child into a vehicle. The child's laughter sings into my ears. The sun is warm on my head and a breeze slips past my face. In a group of men near orange cones, a machine roars *DUT-DUT-DUT-DUT-DUT* and chips away at the cement. The alluring aroma of spicy human food meets my nostrils.

What does that food taste like? What is it called? How is it made? What does it feel like to have a friend? A lover? What is like to have someone like Sunny Day waiting at a home for you at the end of the day? What is it like to have a human home made of wood and stone and metal?

I pause, watching diners at outdoor tables eat and laugh. And live.

I made the wrong choice, all those ages ago.

But if I hadn't made that choice, would I ever have met Sunny Day? But what if I had chosen to become human, and Sunny Day could have become my—what was the word? I stop walking and tuck the flowers under my arm to pull out my notebook and flip to my notes. What if she had been my lover? Or girlfriend? Or my...wife?

My vision is blurry. I press my finger to my eye, and it comes away wet. Tears, just like a human's. That thought makes everything blurrier. I blink and wipe them all from my face so I can see the flowers from Sunny Day clearly. There must be almost a hundred petals in one bunch—no, she called them sepals—just like I feel like a hundred emotions in one human-like container. This flower is perfect. It's like her in every way, and I am—

I swallow hard. I don't know what I am anymore.

A chime sounds.

I have to go. What do I do with the flowers? All I wanted was to see her again. I didn't expect that so few of the human oddments would purchase such a wealth or that one human would unlock my soul's heart and break me open.

The chime sounds again, and I really have to go. I pluck a couple of sepals from the green and flowers from the white and stuff them into my breast pocket.

"Good afternoon," an elderly woman says as she approaches me from the opposite direction down the sidewalk. She seems very tired, or very sad, but her pink hair is cheerful in spite of it. I make a quick decision as she walks even with me.

"Good afternoon." I hand the flowers to her. "These are for you."

She stops, her wrinkled eyes wide and suspicious. "For me? Why for me?"

I have no answer ready. But then she smiles, and I smile back. "To make you happy."

She smiles bigger. "Thank you! What a thoughtful thing to do." She smells the flowers, and my chest tightens. I didn't even smell them before I gave them away. I vow to smell the ones in my pocket later, but I have to tend to my mission now.

"Good afternoon." I nod to her as some of the humans who passed me before had done, and I rush past her and around the corner. I run into an alley and slip into the veil toward my next assignment.

But how will I comfort a soul who is leaving this place, now that I have *felt* why they grieve?

CHAPTER

EIGHT

Both chrysanthemums and rosemary protect against evil spirits.

I stand back in my shop, barely seeing anything. Did I imagine that he wanted to kiss me?

No. I *know* we had a moment. He wanted me as badly as I wanted him. Pure desire emanated from him and enveloped me. My whole body is freaking out from it. I fan myself then take down and put back up my hair.

I wish he hadn't left like that. My heart hurts at the thought that I've hurt him. I wish I could give him a bouquet that means *you confuse me, arouse me, and I'm sorry I hurt you*: red carnation for hurt love, sainfoin for confusion, coriander for lust, and rue, of course. That's for regret.

Do I have any funerals coming up at All Saints Church? What a ridiculous thought—that because I've seen him there twice, he'll be there again. It stops me in my tracks on the way back to my counter. But...the way he just disappeared...

The bell over the door behind me shoots adrenaline through every circuit of my body as I whirl around. But it's not him. It's Bev, smiling and waving as she enters.

"Hey Bev, how are—" She's holding the flowers I just gave to Cor. "Wait...where did you get those flowers?"

"You wouldn't believe it. This handsome young stranger just handed them to me down the street. He said it was to make me happy, but it feels like a sign. It's Ginnie's favorite." She smells them with a wistful sigh. "But I can't really bring them home. Orpheus might get into it, and I can't have him getting sick. I saw your sticker on them and thought I'd bring them back so you can sell them again. Do you know what his name is so I can thank him properly?"

I take them, but I'm so confused. "He told me it was for his mother."

She winks at me. "Maybe he just wanted an excuse to buy flowers from you."

"Ha. I doubt it. You know the right man for me has never been born."

Bev smiles weakly at my standing joke, one she's heard a hundred times before.

"But..." I persist. "Didn't he seem a little odd to you? Something not quite...usual?"

Bev's laughs devolves into a cough. "He was wearing a full wool suit in the middle of July, so his levee isn't holding back all the floodwaters, if you catch my meaning. But he sure was good-looking. You know, for a man. Didn't you think so?" She pulls a water bottle from her bag.

"Yeah, he's gorgeous." And his lips taste like honey. "But he just doesn't seem, I don't know. Like a regular person." I turn back into the shop and walk to the counter. "He was at two different funerals in the past two weeks, dressed the same way he was today." I laugh. "I mean, is he a ghost or some kind of angel of death?" I start taking the bouquet apart and look up to be sure Bev isn't questioning my sanity.

But she's still standing by the door, her hand on a display shelf. "I think I'd better head home. I'm not feeling well all of a sudden."

I freeze. "Bev, are you okay?"

She crumples to the floor.

"Bev!" I grab my phone and run to her. Dial 911 while I feel for a pulse. It's there, but weak.

"911, what's your emergency?"

With shaking hands I put them on speaker. "3313 Azrael Street, Sunny Day Flower Shop. My friend just collapsed. She's in her eighties. Please come fast."

"What is the phone number you are calling from?"

I rattle off my number and grab a heart pillow from a display and gently lift her head to place it underneath. "Are paramedics on their way?"

"Yes, they're on their way. Is the patient conscious?

"Bev?" Her eyes are closed, and she's not reacting to me. But her chest is rising and falling. "No, I don't think so. But she's breathing."

Bev opens her eyes and turns her head away from me. With a soft smile and even softer breath, she says, "It's you."

I freeze. There's no one in the shop with us. "Bev! Beverly, look at me. Stay with me," I cry. "Help's coming."

Movement on the other side of the door. The paramedics must be—

Cor steps through the solid glass door, and my heart slams against my rib cage. I'm not even surprised, I'm *betrayed*. He tilts his head and frowns sorrowfully at me.

"No!" I roar, placing my body across Bev's. "You can't have her," I shout.

"Ma'am, is there someone else there? Are you in danger?"

I ignore the dispatcher because Cor is walking slowly toward us.

"All is well, Beverly. All is well, Sunny Day," he says quietly.

"What are you?" I yell. "The Grim Reaper? The Angel of Death? Are you coming to steal her soul away?" He kneels before Bev, and his gaze shifts to her. She's staring back at him so peacefully. His mouth is moving, but I can't hear anything he's saying.

"Don't listen to him, Bev. He's trying to steal your soul!"

"Ma'am, can you repeat that, please?"

His brows lower as his gaze flicks to me, but his expression smooths as he keeps talking to Bev. He holds his hand just beside her head with the gentlest expression on his face.

He feels right, but this is all wrong. "Don't touch her!" I slap at his hand, but my hand goes straight through it. "Go away!" I cry. "You can't have her!" I grab a handful of chrysanthemums and fling them at him, but they go right through him, and he doesn't even seem to have noticed.

"Ma'am, I need you to tell me what's happening. Is someone threatening you?"

Bev smiles at Cor, closes her eyes, and all of the air leaves her body.

"No!" I cry. I throw a potted rosemary right through his chest. My tears have made a prism of the world, and in its refraction I see Cor stand up with his hand outstretched. A pale, insubstantial ghost of my friend separates from her body and stands, too.

All the hair on the back of my neck raises, and I stagger back. "Hurry!" I whimper at the phone, rooted to the spot. "He's taking her soul!"

"Ma'am, I need you to stay calm and tell me what's happening. Who is there with you?"

Bev reaches her hand toward Cor. Her mouth moves, but I can't hear what she says.

"Don't take his hand, Bev! Please, don't take his hand!" I cry.

Her ghostly hand hesitates, and she turns to look at me.

It feels like all my blood drains from me at the supernaturally piercing gaze of my friend. She turns back to Cor and gestures to me. I can't hear what he's saying to her now, but he puts his open hand closer to her. She smiles and nods and puts her small hand into his big one.

"No! Don't go with him!"

But they ignore my sobbing screams. They turn toward the door together and step forward. Their luminous lights go out, and I'm alone.

"What did you do?" I shout to nothing.

"Ma'am the paramedics are arriving now. Can you tell me what's happening? Are you safe?"

I'm sobbing with grief and fear and relief at the red and blue lights appearing outside my shop door. But they're too late. Bev's body is here, but she is gone.

CHAPTER
NINE

COR

Edict Three: Souls must take your hand to cross the veil.

"I can't wait to see Ginnie!"

I smile. Beverly's soul may be the most talkative and excited soul I've ever encountered on the short walk through the veil to paradise. "Ginnie will likely be the first you reunite with, as well as your parents and your brothers."

"What about my old cat, Possum?"

I smile. "Of course."

"You scared the hell out of my friend, you know."

"Your friend?" I recall Sunny Day's tear-streaked face, and my cord to her is quivering. The waves of her fear and horror still chill both her and me, and my chest is tight with pain. "Do you mean Sunny Day?"

She plants the fist of her hand not holding mine on her hips. "Yes, I mean Sunny Day. She's probably in her shop still scared out of her wits that you're some kind of demon who hurt me."

I gasp. "I'm no demon." But Beverly's assessment is true. Sunny Day was so frightened that she almost talked her friend out of taking my hand.

"I know that *now*," Beverly says, "but she doesn't. Poor thing's all confused. You have to go back and explain everything to her."

I shake my head. "I'm not allowed. But...I don't know how she could see what was happening." She shouldn't have been able to. Although...the realization hits me. "I think it was my fault that she could. My mistake to appear to her in the first place. And my mistake to *keep* appearing to her."

It was also my mistake to want...

What I should not want.

"So I was right! You *are* sweet on my Sunny." Her sly smile lights up her face. "I can tell what a good soul you are. Promise me you'll go back and make things right with her?"

"I don't know if I can. I've already messed things up so badly." As it is, I'm fighting my impulse to go straight to Our Heavenly Mother and beg for her forgiveness and help. She never angers, but what if she takes me away from my duties and I never see Sunny Day again?

"Well, I think God wants us to love each other. Surely She'll understand why you did what you did."

I narrow my eyes at Beverly. "You knew God is a woman?"

She smiles. "Obviously. What else could She be?"

I return her smile and part the veil: we've arrived, and her whole being lights up. Faster than a thought, Beverly is in the arms of her wife, and their beautiful, joyful reunification brings tears to my eyes and makes the place on my belly that connects to Sunny Day ache.

I swallow hard. More than anything, I want to soothe Sunny Day, to comfort her and ease her suffering. But explaining myself would violate Edict One. And if I can't tell her the truth, what else could I possibly say that would ease her mind?

I record Beverly's homecoming in my notebook. She's right, and I know it. I can't leave Sunny Day in such pain. I don't know what will come of it or even what I will say, but I have to go to her. I take a deep breath and slip into the veil.

CHAPTER
TEN

SUNNY

Bright red and yellow dahlias (for kindness), blue delphinium (for an open heart), sunflowers (because they're my favorites), and hydrangeas; always hydrangeas, for Ginnie.

Thank all that's holy that the first responders didn't cart me away for psychiatric evaluation, because every one of them side-eyed me the entire time they were in my shop despite me dutifully answering all their questions: no, there wasn't anyone else in the shop; no, I didn't really see a specter come for Bev's soul; and yes, it's wild what a traumatic event will make you imagine.

Except I didn't imagine any of it.

I pull out the binder from under my counter that I never wanted to need, the one in which Bev has already laid out what flowers she wants me to deliver to her funeral.

The streetlight through the door shade illuminates the ordinary, empty expanse of my wooden floor where everything went down, but it was unspeakably miraculous less than forty-five minutes ago. I watched my friend die, and I'm devastated that she's gone. I wipe fresh tears from my cheeks.

But.

But I watched her soul get up and carry on. She confirmed one of the biggest mysteries of life while Cor raised so many questions. A shiver slips down my spine. All this spirituality shit *is* real, and Cor's really not human.

I relight my incense to Áine and say a prayer for Bev. I don't remember everything I yelled at him in the cold chill of the moment, but I'm calm enough now to admit that whatever or whoever Cor is, he's not evil—if Bev's smile and trust in taking his hand is any indication. She always was an excellent judge of character.

I should go home, but I can't make myself leave without checking to be sure I have all of Bev's flowers in stock, or if they must be ordered. I wipe fresh tears from my cheeks and open the binder.

An unfamiliar pink envelope falls out.

And Cor appears on the other side of the counter out of nowhere. I scream and scramble backward, knocking over a bucket of lilies that spill all over the floor. "Get out!" I yell in reflex.

His eyes widen, and he disappears.

I take a deep breath and press my hand over my hammering heart. "I meant, knock like a normal person!" I shout.

Immediately there's a knock outside my door, and a now-familiar silhouette stands back-lit in the door's window shade.

My heart rate isn't slowing down, but at least he did as I asked. I stomp to the door and pull the shade *marginally* aside. Outside the glass, Cor's eyes are mournful. "What do *you* want?" I ask ungraciously.

"I want to comfort you. May I come inside?"

"You swear you're not gonna kill me, or take my soul, or...whatever you did to Bev?" My voice trembles on my last words.

His brows furrow and his soulful eyes are tortured. "I've never hurt anyone. I would never. And I can't bring you...you're not dying."

I blink at him. *All is well*, he'd said to me when we met, and to Bev before she died. At the funeral, he said he knew the deceased woman from a...a *short trip*. I study his earnest eyes.

Oh.

Ohhh.

I unlock the door and open it, standing to the side to let him pass inside then locking it once he's in. The big man stands frowning near the door like a chastised puppy.

"Are you an angel?"

He frowns, but shakes his head, no. "I'm not allowed to tell—"

"So then you must be a guide, right? Like a ferryman." I fold my arms and stare up at him. It's the only thing that makes sense, and he's just spooky enough for it to be true. "You bring souls to the other side, don't you?"

His eyes widen, and he looks so freaking guilty. But then his whole demeanor relaxes, and he briefly closes his eyes on a deep exhale. "Yes. I am."

"What's your real name? It can't possibly be *Cornflower*."

His smile is slow and hopeful. "You won't be able to hear or understand it."

"Try me."

"I am called ———." His mouth opens at the place he should say his name, but it sounds for all the world like just an exhale.

"Your name is..." and I exhale really loudly.

He smiles and shakes his head. "It's more than breathing out, but it's not a sound. It's a soul calling to another soul."

So he himself *is* a soul. I eye him up and step closer. "Don't disappear on me."

"I don't disappear."

"*You don't disappear,*" I scoff. "Where do you go when I can't see you? How do you walk through walls? What are you made of?"

Those dark eyebrows furrow again. "Sunny Day, I can't..."

I cross my arms. "Just call me Sunny. Look. I've had a really hard day, and I think I deserve some answers." As frustrated as I am, my gut is pulling me to him, viscerally and emotionally. I want him, and I need him, and I cannot fathom why. "I thought we had something here." My voice is small as I waggle my finger back and forth between us. "But you can't be honest with me?"

"I'm trying to be," he says, gently frustrated. "But I have rules to abide by."

I bite my lip. Goddess help me, but I believe him. "Okay. Answer what you can. Is Bev okay? Is she safe?"

"Yes. She is home."

Fresh tears fall through a smile. "With Ginnie?"

He nods with a smile. I step closer and lay my hand experimentally against his chest. My hand hits solid, suited flesh, and a muscle feathers in his jaw. "What are you?"

He pauses and takes a deep breath, apparently considering his words. Finally, he says, "I'm a human soul, like you, but one who's never experienced life."

I cock my head, studying him. "You're pretty...solid. What are you made of, if you're not, like, alive?"

"Of energy, the same as you." He lays his hand over mine, so gently. "But my body is held together purely with divine love, so I can do things and go places you cannot."

"Like disappear and travel through the air."

He bites his lip. "It must appear that way to you."

"Well, don't do it now, because it'll freak me out."

"Okay," he says softly.

I look up into his eyes, and I'm overcome with the strangest sense of belonging and safety. And it doesn't feel only spiritual, as in he's a supernatural entity who ferries souls to their afterlife and therefore he's a gentle, trustworthy being—because wow, what a responsibility. It's also that he's inexplicably *my* gentle, trustworthy being. I reach up and lay my hand against his face, and I want to kiss him again.

If the overwhelming desire I feel radiating from his gaze and presence—and pressing against my belly—is any indication, he feels the same. His gaze at my lips is as hungry as mine feels.

Do I dare let myself fall for someone so otherworldly?

Yes. Yes, I do dare. I move in closer, but he dissipates from under my hand.

I yelp. "I said not to do that!"

He reappears in my little alcove near a table I use with clients, his face all contrition among the flowers. "I'm sorry. I got, as you said, *freaked out.*"

I approach him again. "By me? I'm just a normal human woman."

His dark, earnest eyes darken still, and he shakes his head, no. "There is nothing normal about you, Sunny. You are *extraordinary.* You are light and warmth and love." His eyes move all around my body. "Your beautiful soul shines through your mortal body. You've touched the lives of countless humans with cheer and compassion—so many smile every time they think of you, on both sides of the veil." He smiles himself, and it's radiant. "I have been serving for nearly three decades, but only you awoke this longing in my human soul. Longing to love and be loved. Longing to touch and be touched. Longing to live."

I smile at his lovely words, spoken with such gentle ardor. To love, be loved, and live. Isn't that all anyone wants? Even though it always ends the same. My smile devolves into tears. "I'm sad about Bev."

His frown is gentle, and I know he's feeling my sorrow right along with me. "I'm sorry that it was her time. But as you saw, life goes on in beautiful ways."

"Will you hold me?" I ask quietly.

My feet leave the ground and I'm dipped sideways as he lifts me in his arms, bodyguard style. He stands still, observing me as if awaiting further instruction.

It surprises me into teary laughter, but I don't explain that this isn't what I had in mind. Because it's wonderful. I wrap my arms around his neck, lay my head on his shoulder, and press my face against his neck. It's warm, and the roses-and-incense scent of him settles deep in my chest and through my whole being.

He lays his head against mine, and we stay this way for long minutes as my crying runs its course. I feel steadier and more supported than I've ever felt in my life, and not just because he's holding me up off the floor. His pulse is steady against my lips, and I have the impulse to kiss it. In fact, with his thumb gently rubbing against my thigh, I have the impulse to do so much more with him.

A wise woman on Instagram once said that when you have the option to do a spiritual thing or a human thing, do the human thing because that's the experience we're here for. And right now, I need something life affirming, overwhelming, and deeply passionate.

I press a long, warm, lingering kiss against his neck, and the moan that breathes from his mouth against my hair sends a delicious ache straight to my core. I lift my head and gaze into his black-fringed eyes. "Can I kiss you?"

He licks his lips. "Yes, please."

CHAPTER

ELEVEN

COR

Not-Quite Edict Four: If something has gone amiss, talk to Our Heavenly Mother.

Sunny's mouth gently presses against mine, warm and soft and thrilling. I don't know how to do this, but she moves her lips slowly, coaxing me to learn, and her soft whimpers encourage me. Her arms wrap around my neck, and her fingers skim my beard and tangle in my hair. Even though her sublime body is pressed against me in my arms, it isn't close enough. I pull her tighter, consuming her mouth with kisses, my new favorite thing. Sunny is of my heart, connected to my soul, and I kiss her with a hunger for her flesh—to devour without harm, to possess without subjugation—that I did not know was possible to feel.

I also did not know that my body could respond with such delicious, insistent aching, making my sex hard between my legs. Sunny is squirming as she kisses me, and her arousal envelops me. It's a commingled need and a blessing.

I set her down, and she presses the softness of her breasts against me, murmuring, "I want you" between kisses on my mouth, my neck. "I want you," she pants again, her green eyes unfocused and connecting through my eyes to my soul. "I want to make love with you."

"I want you, too, Sunny. Will you teach me how to please you?"

Her dazed returning smile beams with affection and removes all doubts. "I'll teach you *everything*," she murmurs. Her teeth catching her luscious bottom lip on the V of the word sends a jolt of pure desire to my sex.

Her eyes dark, she unbuttons my suit, my shirt and my pants. In minutes she has laid my body bare and tingling in the cool room. Her gaze unabashedly reviews me from head to toe and back again, then she pulls my face to hers to kiss it and runs her palms along my skin, across the muscles of my shoulders, down the dark hair of my chest that leads below my belly to where I want her hands the most, although I am still afraid to touch her. But she doesn't delay. One hand slips around to grip my bottom, and the other wraps around my sex and slides down and up again.

My knees are weak with the magnificent aching pleasure, my breath hitching. "My body never did this until I met you," I murmur raggedly against her mouth. She grasps me tighter and strokes the tip with her thumb, and the deepest, lustiest moan breaks from my throat. My fingers are desperate to learn her pleasure. "Can I touch you?"

"Yes." Her hands leave my body and untie a ribbon at her chest. She pulls her dress off over her head and her full breasts spill free. She slips off her underwear then stands before me gloriously naked, her skin freckled and pinkened and so lush that my hands and tongue want to explore every inch of her sweet flesh. My gaze catches between her legs where I only vaguely know what awaits me, but I desire the mystery more than anything.

"Teach me how to pleasure you." The demand leaves my mouth gruffer and more commanding than any other words I've spoken in my entire existence, but it lights a fire in her eyes.

Her hands gently guide me to sit on the table, and she turns around and sits on my lap, her bottom pressing against my erection. Holding my gaze, she takes one of my hands, kisses the palm, then fills it with her supple breast, squeezing herself through my hand and guiding my thumb and forefinger to pinch her nipple. Her eyes close in pleasure, and a soft cry breaks from the back of her throat as she grabs my other hand.

Her feet perch on my knees, and she spreads her legs open, dragging my hand down the soft skin of her belly and further until my fingers slip into the deep, hot folds of her sex. Impossibly wet and velvety, it's the most miraculous thing I've ever touched. She whimpers and squirms her lovely body on my lap as my fingers press into her softness, exploring every crevice. Her hand guides mine to a firm spot at the apex of her sex, and she moans when I rub my fingertip gently across it.

"Slip around...circles..." Her breathy commands are ragged as I obey. "Oh my god. *Yes*. And then—" She drags my fingers down and guides two up inside her body. The shock of her snug, wet heat hugging my fingers makes my sex twitch against her inner thigh, and soft moans emit from her throat. But when she pulls my fingers back up to swirl around her bud, she gasps and whimpers in quick little cries. I no longer need her hands to guide me, because giving Sunny pleasure feels like what I was made to do. She presses her head back against my shoulder, her every breath a frenzied cry at my work. And when I plunge my fingers back inside her while my thumb circles her, she cries out louder, and her sex pulses around my fingers.

Her ragged breathing slows as her whole body relaxes in my arms. For a moment, she is too overcome to do anything but grip my hand against her sex and breathe.

"Cor," she breathes. She pulls my hand away then turns around and straddles me while grasping my sex firmly in her hand. "Are you ready?"

"Yes," I pant. "I *require* you. Now."

She kisses me hard, and then the tip of my sex is at her entrance. Suddenly, her snug, wet sheath consumes my sex, and I have never felt such ecstatic aching. I'm moaning and thrusting up into her, and my aching breaks and climaxes into the most satisfying throbbing.

"Oh!" She exclaims softly. "That's okay. It's your first time. I didn't expect you to last—*Oh!*"

I thrust my hips up against her, chasing the ache that is already building again. Because unlike the human biology I learned about, my sex is not refracting. It is hard and needy, and I am not finished claiming my lover.

"Yes, Cor," she cries. She's gone feral, her luscious breasts bouncing against my chest, her hands in my hair as she cries out and rides against me. My fingers dig into her hips as she grinds them in tight circles. Her breaths are cries now, her fingernails digging against my shoulders. She mewls, and her sheath contracts around my sex, breaking me into another soul-consuming climax.

It's still not enough.

Sunny's eyes flutter open, her lovely face flushed and wild as she gazes deep into my eyes. "◊≳ƒ÷⋔," she breathes.

Something breaks lose inside my soul. *"You said my name."*

Suddenly I'm on my feet and pressing her back against the wall with her legs wrapped tight around my waist. I grind into her paradisiacal sex harder and deeper, my hands and mouth consuming her kisses, the sweet taste of her flesh, the bite of her teeth against my lips as she entreats me, *yes* and *more* and *please.*

The powerful waves of her climax undulate around my sex, and I'm throbbing inside her, completely spent and satiated.

For now.

My legs are a little shaky—another new sensation—as I sit back on the table.

She lays her head against my shoulder, and her heart is a pounding drum beneath her pressing breasts. If I stay inside her much longer, I will give in to my desire again.

"Wow," she breathes. "That was...wow. I swear, I could almost feel your pleasure wrapped up in mine. Like we were almost one person."

I smile and kiss her brow. "That is the way of soul mates, I'm told."

She lifts her head, bemused. "Soul mates? Like in some fairy smut novel?"

"What is a fairy smut novel?"

Her laugh is musical. "Don't worry, I'll get you to read my entire stash. They'll be an excellent learning experience for you." She waggles her eyebrows at me with a giggle before laying her head on my shoulder. "I'm ready to go home. You'll come with me, won't you?"

I brush hair from my eyes. "I would be honored, but..." I swallow hard. "I have to go."

She raises her head with a soft frown. "For how long?"

I press a kiss to her forehead. "I do not know."

Her beautiful face falls, and she places her hands on either side of my face. "Cor, are you saying I might never see you again? That's not fair."

I kiss away the new tears staining her cheeks. "My Sunny, I will do everything in my power to come back to you, but I fear what Our Heavenly Mother will say about our love. I've broken so many—"

"God's a woman?" she blurts.

I close my eyes. I have revealed far too much, but I nod. "Yes. But I have broken so many rules, and I have to do the right thing now."

"But you *have* to come back to me," she whispers into another kiss.

I wrap my arms around her and kiss her deeply. "My heart will stay with you for however long we're apart."

Sunny nods through her tears. "And my heart will go with you," she says gently. She stands up and helps me gather my clothes.

In a few moments, I'm dressed, but Sunny's still beautifully naked, adjusting my tie. Her smile is so sad it breaks my heart.

"Come back to me, okay?" She kisses me again, and then I step through the veil to see the Mother of all.

EPILOGUE

SUNNY

Fluffy, sweet-smelling peonies can capture the full range of a human life: a joyous birth (white peonies), the gentle blush of first love (pink peonies), congratulations and good luck (light pink peonies), passionate love (red peonies), dignity and royalty (purple peonies), anniversaries and wealth (coral peonies), and a peaceful death (yellow peonies).

After Cor leaves, I dress quickly and freshen up in my store's bathroom before heading home. My heart is soaring and aching all at once, like I'm on the precipice of the best period of my life or the worst, and I don't know which it will be.

I reach for my purse on the counter, and the mysterious pink envelope catches my attention. I'd completely forgotten about it when Cor came to me. Slouching onto the stool where Bev sat so many times, I cleanly slice the envelope with a letter opener to find a card covered in hydrangeas. Inside is Bev's beautiful cursive, and every word I read makes me cry harder:

Dearest Sunny,

Ginnie and I have treasured your friendship all these years.
We've seen how hard you worked, how kind you are to
everyone. You were there for us when we needed you,
and your store has been a bright spot in my gray world
after I lost Ginnie. She and I decided years ago that since
we didn't have kids, we'd leave you everything we had.

I gasp, and the note continues on as if she'd heard me.

Yes, my dear. We're leaving you our home, where we lived so
happily for so long. We're leaving you our assets so you
can move your shop to that gorgeous location up the
road from me where you always wanted to be. Ginnie
and I love you, Sunny, and we wish the best for you. All
my love, Bev Sweet.

PS. Don't worry about a thing, and don't cry for me. My
lawyer will take care of everything, and I am with Ginnie
where I belong.

Another post-script is scrawled in a different pen color at the bottom:

PPS. Please go check on Orpheus—he's yours now too, if
you'll have him. I'm afraid I've got him spoiled on that
expensive Posh Pussycat brand of food, but he's worth it.

"Oh my gosh! Orpheus!" My mind skips ahead to Bev's painted "Smash
the patriarchy" hide-a-key rock in the petunia pot on her deep porch and
the orange kitten that must be starving by now. But I make sure to tell her
how I feel as I put out my incense and rush to my car. "I love you and
Ginnie, too, Bev. Thank you from the bottom of my heart, and I will spoil
Orpheus absolutely rotten, too."

FIVE YEARS LATER

THE WEDDING I'M PREPARING FOR HAS OFFICIALLY BEEN DUBBED "THE PEONY Wedding." The grooms have been growing them together for the past five years—about as long as our shop has been in its new location—and they donated a frothy wealth of them from their garden for their big day.

Cor comes from the back room of our Sweet Sunny Day Flower Shop —the addition of Bev and Ginnie's chosen last name was Cor's brilliant idea—with a bucket of the reddest peonies. His apron looks so cute over his t-shirt and blue jeans that I just might have to tear them all off in a minute.

"Hey hot stuff, where are you going with my peonies?"

He grins. "Hello, my beautiful love. I thought you might need these next." He sits the bucket on my counter and wraps his arms around me from the back, kissing my neck.

"Why thank you—I do." I kiss his lips and again thank the goddess for letting him come back to me and for allowing him to continue his psychopomp work, which is so important to him. I lean back against him and sigh contentedly at how our lives are now.

When he left me that night all those years ago, I was so afraid I'd never see him again. I waited for three excruciating days. Meeting with the lawyers, overseeing the preparation for Bev's services, and crying every night for him to come back to me.

And then, like an answered prayer, he appeared in my apartment the night before Bev's funeral. He couldn't tell me much about what happened on the other side, but he told me that he went before Our Heavenly Mother, who listened to his contrition over breaking edicts and not-quite-edicts and granted his petition to stay with me and love me. Apparently, she'd sent him into service as a psychopomp hoping that he would find the human experience he thought he didn't want.

My gaze falls on the mural on the wall of our flower shop. It repeats the only words he could relate to me that she spoke: "Love above all."

I run my hands along Cor's arms around me, my body flushed with desire. He is right there with me, his hardness pressing against my backside.

"We won't open for another hour," he murmurs into my ear.

"Say less, lover." I turn around and wrap my arms around him, and he lifts me and brings me into our office, to the sofa there that has weathered many afternoons—and mornings, and evenings—of our lovemaking.

He sets me down and kisses me like the delicious snack I am, then searches his eyes and runs a finger along my forehead, no doubt soothing a wrinkle away. We smile in common understanding—he's using a loophole in the rules to keep me young and fresh like his flowers, and if we're lucky, we'll be able to live in this earthly slice of heaven for years and years to come as he continues his duties. My smile curves wickedly at him. I like to think I'm part of his reward for all his hard work.

Kneeling before me, he reaches under my skirt and pulls my panties down my legs, tossing them behind him. His firm hands spread my thighs apart with a smile that would make my panties drop if they weren't already off, and he pulls my bottom to the end of the deep cushion.

When his open mouth presses hot against my core, I unravel. He's more talented than any fae lord or brooding, mythical king, and me and my smutty novels have taught him a thousand ways to engulf us both in pleasure. He's so slow and deliberate at his feast between my legs, leaving me a gasping, quivering mess even before he joins me on the sofa and fills me with his hot thickness inch by blessed inch until I am impossibly full, aching with the need for him to move inside me.

I thrust the tip of my breast into his mouth, and he greedily sucks it in, pinching me in his mouth and flicking his tongue to make me moan. His appetite for my body is vast and insatiable. Climax after climax barrel through me in heavy, consuming waves, and I wrap my arms around his head, my hands in his hair, exhaling in a long, languid moan.

When the powerful waves of his first climax undulate inside me, he breathes into my ear something that sounds like *me*. I kiss him like I'm afraid he'll disappear again, but he doesn't, and he won't.

He is mine, and I am his, and we are home.

About Holly Rose

Holly Rose is the author of *Follow Your Bliss* (The Dream House Girls #1), *Until the Stars Fall* (Interstellar Witches #1) and *The Knight of the Trove* (The Knights of Mellora #1).

She lives in Louisiana with her husband, two sons, and two cats, where sadly, there are no dragons. She eats too much cheese fries, loves stargazing, and writes books about people falling in love.

Learn more at writerhollyrose.com.

BRIDE OF THE DRAGON PRINCE

MEGAN VAN DYKE

CHAPTER ONE

The dragon was restless today. He had been the last few weeks. To be fair, so was most of the city, but Briannis usually didn't have to worry about her neighbors carrying off one of their cows for a meal.

She glanced up as the dragon glided over the fields, wings stretched wide. Light glinted off his green scales. Her heart raced at the sight, at powerful haunches, sharp claws, and tail that could destroy a building in a single swipe. Its wings beat once as it passed over, sending a sudden gust fluttering her long, frizzy hair. Briannis squinted against the wind then whipped around to watch the dragon as it sailed along on the breeze.

She should be scared. She should have screamed.

Any sane person would, right?

But just like every other time she'd glimpsed the dragon over the years, it was tingling excitement that caused her pulse to flutter and body to warm, rather than fear.

What would its scales feel like under her fingertips? Could its fiery breath really turn a tree to ash in moments?

Truth was, Briannis had spent her life around large animals like the cows at the family dairy, and wasn't a dragon just an even larger beast? Was it really so dangerous and deadly as everyone believed?

Though it had taken a cow a few months back. A scowl formed on her face as she watched him. *If he makes one more low pass over the fields...*

Not that she could do more than send unhappy thoughts his way if he did bother their animals. No one would dare mess with their guardian. The Fates would surely punish anyone foolish enough to do so.

Thankfully, he continued on, flapping his massive emerald wings until they carried him away from the fields and up into the mountains where he was said to live.

Briannis let out a sigh and patted Una, one of her family's many cows, on the head. "Looks like he's gone now." Briannis scratched between her ears. "No need to worry." The cow stomped and tossed her head, nearly knocking her into the wooden fencing.

Most humans and animals alike feared the dragon. Why, earlier that morning when she'd been making a small delivery of a new batch of cheese, Briannis had seen dozens of people scream and hurry for cover at the mere sight of him flying above the city.

Ridiculous.

He didn't eat people.

Well... She grimaced. *Except for today.*

The streets had been thick with tension—and people—this morning thanks to the ceremony that would take place in the square when the sun was highest.

Briannis glanced back at the sky, squinting against the brightness. "Damn," she muttered, giving Una one last pat. "Aunt Davina is going to kill me." She'd taken much longer delivering her latest blend of cheese than she ought to have.

The family home lay at the end of the lane. Briannis ran toward it, the cool spring breeze a balm to the sweat rising on the back of her neck. What once had been a small home had been added onto over the years. As the family's dairy business grew, so did their residence...and the number in their household. How Aunt Davina managed to be such a successful business woman *and* a mother to so many little ones she couldn't say.

Well, actually, she could. Her business success let her hire help, but it had been her strong will, determination, and excellent taste in cheese that had built their modest farm into something enviable.

As a grown woman of six and twenty years, Briannis could have moved out long ago; however, Aunt Davina and Uncle Euan had been parents to her since her own had passed when she was but eleven. They treated her like one of their own, even instructing her in the running of the business. It was no secret that her aunt saw her as her future successor.

Briannis banged through the main door, aiming for the stairs up toward her room, but was stopped in her tracks by a scathing, "There you are! You're late."

Aunt Davina scowled. "Of all the days." She tsked. "I knew I should have sent someone else with that delivery."

Briannis shoved her unruly red hair—the same shade Davina's had been before it became streaked with grey—behind her ears and joined her aunt in the front parlor. "Maybe this will change your mind." She untied the little pouch around her waist and upended the contents into her palm.

All her aunt's focus zipped to the five gold coins in her hand. Her anger vanished, replaced by a raising of her brows. "I see. Mr. Stoutwell liked your newest blend. Enough to pay for the next wheel in advance?"

"Enough to pay double, *and* promise the same amount for the next three wheels." Briannis beamed with pride. She knew that blend was going to be great. Much like her aunt, she had a knack for flavors and it had yet to lead her astray.

Her aunt's lips parted in wonder. "Oh my."

"Though I think today being the Choosing had something to do with it," Briannis admitted, her joy quickly fading. "Given what happened with Merilee..." She swallowed. It was still hard for Briannis to think about the bright young woman they'd lost. How much harder was it for Mr. Stoutwell given she'd been his only child?

"Fates give her rest," Aunt Davina replied with equal somberness.

Every five years the city held the Choosing where all unwed young women aged 18 to 30 were required to present themselves as a candidate to become the dragon's bride. No exceptions. Two Choosings ago, it was Merilee who was selected.

It was supposed to be an honor to wed the dragon and ensure his favor, therefore granting prosperity to the city. But dragon brides never lived much beyond their wedding day, if at all.

With a sigh, the hard set of Aunt Davina's expression returned. "The Fates will be against us if we don't get you to the Choosing on time."

Because Briannis would be one of the candidates, just as she had been five years ago. She hadn't been worried. Not at all. But now that it was almost here, there was a tightness in her throat she couldn't quite swallow down.

"Your dress is all laid out upstairs." Davina waved her enthusiastically in that direction. "Go on. The dragon waits for no one."

CHAPTER

TWO

The city was always strange on Choosing days.

Somberness hung heavier in the air than humidity at the peak of summer. But bubbling just under the surface was a tremor of excitement, the hustle and bustle of townsfolk preparing for the festivities to follow. Even the air held a hint of sweetness from all the flowers carted in and cakes being baked. Because after the dragon's bride was selected, the other women were free to wed. And they always did—in masses.

After all, the few months after the selection of the dragon's bride were the only time they could. Once the winter snows returned, the elders would put a stop to it until the next Choosing in five years. The dragon always had first pick, and to slight him by marrying before one could be chosen as his bride? Well, that was to invite his wrath upon the land.

It had happened before. Some said the plague that took Briannis's parents and younger brother, along with a host of others, was because Niama wed Gerrick in secret a year before her first Choosing.

The wagon jolted as they rounded a turn and neared the thick press of people near the city center. Briannis gripped the wooden seat hard to steady herself where she rode at the front next to Uncle Euan.

"Euan!" Aunt Davina squealed. "Don't tip her off now that we're finally here."

"Well, if you all hadn't taken so long readying yourselves…" he grumbled as he slowed the horses. They approached a few other parked wagons and came to a stop. It was as close as they were going to get.

"Hmph!" Her aunt stood in the back of the wagon and brushed off the skirts of her dress before leaping over the side to the ground like a woman younger than her years. But that was Aunt Davina. She had more determination and enthusiasm than most women half her age…in everything.

"Next time, you can wrangle these young ones." She scowled at her four children before shaking her head with a sigh and holding out her arms for them to jump off into them. Ranging from five to sixteen, they were a handful. Each had the fire of their mother that burned just as bright as their red hair, a trait Briannis shared. Quite the opposite of her uncle, who was calm as the stream that trickled through their fields and had brown hair dark as the soil. He had a talent with animals and Briannis had learned much from him. If only she could develop his patience too.

"I should probably go on ahead," Briannis said after she climbed down. The city center was an open park filled with grassy fields, artful flower beds —which might currently be getting trampled by all the people—and a few large shade trees with sprawling limbs and thick roots dotted here and there. Various pathways converged in the middle where a large circle of flat stones known as the Seal of the Fates was inlaid in the ground. Any matter of significance happened there, from weddings to trials, and of course, the Choosing. A large stage had been erected on top of it for the ceremony. Already, young women in white were ascending the stairs and lining up.

Aunt Davina looked over her shoulder toward the stage and muttered a curse.

"I'll find you all after," Briannis promised with a smile and a little wave.

"Briannis!" Her aunt called. "Wait!" Aunt Davina's lips twitched. Her throat bobbed, and the woman's controlled expression faltered and dimmed.

Briannis blinked, stunned. That couldn't be tears in her eyes, could it?

Before she could take a closer look, her aunt pulled her into a crushing hug that half knocked the breath from her lungs.

"I love you, dear girl," she whispered, petting the bright, autumn waves of her hair that they'd painstakingly tried to tame before their departure. "If the worst should happen—" She let out a choked sound, which turning into an *oomph* as the younger ones joined in on the hug, clinging to their sides and legs. Uncle Euan was the last to join, wrapping his big arms around them all.

Briannis's throat grew tight. Something prickled at the corners of her eyes. Suddenly, all the courage she'd taken for granted seemed to crack and crumble at the onslaught of affection and her family's fear.

What if she was chosen? What if she didn't see them again? The urge to cling to those she loved had never been quite so strong. But there were so many women...the odds were so slim...

With a deep breath, Briannis started to pry herself from their embraces.

"Really, I'll be fine." She blinked away the beginning of tears trying to form. "It's not my first Choosing, after all." But it would be her last.

Though next time Catronia, the oldest of her cousins, would be in the running, and that was suddenly more terrifying than being chosen herself. Briannis forced that worry to the back of her mind. There was nothing to be done about it. "I'll see you all after. And then maybe we can find some of those sweet cakes you all love?" She ruffled her youngest cousin's hair and gave them all a smile full of all the blinding confidence she no longer felt.

Finally freed, she turned and headed off, ignoring the sweet words they called after her that tried to tear open her heart. It wouldn't do any good to be a sobbing mess on the stage. Some women would be, but not her.

The crowd parted for her and she hurried toward the stage. But as she neared the stairs where the women were ascending once their name was checked off the register, someone grabbed hold of her arm.

The unexpected touch caused her to jolt and twist in an attempt to get away.

"Briannis!"

She stilled at the sound of her name. "Ian?"

Sunlight caught in his blonde hair as he tipped his head to the side. His strong jaw lifted in an expression caught somewhere between a grin and confusion. "I've been calling after you. Did you not hear me?"

He removed his hand from her arm. Though broad and strong, it wasn't calloused like those of the men who worked the fields. The softness was a reminder of the privileged life he was born into as the firstborn son of a wealthy merchant.

"Over all this?" Briannis nearly laughed as she gestured around. It was far from quiet with everyone pressing in toward the stage and talking with a mixture of worry and excitement. "Besides, I'm almost late. The ceremony will be starting soon."

"That's what I hoped to talk to you about." He took both of her hands in his.

A sinking feeling bloomed in the pit of her stomach. She looked toward the stage, practically begging the elder taking down all the women's names for help, but the woman didn't notice her.

"Soon you'll be free to wed," Ian said, drawing her attention back to him. "And you must know how I feel about you." A flush rose to his fair cheeks.

Oh no... Not again.

"So before anyone else can ask you, I—"

"Oh, Ian," she chided with her best bashful smile. "You know it's bad luck to talk about such things before the ceremony."

His throat bobbed as he swallowed thickly. "Bri, I—"

She shook her head and tugged her hands away, trying to hide her grimace. She *hated* that nickname. How could he not remember that? "We'll speak after," she promised and hurried away.

He was a nice man, wealthy, respected, reasonably handsome, and by all accounts kind, but not *her* man. He wanted a happy little wife who would bear his kids, see to the family's well-being, and not seek anything for herself beyond that. That was certainly not her. She had too much ambition. Had already worked too hard to learn everything from Aunt Davina in the hopes of continuing the family business. She wasn't about to give that up for some man she didn't really love, no matter the potentially comfortable life he offered. Why couldn't he understand that?

For months, she'd held out hope he'd come to that conclusion on his own, but no. She'd have to break his heart definitively this time...after the Choosing.

CHAPTER
THREE

Briannis made it to the end of the short line of women still waiting to ascend and let out a heavy sigh. *Finally.*

She'd just started to pat her frizzy hair back into submission when her relief evaporated. Finola, oldest daughter of the Lord Provost, whose family had been head of the city for generations, stalked her way with a scowl on her narrow, pinched face. Unlike the other women, she hadn't been in line, but had lingered near the record keeper at the base of the stairs, probably hoping to be the last one up and make some sort of grand show of her *bravery* as she joined the others.

"You were just speaking to Ian," Finola started in without preamble the moment she reached Briannis at the end of the line. She leaned in entirely too close. "What did he say?" The words flew out in a rush.

Every young woman had to go through the Choosing at least once, even the Lord Provost's daughters. At just two and twenty, Finola would have another Choosing in her future if she didn't marry, not that she'd ever let it come to that. Unfortunately, she'd gotten her mind set on the only man who didn't appear to be interested in her.

"Nothing much," Briannis lied smoothly. "Just wished me luck today."

Finola huffed, her chin jutting as she crossed her arms. "You know he's going to marry me, right? He'll propose the moment this is over."

Briannis did her best not to let her exasperation show as the line advanced and Finola stood, blocking her way. "I'm sure he will." She didn't mean for her voice to be laden with skepticism, but it flowed out anyway. Maybe he would propose, but not to Finola. A pity he didn't like her instead. It would have saved them all some trouble. "And I wish you all the happiness together when he does," she added with full sincerity.

The comment seemed to take the younger woman aback and her arms loosened a little. But she couldn't just leave things alone. Sliding into line in front of Briannis, she added. "Well, good, because it'd be a shame if you got the wrong idea about him and ended up with your heart broken."

Briannis bit her tongue to keep her smirk hidden. She managed to wait until Finola gave another huff and turned around before she shook her head and rolled her eyes.

Finally, Briannis reached the record keeper. "Briannis Andrews."

The elderly woman scanned the long roll of parchment in her weathered hands, clicked her tongue when she found Briannis' name, and added a mark beside it. "Good. Up with you now."

She'd barely lifted her foot to ascend the handful of stairs when cries erupted from the stage. A stiff burst of wind had Briannis squinting her eyes and glancing up as the dragon swooped overhead before turning skyward toward the blazing sun.

It was truly beautiful when light shimmered across the prismatic sheen of his green scales. Something so beautiful shouldn't be so deadly...or demanding of innocent lives.

A few of the women had dropped to the stage and were picking themselves up again, brushing off their white sheath dresses.

The Lord Provost's voice boomed as he tried to ease the nerves of the crowd, mentioning something about the dragon being eager for his bride and how they must get on with it without delay. He lifted a fine leather sack cinched tight at the top. "Each of these lovely young women will select a stone from the bag. They have all been painted in various colors. Only one will indicate who the Fates have bestowed the honor of becoming the drag-on's bride and granting us all safety and security for years to come."

"An honor," Briannis muttered to herself. The phrasing always sat a little bitterly on her tongue.

The Lord Provost turned toward the older woman who had been collecting names. With a single, tight-lipped nod she conveyed everything he needed to know. All the expected young women were accounted for.

And so it began. One by one, women reached their hand into the bag and withdrew a stone. They must be small, as each kept her fist closed tightly around it. Painful quiet settled in. What color signaled doom? They hadn't said yet. Even if a woman peeked, she had no way to know if she was safe.

It felt like ages before the Lord Provost finally closed in on her at the end of the line. Her feet ached from the too-tight fancy shoes her aunt had insisted on—no woman under her care would dare wear boots with their dress, as Briannis had planned.

The Lord Provost stopped in front of his daughter. Rather than show worry or fear, he beamed at her and she at him. A show of courage for the crowd? Still, something about it picked at her as Finola thrust her fist into the bag and then drew it out a moment later.

Finally, it was her turn.

"Last one," the Lord Provost said with a now tight-lipped smile as he held out the bag between them.

Briannis reached in, easily finding the last stone, and closed her fist around it before withdrawing.

The selection complete, he walked back to the front of the stage and began speaking again about the legacy of the city, the selection of brides, and how the sacrifice had protected them for generations. But all Briannis really wanted to know was *what color?*

The little stone felt like a boulder, the sun overhead was too hot, and though she kept panning the crowd looking for familiar faces, they all blurred and she couldn't see her family anywhere.

"The bride of our guardian dragon shall be the one who presents a stone in his color—green! Now, ladies,"—the Provost turned toward them—"reveal your stones."

Briannis turned up her palm and unfurled her fingers.

Finola screamed. A horrible, shrill sound that made Briannis jolt and nearly drop her stone.

But the other woman wasn't staring at her own stone, a pearly white ball in her outstretched hand. Instead, her wide brown eyes were glued to Briannis' open palm.

She hadn't even looked. There hadn't been time. But sitting there, gleaming in the light, was a smooth, oval stone that was unmistakably green. Not the bluish tint like mold on cheese, nor the deep shade of fir trees in the mountains, but a bright glimmering green like the dragon's scales.

A buzzing hum filled her ears, drowning out whatever the Lord Provost said. Her legs wobbled.

It couldn't be. There was no way. Surely the Fates would have warned her, given her some hint. Figures closed in around her, blocking her view of the crowd, one she was suddenly desperate for. She had to find her aunt and uncle—had to.

Sound returned. Distantly, she heard someone screaming her name. Her heart rate jumped even higher as the elders closed in, the Lord Provost directly in front of her. Everything in her said to run, to flee, but they'd already ringed her in, the other women falling back—some sobbing, others celebrating.

"It's a mistake. I can't—" Her gaze darted, searching for an escape, a way out. She had so much to do, so many plans.

"I'm really sorry about this." The Lord Provost shoved a dark cloth toward her face. A sharp scent stung her nose. And before she could even gather her wits to pull it off, the world slipped away.

CHAPTER

FOUR

Briannis was soaring, arms spread wide, her fingers trailed through tendrils of cloud as the wind whipped her hair behind her head like ribbon of flame. Her heart was light, her burdens gone. Joyful laughter bubbled from her lips. But she wasn't flying, not truly. She was not a bird and had no wings. Between her thighs she felt the flex of thick muscles, the strength of something even more powerful than a horse. The emerald dragon beat its powerful wings, drawing them higher, yet she had no fear. She was safe with him.

And then the dream shifted.

The wind trickled to a breeze which teased her now bare skin. The shape between her thighs was still powerful, but narrowed. Scales had become skin. And when she rocked her hips? A moan tore from her lips at the almost painful fullness spearing her core. She curled her fingers, dragging them down over the hand planes of a muscular chest. Then something —*he*—gripped her waist, the contact jolting through her like falling into an early spring stream.

"Briannis." Her name hissed from a shadowed face.

A scream tore from her throat. She jumped up. Slipped. Fell.

And fell. And fell. And—

Briannis sat up with a gasp, heart and head pounding in discordant tempo with one another as she sucked in deep steadying breaths. She clutched at her forehead.

A dream. Only a strange and disturbing dream.

Though the most alarming part might be the way she still ached between her legs, her body yearning for what had only been illusion. And how strange that she'd been more startled by a man than the beast.

"Damn ceremony giving me nightmares."

Her hand dropped to her side and planted on cool, hard stone.

Stone. Not her bed.

All at once, memories rushed back, hitting with such ferocity that she nearly lost her breath all over again.

She knew what happened to the women who were chosen. They'd all heard the stories. She had even seen part of it herself at the last Choosing.

Once the woman was selected, there was no long goodbye. Nor a quick one. It was supposed to be easier that way. A bitter laugh pushed between her lips. There was nothing easy about goodbye, but being denied even that? Agony.

Briannis hunched in on herself, tears blurring the halo of her vision as she gathered her bearings.

There wasn't much to see in the dim light. The grey stone walls framed a path a little wider than she was. The flames of a lone torch flickered against the iron bars driven from floor to ceiling blocking the way toward the exit, the multitude of locks and chains holding the door firm.

There was no chance of escape.

One woman, Sheena, had done that long ago—found her way out and hobbled back to the city. She was returned not long after with guards set watch to keep her from fleeing. But the dragon knew. That short escape had been enough to doom the city to a string of fires that year that had burned much of the city and half the fields. The starvation that ensued... Well, no wonder there were bars now.

She glanced the other way, straining to see into the gloom as light gave way to shadows. Somewhere in that direction was the dragon's lair.

A shudder wracked her body. All her life she'd been secretly fascinated by the dragon, but the thought of becoming its latest snack was a nightmare made real.

But...

Briannis shoved to her feet.

The dragon had been flying around the city—maybe it wasn't in its lair.

This narrow path wasn't big enough to fit a creature such as that. It had to have another way in and out, and if she could find that, perhaps she could escape.

Briannis shook the metal gate, just on the off-chance it would give way, but of course it didn't. And the torch was too far away on the other side of the bars for her to grab. She sighed as she turned her back on it. The Fates really were against her for some reason.

Her white dress was now damp and dingy from where she'd been lying on the floor, and it kept trying to tangle around her legs as she shuffled into the darkness, hands on the cool walls to steady herself.

As she stumbled on through the pitch black, a conflicting little voice in her head kept telling her to turn back, return to the entry tunnel where she'd been unceremoniously dumped. Though what would she do there? Wait to die of starvation?

No. The only real choice lay ahead.

At first, she thought her mind was starting to play tricks on her. But no, those were real shapes ahead—dripping stalactites no wider than a shaft of wheat and more of the grey stone—illuminated by dim blue light.

A few more steps, and she stilled momentarily, before hurrying forward toward a swash of blue along the wall. "It glows." She ran her hand over the strange moss in wonder. Immediately her mind began to debate whether it was edible, its flavoring, and what it might taste like incorporated with cream or blended into a smooth cheese from their dairy.

Her chest grew tight as her hand fell to her side.

There would be no more dairy for her—no home at all. Even if she escaped, she couldn't go back. She'd have to go somewhere else. But where?

Briannis shoved the thought away. One thing at a time.

There was more moss as she moved along, enough that she hurried her steps. The tunnel grew wider before abruptly opening into a massive cave.

As she skidded to a halt, small stones tumbled down the path ahead of her, each *clink* loud and damning. Her heart leapt into her throat as she glanced around for any sign of the dragon. It was brighter here. Daylight lanced in from a crack in the ceiling above. Flowering green vines draped down through that opening, though none were low enough for her to consider climbing up. The closest was at least two stories above her head. The trickle of water somewhere nearby gave her an odd sense of peace. If this was the dragon's lair, and it was home, surely she would see or hear it.

The ceiling may not be her salvation, but across a still pool of water, there was something else that might be. The beginnings of another tunnel beckoned, and she made her way toward it, senses alert for any sign of danger.

Every breath felt too loud in the cavernous space, but luckily nothing swooped out to eat her before she reached the edge of the pool. She pulled her bottom lip between her teeth as she glared at the tunnel. It was definitely wide enough for a dragon to fit in if it pulled in its wings. Not ideal. Neither was swimming across the water to get to it, but what choice did she have?

Briannis pulled off her flimsy shoes and dipped a toe into the pool. Shivers raced up her leg before she jerked it back. *So cold!*

She scowled at the water, dreading the plunge, when she noticed something among the greenish rocks below. Gold shimmered in the depths of the pool. "A ball?" She leaned in, pulled toward it like some string around her middle was given a soft tug.

Green slid over the top of the gold then retreated.

Briannis screamed. The shrill cry echoed through the cave. The invisible string around her middle seemed to snap as she flung herself back from the pool, slipped on the wet stones, and fell to the ground.

It wasn't a ball. Nor a stone.

The still pool was suddenly a mess of waves, the center rising.

Briannis scrambled backward. The dragon broke the surface, its wings flying wide and spraying water in all directions.

It was glorious and horrifying in equal measure. She'd always thought of the dragon as a wild beast—one that sparked more curiosity in her than fear. But in that moment, she was the startled animal fleeing from a predator, and her body knew it. Terror tightened her throat. Her chest felt like it might contract or explode at the same time. She barely felt the rocks under her bare feet and palms as she tried to shove herself upright to flee.

The dragon had seen her. It knew. She had to get back to the tunnel.

CHAPTER

FIVE

Without another backward glance at the rising beast, Briannis clambered across the rocky cavern floor, cursing the wet skirt of her dress as it tried to tangle around her legs.

A thump filled the air. Not a heartbeat later, a strong burst of air pushed her hair in front of her face and nearly sent her to her knees once more.

A second thump. And then rock crunched in front of her. Wind blasted her face. The dragon had landed between her and the tunnel. Its lizard-like head tilted to the side in appraisal, golden eyes blinking.

Another scream tore from her throat.

Arms raised in front of her, she retreated. "Please!" A stone sliced at her foot and she whimpered. "Don't eat me!"

A deep grumble emanated from the dragon. "Eat you?" A stream of air huffed from its snout.

Briannis stilled. Had it just...spoken?

"I don't— I wouldn't taste good," she amended. Was she really trying to reason with this thing? Maybe she'd hit her head along the way and didn't remember it. "But cows are delicious. Beef yummy. I could give you one? Ten?" She winced. Sacrificing the family cattle felt like a betrayal, but if it saved her life...

The dragon seemed to settle, lowering its bulk toward the cavern floor. "They think so poorly of me."

Her heart leapt at the sound. No, not a sound. She didn't hear the words. Rather, she felt them, almost like they were spoken into her soul, echoing somewhere in her mind.

"At least this one hasn't died of fright." Another puff of air left the dragon's snout as it lowered its head.

Briannis blinked, dumbfounded. *Did it just...sigh?*

The dragon's wings ruffled. "I do not sigh."

She yelped. "You read my thoughts?"

Though it had been moving little before, the dragon turned preternaturally still. If not for the trickle of water and the fluttering of an errant bat waking up, she might have thought the world frozen save for her.

Finally, the dragon blinked. "You... You hear me?" The voice in her head asked. Though not spoken aloud, the dragon's tone held a mix of awe and disbelief mingled into the deep voice that was unmistakably masculine. Rough and edged, it fit with the sharp looking spikes and ridges rising from the crown of its head and down the sides of its neck. To say nothing of the wicked claws at the tips of its feet and wings.

"Yes?"

A shudder wracked its body. Its head swung side to side in the strangely human-like manner of someone trying to clear their thoughts. "Can it truly be—"

The thought shut off abruptly, like a door slammed between them. The dragon stretched its neck forward, gaze intent.

Briannis flinched and stepped back. Her heel landed on something sharp and she hissed in pain.

"Don't harm yourself!" The voice rushed back into her mind.

She scowled. "I'm not trying to."

Its head reared back as its nostrils flared. "I smell your blood."

She stared down at her body. Her hands bled from little cuts and scrapes. She raised one foot and stared as blood trickled from her heel down the sole of her foot to drip from her big toe. Something about the sight unlocked her pain—a sharp throbbing buried under her fear and the shock that followed the revelation of the voice inside her head.

"Damn." All at once her instincts cried out once more that she was prey. And worse, she was bleeding in front of a very real predator. So what if it spoke to her? She spoke to animals all the time, even ones that ended up as dinner.

"Come here," the dragon commanded.

Briannis pulled her hands toward herself. "I will not be easy prey." She twisted to look behind her, searching for another opening she'd yet to spy.

"Stop!" It rumbled, seeming to sense her panic. "I have no desire to ea —" The thought ended in a real grumble that echoed through the cave. "I do not want you as my food."

Something about the strange wording and the desperation laced into it had her glancing back at the dragon.

"I will not harm you."

Impossibly, it felt like truth. But this monster had killed all his brides. Why not her?

The dragon must have heard her thoughts because he reared his neck back and bared a mouth full of long fangs. Its tail whipped into a wall, sending a few stones tumbling. "I did not kill them!" he yelled into her mind.

The force of the thought was so strong it left her bracing and panting for breath.

"You didn't kill them?" But they hadn't returned. Only the one, who was sent back. Merilee, Alivia, and the all the women before, none were seen again. Although... Briannis glanced around. If this was the dragon's lair, she didn't see any skeletons. Unless he ate them elsewhere or consumed the bones, too.

"I. Did. Not. Eat. Them."

Briannis gasped as a small stream of flames flickered from the dragon's open mouth, sending a wave of light cascading through the space before it snapped its jaws closed again.

"Okay, okay," she said. "You didn't eat them."

The dragon huffed again. "You don't believe me."

Damn whatever force projected her thoughts to him.

"Come and let me heal you."

"Heal me?" her brows pinched in confusion.

"Or promise not to flee and I will come to you." The dragon shuffled a lumbering step forward and halted, head tilting in question.

Walking on an injured foot over rocky terrain was less than ideal, and the area he perched was filled with sharp looking boulders. It couldn't be comfortable—for her or him. "Fine. I won't run." She held her head high, summoning her bravery. Either she could trust him, or he lied and she was about to be dinner.

"Dragons do not lie," he grumbled as he slowly advanced.

The closer her got, the more she craned her neck to watch him. He was twice her height with his head held high as it was then. His wings were even wider than he was tall. It was hard to tell in the fading light—barely any filtered through the crevice anymore and only the glowing moss on the wall illuminated the space—but she thought some of the membrane of his wings might be translucent if he were out in the sun. The dragon's sharp claws clicked on the stone as he took a final step and stopped in front of her, staring down with those golden eyes.

"So, how does this work?" Briannis asked, trying to sound brave. Her heart still beat at a frantic pace. If he could smell fear like wolves were said to do, she was probably downright pungent.

The dragon lowered himself until his head was level with hers. Then to her surprise, lowered it further. "What is your name?"

"My name?"

His head bobbed in an unmistakable nod.

What could it hurt? "Briannis."

"Briannis." The not-voice hissed out the last syllable in a way that curled around her middle before sending a pleasant shiver down her spine. "Sit, Briannis. Then hold out your hands to me."

It was even stranger speaking to him this close. His mouth didn't move. The silent words didn't echo back through the cavern like hers did.

Briannis did as he asked, sitting carefully on a smooth rock and then turning her injured palms up toward him. *Putting blood right in front of a predator's nose. You really have lost it.*

The dragon grumbled, sending a wave of warm breath wafting across her face. Briannis scrunched up her features in anticipation of a putrid scent only to be met with a surprise. It was smokey, yes, but in a pleasant and comforting sort of way like a warm fire in winter.

A long tongue slipped from the dragon's maw and lapped at her palm. Briannis gasped at the touch—light, soft, and not wet like a dog's. The forked end tickled her skin, and of all thing she nearly giggled despite the tinge of pain from contact with the wounds.

"You truly thought I ate them? The other women before you?"

Briannis's humor died. What an odd question to ask while he was... whatever he was doing to her hand.

"Yes. It's what happens to the dragon's brides."

He snorted again at that, enveloping her in smoky warmth. "Foolish. Do humans remember nothing?"

"We remember quite a lot," she replied, indignant.

The forked tongue retreated. "Your hand." He bobbed his head toward it.

Briannis blinked down at it. It was clean, but more than that, the wound had sealed, only a hint of pink showing where the cut had been. "How did you—" Her mouth gaped as she searched for the words.

"My saliva can heal." He nudged her other hand with his snout. "May I?"

She let the healed hand drop and angled the other one toward him. "Yes. Thank you." She shook her head, still trying to wrap her mind around what happened. But something else nagged at her just a much. "What happened to the women, if you didn't eat them? I don't see them here."

"I took them away."

"Away?" she echoed.

"To new homes. After the one was sent back broken and left to die..." The growl that tore from his through rumbled the very cave.

Briannis swallowed. Did he mean Sheena? She'd been sent back after she escaped but, broken?

"Brutalized. Bones broken." He snarled, and Briannis shook with fear despite herself. "Half bled out. I could not save her."

"Good Fates," she cursed.

A softer grumble left the dragon before he settled his head back near her hand and began to work on her second palm. "Sheena," he said after he finished. "I shall remember that name." The dragon dipped his head further until his chin was nearly on the ground. "Your foot?"

Tentatively she uncurled it from beside her and held it up toward him, wiggling her bare toes as she did. "Why demand us just to send us away?"

His gaze held hers. "Tell me what you know of me, Briannis of Grimshire."

She opened her mouth to speak, but then his tongue lapped at her heel before trailing up over her sole. Briannis squealed and wiggled at the tickling sensation. He did it again, and the sensation was even stronger. Without thinking, she kicked her foot...straight into his snout.

CHAPTER

SIX

The dragon whipped its head back with a grumble.

Oh no. The sound may well have doused her in ice. *Did I really just kick him?*

Faster than she could blink, he swiped out with his front paw and grabbed her ankle. His claws clicked together but never scored her skin. For a few heartbeats, they were locked in a frozen staring competition. The dragon's grip on her ankle flexed, drawing all her focus to that point of contact—his warm, smooth scales against her skin.

For reasons she couldn't explain, that touch did something to her. A warmth settled low in her stomach and suddenly she was aware of the way her dress stuck to her curves from the dampness and how it had ridden up to her hips when she raised her leg. Maybe he heard her thoughts, because his gaze dipped to the juncture of her thighs and the thin undergarments exposed there. She wiggled her hips in a failed attempt to shield herself.

His nostrils flared. "Do try to hold still."

"It tickles." The huskiness of her voice startled her.

He tilted his head and lapped at her heel again, this time keeping his tongue away from the sensitive arch of her foot. "Tell me. What do you know of me?"

Watching his tongue lap at her skin was doing things to her that she didn't want to think about, especially with the strange ability of him to hear her thoughts, so she did her best to relax and stare at the ceiling as she talked. "You're our guardian dragon, and have been for generations. You protect Grimshire from enemies and invaders, plague, drought, and other ills. It keeps us safe and thriving. But in return, you ask for a bride every five years from the unmarried maidens of the city. The Fates select your bride and the citizens deliver. If we fail to do so, we are punished. Or like Sheena's year, when she left…" Her brows pinched as she considered what the dragon had said, how upset he had been at her mistreatment. "We were punished because she left? Or," he'd stopped lapping at her foot and she sat up, "was it because of how she was returned?"

The dragon crossed his forepaws on the ground and laid his chin atop them. "Neither. I rarely punish you humans, even when they deserve it."

"You… don't?" The impossibility of it struck her as even more strange that their odd method of communicating. All her life—all the lives of everyone in the city—were built on tales of the dragon: the rewards for submitting to him and the risks if they did not. He was the threat that kept enemies away and encouraged children to obey their parents lest the dragon catch them out of bed at night and seek to punish naughty behavior. The need to deliver a maiden bride kept women from wedding their loves or seeking pleasure. Same for the men. To deny the dragon was the greatest offense.

"How could so much be forgotten? So misunderstood?" He closed his eyes as if in pain. "No wonder things changed. No wonder the promises were not kept."

"What changed? What promises?" Briannis inched forward, rising on her knees.

He blinked open his eyes. The depth of emotion in them rocked her.

This dragon, this creature they were taught was both protector and monster, hadn't eaten her. He'd healed her.

"Thank you, again." Did anyone thank him for all that he did? Not to his face surely. And that made her wonder… "Do you have a name?"

He stared back at her, as if she should know.

"We just call you *the dragon*," she admitted, cheeks heating in embarrassment. "But that's not it is it?"

"Noctokozain."

"Not-co—"

"Zain will do."

"Zain." It fit him. It really did.

The dragon—Zain—almost seemed to smile. His mouth opened and he released a long puff of warm breath which surrounded Briannis like a comforting blanket. She found herself leaning into that warmth. Yearning for. Especially as it faded and the chill of the cave returned.

"I suppose all your brides get to learn your name." Briannis shoved her frizzy hair behind her shoulder.

Zain stretched his wings before tucking them in closer to his sides. "I have not been able to speak to any of them. Only you."

"What?" Briannis replied, taken aback. "None of them?"

He shook his head.

"Then how can you speak to me?"

He raised his head slightly, bringing it level with hers. Warmth radiated from him, leaping the few inches that separated them. "You are—" The thought slammed off abruptly.

She leaned closer. "I am what?"

"Cold." He raised a wing. "Come, you'll be warm near me."

Her eyes narrowed. She was pretty sure that wasn't what he'd been planning to say at first. But she was cold. Though she would have balked at the idea hours ago, she found herself inexplicably yearning for his warmth and closeness now. The rational part of her said she was just curious about him. How many times had she thought about him over the years? Desired to get a look at him up close and study him? That was why she took his invitation and came to sit next to his chest—or at least that's the reason she gave herself. The green of his scales lightened as they flowed down toward his underside, transitioning into a paler green bordering on tan, almost like the first leaves of spring.

It *was* much warmer near him.

A soft gasp slipped from her lips as his wing curled over her almost like a blanket and urged her to lean back against his side. She did, settling into the crook of his shoulder. He'd turned his long neck until he stared at her, blinking. "Better?"

"Yes. Much." There'd be no chance of her getting cold there. Maybe the opposite. "Will you tell me about you? Whatever we have lost?"

His chest expanded, moving her forward, then back as he exhaled in a deep sigh.

Briannis's lips quirked up. *And he said he didn't sigh.*

Zain's eye's narrowed before he breathed a puff of hot air at her.

She giggled in return. Giggled...when only minutes ago, she thought she might die. Thoughts of her family rushed to the surface. They probably thought she was dead. Or dying. All Zain's warmth wasn't enough to keep the cold of that revelation away.

"I wasn't always a dragon."

Now *that* snapped her from her tormented thoughts.

"At least not fully," he continued. "I was born to a family far in the south with the ability to shift into dragon form. But my normal form was human."

Human. Briannis gaped. She knew of no other dragons, and certainly no humans who could become them.

"Yes. A surprise, I know. As my father's heir, it was my job to travel and build relations with other kingdoms."

Heir? He was a—

"A prince, yes," he answered her thought. "On one of my journeys I met a young and beautiful witch. She desired me—or rather, my crown. I might have been a young fool, but even I could see that. When I rejected her, saying that I would only bind myself to my fated mate, she placed a curse on me. If I would not wed her, then I would have to wait for my mate...as a dragon."

"What a selfish bitch." Briannis hugged her arms about herself. For some reason, the story brought to mind Finola's face. Another selfish woman who wouldn't hesitate to damn someone for denying whatever she desired, feeling entitled to the very ground she walked upon.

He laughed, chest rumbling. "Indeed. Unfortunately for me, she was powerful. My one blessing was that I could communicate with my family when they were also in dragon form. I told them of my plight, and they sought out any who might be able to help me find my mate. Eventually, a powerful seer was able to give me direction. My mate did not yet walk this plane, but she would come from the city of Grimshire far to the north."

"Here?" Briannis sat up straighter. "Then your brides—"

"You're getting ahead of me, but yes. My brother made the journey with me, for he could still become a human and speak when I could not. He described my plight to the leader of the city, and an agreement was forged. I would stay and live in the mountains, protect the city in any way that I could. In exchange, the young maidens of the city would be presented before me each year so that I could determine if any were my mate."

So long he waited. Briannis absently stroked the scales of his leg. "But that's so different than now."

"Mmm." He dipped his head, lying it on the ground. "Time has a way of breaking down truths, wearing them away until they are a twisted shell of what they once were. Some pieces remain, but others..." His tail whacked into a pile of stones, sending them scattering and splashing into the nearby pool.

"The agreement held for a while. I would land outside the city and the women would come before me. But none were the one I sought." Sorrow laced his tone.

Briannis's hand stilled on his scales. "How did you know? That they were not your mate?"

"Mates are a rare blessing. Some of my kind search their whole lives to never find one. But my father found my mother—a human woman he met in a small fishing village. He said he felt a pull to her, a force tugging him in her direction. And once he was near her, there was an undeniable urge to join with her."

"Oh." A rush of heat flew to her cheeks as she pulled her hand away from him.

"I never felt that pull, that desire. But I protected the city all the same from any enemies who could threaten my future mate."

"Plagues? Drought?" Briannis asked, leaning forward.

Zain shook his head. "A foolish human wish. No dragon can stop a plague. Perhaps burn a field to purge a fungus, but no. Not as I assume you mean it."

Her head fell back against his side as she pinched her eyes shut. So the plague that killed her parents wasn't a punishment. It had nothing to do with the dragon at all, nor could he stop it.

"You have some experience with loss," he said into her mind.

She pulled her legs to her chest as she opened her eyes to look at him. "Yes. It was years ago now but..." But some pain never truly went away. "But yes, I do. What happened to your family? Could they not clarify the agreement when it changed?"

"My brother used to come every few years."

Years? Her eyes bulged.

"We have a longer life than humans, and it's a long journey." His leg moved in something like a shrug. "As the new heir, he had many responsibilities. I do not blame him for not lingering with me. But the final time he came, there was a misunderstanding. Many had come for some festival in the city, and my brother arrived in dragon form. There was panic among the foreigners." Bitterness filled his tone. "During the chaos, he was attacked and captured."

Briannis's chest grew tight. The dragon behind her seemed to shift and tense.

"He fought back, with lethal consequences. By the time the locals freed him and came to me, many humans had died, and my brother..." Zain's head dropped. "He was beyond saving."

"No." She clutched his leg again.

"In my anger and grief, I..." He glanced away. "That was when the fear began. When things changed for the worse." He laid his head down and closed his eyes. "One misunderstanding can be a like a rock tossed into a pond. So small, but the ripples can be so large and grow and as they spread."

"I... I'm so sorry." She knew the pain of loss. Of seeing loved ones suffering and being unable to save them. It was torture. The kind that left its scars on your heart.

Briannis snuggled in against his leg. "So now we just give you one bride every five years, which probably makes it impossible to find your mate, right? I mean, what are the odds?"

A deep grumble left his chest, which she took for agreement. Absently, she noted that he was much better at shielding his thoughts from her than she was from him.

"Why not just swoop down to the middle of the square so you can check out all the women?"

He lifted his head and drew it closer to hers. "How do you think that would work out?"

She swallowed, thinking of the way the women had dove toward the stage, the way everyone in the city seemed to panic when the dragon flew too close. "Okay, terrible idea. But it's so unfair to you and to all of us. The women who were picked and sent here—" Fates, they understood so little. "They really did not die?"

Zain looked away and lowered his head to the ground once more. For a moment, she thought he would not answer. "Some did, though I did not kill them." He cracked open one golden eye. "I could not speak to them like you. Some died of fright. Others in attempts to escape. The one who was sent back, Sheena, I could not get to her to heal her. She died of her wounds."

Somber truth filled the air with heaviness until finally Zain continued. "Most lived."

A held breath whooshed from her lungs. They lived. It was as much a revelation as if one of the Fates took human form and appeared in front of her. Or a dragon speaking into her mind...

"Before the *incident* with my brother, none were taken. The years after were...strange. I cannot say how it happened exactly, but the fear spread and grew. No longer would the women come before me, or any humans at all. They fled. Time passed. I fell into despair. And then there was a particularly bad drought. Many died and I could not help them. I feared then the city as a whole would be lost, and I too would be doomed forever. Soon after, the sacrifices began. Women sent to the hills. I would return them to the city if I could. Though some struggled. There were a few times in a row when I failed to help them, to return them. Another drought struck. That was the year they sent Sheena." His eyes slid closed. "She survived. At first.

She left and found her way home. But shortly after, lightning ignited a fire that burned much of the city and the fields. The people must have believed it was me. That I was angry and caused the fire. So they sent her back, injured and left to die as a sacrifice to the dragon."

Briannis shook her head at the ironic tragedy of it all.

Zain opened his eyes again and stared at Briannis. "So then, I started taking the women away when I could. Across the sea. Somewhere they could be safe and live but not return here."

"There was a woman ten years ago. Blonde. A little plump. Very kind." A spark of hope burned deep in Briannis's chest. Could she be alive? "Her name was Merilee." Not that he likely knew it, but she felt the need to speak it anyway.

"I remember her," Zain replied. "She was frightened and cried much."

Briannis held her breath.

"But I was able to take her safely to a new city."

"She's alive!" Briannis nearly spang to her feet at the joy of it.

He nodded. "She was two years ago, when I was last there. The people there think me some sort of God, I believe, and the women I bring are sacred. They are treated well and come to see me when I visit."

She laughed in disbelief. All this time, the town mourned them as dead. She could change that, let them know that their family members lived. And not just lived, but thrived! They weren't the only people she could help. "I can help you find your mate!" She flung out an arm in her exuberance and grazed his wing. Zain's body shuddered.

"So sorry." Briannis whipped her hand back. Damn. Her nails were probably sharp thanks to scrambling around on the rocks. "But I really think I can help you," she hurried on. "I can explain what happened. Bring back the old tradition so that people will not fear you and you can meet everyone to see if anyone is your mate. Just take me back and—"

A loud grumbling roar silenced her. Zain had thrown his head back and bared his fangs. Briannis stilled, fighting the urge to bolt. His wing tucked in closer and she shuffled back toward his side instead. "I will not risk you with them."

Oh. *Oh.* "You think they'd treat me like Sheena?" Would they? If she came walking back into the city claiming to have spoken to the dragon...

Her heart sank. He was right. They'd think she lost her sanity in the escape. No one would listen to something so outrageous. But what if he went with her?

Zain grumbled again. "No."

"But how will you find your mate?"

He stared at her for a few moments before looking away. "We will discuss this another time. The sun is setting quickly." He glanced at the ceiling above. "You must be tired."

Sleep had been the last thing on her mind, though now that he mentioned it, she really was exhausted, especially after rising so early that morning and the fear of earlier burning away her energy.

"Fine. But we'll figure something out. There must be a way." She glanced around, suddenly unsure. "Where should I sleep?"

Deep laughter rolled through her as Zain tucker his wing closer. "Right here. I will keep you warm."

CHAPTER

SEVEN

Briannis woke to the mouth-watering smell of roasting meat.

Sleeping on a rocky cavern floor next to a dragon should not have been comfortable, yet she felt strangely refreshed as she yawned and stretched her limbs. Blinking awake, she spied a hulking figure beyond the burning branches a few feet away. Her body locked up, then relaxed as memories of the night before flooded back.

Zain blinked his golden eyes at her. "Good morning, Briannis."

He'd clearly been up and busy long before her, though he'd somehow managed not to rouse her. How a dragon as big as him could move around without sounding like a thunderstorm, she had no idea.

Slowly, she tore her gaze away from him and to the fire. A few sizable branches lay in a haphazard heap. Directly on top of them was the source of the smell. "Is that..."

"Mountain goat."

She sighed in relief.

"They are quite tasty." He crossed his forelegs in front of him. "You would prefer something else?"

"No." She'd never tried mountain goat, but it smelled decent. The sight however… Blackened and charred, it was unrecognizable, except—yep, that was a hoof at one end.

"Apologies. I am not used to cooking."

Briannis shoved to her feet and approached the fire. "Oh no, it's fine. This is very sweet actually." It was. He'd made a fire and tried to cook meat for her, when it was clear he was unused to doing so. She had a feeling he probably preferred his meat rare. "I appreciate you thinking of me."

Something that sounded more like a purr than a grumble rumbled from his chest. Zain adjusted his hind legs, shifting his posture but not rising.

Briannis tried to wall off her thoughts as she edged closer to the meat and used the cool end of a large branch to knock the charred leg from the fire. She was hungry. Her stomach rumbled at the savory smell despite the charred tinge in the air. And he'd done this for her—the fire, the fresh kill. It would be rude to ignore the offering.

Heavy silence hung in the air as Briannis tended to her full bladder and waited for the meat to cool. Her underthings were in worse shape that she realized, and she couldn't stomach putting the stained and dirty material back on, so she left those off. It might be improper in the city, but she couldn't fathom a dragon caring.

When the meat no longer threatened to burn her fingers, she started to pick past the char looking for something edible. Zain shifted a few more times, almost like he sat on an uncomfortable rock, yet decided not to move. Whatever thoughts floated through his mind were shielded from her. Though she tried to keep hers to herself, she may have failed. What happened next? How could she go home without the city panicking? How would they find Zain's mate?

Briannis tore free a chunk of meat in a most unladylike way that would have had her aunt scolding her manners and plopped it into her mouth. A moan slipped past her lips. She closed her eyes at the smokey, meaty goodness. Maybe dragon fire added extra flavoring, because it was surprisingly delicious.

When she opened her eyes once more, Zain stared at her intently. Something, not quite a thought, but more a feeling, rushed into her mind.

Pain. Need.

She swallowed the bite and lowered the next one she was about to plunk into her mouth. "Are you…are you hurt?" Guilt swarmed in her belly. If he'd gotten hurt hunting for food for her…

"Not hurt." The short phrase came across like it was bitten out between clenched teeth.

Briannis took a few more bites. Zain kept shifting. He didn't speak, only stared at her as she ate.

"Something is wrong." She laid down the rest of the goat leg.

This time, he did not answer.

She stood, frowned at her greasy fingers, shrugged, and then wiped them on her dress. The thing was already dirty and ruined anyway. Briannis approached Zain slowly, like she might a wounded animal.

"Is this about taking me away?" She held out her hand as she approached. "Because I've thought about it, and I don't want you to." She laid her palm on the hard flat plane that would be the bridge of a human's nose. A shudder ran through his form as he closed his eyes.

He lids flew open. "I won't let them hurt you."

"Well, I'd prefer they didn't too, but you can't carry on like this." She dropped her hand and squared her shoulders. "And sacrificing our women? The lengths that we're restricted and controlled all to be a pure offering? It's not right!" Her voice rose, echoing back through the cave. "It's not even helpful. It can't continue."

"I agree."

She blinked, taken aback.

"And it won't."

"What?" Her brow furrowed.

Again, he shifted his back legs.

Briannis narrowed her eyes and stalked down his length. He was hiding something.

Zain snapped his wing down to cover himself.

Briannis placed her hands on her hips and twisted back toward his head. She projected her thoughts as loud as she could. *Something is wrong. Stop hiding.*

A deep grumble was his only reply.

"Don't you grumble at me." She waved a finger at him, much like she did her cows when they were testy. "You'll find I'm nothing if not stubborn, and I'm not letting this go, so what is it?"

When he merely blinked at her, a thought struck so hard that she gasped. "Are you—are you dying?" Oh, blessed Fates, was that why he said it would not continue?

A sound floated down their bond and when she wrapped her head about it, her concern faded into a frown. He'd laughed at her. Laughed!

She crossed her arms and tapped her foot while she scowled at him.

Zain's humor dwindled and finally he said, "I fear that if I tell you, it may make you...uncomfortable."

"Because letting me think you may be dying and then laughing at me is so much better."

He laid his head on the ground in a sign of submission. "Know that if I tell you, you are under no obligation to help me. I can take you somewhere you will be safe and cared for."

"I'm not running away. I want to—"

His loud grumbling growl cut her off. Her scowl deepened but she stayed quiet.

"I ask for nothing but your safety and happiness."

She shifted from one foot to the other. The way he said that, the emotion...it felt so deep for someone he'd only just met. Briannis sighed and loosened her crossed arms. "I think it's best if you just tell me what's wrong and we'll go from there."

Zain dipped his head and then let out a deep huff that was definitely a sigh. "I think it may be easiest to show you."

He slid his wing back, revealing his lower half. The he moved, rolling onto his side, lifting one hind leg.

It took a minute for Briannis to comprehend what she saw—the thick pink lengths sprouted from a slit in the scales between his hind legs. Her eyes widened. Heat rushed to her cheeks. More strangely, moisture flared at her core.

"You're—" She licked her suddenly dry lips and forced her attention back to his face. "How have you, um, handled this before?"

"I haven't." He adjusted his posture, settling back fully onto his hind quarters and lowering himself until his erect cock—*cocks, Blessed Fates, there were two of them!*—were hidden from view. "In dragon form, we only grow aroused for our mate."

His mate...

Briannis gasped. "Oh!" She clapped her hands over her mouth before lowering them. Pure joy sparked in her heart for him. "That's why the bride ceremonies don't need to continue! You found her! Oh. Oh my. I can help with this. I can speak to her on your behalf. Let her know you're waiting for her. It may be hard to get her to convince her—" She shook her head. "Actually, I'm nothing if not convincing. If I can sell cheese to every shop in the city, surely I can talk a woman into falling for you, right?"

He just stared at her, seemingly unaffected by her enthusiasm.

"Why are you not excited about this?" Briannis asked, truly confused. She stalked right up to him, barely an inch from his maw. "This is what you've been waiting for! Your curse can be broken!"

He nudged her gently with his head. "My mate has to want to break my curse."

Her shoulders slumped. "And you worry she won't. I mean, I'm sure the idea of the dragon being your mate might be surprising to someone. It's certainly out of the ordinary. But I'm sure most women would be honored to be your mate."

Briannis gasped and jolted as something touched her calf through the material of her dress. A quick glance and her panic subsided. His tail. The end of it slid down her leg again, almost like—

The heat in her face spread down her whole body. Almost like a caress.

"Briannis." The richness of her name in his husky timber sent a shiver down her spine.

Her gaze snapped to his. "It's me," she said, barely a whisper. "I'm—"

Your mate.

"Yes."

Her legs wobbled and she nearly sat. If not for his tail wrapping further around her, almost holding her up, she would have.

His mate. I'm his mate.

Somewhere in her mind, she felt a door close. Almost like Zain was giving her privacy, making sure her thoughts stayed her own. *His mate.* He was giving his mate privacy. Just as he'd given her food. Comfort. Healing.

"Is that why you can talk to me?" Of all the questions tumbling through her mind, that was the easiest.

"I cannot be certain, but I believe so." Another comforting stroke of his tail down her leg.

"How long have you known?"

"Since last night. When you could hear me, I wondered. It's a trait some mated pairs possess. And then the more time I spent near you, the more my body echoed what my mind was already piecing together."

So, recently. She tentatively reached out and cupped his cheek. The smooth, warmth of his scales under her palm was comforting. It gave stability through the shock slowly settling into her bones. *His mate.*

"Though, I'll admit, things had felt strange the last few years."

"Strange? How so?"

"I felt... a pull. An interest in the city that I had not felt since the early days. I think perhaps, deep inside, I knew my mate waited for me, though I did not realize that's what it was. Maybe I should have known, but after so long..." He leaned into her touch. "Even last night, I was in denial. Until my body confirmed what my mind refused to."

All night. He'd been like that. Even this morning, when he'd hunted for her. Made a fire. *Cooked for her.* She stroked his cheek. "No wonder you're uncomfortable and in pain." She knew it had to be something, though she'd never considered this...

Something knotted in her belly and she squeezed her thighs together. She could help him. Heal him. Break his curse!

"You found me, but you're still a dragon."

He dipped his head and closed his eyes. There was still something of a door between them, cracked enough to let his thoughts flow to her but perhaps not the reverse. She could feel the emotion churning in him. Hope and sorrow blended as one in a wave of feeling.

"Well. We'll fix that. We'll find a way. But first—" Her words grew thick and she had to swallow before continuing. "Let me help you."

He reared his head back, jerking away from her touch. "Briannis." His tone held astonishment. Desire. But also something too much like fear for her liking.

"You healed me. Did you really think I would leave you in pain?"

"But my suffering is—" He brought his wing down, tucking it against himself and blocking his hind section from view.

Briannis escaped the curl of his tail and stalked down his body. She clicked her tongue before stroking his wing. Like the last time, he shuddered. And now she understood. It hadn't been pain the night before, but pleasure.

"Can you honestly say you don't want me to touch you?" She tossed over one shoulder.

"No. I want—" His tail curled around her again, almost like he couldn't help himself. "I want that more than anything."

To her surprise, Briannis did also. Well, maybe not *anything*, but she was certainly eager to help him. And curious. And maybe more than a little aroused herself at the thought of what that would entail. She patted his side. "Then be a good boy, move your wing, and let me help you."

His chest rumbled under her palm. "Careful, little mate." He did as she asked, and this time, when she caught sight of the lengths between his legs, she didn't look away despite the burning ache in her chest or the way her core practically throbbed at the sight. This time, she let herself study him.

She'd seen human males a few times, but those cocks were mostly flaccid and uninteresting, glimpsed during a dip in the river in summer or when she'd helped with the infirm during a particularly bad bout of illness. Only once had she seen a man in his pleasure—through a crack in the door by accident when delivering cheese. A woman had been on her knees before the man. She stroked his cock with her hand, then her tongue, then both. Briannis had been so transfixed at the sight, so captivated by something that was supposed to be forbidden to her until after her final Choosing, that she watched through that crack far, far longer than any decent person should.

But Zain's cocks were nothing like that man's.

Each was a dark pink, bordering on red. A far cry from the pale green of his scales. Both protruded from a slit between scales, one on top of the other. The top cock was a little more narrow and slightly shorter than the bottom one which was almost as thick as her forearm. Along the lengths of each were ringed ridges leading to the flared tip where moisture sparkled.

Did dragons take their mates in their dragon form? Would something like that even fit in a human? The thought aroused and terrified in equal measure.

If Zain listened in to her questions, he said nothing, just left himself open to her perusal.

When his voice came through their bond again, he began, "If you do not wish to—"

Briannis nearly laughed. "Stop being a gentleman and read my thoughts again."

The door between them opened. And through it, she shoved the thought of her on her knees beside him, licking one cock and then the other.

Zain bucked, his tail nearly sweeping her off her feet. "Briannis." Her name was a choked sound.

"What was it you told me last night?" she asked with a little smirk. "Sit. And be still."

Briannis stalked the short distance down his length and dropped to her knees before him. Her whole body was warm, and it had nothing to do with the pleasant heat radiating from his scales. Zain had bent his head in close to hers. His smokey breath caressed her skin, only increasing the slickness building at the juncture of her thighs.

Tentatively, she reached out and took his thicker length in hand. A shudder coursed through his body. His eyes slid shut. "My mate. My mate is touching me."

The thought was so vulnerable she was sure he hadn't meant to share it, but it gave her the confidence she needed to stroke down his shaft, marveling at how he was soft yet shockingly firm all at once, how her fingers slid over each ridge, how he was so big around that her fingers could not touch.

She ached—ached!—at the thought of that length trying to nudge inside her. Impossible. Painful. Yet…there was an undeniable allure to the thought.

Briannis took the smaller, but still startling large, cock in her other hand. It was ridged, like the first, and a bead of something shimmery lingered at the tip. She ran her thumb over it then spread the slick down his length.

When she looked over at his face, his eyes were open once more, mouth slightly parted to reveal his fangs. It should have been terrifying, but she had no fear of him.

"Good?" She asked, stroking both lengths.

"Yesss..." A hiss of pleasure accompanied the response. "Any touch from you would be a delight."

She grinned. Inexperienced though she may be, at least he enjoyed it. His tail curled behind her thighs, tucking her close. Briannis shoved her unruly hair behind her shoulders and leaned in. Before she could second guess herself, she lapped at the thick cock straining in her grip.

A deep groan slipped from her dragon. It was all the encouragement she needed to sample him again, licking up his length while her hands glided up and down like she'd seen the cook do to her lover that once.

"Your smell. That scent," he said into her mind. "You enjoy this."

She stared at him through the fall of her red waves which had slipped back over her shoulder in her eagerness. "I do enjoy you." She flicked her tongue across his wide tip. Who would have ever thought she'd say something like that about a dragon?

His claws dug into the cavern floor.

It was intoxicating how her touch affected him, how a common woman such as herself brought a dragon such pleasure.

His tail flicked away, and then it was back, but not wrapped around her as it had been. The tip slipped between her legs, finding the opening of her dress and travelling under the fabric.

Briannis gasped as the new sensation, drawing back. Before she'd fully understood his aim, that tail surged up between her thighs and slid across her slick center. "Zain!" The one touch set her nerves alight. He moved it again, and a moan slipped from her lips. Her hands tightened on his cocks, perhaps too much as he reared his head back with a roar.

She loosened immediately. "Did I—"

"No." He bit out, lowering his head. "I delight in you." His nostrils flared. "My mate is wet for me."

"Yes." She bit down hard on her bottom lip. So embarrassingly wet. No human man had ever made her feel that way.

"This is—" A shudder ran through her form before she started stroking his lengths again. "This is about you. Easing your pain."

That delightful tail slipped through her folds, right over the taut bud between her legs. "Pleasuring my mate is a dream. A joy. How I have yearned for you..."

"Zain," she whimpered again before turning back to his cocks and wrapping her lips around the tip of the narrower length. His smokey, musky taste was a delightful enigma as she sucked on that flared tip.

His tail continued to tease her. The thoughts slipping from him between their bond became groans and feelings—incoherent as hers. All the world narrowed down to his hot lengths, the two in her hands and the scaled one sliding between her legs. So thick. So warm.

The knot of desire in her core twisted tighter with each stroke. Sweat broke out across her skin, causing the fabric of her dress to stick. She wanted it gone, but she dared not stop. Briannis rocked her hips, baring down on the length of his tail. Blessed Fates, how could just his tail make her feel this way? Smooth scales slid over her clit, sending hints of ecstasy racing under her skin. Her pleasure felt like a dam about to break.

Without removing her lips from his cock, she shouted down their bond. "Zain! I'm... I'm about to—"

"Let go, my mate."

"But you—"

"Let go," he ordered.

His tail retreated and she nearly screamed in frustration. How dare he tell her to let go and then—

Suddenly, it was back, not slicking through her folds and over her clit, but sliding into her hot center. The unexpected thickness, fullness of him sent her over the edge. Briannis shattered. His cock slipped from her lips as she threw her head back with a cry of pleasure. "Zain!"

Her scream echoed through the cave. The muscles of her core clenched around his tail as he held the tip still within her, almost like he knew she needed it—maybe he did.

"My mate, my beautiful mate," he crooned.

"Zain," she panted. His name was the only coherent thought she could form.

His tail slipped from her and she all but collapsed into a heap, body still twitching from her release. In her ecstasy, her hands had fallen from his cocks. Panting, she shoved her hair out of the way. They were still erect, still straining. She reached for him again, determined to finish what she started.

But that wicked tail wrapped around her middle and pulled her back.

"Zain?" She asked, unable to disguise her sudden hurt. She'd tried to relieve him. She'd really—

"You are glorious, my mate. Your touch is everything. But I believe I need...something else." His attention dipped to her lap then trailed back up her figure.

Her mouth parted in understanding. She panted as she held his stare. She wanted to—wanted him. But could she?

"Will you try for me, Briannis?"

"Of course," she said at once. Of course she would try. She climbed to her feet on shaking legs. His tail was there again, stroking her calf, almost like he couldn't help himself.

He moved his head until it was an inch from hers, so close it was almost hard to look him in the eye. "If it hurts, we will stop. I will not risk you."

She stroked his face. "I'm not afraid of a little pain."

"Briannis!" He growled.

With a smile, she placed a kiss on his nose. "If it's too much, I will let you know."

He huffed air through his nose, blowing her hair back. "I will find it in your thoughts if you lie."

"Then you'll also know how much I enjoy your touch."

His tongue flicked out, licking her face in the strangest kiss of her life, but also the most touching.

"Well, I should get rid of this." Briannis stared down at her ruined dress with a laugh.

"Mmm." Zain nudged her gently with his nose. "Yes, let me see my little mate."

She tugged the dress over her head and tossed it away. She'd already discarded her underthings, which only left the band of fabric over her breasts.

Zain had risen to stand, his erect cocks hanging precariously close to the stones between his hind legs. He lowered his head to the red curls between her legs and inhaled. A rumble of pleasure sounded in his chest. "Fiery inside and out."

The comment made her body flame anew. Carefully, she unwrapped the length of fabric over her breasts, sighing as it fell away. She did hate binding herself, though it'd been necessary given how little the ceremonial dress concealed.

Feeling bold, Briannis pushed her hair behind her shoulders and stood proudly bare before him.

"Beautiful." His tongue flicked out to tease one nipple.

She giggled at the touch. The laughter vanished as his front paw closed over her bare hip. The tips of his claws grazed her skin but did not hurt. Their gazes locked, and she suddenly remembered what they were about to do.

"If you have any second thoughts..."

"No." She shook her head. "None."

Her nudged her head with his. "Then lay down, my Briannis."

Lack of experience had never given Briannis hesitation in life. It was just an opportunity to learn more. And this was something she had yearned to learn about even before her aunt had stoically explained the basics of it to her years ago—mostly as warning of what not to do to anger the dragon. How ironic that she had a feeling her dragon didn't care about her purity at all, just her.

While she didn't know how humans typically lay down to mate, she'd seen her animals do it many times. So, Briannis got down on her elbows and knees, legs slightly parted, rump raised in the air toward Zain with her pussy on full display. "Like this?" she asked over one shoulder.

His tongue flicked out, almost as if he licked his lips. "How you undo me." His emerald wings flicked and stretched. Zain stalked forward until she loomed under his bulk. Clawed feet dug into the ground on either side of her, both ahead and by her own legs.

Briannis's core throbbed in anticipation. She fought the urge to rock her hips as he slowly lowered himself. A sharp gasp tore from her lips as the head of one cock slid against her thigh. Then it was moving up, spreading a hint of his moisture across her skin. Unable to resist the temptation, she dropped her head to stare between her legs. His large cock hung between her spread thighs. The slightly narrower one slipped against her folds, making her groan.

Zain kneaded his clawed feet in the ground as he adjusted his hips, attempting to position himself just so.

Suddenly, the head of his cock notched at her opening. "Yes. There," she whimpered. Briannis bit her lip, torn between bracing and trying to make her body relax.

Ever so slowly, he pushed forward. The head of his cock stretched her opening. Her body both delighted in the tease of fullness and yearned for completion. Compared to the end of his tail, this appendage was thicker. It didn't want to slide into her easily.

Zain pushed again. A small whimper escaped as the head of his cock stretched her opening.

He halted. "Briannis. I think we should—"

"No." She smacked a fist on the ground. "I'm fine. We can do this." Something in her, more than lust or carnal desire, said they *needed* to. She rocked her hips back, forcing her body to stretch around his girth. "Please. Fill me, Zain. Fill me with your cock."

A grumbled accent filled the air and then he gave a gentle thrust forward.

Something within her finally gave way, letting his thick length inch inside. Tingling pain raced through her, but mingled within was triumph and the most delicious fullness.

Zain let out a roar of pleasure. "So tight. My mate's pussy is so tight and wet."

The slickness of her earlier release helped ease his passage as he pushed in further. And that's when she started to feel the ridges along his length. The extra stretch, the slight release, and the way they brushed against her inner walls? Bliss. Briannis moaned as he sank slowly deeper, filling her, stretching her. She started clawing at the ground herself, needing more but wondering at the possibility of it. Her walls ached, but it was a burn she craved as much as air.

The deeper he slid, the more she started to feel his second, broader cock. The length slid against her clit, sending bright waves of pleasure coursing through her.

"Fuck. You feel so incredible." Zain's claws tore up the ground in front of her as he fought to control his entry.

Every time she was certain he couldn't go any deeper, his cock would slip further in. It was a delirious yet blissful agony as her body stretched to accommodate him while he seemed to fill more than just her body but her whole sense of being. Finally, when she was a mewling mess, her cheek pressed to the cool stone, he halted.

"Briannis?" Her name was a strangled hiss, both a question and a plea.

"Yes, Zain. Yes." Whatever it was, whatever he asked, she wanted it. She could take it.

He pulled back, each ridge of his cock sliding through her aching pussy. And then he surged forward.

A scream tore from her lips. Bright pleasure surged through her as sharp and hot as lightning and tingling with its own burn. She welcomed it, wanted it. He must have seen that in her thoughts, because he began to move in a steady rhythm, driving his cock in and out of her while the bigger one grazed her clit with each surge forward. It was maddening. All-consuming. Briannis dug her fingers into the cavern floor, grasping for purchase as each thrust left her rocking forward.

"Zain!" His name was the only word she could find as he drove her steadily toward a looming precipice within herself. She was there, but not. All sensation was pulled to the awareness of their joining, his hot cock inside her, another caressing her, and warmth from his body jumping to hers.

"My beautiful mate." His voice in her mind was like a caress down her spine or breath along the shell of her ear. "You take me so well."

The praise shoved her off that internal cliff, and she was falling in a tumult of bliss. No. Not falling at all—flying. It was like her dream. She soared through the clouds in pure, mindless bliss. Freedom. That's what it was. Bright, burning, and wonderful. Briannis gasped as she came back to herself, her core still clenching and spasming from her release. Zain continued to move, drawing out her pleasure until tears ran down her face.

"Fuck." His awareness rushed into her mind. "So tight. I—" The dragon roared, a sound louder and more guttural than any before.

The bellow shook the ground below her. Distantly, Briannis heard rocks fall and tumble, but she was not afraid, not with her dragon protecting her. He would never let harm come to her, his mate. She knew it with soul-deep certainty.

With a last deep thrust, he stilled inside her. Briannis gasped as a sudden burst of heat spilled within her, spreading through her still tingling pussy. She groaned with pleasure at the new sensation, even as hot liquid dripped down her thighs. His come, she realized distantly. So warm and delightful, just like the rest of him.

Boneless as she was from her release, Briannis closed her eyes and laid her head on the smooth stone ground, savoring the new feeling of his completion. His cock slipped from inside her, sending more liquid splashing to the ground between her knees. Something warm and almost heavy covered her back—his underbelly?—though he was careful not to crush her. Then, something brushed her arm and her brows pinched at the sensation. Not scales. Nor his wing. She cracked open her eyes.

"Briannis," a very real voice panted right in her ear.

She screamed. Not of bliss, but terror. Instantly, she was scrambling forward, clawing her way across the stone floor and out from under the very real person who had suddenly appeared atop her.

"Wait!" the deep voice cried. "Briannis!"

She twisted to look over her shoulder. Through the fall of her hair, she spied a figure on the ground. Male. Muscular yet lean. Naked. Very naked, and with a half-firm human cock. He tried to rise, wobbled, then fell.

"It's me," he grunted.

Briannis turned fully and shoved her hair out of the way. That voice... It was different out loud, but yet, familiar. "Zain?"

She gaped at him where he sat a few feet away. His hair was dark, a deep brown like the soil of their fields. It framed the strong, angular features of his face and the scruff on his jaw. The skin along his form was a light golden bronze, not a tan line to be seen. But the eyes...

Those golden eyes, she knew.

"Zain," she repeated with confidence and awe.

"Yes," he said between heaving breaths. "I—" He held his hand in front of him, staring at it like it was some strange new thing.

Briannis raced to him and dropped to her knees at his side. "You're human! Your curse?"

The corners of his lips turned up in a slow, devastating smile that had her insides doing somersaults. "It seems my mate freed me."

She'd freed him. Saved him. This was Zain. *Her* Zain.

She let her gaze wander over his form, taking in the man that had only moments ago been a beast. A smattering of dark hair covered his muscular chest and arms. That was what she had felt that had alerted her something was different—the brush his arm against her, hair and all.

Zain did the same, taking her in with human eyes. She could almost feel his gaze as it coasted across her skin. His nostrils flared and eyes widened as they passed over her nipples peaking through the fall of her hair, and then lower…

Heat surged to her cheeks. There she was, naked before him, his come still on her thighs. How strange that it hadn't bothered her at all when he was a dragon, but being naked in front of a human was suddenly awkward.

"I can't hear your thoughts anymore," she said, voice thick. Anything to distract from the butterflies in her center.

He stilled, then his brows pinched. "Nor can I." His voice was rough, hard like stone yet warm as the fire he'd breathed as a dragon. "A dragon trait between mates, I assume. I'd never had the ability before you."

A pity. She'd love to know his thoughts in that moment—about her, himself, everything.

Zain drew his hand hear her face, flexing his fingers. "May I?"

"Yes?" She wasn't quite sure what she agreed to.

But then, hand shaking a bit, his fingertips touched her face. She sucked in a breath at the contact. It was so light, almost like he feared hurting her.

"Briannis." He slid his fingers out and across her skin until his entire palm cupped her cheek. She leaned into the touch. "Being able to touch you like this…to be so close." He shook his head. "This is a blessing. You're a blessing. A gift from the Goddess herself."

She pulled her bottom lip between her teeth and fought the urge to look away. She didn't deserve such praise. What had she done but merely tried to help him as he had her, and then given into their mutual desire? Perhaps most women wouldn't have bedded a dragon, but she had never been considered typical among the women of the city, not with her focus on the family business and lack of interest in finding a husband to wed the moment she could.

"The Goddess sent you to me. At last."

Briannis swallowed thickly. She'd wondered about that the night before as she'd fallen asleep beside him. Had the Fates truly chosen her? Or his Goddess, whoever that was? Knowing she was his mate, it now seemed possible, but last night, after replaying the Choosing over and over in her head, she wasn't so sure.

"It may not have been her," Briannis admitted.

Zain dropped his hand. "What do you mean?" His whole expression dipped into a confused frown.

"I think..." She sucked in a deep breath before admitting her suspicions. "I think another of the women planned for me to be picked." She couldn't stop seeing Finola's face, hearing her exclamation of shock. It was before Briannis herself had seen the stone, so how could she have known? And that look she shared with her father...being at the end of the line...it was too much of a coincidence to be believed. "I think she placed the stone in the bag knowing I would draw it since I was the only one left. She wanted me gone." And she definitely wanted to save herself.

Fury blazed in his eyes. "This other woman. She sent you, expecting you to die?" His lips pulled back in a very beast-like snarl.

It sounded really bad, but... "I think so." Briannis winced. "Though I can't be sure."

"She threatened my mate." Zain shoved to his feet. Immediately he began to wobble. His arms flailed as he sought balance.

"Zain!" Briannis jumped up and grabbed him before he could fall. "Sit back down before you hurt yourself."

"This body..." Zain grumbled, but allowed Briannis to help him. "Human legs are different. It's been so long."

She could only imagine. "Take your time. There is no rush."

"Why would that woman do such a thing?" he asked, still riled.

Briannis sighed and shook her head. "Finola is spoiled. Whatever she wants, she gets. There is a man she wants, but he prefers me instead, and—"

"You have a mate already?" Zain's expression shuttered. He looked away. "I should have—"

"No!" Briannis rushed to assure him. She cupped his face between her palms and turned it toward her. "No. It's nothing like that. We were not together. I did not care for him like that. He's a nice man, a good man, I think, but he was not for me." She watched as the revelation sank in, as his fury and heartache melted away. "Though," she continued, "he had trouble admitting that to himself. Much to my frustration, let me assure you. Finola wanted him. She was convinced they belonged together and I was keeping them apart."

His lips thinned. "So she planned to remove you."

"It...it seems that way." She hunched in on herself. She didn't want to believe ill about others, even someone like Finola, but it was hard to revisit the Choosing ceremony and see it any other way.

"But enough about that." She shrugged, trying to pretend it didn't sting as badly as it did. "What do we do now?"

A strange expression broke over Zain's face, and then, of all things, he laughed. Not a chuckle, but a deep belly laugh, head thrown back and wide grin upon his face.

Briannis couldn't help it, she smiled too. "I didn't know it was such a strange question."

Finally, he reined in his laughter, and when he did, he cupped her cheek more confidently this time and leaned in until they shared the same breath. "I never thought past this moment. At least, not in a long time. It's been so many years...I thought I might never find my mate. Finding her—you—was my dream. As far as what came after? I...I don't know."

"Your family..." she began, then almost thought better of it. "You said what happened to your brother, but the rest? Are they out there, waiting for you?" After so long? Did they live that long?

His shoulders dropped. "I don't know. None visited me after that. If they're out there still...I'm not even sure I could find them."

"If there's a chance they're out there, it's worth taking, isn't it? I mean, if you loved them. If I could see my parents again, my brother, well, I'd have to try." It hurt to talk about, even after so many years. But in his position, if there was even a hope of being reunited, she'd want to take it.

He leaned back, expression downcast. "I know you miss them. I saw it in your thoughts before. And the rest of your family." He looked away.

"But now I can let them know I'm safe." She grinned at the thought of it. What a shock they'd get when she returned. To be able to give someone back a loved one they lost...it was a dream.

Zain's attention snapped back to her. "Briannis." He opened his mouth to say more. Closed it. The expression on his face was a dagger to her heart.

She leaned away from him. "You don't want me to go back." Her chest squeezed tight. Suddenly everything felt wrong.

"If they see you—if they try to hurt you—" He shook his head, reaching for her. "I can't let it happen." His expression turned fierce. "I won't."

He'd fight for her. Protect her, even from them.

"It won't be like with Sheena," she began. "We can explain—"

"You think they'll listen?"

Irritated, she stood with a huff. "So I just, what? Leave forever?" She crossed her arms and turned away from him. Leaving everyone she loved to think she was dead was not an option.

Behind her, she heard scuffling, likely Zain trying to stand on his human legs once more. The urge to turn and help him was near overwhelming, but she was nothing if not stubborn.

Another moment passed. Then two. Suddenly, she jumped as his palm landed on her hip from behind. The motion had her tipping back into his hard, bare chest, but thankfully they didn't tumble to the ground. Zain's hand slid up to her waist, like she was his anchor, the only thing holding him up, but at the same time, he managed to hold her against him.

"Briannis." Her name was a whisper at the shell of her ear, one that sent a shiver down her spine. "I can deny you nothing, but neither will I lose you, not now that I've finally found you." His fingers tightened possessively.

"I may be a man again in form, but I've been a dragon for a long time, and dragons hoard what is theirs."

Those words in his rough, deep voice made her knees go weak, but she could not give in. "They're my family."

"I know." His cheek rubbed against hers. "And if you must go, I'll go with you."

She let out a short gasp, hope brightening within her.

"But if they try to harm you, I will defend you," he vowed. "I will not hold back."

An idea struck her. Briannis twisted in his arms until their chests pressed together. She gazed up at him, sharing his heated breaths. "Can you still become a dragon?"

His eyes widened. "You would have me unleash dragon fire on them?"

"No!" She gently smacked his arm. At least...not unless they had to. "I have another idea. One that may convince the people without the risk of bloodshed."

At that, his brows raised. He canted his head to the side, waiting, but she was waiting on him too. His features pinched as if in thought. "I think..." His arms unwound from around her. "Well, there's one way to find out."

Briannis hurried out of the way.

Zain watched her, his gaze never wavering, as the air around him started to shimmer and warp. It reminded her a bit of the way the air near a fire, sparks and all. She gasped as he ignited in flame and where his body once stood, his dragon form loomed instead.

"Worried, little mate?" came the crooning voice in her head.

"Zain," she whispered in awed wonder.

He stretched his long neck forward until his face was just before her. She threw her arms around it in an awkward hug and leaned her head against his snout. "Only for a minute," she replied through their mental bond.

Laughter answered her.

She raised her head. "Can you become a man again just as easily, or do we need to..." She trailed off, biting her bottom lip.

Zain nudged her with his snout. "Only interested if I'm in need?" he teased.

She scowled at him. But then it transformed into a smirk. "You can read my thoughts. You tell me." The memory she projected toward him was of minutes ago, her on her hands and knees as he filled her.

A deep rumble left his chest, followed by a puff of smoky warmth that surrounded her in delicious heat. His tail flicked back and forth like a cat ready to pounce.

"Oh, the things I plan to do to you." Zain sent an image back. Once more Briannis was on her hands and knees, but it wasn't just one cock buried deep inside her. A surge of moisture built between her legs. Her pussy clenched tight with want despite the improbability of what he showed. The smaller cock that she had taken before dipped into her puckered hole, filling her in new ways. And the larger? It stuffed her pussy, stretching and filling her until its girth swelled her pelvis.

"Not impossible," he chuckled. "Your body will adapt to mine. Just as your lifespan will lengthen to mine should we choose to bind ourselves together as mates."

"My lifespan?" she echoed. Fates, she hadn't thought of that.

He nudged her with his snout again. "You'll have plenty of time to decide later. One plan at a time."

Perhaps. But she didn't really need time. Wild as it may be, having just met him, she already knew.

The air shimmered, and suddenly he was a man again, the transformation back to human much faster than to dragon. Zain wobbled on his human legs again. Briannis grabbed his arm to steady him, but he was already falling and pulled her along with him.

With a grunt, he took the brunt of the fall, her landing atop him.

"Have to work on that," he groaned.

Briannis sat up. Only then did she realize her legs straddled him. As she moved, her wet core slid over his very hard cock, transforming his groan into something else entirely.

Zain grabbed her hips, holding her atop him. "This. This I could get used to." He subtly rocked his hips, thrusting between her folds.

A little whimper escaped her lips as she stared down into his hooded eyes.

"I want to hear your plan," he panted. "But I have one of my own I'd like to see through first, if my lady is willing."

"You know, I've never had a human before." She ground her hips again him. "I think I'd like to try."

CHAPTER

TEN

Briannis snuck into her family home just after dusk two days after the Choosing. Her uncle stared at her like she was a ghost. Her two youngest cousins screamed and fled. It was her aunt who recovered first, standing from her place at the dinner table, eyes still red and slightly puffy, and spoke with awed certainty. "It's you. It's really you."

The next few hours had been a blur of emotion and words as she explained all that had happened in such a short time, washed, ate, and savored each hug and embrace. To her relief, they believed her, and were eager to meet Zain and welcome him to the family. However, he'd already left to carry out part of their plan, one she explained to her aunt and uncle after the little ones had fallen asleep.

Two mornings later, Briannis hid under a blanket stretched over part of their wagon as her aunt and uncle drove it into the city square. They'd eagerly agreed to help, and to leave the kids at home under Catronia's care. Thank goodness for that.

They'd expected crowds. After all, it was now wedding season, and ceremonies would be held almost back-to-back on the Seal of the Fates in the center of the square, with celebrations to follow in homes, taverns, inns, or wherever the happy couple saw fit. But this? Briannis swore under her breath as she peeked out between two slats on the wagon's side.

"This may be as close as I can get us," Uncle Euan said as the cart rocked to a halt. "I thought things would have thinned out by now."

"I believe I know why," Aunt Davina said tartly. "Look at that ridiculous sign."

Briannis searched her narrow view. *Where...?* She gasped when she saw it, jerking back from the opening before leaning forward again to make sure she hadn't imagined things. But there could be no mistake.

Painted on a board between two high posts were the words "The Wedding of Ian Wallace and Finola Balfour."

Her chest burned. Briannis felt like she might be sick. It shouldn't hurt. She didn't even like Ian in that way and she had Zain, but knowing that Ian had been asking to marry her one day and was marrying someone else less than a week later really stung.

Sharp nails dug into her palms. Well, at least she didn't have to feel too bad about what was about to happen. Minutes passed as they waited. Briannis tried to focus on her breathing to calm her nerves as even more people filled into the square dressed in all their finery. Through a crack in the dense crowd, she spied *him*, awaiting his bride.

"Bastard," she and her aunt said at the same time. In so many ways, they really were the same person.

But at that moment, a scream went up through the crowd that brought a grin to her face. Only one sight would have people looking up in fear like that.

"That's the sign," Uncle Euan said, as if they hadn't noticed.

"Ready?" came her aunt's reassuring voice.

Oh yes, she was so ready.

Briannis nudged some wax-coated wheels of cheese out of the way so that she could scoot to the end of the wagon. With her bright red hair tied up and hidden under a scarf, she slipped out into the crowd.

No one noticed her. Or if they did, they clearly didn't realize she was the woman who had just been sacrificed a few days ago.

Zain swooped by again overhead, stirring up the crowd and sending some hurrying toward the edges of the square. But Briannis kept straight on toward the center.

"He's getting lower!"

"Fates save us!"

Zain glided low toward the Seal of the Fates, the circular stone formation inlaid into the ground in the center of the square.

"Watch out!"

"Run!"

People hurtled past Briannis, one slamming into her shoulder and nearly knocking her down. Zain saw it, his fury radiating through their bond as he roared at the people below. He slowed his descent, wings buffeting them with sharp bursts of air. One caught her scarf and ripped it away.

The center of the square had emptied by the time his clawed feet landed on the stonework.

"It's her," someone yelled. "The dragon has rejected her!"

Briannis clicked her tongue as she spied the older man pointing at her from a cluster of people some distance away. Men and their assumptions.

"Bri?" The shocked gasp had her looking to the left.

There Ian stood, his arms wrapped protectively around his would-be bride in a dress so large and voluminous it was a shock he could find her in all the fabric. Finola gaped in horror—at her or the dragon, she couldn't say. Her father, the Lord Provost, stood just behind her. His fury was easy enough to read.

No sense waiting anymore.

Briannis spread her arms wide to demand attention, not that all eyes weren't already on her and Zain. "The dragon is not to be feared! He is not here to destroy or in retribution. We are here to let you know the curse has ended."

"Curse?" The Lord Provost stormed forward. "What curse? This is nonsense!"

No sooner had he separated from the ring of people around them than Zain turned his draconic head his way and growled. The Lord Provost stopped immediately. Not a complete fool, then.

"Long ago, a pact was formed between the dragon and our city. His protection in return for helping to find his mate, who would be born here," Briannis shouted. "But over time, the legend changed and we misunderstood. He never wanted a bride as a sacrifice, only to get close enough to find the one that would be his."

"Nonsense!"

"She's a witch!" a woman called. "She bewitched him!"

Briannis's lips pressed thin as Zain snapped his head this way and that, analyzing the threats. This was not going well.

"She speaks the truth!" rang out a high voice from behind her.

Zain lowered his wings and settled his bulk on the ground. Several in the crowd gasped.

In all their panic and fury, no one had noticed the woman on the dragon's back. They certainly did now.

Briannis turned, getting her first real look at Merilee in ten years. She was much as she remembered, curvaceous, with a stunning smile and shimmering blonde hair that was enviably perfect even after a flight on dragonback. The light and flowing fabric of her dress accented in silver jewelry and spotted with gemstones would stand out among any crowd. In fact, her attire outshone the bride, which made Briannis a little more gleeful than it should. Merilee smiled at Briannis as she ran a protective hand over the swell of her belly. Now *that* was unexpected.

She turned her attention to the crowd, grin fading. "You all sent me to the dragon to die, ten years ago. Yet here I stand."

Where the crowd was raucous before, they'd gone eerily quiet.

"He spared my life. Took me somewhere I could live in peace and safety. For he knew I would not be able to come back here. He saw what was done to Sheena all those years ago, what you would have done to me, what you all were just suggesting about Briannis. You're the killers. Not him."

"This is impossible," The Lord Provost said, though his words lacked the confidence of before. "A sham. You can't possibly be—"

"Merilee?" Mr. Stoutwell nearly pushed a man down as he burst from the crowd into the open expanse surrounding them. His wife appeared behind him. One look at their daughter and she clasped her hands over her mouth and burst into tears.

A dragon was no deterrent to a father who thought his child lost only to find her again. He raced forward and wrapped his daughter in his embrace. No sooner had he reached her, then Merilee broke down in sobs. Mrs. Stoutwell collected herself enough to join them, and together they formed a cluster of love as they sank down to the stones.

"I'm to be a grandfather?" Mr. Stoutwell asked, finally pulling back to look her over.

Merilee grinned through her tears. "You already are, twice over."

"Grandbabies," Mrs. Stoutwell gasped.

"I hope you can meet them soon. What with running the inn—"

"Oh, Fates take the inn!" Mrs. Stoutwell said, hugging her daughter close.

"This is touching and all," the Lord Provost began, stepping near, "but how can we really know the dragon isn't just rejecting you both?"

Briannis couldn't stop her eyeroll. *Some people just—* But she was saved from responding.

Zain flapped his wings hard, buffeting the crowd with a gust of wing before the air around him shivered and a man stood where the dragon once had. A very naked man.

People gasped and cried out. One woman near the front literally fainted.

"You know, because I'm telling you," he shouted. He held his head high before turning to Briannis with a smirk on his face.

With an outstretched hand, he beckoned her. He wobbled a little where he stood, still unsure on his human legs. Briannis joined him, quickly savoring the view before taking his hand. He stepped behind her to shield his half-mast cock then wrapped her in his arms for good measure. "As she said, I was cursed. The village then offered to help me find my mate in exchange for my protection. Each year I would get the chance to meet the young women of the village to see if they were the one I sought. And when they were not, I *left them* in peace." The crowd seemed to hang on his every word now. "But over time, the truth was lost. Things changed. But I did not believe the young women should suffer for the misguided wisdom of their elders." He gestured to Merilee. "I saved those I could. Took them to a new life of safety."

"Alivia!" A woman shouted, her voice breaking. "Five years ago, she—" The question choked off into a sob.

"Is safe and well," Merilee said from where she still huddled with her parents.

The sobbing grew even louder. People began to murmurer among themselves.

"But the curse is broken," Zain continued, projecting his voice outward. "Briannis has broken it." He beamed down at her. "I no longer need to meet your women... as I have found my mate."

There was some shuffling, a feminine outcry, then in a voice she recognized, "Bri—"

Ian had his hand outstretched to her, even as Finola clung to his other trying to pull him back.

"It was never going work between us," Briannis said matter-of-factly. "And I always hated that nickname. Both of which you would have known if you'd *ever* truly listened to me."

He gaped like he'd been struck, but Briannis just shrugged. "Congratulations on your wedding day, by the way. Just be wary of getting on that one's bad side, or her father's. They might just try to get rid of you too."

Ian's eyes widened in horror.

"The Fates pick the brides," the Lord Provost sputtered.

Finola's tirade was as much as screech as words. Enough that Briannis almost felt sorry for Ian. Almost.

"Thank the Fates that I am the forgiving sort," Zain said, loud enough for everyone to hear. Then, as his gaze panned the crowd. "But should any ill will befall Briannis or her family, I won't hesitate to unleash my wrath."

As if to make his point, Zain stepped away from her and shifted into his dragon form once more. The crowd cried out at the sudden change, but the moment the shock wore off, their attention shifted from him to the Lord Provost, who Zain pinned with his draconic stare.

"Good boy." Briannis gave an affection pat on his leg.

A note of satisfied pleasure rumbled from his chest. That long tail wrapped around her waist and tugged her close.

"Do you think they'll listen?" she asked through their bond.

"One can only hope," he replied. "Do you think I should breathe some fire to remind them what I'm capable of?" She could almost see the smirk that would have been on his human face.

She grinned up at him in return. "I think they've had enough shock for one day."

"Well, then. No point in lingering." He lowered down and Briannis climbed up on his back between his wings. "Where to, little mate?"

"Somewhere we can plan how to find your family?" she suggested.

"Hmm... Perhaps. Though didn't you promise to let me taste your family's delicious cheeses? If we're going to return here and help run the business, I should have some idea of what I'm getting into."

This time, she laughed, throwing her head back as they soared through the clouds then swooped back down over the city. "Very true. And you must be hungry after such a long flight."

"For cheese. And something more."

Moisture grew between her legs at the suggestion. "You're insatiable."

"For you?" He banked, taking them toward her family farm. "Always."

"Well then, cheese first, dessert later."

He chuckled. "Agreed."

ABOUT MEGAN VAN DYKE

Megan Van Dyke is a fantasy romance author with a love for all things that include magic and romance, especially fairy tales and anything with a happily ever after. Many of her stories include themes of family (whether born into or found) and a sense of home and belonging, which are important aspects of her life as well.

When not writing, Megan loves to cook, play video games, explore the great outdoors, and spend time with her family. A southerner by birth and at heart, Megan currently lives with her family in Florida.

Learn more and join Megan's author community at authormeganvandyke.com.

JUST ONE SIP

JEM ZERO

CONTENT NOTES FOR JUST ONE SIP

Homophobic slurs, sex work, attempted sexual assault, drug use (both with and without consent), gore, bodily functions (vomit, blood, etc.), mild existential stalking, explicit sexual content and consensual sex

CHAPTER

ONE

SHARD

"**S**mells like fart in here," Rooney announces after kicking open the backstage door. He inhales deeply, wrinkles his nose, and gags in quite the exaggerated fashion.

Lounging on the couch in my best approximation of a confident sprawl, I stroke the twink in my lap from the top of his curly blond head to the flat planes of his bottom. Previous to taking this form, reconnaissance indicated the value of having a significant object to attract attention. It's an exercise in exceptional patience waiting for Rooney to question my appearance, but I've existed long enough to know stalking up and demanding engagement is *not* the way to draw someone's interest.

That's alright. I can be plenty interesting.

One of Rooney's fellow dancers parries, "It didn't smell bad before *you* arrived."

Rooney rolls his eyes, then slides out of his long leather jacket and tosses it on the couch without sparing me a glance, even though it clips my lap ornament's shoulder. Frustration has me digging my fingertips into his thigh, but he remains sitting placidly, eyes trained on Rooney, as mine are

The slender man doesn't yet notice our combined stare. No preservation instincts, this one. A jewel like Rooney should protect himself aggressively, but a week spent learning everything about him from the mold in his fridge down to his molecular makeup has taught me the concept is foreign to him.

Admittedly, that recklessness is one of many elements that draw me to him.

Rooney whips off the t-shirt he was wearing under his jacket and tosses it in the opposite direction, at the ledge beneath a wall-length mirror. It hits the surface, then falls to the floor. He sniffs under his arm, then shrugs. "My moped broke down again, so I had to walk."

Frowning at my oversight, I project a sliver of my consciousness through a crack in the ceiling, navigating the streets to Rooney's crumbling apartment building in an urgent slither.

While I'm usually proactive about warding unnecessary inconveniences from Rooney's dogged shamble toward survival, my earlier focus was spent on launching my plan to secure his desire. I make a note to improve my skill at splitting focal points—something I've never had to worry about before, but Rooney is a special case. When I'd secretly embedded a small opal of my being in the nape of his neck, I hadn't been prepared for the sheer volume of risk-taking behavior.

Walking through this decrepit city with no protection is but one in a long, long line of ways in which Rooney is careless about safety, as if he has no regard for his own life.

One day he will be ready to accept my protection, but to make that happen, first he needs to *know me.* But I won't have the chance if serious harm comes to him first.

Working to keep my eye on the changing room while my consciousness approaches Rooney's chained-up moped, I select a knowledgeable soul fragment from my collection, directing it to worm inside the mechanisms. The machine is run-down offal, but while I would like to make it entirely new, he'll certainly notice the unprecedented appearance of a different vehicle. Instead, I rewind the machine's guts until they're as fresh as the day of their manufacture, strengthening the rusty chain affixing it to the bike rack as well.

That handled, I return my full attention to the scene in front of me. Rooney has taken several steps away from the sour dancer, dismissing her as a threat by showing his back. "Whatever, Sara," he's saying. "Your pussy definitely stinks. Can't say the same about mine."

A few of the other performers titter.

Sara's retort is outraged, but Rooney raises his voice over hers, adding, "Maybe it wouldn't if you stopped using those scented douche kits that throw off your pH!" His cheeks flush, olivine skin going rosy.

Unwilling to watch my jewel descend into further distress, I decide to act.

My prop stands, tossing his blond curls and heading toward the studio exit. I steer him just enough to the left that his shoulder bumps Rooney on the way out; he doesn't turn at Rooney's cry of incredulity, simply continuing on. The moment he's through the door I dissolve him, eradicating the soulshard I used to create the puppet. Rooney storms after him, seeking on a confrontation he won't receive.

"Where the fuck did that little faggot go?" After looking around and finding nothing, he returns to the gaggle of unsettled dancers and snarls, "Who even was that?"

Nova, the mature woman whose name I know because she demanded I identify myself before I could enter the changing studio, tips her head in my direction. I train my lips into a smirk—not a smile—in time for the impact of Rooney's gaze, hazel eyes landing on me with the *thunk* of twin blades. I'd hoped he'd be less agitated upon meeting me—in my current form, at least—but I can't object to the display. Rooney wears rage like a cloak of peacock feathers.

"And who are *you*?" he demands.

"Shard," I answer, letting the word hang suspended between us, watching his features twitch with irritation when I don't elaborate. Mostly because I don't *have* anything else to say—I've never remained in proximity of a human long enough to need more of a name.

"He bought the club," Nova informs him.

Rooney balks. "George dipped? But this shithole was his baby."

Don't I know it. It took more than a few layers before the former owner lost enough of his soul to no longer care about the strip club he founded—named *Caution*, aptly—but I was determined to have it, and rewarded the old man generously for his sacrifice. Perhaps I'll give it back someday, though I can't say the same for the fragments of his soul I had to consume. They felt greasy, but interesting enough.

Rooney eyes me with open suspicion, taking in my crisp pinstripe suit and backswept dark hair. My hewn jewel likes put-together men, as great a contrast from himself as he can find. I made myself in that image, different from the petite redhead I'd been when we met. He'd kissed me in the darkness of the dance floor, letting me ride his fishnet-clad thigh until desire was a knot in my throat, but had declined my offer to go further.

The flicker of a taste was enough to claim me irrevocably. I needed to know more about him, the man with a loud laugh and crass tongue, who scowled when unwarranted and snorted in amusement at my pout when he turned me down. He was gentle, at least. Not quite kind, but not cruel either. *You're not my type,* he had explained without apology.

I couldn't tell him I'd never had to worry about being someone's "type" until this exact moment. Sampling human life—their culture, their experiences, their *souls*—is how I chart my continued existence in this dimension, but I'd never latched on to someone teeth-first, prepared to die rather than unlock my jaw. I'd been ready to beg for another kiss, the opportunity to press my chest to his and feel his fever-bright soul pulse like whalesong.

Instead, he'd kissed my forehead, the brush of lips an indelible signature, a *brand.* Although he melted into the crowd after that, I maintained awareness of his movements until he reached the heavy door marking the exit, and in a moment of liquid desperation, I fractured. Myself. It was different from chipping shards from a human's soul. I wrenched free a substantial piece of my being—messily and not enough, but the seconds were too thin—and smoothed its jagged edges with the molten-need subsuming my core before burying it under his skin.

I've been desperate for more ever since, seeking a way to put myself in his path again. The problem remains that Rooney is flightier than a strutting cockerel, phasing through a tangled network of parties and men and drugs, never lingering in anyone's grasp.

Rooney props his fists on his hips. "What's someone like you buyin' a club like this for?"

I laugh, not meaning to be cruel or condescending, but I close my lips around the sound in fear of it coming across as such. "I've a soft spot for the ramshackle," I explain, cryptic enough to knot Rooney's brows inward.

"Gonna price us out of it," Sara says like bitter pith.

"He'd better fuckin' not!" Rooney speaks with the bravado of a powerless man who has nothing to lose, commanding without even addressing me properly.

Such bold confidence is intoxicating. My primordial nature begs for a more intimate taste, but I beat it down viciously, silencing the urge. Unlike my own, the bladed edges of Rooney's soul are far too precious to risk dulling, no matter how careful my excision would be.

Lifting my hands in easy surrender, I say, "I have no intentions of firing anyone." And I don't intend to keep Caution either; I'm only here as long as it takes for Rooney to welcome me into the gaps. No cost is too great.

"We open in fifteen minutes," Nova says, disrupting our staredown.

Rooney redirects his attention, leaving a gaping wound in its absence. I grind my teeth with the effort it takes to hold back, but hold back I do, settling for watching the swoop of his spine as he shucks his pants and boots. He's wearing sinfully tiny shorts underneath, so tight they expose the bulge of his little cock. After tying his long hair and pushing his bangs back with a headband, Rooney dusts his face with iridescent highlight powder and smears shimmering oil from his neck down, leaving him fragrant and glistening. The concealer he paints over the scars beneath his pectorals makes me frown; he shouldn't have to hide his seams.

Once painted, he removes a roll of caution tape from his bag and wraps it messily around his hips, securing it with a gummy substance that he bitches about liberally during application. He loops it over one shoulder like a philosopher, then finishes with a pair of neon yellow platform heels. At the end, Rooney blooms, not a flower but a stem of poisonous mycelium: bright, brilliant.

Dangerous.

I've seen Rooney dance before: once from the audience with physical eyes, before becoming frustrated with their limited scope. The next night, I put myself into his muscles, feeling him flex and twist as if he was an extension of my own being. Inhabiting his body should have been enough. Far beyond the simplicity of human sex rituals, entering someone is the greatest form of intimacy I know outside of consumption, but as I refused to take from Rooney, even that proximity only left me wanting. I need more than his spectral presence, which could be taken without his knowledge—I need Rooney to *give himself to me*.

So I wait, and I watch, standing behind the raggedy curtain, a backstage hoverfly. Rooney flirts and smirks and grinds, scaling the spinning pole mounted on a circular platform, central to the dark room, connected to the main stage by a worn catwalk. Desperate men crowd the sides, thrusting sweaty bills at Rooney, begging for even a flicker of his attention.

I know what it's like to be desperate for him, in ways these men could never imagine.

So I watch, and I wait.

ROONEY

If pressed, I wouldn't be able to tell you if it was the fried shrimp or the shrooms that got me. Either way, I'm locked in my bathroom, bent over the toilet with drool dripping down my chin. Along with some other stuff I'm not okay with interrogating.

To make matters worse, the drugs are still doing their thing, leaving my head spinning and colors flying. Now, I've been in some pretty gross situations. I work at a strip club, and mystery fluids aren't unknown to me. However, hugging cold porcelain while the party rages outside my bathroom door is less than ideal, because I don't know who's planted their pimpled ass on the seat I'm currently resting my cheek against. Unfortunately, my chest hurts too much to move, and the pack of wet wipes I keep for these situations is a foot and a half out of reach.

As another contraction of my abdomen makes me heave bile into the foul-smelling bowl, I find myself wondering: is this what rock bottom feels like?

No, probably not. I can go lower.

Seventies flower power aesthetics in garish disco colors whirl behind my eyes like a naked bore on a car after its wheels and rims have been stolen. I risk reaching for the wipes, but moving immediately makes my stomach lurch, so I wrap my arms around my middle and groan in defeat. I could die like this and no one would find me until they desperately had to shit and decided to bust the lock in. It's flimsy. Flimsier than my connection with every single person infesting my apartment right now.

They only come over because I don't give a shit what they do here, and I only host these shindigs because I can't afford groceries after spending all of my jock strap money on rent. People bring drugs, alcohol, and snacks in exchange for admittance, and I can eat their offerings for the night and maybe get laid. Win-win. Except for when I get got by a foul batch of fried seafood, of course, though it's not the first time and I guarantee it won't be the last. I can't afford to be picky.

"If I die like this," I mumble to myself, "at least I won't have to see this retro shit anymore."

"I'd entreat you to avoid death as adamantly as possible," a voice says to my left. I squint enough to see the blurry shape of a male hand plucking the package of wipes from the floor. The owner of the hand continues in a smooth baritone: "The world's light would be greatly diminished without you."

Blinking tears out of my eyes in hopes of seeing him better, I mutter, "The fuck it would."

The man doesn't respond. He removes a wipe and gently, carefully, adjusts my head so he can dab at my mouth, wiping away the sick. Then he tosses the wipe into the plastic bag I use for trash and produces another. "You've made a proper mess of yourself, Rooney."

"At least it's just shrooms and shrimp, rather than a needle," I slur. "How did you get in here?" That should have been my first question.

He only hums.

I allow him to clean the rest of me, distantly wondering about the ease of my acquiescence. Allowing intimacy like this isn't usually my thing; I hate it, and run from any man who tries to "take care" of me, especially if he's gotten it into his head that I need saving. From this city, from my life, from my*self*. No, I'm fine. Well. Not right now, but usually.

As the mystery man brushes damp bangs out of my eyes and re-ties my ponytail, I sense my nausea beginning to ebb. By the time he's finished straightening my clothes it's disappeared entirely, and the chewed-up technicolor peace signs I've been trying to ignore have given way to blooming fractals in a spectrum of blues. It's refreshing after the drug-induced assault of visual—and physical—vomit.

I feel brighter than I have all week when I turn to study my helpful stranger, only for concern to lodge in my chest when I notice him looking a bit green. Maybe the smell is getting to him. Quickly closing the toilet lid, I flush and attempt to stand. He assists me in rising to my feet, but when I tilt my chin upward, finally trying to get a clear picture of my unexpected rescuer, he turns away.

"Hey," I say softly. I bite my lip, debating on whether to thank him or not. I'm a rude person by nature, and I don't play nice with other kids, even the kinder ones. Still, there aren't many guys out there willing to clean up a burned-out stripper's puke.

Still blocking my view with his impressively wide shoulders, the man paws through a cluttered shelf until he finds mouthwash, then fills the cap. When he hands it to me I am rewarded with the proper look at his face I'd desired. What I see has my mouth tugging into a perplexed frown. The handsome face looks familiar, but I can't place it. That's when I become aware of his clothes—a well-fitting business casual shirt with the sleeves rolled up to his elbows and speckles of yellow bile staining the subtle cornflower blue. No one who attends my parties has any excuse for showing up wearing *that*.

Irritation surges in my chest, burning almost as bad as my stomach acid did, but before I can make a point of demanding the sorely out-of-place man's name, he takes my hand and levers the cup of mouthwash to my lips. I have no choice but to part them or risk a river of bright green spearmint down my front. Stinging fluid floods my mouth, and I glare at him while I swish. He watches me with a half-smile. When I bend to spit, I feel his thumb ghost down my neck. I come up for air ready to cuss him out like a hissy stray cat, but he's no longer in my peripheral. Spinning, I find he's no longer in the bathroom at all.

Somehow the bastard slid out without me noticing, and didn't spare me a parting word.

True anger heats my nerves, and I storm across the bathroom, seizing the doorknob with intent on pursuing him, but stop when it refuses to turn. I jiggle it a few times, then move my palm to inspect the mechanism, wondering if the latch got stuck. But no. The lock itself is still engaged.

How the fuck did he get out without me hearing the door? Without unlocking it? And somehow magically re-locking it from the outside? It doesn't fucking make sense.

A hard knot of fear lodges in my throat as I thumb the button, which responds with ease, not sticking at all. I step out, scanning the collection of fuckheads crowding my tiny apartment. None of them look like the man who helped me. None of them even glance in my direction to ask if I'm okay.

I don't know what I would say if they did.

I'VE BEEN PARANOID SINCE THE PARTY. I KNOW THE KIND STRANGER WAS JUST A hallucination, and I'd thoroughly cussed out the guy who gave me the shrooms for lying about whatever he spiked them with. Yet I remain ill at ease, looking over my shoulder, feeling like I'm being watched. I can't stop wondering if the guy will appear again, that phantom cooked up by my sick brain. I can't use that mouthwash without shuddering, sharp spearmint reminding me of air caressing my bare throat. My heart pumps overtime when I spot anything with that eerily familiar medley of cool blues.

I did some research on psilocybin-induced psychosis. If I had money to see a neurologist, I might have briefly considered seeking one out, but a quick search on *that* confirmed that no fancy brain doctors would come anywhere near this pisshole city. Shame. Or not, since I couldn't go anyway. Wouldn't? I dunno.

What I do know is: if this paranoia doesn't fucking cool it, I'm going to go *apeshit*.

But it lasts past Wednesday, a quiet night at Caution, and into Friday, when it's much busier and more difficult to ignore the sensation of being... witnessed. Guarded almost, which—fuck *that*. I almost hope my drug-induced stranger pops up again so I can demand he get off my jock.

During my first lap dance of the evening, I glance over my shoulder and freeze for a second, swearing I see his face at the back of a gaggle of leers. The pervert beneath me grunts in annoyance, and when I start moving again, the face fades into a ripple of shadow. I grind against the dude's boner, trying not to frown as the memory of that horrid twink the other day returns to me. He'd disappeared too, gone in the swing of a door, and I doubt he had time to hide behind one of the speakers. Except that couldn't have been psychosis, because the others saw him too.

Something is happening, which is an alarming thought considering I don't—and never have—believed in spirits, a higher power, or the afterlife. Even as a kid I understood that death is followed by nothing but shitting your pants on the way out. Unless superpowers are real, I'm gonna have to recalibrate that metric.

I don't usually drink on the job, but the very instant this pathetic little creep comes in his khakis, I pop up and stalk toward the bar. While on the floor I try to tone down what a rude motherfucker I am in interest of actually making money, but right now I don't care. I need a shot of something stronger than Everclear.

By the time I'm up in the pole queue, I'm proper drunk. I strut onstage with only a bit of stumble, barefoot because I don't trust myself in heels while this slammed. My set is...fine. I keep my eyes closed instead of flirting with the audience, peeking through my eyelashes only when I need to make sure I don't hit the pole at the wrong angle. That'd be more embarrassing than breaking character during a lapdance, and I'd certainly get a word from Nova about it, on top of being mocked by Sara and the other little bitches who hate me, all for very legitimate reasons. If George was still around I'd catch an earful from him, too, so I ought to be grateful he's gone, except our new boss is a total blind spot. I barely remember what he looks like, since I've only seen him the once.

I make it through my set without any crises. Nova gives me a suspicious look when I hurry offstage with a touch more wobble than before, but she's up next so I arrive at the dressing room unaccosted. Nobody inside pays me any attention. I chug from a lukewarm bottle of water, because George was too cheap to buy a backstage fridge, then change into a shimmery silver jock strap. I have to pack the crotch because my t-dick is too small to make a proper bulge, but I'm gonna need to work a bit harder to get enough tips to buy gas. My moped thankfully started working again after I kicked it a few times. I raid our small costume closet, finding a slightly-too-large pair of gladiator sandals covered in gold glitter. The silver and gold clash, but better than crashing and burning on heels; it'll be fine in the dark.

Despite my efforts, the tips suck for a Friday, even though I let a group of patrons even drunker than me slap my exposed asscheeks at a crisp fifty bucks per swing. Then I see him: my boss, watching with a slight frown. We aren't supposed to let people touch us during shifts, even with permission, and George would penalize anyone who got caught allowing it with an additional fee taken from our tips. Reluctantly, I wave a few disappointed jerks away, bemoaning the lost income.

All said, it's a worthless disappointment of a night, and gets worse when the bartender cuts me off after the club closes. "It's not your fucking job to babysit me," I inform him with a scowl, but he doesn't budge, so I stomp my little gladiator sandals back to the dressing room to get changed.

Most everyone else is gone by the time I'm done wiping mascara and highlighter off my face. I use a makeup remover wipe on my top scars, scrubbing off the foundation I use to hide them every night. No one gets to know I'm trans without my say-so, and even with my undersized dick (because bottom growth isn't *that* miraculous) most of the patrons have no idea they're horny for a man with a pussy.

As I'm tugging on my jacket, a deep voice rumbles behind me: "Rooney."

I recognize that smooth baritone. It was so relaxed last time I heard it, but this time it's tense. A warning. The mirror gifts me the image of a frowning man in a nice suit, arms crossed over his chest.

My new boss.

"Sir?" I croak.

Displeased expression aside, Shard is handsome, tall and tanned with a strong jaw and dark waves of hair styled to sweep behind his ears. A curl lingers on his forehead, framing his furrowed brow. Like Superman. Last time I saw him, he disappeared through a locked bathroom door.

My caring stranger.

Without calling attention to my gawping stare, Shard says, "A word, please?"

SHARD

Rooney is a disheveled mess.

I feel tense and unstable, and while I'm trying not to alarm him, it was only yesterday I recovered from consuming his...distress. I was careful not to take more than the illness, denying myself even the most infinitesimal taste of his soul. Rooney is brilliant in his untouched state, and I don't know if I'd be able to stop myself were I to sample him. It'd be unforgivable to dim his light, and devouring too much of a person's soul, well...it doesn't kill them—usually—but it leaves them empty. A shell. Soulless walking puppets with no joy, no desire. I can't risk it.

Although I try not to frighten him, the way he's clenching the counter while he meets my eyes through the mirror says I'm not succeeding.

"Can I help you?" Rooney asks, a parody of his usual disposition. There's a slight slur in his words.

"You..." I falter. Not knowing what I ought to be scolding him for, I send a sliver of *insight* to slip through his pores into his meat, shimmying through the plates of his skull so I can enter his mind. Invading someone so intimately produces an odd sensation, so I don't do it often, but presently I have a good reason. I paw through his thoughts, seizing the tail of his insecurity and fear, drawing it out when it tries to escape under a nest of bravado.

What is he worried I'll say next?

"Allowing patrons to touch you is against the club rules," I spit out. I did not have time to consider the statement before speaking, but once it's freed, I feel right about it. I *don't* want other men touching Rooney, especially none of these degenerates, and fortunately there are already guidelines in place to obscure my jealousy.

"I'm sorry, sir," Rooney responds immediately. By the twitch of his eyelid I can tell it rankles to present a submissive front, but the fragment that hasn't left his mind yet informs me of his apprehension. He's thrown off by my foreign presence, the power I have over him.

I don't want my jewel feeling subjugated by me. He's more powerful than he knows.

Clearing my throat, I say, "Don't sound so nervous." I withdraw the remaining fragments of myself before he responds, suspecting it wouldn't be appropriate to spy on his thoughts before he voices them. "You don't have to worry; I'm not going to dismiss you."

Stubbornness shapes the set of Rooney's jaw. "Forgive me if I don't automatically trust you."

"Trust me? No," I say, struggling to keep my resolve from dissolving under the acid of his sneer. "But believe me, as a businessman, I wouldn't terminate a valuable worker over such a small offense."

"You could get fined for it," Rooney argues. "The cops do stings for prostitution an' shit in this area all the fucking time."

Unbidden, a fragment of *jealousy* chases a line of fire up my throat. I swallow it down. "Were you planning on fucking them?"

Rooney huffs. "Ew. No."

"Then I rest my case."

He scowls down at the counter, fists clenching until his knuckles are white.

I can't hold back a quiet chuckle. "You seem displeased. Are you angry about being confronted?"

Rooney's head snaps up, and after a moment of watching me in the mirror, he spins his chair around, then throws one knee over the other. He gives me a shrewd look before speaking. "I'm not scared of you."

"I don't recall asking if you were," I reply, mildly taken aback.

"How could I be?" he continues. "Not when you—" He cuts off with a soft hiccup. I wait with bated breath for his next words, but he doesn't seem inclined to continue.

"When I what?"

His teeth sink into his plush lower lip. I take two steps toward him, falter on the third, plagued by uncharacteristic trepidation. Rooney catches my gaze and holds it with such intensity the desire to curl around the orbs of his eyes is nearly unbearable. I want to clutch his ocular stems and peer through them, experience whatever he's seeing in me.

"When you nothing," he finally says, sighing. He rubs his temples. "Nothin' but a bad trip."

Disappointed, I frown. "You're drunk," I point out, in case he thinks I haven't noticed.

"I'm not," Rooney protests, trying to shoot to his feet, but wobbling on the way up.

I can't help myself. I devour the distance between us, reaching to steady him even though I'm sure he could have managed on his own—he doesn't need to be alone anymore. But the moment my hand brushes Rooney's elbow, he stiffens. His hazel eyes harden as he jerks his arm close to his body, clutching the spot I touched. Not wanting to crowd him in a clear moment of distress, I move several paces back. We size each other up, Rooney's features shadowed in suspicion. I wish he'd say something, but he doesn't.

When the silence begins to itch so profoundly I can't bear it any longer, I surrender to voicing the only thought I have left: "No more drinking on the job. Understood?"

Rooney's mouth drops open. "No more— Who the fuck do you think you are?"

"Your boss," I respond, a smile tugging my lips.

Cheeks flushing with discomfort, Rooney snarls, "I know that. But you're not my goddamn *mom*."

"I never claimed to be."

Leaving that hanging, Rooney descends upon his street clothes. He yanks a worn graphic tee over his head, mussing his long bangs and the shaggy tail at the base of his skull. He shoves his wiry arms into the sleeves of his hoodie, leaving it hanging open rather than covering his front. Then, snatching up his bag, he storms toward the exit, avoiding looking at me all the while.

"Rooney."

He pauses in the doorway, but doesn't turn around.

Sighing quietly through my nose, I wonder out loud, "How are you not freezing?"

Rooney purses his lips, seeming to consider for the first time his lack of weather-appropriate clothing. "I'm used to the cold," he says quietly, then tugs his hoodie closer to his core and stomps outside. I watch him through the heavy door until he escapes the radius of my perception, and while my own core clenches with the need to keep him in my atmosphere, I know I have to let him go.

For now.

ROONEY

The meaty guy who invited me to this club is pure unwiped asshole, and would be better served by a crabs-infested brothel than an upscale lounge. And honestly, I'd rather be on the floor selling shots in my underwear than sitting on his lap right now. I forgot the douchebag's name five minutes after we met, so ever since I've been mentally calling him Bowlcut McFuckface. Three guesses why.

Unfortunately, this is a class establishment, not a strip club, and I'm too bitchy to be an escort. I barely kept my tongue behind my teeth long enough to get my first drink, much less the fish scale cocaine Bowlcut promised me if I was still with him by night's end. He'd better not be expecting a fuck for it, but I'll swing a blowjob if it gets me a to-go bag. Long as he washes first.

But even the blowjob is off the table when I get back from using the bathroom—clean, without used condoms on the floor, a full trash can, broken latches, or suspicious sounds coming from any of the stalls—and find his VIP booth empty. The waitress wiping off the table gives me a pitying look that grinds my molars, resentment sawing something ugly in the back of my throat.

"They left, hon," she says, in case I had any doubts. She cocks her hip and props the ball of her hand on it, inspecting me.

My closet isn't well-stocked, bereft of anything suitable for this establishment, so I dressed like a skank. Which I usually do, but I played it up, sheer tinted tights with tight black overall shorts and a teal crop top underneath. Red's more my color, but I've been drawn to cool shades lately.

Either way I look like a whore, which is insulting not because I have anything against prostitutes; rather, I don't have the range. I'm good at two things: pole dancing and talking shit. I can tell preemptively neither of those are gonna save me from being booted out on my ass.

"Do you know anyone else here?" the waitress asks, carefully. Unlike at Caution, people who work here still have to be polite.

Fuck all that.

"Piss off," I tell her, then huff my way to the vestibule.

I keep my chin tipped up as I leave and gaze forward, not giving the bloodhounds guarding the wealthy patrons any reason to manhandle me.

It's not until I get to the exit proper I remember I left my trench coat in Bowlcut's car. Genuine leather doesn't stop working secondhand, and it's the nicest warm thing I own. Owned. I only wore it because Shard's callout about stomping around in halfway-to-nothing affected me more than I wanted. I don't need my nosey boss to care how cold I am, and I'm about to be very, very cold.

First thing I do when my boots hit the sidewalk is pull up my banking app, hoping there's enough to afford a ride home. There's a whole lotta jack shit in my checking, and the bank closed my savings last year for being perpetually empty. I check the price on three different rideshares, but this squeaky clean suburb doesn't associate with my town's crumbling infrastructure, and there are too many numbers between the decimal point and the dollar sign.

I feel broken down for the first time in a long while. I've gotten used to most setbacks, but this one is hitting deeper for some reason. Abandonment gets me sometimes—rarely, because I don't give most men the opportunity, but apparently it's too sharp an edge to be ditched by a guy who has to lure strippers into dating him with promises of fancy cocaine. Apparently I'm not worth even that.

With nothing left in my tank, I search walking directions to Caution, which is closer than my apartment. The cold stings my face and arms, and every windy slap feels like claws raking over my exposed sides. I'll blame that for the tears gathering in my eyes. At least no one's here to see—

A shiny SUV in a garish shade of royal blue turns into the crosswalk, blocking me from the curb. I stagger, reeling with indignation so hot it hisses when it touches the cold. To make matters worse, the car stops in front of me. A snarl cracks my bottom lip, but the pain amplifies my rage.

"Yo, dickhead, what the fuck do you think you're—"

The tinted window rolls down, and across the sleek leather passenger seat I see the driver, none other than *him*: Shard, my fucking boss, the guy who appeared in my bathroom, the guy I can't stop fucking seeing when I blink, a wash of iridescent blues that calms me as much as it frustrates me.

"What're you doing here?" I demand, though it's weak, my usual energy bar so low there's crisis blinking in a dangerous red.

Shard pushes the passenger door open. "What do you think?"

Deeply conflicted, I gnaw the split in my lip. "Have you been following me?"

Shard doesn't answer; he just watches me with eyes such a vivid blue I can't place the shade.

I try to wait him out, but eventually the cold makes the decision for me. Avoiding him, catching hypothermia on my walk back to the club, and eventually dying in a dirty alley won't get me answers, so I huff and hike my leg up onto the footrest so I can climb into the passenger seat.

As he drives, Shard's eyes remain on the road, hands positioned precisely on the wheel, and I bet he adjusted all his mirrors before turning the key in the ignition.

With exhaustion dragging me down, I ask, "Don't you have anything better to be doing?"

Again, Shard doesn't answer.

At last, I sigh. Too many coincidences say I'd rather be wrong and able to blame it on brainfreeze than living in denial. "You really did show up in my bathroom, didn't you." It's not a question.

A small smile brings life to the corner of Shard's mouth. The attention he's paying the road doesn't waver, but even though he doesn't look directly at me, I feel intimately perceived all the same. "Sharp boy," is all he says.

We're quiet the rest of the drive.

CHAPTER

FIVE

ROONEY

Going to Bowlcut McFuckface's apartment at three in the morning is the worst idea I've had in a while, but Friday evening he texts me apologizing for ditching me at the fancy shitass club last week and asks for a do-over. Says he has my coat, which is manipulative as fuck, but it works better than the fishscale would. I want my shit back, damn it. So, after I get off shift at two, I gather what's left of my wits and hop into the taxi he sends to take me to his penthouse.

The elevator is nice; the guard at the fancy desk was not. Bowlcut didn't deign to meet me in the foyer, so I fidget my way to the top floor, trying not to dwell on resentment. Why does this pungent turd get to live in luxury while nice people like Nova have to strip for a living in a club located a block down from the biggest crack den in the city? I'm not mad on my own behalf. I deserve this life. Never was destined for anything better.

Bowlcut's décor leaves much to be desired. It's a mishmash of expensive-looking gaudy shit, none of which matches with any element of elegance or, I don't fucking know, fengshui.

When I wander deeper into the penthouse, it's to see Bowlcut lounging on an ugly-ass couch with a highball glass in his hand. He's got his bare feet propped on an expensive-looking coffee table, one that doesn't deserve to be molested by his pale, sweaty skin. Neither do I, in fairness, but I don't suppose it matters, since I'm here and all.

"Rudy!" he greets, lifting his glass so the amber liquid sloshes inside.

I don't correct him on my name—it's only fair he fuck it up when I didn't bother to remember his, not even something that rhymes. I guess actually *wanting* to fuck someone lifts the bar an inch or two.

"Come sit next to me," Bowlcut says, patting the leather cushion with a hand so moist it leaves sausage finger-shaped smears on the matte black surface.

Thank god I wore leggings here. The evening cold was so severe it forced me into my only pair of jeans for the moped ride to Caution, even though I hate the feel of denim against my skin. Then, at the end of the night when I was loath to climb back into them, I found the leggings folded neatly with the rest of my belongings. Blue-toned grey, the inside lined with soft fleece. I didn't question their appearance, since it seemed obvious, and was happier than I'll admit pulling them on before leaving the club. I paired the grey with a baby pink off-shoulder crop top to maintain the slutty persona I knew Bowlcut would expect when I arrived.

Now I'm here, resenting him for getting hand-grease on the ass of my new leggings. Couldn't enjoy the fresh, stain-free fabric for more than an hour before sullying it, which is about right for my grody lifestyle.

I settle gingerly next to Bowlcut on the couch, offering a grimace in place of a smile when he hands me an empty highball glass. I watch him swish the contents of a half-full bottle of double-malt whisky, then hold out the glass to receive a suspiciously generous pour.

"Thanks," I mutter before throwing a mouthful back. I gag against the burn, embarrassed but unable to conceal my reaction. Must be stronger than the cheap watery garbage I'm used to.

Bowlcut watches me ride out the flare of heat with an odd intensity, offering me a napkin only after I've sputtered all over myself. "Good?" he asks.

I choke out an insincere "Great," muffled behind the napkin swiping across my spittle-slick lips. "Where's my coat?" is the first thing I ask once I've composed myself.

Frowning, Bowlcut says, "It's in the closet. Why don't you relax, and I'll grab it."

Unable to inform him there's no way I'll relax in this poorly curated cumdump of a penthouse, I nod. Then I take a smaller, much more careful sip of whisky. Bowlcut's expression tips into a satisfied smile, and he departs with an overdone swagger.

Careful only to avoid dripping on my own hand, I set my glass directly on the surface of the fancy wooden coffee table. Across the way there's a wall-length window, but much of the late-night cityscape is blocked by a TV screen so large it's tacky. I don't possess any appreciation for classy things, though, knowing they're far above my societal rank, so I stare at the dark, blank surface rather than admiring the lights beyond. Who wants to gaze in awe upon a city that treats them like a penniless trollop anyway? Not that it's unfair, considering that's what I am.

Still, the stars are more visible here than the soggy-newspaper sky above my apartment. Smog and smoke from weed and burning trash cans, light pollution turning the sky dingy grey instead of properly dark. A bruise upon the atmosphere. Here, with the windows so high, I don't even have to tip my head to see the purplish-blue swirls embracing pinprick stars in the black canvas.

I heard that stars twinkle due to meteor showers whizzing through space between us, blocking their ancient lights from our tired eyes. Some of the stars beyond this window might be dead by now and I'll never know. It feels oddly sentimental; I know the feeling of burning out while people watch.

A heightened sense of alarm washes over me when those precise points of light, the ones I keep telling myself I'm not going to stare at, begin to blur. The stars can't all be shooting at once, right? That would be... apocalyptic, but I've no idea what force could send stars smearing across the slate sky like lines of chalk that failed to teach an important lesson.

"Doin' alright there?"

I turn from the window, my eyes struggling to focus when they settle on

Bowlcut, who is leering a bit too suspiciously for me to reason I magically became a lightweight on the drive over.

"Just great," I tell him, before returning my gaze to the no-longer-sacred night.

Maybe it'd be nice to leave the city, if I could ever get out. Strip away the layers of grime and smog obscuring the moon's glow, meet more stars and hope some of them are still alive... Shit, there's a whole fucking *universe* out there. And here I am, in a pretentious, shit-assed city, inside this pretentious, shit-assed apartment building, sitting on some dude's pretentious, shit-assed couch, fairly certain I just got roofied.

Damn.

Bowlcut looms, scanning my prone form. The plush leather cushions have all but swallowed me, leaving me stuck staring up at him, his round face obscuring the view. His shadow falls over me. "You don't *look* great," he says, seizing my chin with damp fingers so he can inspect my face.

After only a brief, half-hearted struggle, I go slack, somewhere between horror and acceptance. This fucker can't defile me any more than what I've already allowed from the rest of the world. It won't be the first time I've been raped, although the GHB is new. What's another level of regret?

But then there's a flash of blues, a cooling bath of light, and a shadow rises behind my assailant. It's Shard, but different than I've ever seen him. His chest is bare, and several stretches of his body are nearly transparent, fractals of light winking in their depths. Like stars.

"Get your *foul hands* off of him," Shard snarls, hundreds of voices whisper-screaming just below the familiar baritone.

"What the fuck is that?" Bowlcut cries out, staggering backward.

Shard snatches the front of his shirt, reeling him in. "A being whose jewel you dared to touch," he answers. Then his mouth falls open, far wider than human anatomy could, exposing sharp rear fangs at the back of an unexpected maw. His lips thin as his jaw unhinges, and in one great gulp, Shard rips Bowlcut from throat to navel, tearing a massive chunk from his portly frame. Strips of meat and sinew stretch until they snap, leaving bits of skin and intestine hanging from the fresh corpse's crushed ribcage. When Shard's jaw closes around the hunk of torso, his teeth crack its elbow joint, severing the forearm so it falls onto the floor with a heavy thump.

Unfortunately, I'm unable to get my legs out of the way before my new leggings are splattered with blood and fragments of bone. I clap my hands over my mouth. My head spins from the sudden movement and I'm trying desperately not to hurl.

Shard makes quick work of the rest of my would-be rapist's body, devouring every bit, with the exception of the disembodied arm. He sways a bit before opaline eyes lock with mine, his gaze penetrating to my core. The translucent expanses of his skin seem light-years away, even as his solid body draws nearer. His blue-tinted thumb traces the line of my jaw where Bowlcut touched me, purging the lingering sensation of rancid grease.

I try to say something, though I'm not sure what, but I gag around the words. Shard's palm curves to fit my cheek, stroking gently. As if reliving the shrooms-and-shrimp incident, I feel the fog clouding my brain start to fade away, leaving a sharpness in my awareness. Leaden limbs grow lighter, so I'm able to press my hand against my stomach until the nausea leaves as well. Licking my dry lips, I croak, "Did you really just—"

*Stalk me here? Eat a guy in front of me? **Save** me?*

I don't get the chance to decide what I'll ask, because Shard's face shifts from teal to an unflattering chartreuse. His expression crumples, and he reels back, clutching his throat.

Gasping, I yank my feet up onto the couch, folding my legs beneath my chin as Shard staggers down to one knee. A torrent of neon green ectoplasm ejects from his mouth, plopping to the floor in revolting chunks that wobble like hot gelatin. When Shard heaves again, whatever substance his body is rejecting pools on the ground around the abandoned half-arm, which steams upon contact.

A few messy contractions later, Shard appears to be getting himself back under control. He wobbles at his first attempt to stand. Without thinking, I jump to my feet, barely missing the oozing puddle. I find myself at Shard's side, holding his arm to steady him while the palm of my other hand presses against the cool, crystal-smooth space between his shoulder blades. Glancing down, I see the shadow of my fingers through his chest.

"Are you alright?" Shard asks, voice scraping in his raw throat.

"I should be asking you that."

He shakes his head. "Don't spare it a thought. I've been through far worse." He brushes a few strands of nervous sweat-damped bangs behind my ear, expression so tender it alarms me. Emotions I never thought myself capable of eliciting reflect across his features. It gives me a moment to study his eyes—without a pupil or iris, an idiot might call them blank, but I know better because in their depths I see the fiery birth of new stars at the farthest reaches of the galaxy.

CHAPTER SIX

SHARD

It's a gift, Rooney allowing my touch to linger. My hand shakes tracing the contour of his jaw; it's the first time I've touched someone so beautiful, human or otherwise. As if drawn in by gravitational force, I lean down, starving for the taste of his lips. I've only had them once, and never in this body. Keeping my distance has been agonizing, but it's important Rooney desire closeness at least half as much as I do.

To my elation, he tips his chin the slightest incline, putting his mouth in the path of my own. I hesitate a fraction of an inch before my lips brush his, concerned about the lingering taste of the shattered soul my body rejected. I don't want it coming in contact with Rooney's skin.

Before I can focus on a cleansing pass of energy, Rooney jerks forward, hissing. Our chests collide, but not in a desirous way; the ectoplasm has oozed across the floor enough for the edge of the puddle to graze Rooney's boot. Foul and toxic, the substance makes quick work of burning through the leather, that revolting bastard's desire for my precious jewel lingering even after obliteration.

Against my resolution to not touch Rooney without his explicit consent,

I scoop him into my arms without thinking, sacrificing a larger-than-usual soul fragment to fizzle the boot out of existence rather than allow it to further harm his skin. Rooney's eyes widen. If devouring the man about to assault him hadn't already exposed my lack of humanity, this would have obliterated my secret. Had I cared to, I might have allowed him to think the encounter was another drug-induced hallucination. Explaining away the physical disappearance of an object would cross the border of mystery into gaslighting, and no. Never.

Now Rooney will either descend into panic and reject me, or...

Well, whatever he chooses, I'll respect. Even if it results in agony like none I've experienced during my time in the mortal dimension.

"I'll get you another pair," I say, clumsy in my panic.

Rooney stares at me for an infinity, before laughing, a tinge of hysteria fraying the sound. "You can get me the fuck out of here, is what you can do."

I bundle him tighter against my chest, breathing the words, "By your lips, thus shapes my being." It's an ancient oath, pure devotion distilled into a few simple sounds...the weight of which Rooney will not understand.

As expected, his brows tick upward, but I avoid questioning by promptly slipping our bodies through the dimensional layers between which I was formed.

WHEN WE ARRIVE AT MY APARTMENT—NICE, BUT NOWHERE NEAR AS LAVISH AS THE fetid creature congealing on his own floor—Rooney shoots me a pointed look. I don't suppose he's surprised I didn't take him back to his own living space, but he doesn't comment. He doesn't say anything at all, actually. Unusually placid, he allows me to clean him and strip him of his clothes, soured by fear, then tuck him into my unused bed. I don't join him. Physical sleep isn't something my being requires, but more than that, I don't want Rooney to feel unsafe.

I'm not going to remove him from one predatory situation only to slip him into another.

Rooney sleeps solidly for thirteen hours. I watch over him from across the room, never looking away until I sense him beginning to stir. I disappear then, the spot where I sat occupied by a stack of clothing items for him to choose from.

After rolling out of bed, a half-asleep Rooney disappears into the ensuite bathroom to shower. I covered the vanity in every hygienic product I could think of him needing, including some others that I didn't find while examining his belongings, but thought he might like. I haven't any idea what he selects because I leave him to his privacy, even though we both know I could snoop if I wanted. And it's not that I don't want to watch him, but I crave his trust over filling the voyeuristic desire to always be near him.

Never before in my long, long existence, have I cared so much about endearing myself to another being, whether like or unlike myself. Infatuation this rich is rare for my species, maybe even unprecedented. We are few, and asocial by nature. I haven't seen any of my kin since I mistakenly slithered into this dimension and decided to stay.

Fretting and restless in a way I'm wholly unaccustomed to, I put myself to the task of seeing to Rooney's other needs. Rest, clothes...food. I don't eat —the soulshards I shave from humans provide me sustenance—so my first attempt to manifest something edible results in an unpleasant mash, one I quickly dissolve before it can be witnessed. Fortunately, Rooney takes long showers. After seeking ideas from the building's other inhabitants, I borrow contents from a neighbor's fridge and, faced with no other options, teach myself to fry an egg.

I'm trying to figure out what to do with a slice of burnt toast and hard, cold butter when Rooney emerges from the bathroom, dressed in a pair of baggy sweatpants and a long-sleeved shirt, its hemline dripping halfway down his thighs. The items I set out would have fit perfectly; these are items he pulled from *my* drawers. Seeing him draped in my clothing causes a feeling I don't know how to name to surge in my chest.

Rooney's gaze flicks from me to the plate of poorly cooked eggs next to the toaster, there and back twice, before he pads over and plucks the burned toast from my nervous grasp. He meets my eyes, unblinking, and crunches his teeth into the charred bread. He doesn't break his stare even once, leaving me oddly paralyzed where I've been left leaning against the counter. Once he swallows, he lingers a moment longer, then asks, "Could I have a glass of water?"

That, I can do.

By the time I've materialized a glass and filled it with cool water from the fridge, Rooney has tucked into the eggs, using the toast as a makeshift implement. Because why would I have forks when I don't eat? This whole apartment is a show just for him. I didn't expect to feel so off-kilter finally having Rooney here, whereas he seems completely at ease, as if he's figured something out and I'm not yet privy to what.

"So, you're not human," Rooney says after swallowing a large gulp of water and wiping his mouth on his shirtsleeve.

I gawp for a moment, but eventually concede, "I'm not."

"Are you going to hurt me?"

The question chills me to my core. Surging forward, I catch Rooney's waist with one hand and cradle his cheek with the other. "I couldn't fathom such a thing."

Rooney shrugs. "Just had to check," he explains. Then he brushes me off and goes back to eating.

Upon finishing, Rooney puts the plate in the sink, but doesn't wash it. He doesn't have to, because I'll simply dematerialize it later. He does rinse his hands and mouth, then dries with the shirt again, because I haven't provided any napkins or paper towel, damn it all. This is a disaster.

A pause follows. Rooney stands before me, examining me as one would an unusual bug. I've never felt so small before, an insignificant little creature, unworthy of the attention it's drawn.

Just before I give in and beg to know what he's thinking, Rooney traces the line of my exposed forearm with his fingertips. I shudder, flexing my hand when he reaches the rolled-up cuff tucked above my elbow. A flicker of a smile takes Rooney's lips, but I don't have time to be pleased, because a moment later he drops to his knees.

Rooney's hands go to the fastening of my slacks, deftly popping the top button. By the time I remember how to move my limbs, he's slid free the clasps securing the fly; fortunately, he doesn't get the zipper down fully before I catch both his narrow hands in one of my own.

Swallowing hard, I ask in a bone-dry rasp, "What are you doing, Rooney?"

He sits back on his heels and scowls at me. "You ever heard of a blowjob?"

"I— Yes, of course I have. But you don't have to do that."

Rooney pushes his damp bangs back from his forehead. I resist the urge to smooth the tangle this creates. "Of course I do. That's what you're after, right?"

I realize, a sickness flooding from my core outward, that Rooney believes my intentions to be no different than the little man who tried to violate him. If I hadn't already vomited him up and spent half the night scrubbing my being from the aftertaste of his soul, I would have choked on the last mouthful.

"*No*," I say emphatically, pulling Rooney to his feet and giving into the urge to run my fingers through the drying frizz atop his head. "I simply want you to be safe." *And mine*, I resist adding.

Rooney rolls his eyes. "Right." He steps backward, out of my grasp, and crosses his arms over his chest. "Right..." he says again, sounding less sure this time. "Look, I hafta get back to my apartment. There's shit I need to do before my shift tonight."

Ah, yes. Past noon on a Saturday. Caution doesn't open until ten, but I don't point that out.

"I'll drive you home," I say instead, but Rooney shakes his head.

"Not necessary. I'll take the bus—there's a station nearby."

Powerless for the first time in my existence, I trail Rooney down the hall to my room. He shoves his clothes from yesterday into a pillowcase and maneuvers his sockless feet into the new set of boots I created, as promised. He doesn't thank me, and I don't care; I'm not in this for gratitude or because I want him indebted to me. All I want is for Rooney to desire my company the way I'm desperate for his. Maybe not even that, because if it's possible to need someone *too* much, I'm certain I've crossed that threshold. My being wants Rooney more than his fragile humanity can match.

"Later," Rooney says without looking at me, then clomps out the door in those stiff, heavy boots.

ROONEY

I don't bother with the open stares of the other strippers when I walk up to Shard that evening and place a hand on his chest. He's been watching me like a lovesick puppy, and I'm rather sick of it. I push him onto the couch where he sat the first day we met, then drop myself into his lap.

The room quiets, and I sense the moment everyone's attitude toward me turns hostile. Instant judgment, even from Nova. *Did he actually do it?* they're wondering, I'm sure. And even though I haven't actually fucked Shard in exchange for his protection, I would have. I almost did, so none of them are wrong for exchanging looks, silently calling me a gold-digging skank. As if none of these bitches would have taken the opportunity to screw our rich, handsome boss to curry favor.

The difference is, Shard isn't human, and I'm not sure why he's so obsessed with me. I haven't asked yet. It's on the list.

"So, what are you?"

Shard's strong brows crawl up his forehead. I want to smooth my thumbs over the thick, dark hair, chasing them back down. "Are you certain you want to do this here? Now?"

"Don't question me," I say, mildly irate and not trying to hide it. "I figure you'd be less likely to eat me in a room full of catty strippers."

A knot forms between Shard's eyes, surprise turning into…whatever that emotion is. "I'd never molest you in such a fashion. You are the brightest—" He cuts himself off, teeth in his bottom lip.

I have the impulse to scratch his face open so he has no choice but to finish the thought. Rather than violence, I opt to stare at him expectantly until he sighs and wraps an arm around my lower back, tugging me closer. I allow myself to spill against his chest, surprised at the way he holds me tight against him without fondling my ass. Guess he was serious about the *no molestation* thing.

"There is no name for what I am," he says, once I've tipped my nose underneath his chin so I can feel the low rumble in his throat.

"Not good enough," I immediately parry.

Shard laughs, the hard muscles of his chest flexing. "I wasn't going to leave it there."

"You'd better not."

"My species gestates between dimensions," he begins, thumb stroking down my spine. He doesn't worm his hand underneath the thin t-shirt I'm wearing, because my impulse control wouldn't let me wait to get dressed before confronting him. The simple, non-invasive touch isn't making it easy to focus, which is important when he's using words like *gestates*. "Once we're fully developed, we…emerge, I suppose," he muses. I wonder if he's ever had to explain this before. "We're set free amongst the far reaches of the universe, at the edges of infinite numbers of dimensions. Most of us stay there, collecting fragments of worlds that make their way to oblivion. There's a threshold where reality ends, little jewel. But we don't let them disappear. My kin and I, our purpose is to turn those lost somethings into pieces of energy, light, spirit. And once we're full enough, we… expand. Become something new."

"A new universe? Or, uh, dimension?" I wonder, struggling to hold on to his dreamy spidersilk murmurs.

Shard squeezes my hip. "Perhaps. It's as good a guess as any."

"Is that going to happen to you?" The idea of Shard blowing up into his own dimension makes my chest ache in a way I, frankly, do not consent to, but it happens anyway.

But then he says, "No," and chuckles.

I frown, disliking the lighthearted way he wastes my second of worry. "Why not?"

"Because I'm here," he says, gesturing to the dressing room around us, where the girls are tying bikini strings and sucking their teeth resentfully. "I fell into this dimension on accident, ending up on your Earth."

"Are you trapped, then? Can't you go back?"

Shard shrugs. "I haven't tried, and I don't intend to. I found something more interesting to collect."

Swallowing, I force myself to ask, even though I don't want to know if the answer is 'stripper boys who taste good.' "What do you collect?"

"Souls," Shard answers, tilting his head so his slightly stubbled cheek can nuzzle my forehead. I tense noticeably, prompting him to stroke my hair, slipping past the short strands at my temples to the long tail at the nape of my neck. He twists it around one thick finger, voice soothing when he continues, "Not all of them. Don't be afraid. Fragments."

All at once, it dawns on me. "Shards...of people's souls?"

He rumbles in approval. "Yes."

"Does it kill people?" I ask, thinking of the fucker who roofied me. I wonder if anyone found his remains yet, and if I'll be accused of murder since I was the last person seen entering his apartment before we both disappeared.

"Not usually," Shard hedges.

"Only when you want to."

"Yes." Sensing my unspoken question, Shard says, "The foul little man who hurt you needed to be dispatched. There was nothing of him worth keeping, so I spat him out."

Spat is a generous term. I'd have said *violently upchucked*, but I don't correct him. "Thank you for that, by the way." I bite my lip. "Not sure I said that before."

Shard gives a dismissive wave. "Not necessary, Rooney. I wouldn't have allowed it to happen to anyone I was near enough to protect. Though

I would have taken the fragments containing their memories of the events."

"Why didn't you take mine?" I'm relieved he didn't, because the idea of having experiences taken from me without permission makes my stomach churn. They might not all be good—in fact, most of them are actively bad, but they're *mine*. My choices, even the stupid ones. How will I learn from the mistakes I've forgotten?

After a moment of hesitation, Shard answers, "You're different."

"Don't make me shake you," I warn, making him laugh, but I'm serious. I straighten in his lap, tugging his collar so the vibrant blue of his eyes meet mine, only inches separating us. "You've been stalking me for weeks. What makes me so different? I'm just a burned-out stripper."

His sharp inhale steals the air between us; I almost jerk forward to demand it back. "Rooney, you're—"

"Hey, Rooney!" another voice interjects, my name a slap on her lips. I turn to Nova, seconds away from cussing her out for interrupting Shard before he can say what he wants from me, *again*, but she cuts me off. "We open in ten minutes." She radiates disapproval, priming me to expect a scolding the moment she can corner me. Just great.

Reluctantly, I slide off Shard's lap. He looks disappointed to see me go, but I fix my mask and scowl until he fixes his. "I have to get ready," I inform him.

Shard follows me upright, forcing me to lift my chin and pretend I'm not intimidated by his confident stance and powerful shoulders, twice the width of mine. "Go then. I'll be waiting."

"You'll be watching," I correct.

A smile twitches the corner of his mouth. He pats the top of my head, then slides past me, walking toward the exit with long strides. The heavy door unleashes a burst of cold into the dressing room before falling shut behind him.

I pretend not to be bothered by the stares I get when I tuck myself into a corner to rush through make-up application before wriggling into my skin-tight black leotard. I shove my hands between my thighs to fasten the little buttons over my crotch, hidden there so we can piss without getting completely naked. As well as less innocent purposes. It's not until I'm pulling on a pair of red booty shorts, less than two minutes before I have to be on the floor carrying a tray of shot glasses, that I go stock-still.

Did Shard...

Somewhere within that weird existential sci-fi mishmash, did an impossible, inter-dimensional cosmic being call me his *jewel?*

I don't see Shard for the first hour of flirting and lap dances, which raises my ire. He's not lurking in the corners as he has before. No idea what could be more important than stalking me, when it seems he can be aware of me even when he's not physically present. Maybe he's still doing that, but I don't want some distant knowledge that he *might* be paying attention. I want to look into the crowd and see someone who wants more than my ass.

By the time it's my turn on the pole, I'm in a proper horrid mood. How *dare* he? Say all that then abandon me?

Fuck. *Fuck!*

Next time I see that fuck, he's gone. I'll tell him to get lost. No more of his well-intentioned stalking; he can just leave me alone. I don't need anyone to save me, not even a—

Especially not some hyper-focused cosmic bastard.

Too distracted for heels, I stomp barefoot onto the stage and seize the pole, so hopping mad I nearly miss my music cue. But then, as I'm lifting myself up, up, the first spin of the pole gathering momentum, I feel something odd in my shoulders. Power dripping down my muscular arms, greater than the strength I usually wield. Which is not insignificant, but this is *more.*

I cross my legs around the pole, flexing my thighs to hold my weight as I bend my back in mid-air, arms twisting above my head. A thrill runs to the center of my sternum, making me gasp. When it rolls down my abdomen, shock has me nearly releasing the pole and crashing head-first to the stage, but a force separate from myself tightens my thighs for me. I only drop a few inches before jerking to a stop, and a handful of bills rain onto the stage. Guess they thought it was an intentional trick, but I'm too distracted to care.

The next several beats of my choreography are executed through muscle memory alone, improvised with a bit of ass-shaking on all fours. One guy slaps a stack of bills against my crack and for a moment I'm filled with rage so hot I want to kick like a horse, heel slamming into his nose with a crunch and fountain of blood. I'm distracted by a different kind of heat—the man escapes unscathed, and that force drags me back to the pole. I launch myself at it, furious enough to fly, legs flaring, obeying the momentum I gather as the pole whirls in my grip.

Warmth pools between my legs when they cross the pole again. Sweat beads on my forehead, dripping down the bridge of my nose, dampening my cheeks. Another form of moisture dampens much lower down, soaking the crotch of my leotard. Wet, *wet*, I reach under my shorts to unfasten the buttons, fingers slipping because they're tiny and slick. The ravenous crowd howls when I pull the lycra to my waist, exposing my sweat-sheened hipbones. I climb the pole as high as I can reach, whirling, tugging the rest of the leotard over my shoulders and hurling it to the stage, leaving me in nothing but red spandex.

Panting like a bitch in heat, I struggle to finish my routine. By the time I'm done I'm shaking from the tips of my fingers down to my ankles, and I barely make it down the stairs backstage without falling on my ass. I immediately hurry down the dimly lit corridor to the changing room, swaying dangerously, needing to sit down. Nova meets me halfway, brow furrowed.

"Rooney, are you okay? You look like shit." She pauses, lips pursing. "Are you on something?"

I shake my head. "Might be getting sick," I say, gripping my stomach. "I need to get to the—thinkin' I stepped in something. Gotta find..."

"There are wipes in the bathroom," Nova says, her cool gaze saying she doesn't believe me but doesn't have time to argue.

I slam the bathroom door, crash-landing on the toilet seat. I scramble with the pack of wipes, scrubbing the bottom of my feet, my hands, my chest, my face. Still, heat suffuses me. Something I can't name or process. Then, the air shifts, and when I look up from the view of the grimy floor between my knees, I'm somehow not surprised to see a certain large, imposing man leaning against the door with his arms crossed and his rippling teal-blue gaze fixed on me.

Contrary to my resolutions earlier to cuss and kick him in the nuts, seeing Shard fills me with a cool sensation of bone-deep relief.

"Where were you?" I demand, voice rasping. "What the fuck did you do to me?"

SHARD

Although I planned what to say when Rooney confronted me, as I knew he would, I'm briefly overtaken by the blazing desperation in his eyes, pupils so blown only the tiniest ring of hazel remains. He's a creature of provocative fire, one whose immense power will forever leave me at his mercy. I can only imagine how much greater the inferno will grow once I've finally gotten another taste of him.

"I was inside you," I finally say.

Rooney narrows his eyes, tongue flicking out to wet his bottom lip. "Why'd you do that? I could've fell."

A smile softens the hard set of my mouth. "I wouldn't have allowed that to happen."

He huffs. "Still." Rooney leans back on the lid of the toilet, running his shaking hands through his long hair. "What now?"

"You should rest. That...it seems I took a lot out of you." Not that I'm sorry, but I hold back from admitting to that. Either Rooney would be amused or incensed, and I'm not keen on risking his stress levels.

"Gods," he mutters. "That's one way to put it."

I watch him tremble as he stands, avoiding contact as he slides past me to the sink to wash his hands and face. My consideration is intense, almost painfully so. Rooney pulls the tail of hair at the back of his nape over his shoulder, finger-combing it, and at the sight of his exposed neck, my lips stretch into a broader smile.

"Rooney, I've a question."

He frowns at me in the mirror. "Yeah?"

"How haven't you noticed this?"

"Noticed wh—"

I tap the back of his neck, where I embedded the smooth stone of my own being. I could have tracked him with a less noticeable soulshard, but sullying him with contact from another human's soul was out of the question. I was worried he'd discover the bump on his own, but I suppose I can't blame him for being too distracted.

Rooney's hand flies to the spot I indicated, feeling around with hard fingertips. "What the fuck did you do to me?"

Gently, I brush his hand away. "Kept you safe," I explain, even if he might not see it the same way. "It's a piece of me, and it allowed me to find you whenever you were in danger or distress."

After a moment of blankness, Rooney's face screws up into a sour grimace. I won't be surprised if he lashes out, even if I'd prefer he maintain his calm—not because I won't accept responsibility if he views it as an invasion, which wouldn't be incorrect, but because I'm not sorry, nor am I willing to lie and say I am. Every situation I've pulled Rooney out of has grown in severity, and I'll never regret my instinct to protect him.

What I'll do if he demands I stop...is another matter entirely.

"When did you do this?" Rooney finally asks.

"Shortly after we met."

Rooney's eyes flick to the reflection of the bathroom door leading to the changing room.

"No, not then."

"Then when?"

I sigh, pushing a hand through the dark, wavy hair I chose only because it's what Rooney finds the most attractive. Everything about this body was stolen from his thoughts, which I suppose he ought to know before we go any further. "Weeks ago," I say, "you were at a...queer club." I don't remember the name, and Rooney doesn't provide it. "You kissed someone."

Rooney squints. "I kiss a lot of people," he hedges.

Humming, I close my eyes and focus, calling up the image of the petite redhead I was masquerading as when Rooney first caught my attention. I place their image in front of me, appearing as real as the blond I tricked him with my first day at Caution.

When the familiarity hits him, Rooney's lips part. He spins to face me—and the still redhead. "You were— That was *you*?"

"Yes."

"And you—"

"You said I wasn't your type," I admit with a shrug more awkward than anything I've ever felt, perhaps my entire existence. "But I needed more of you. One kiss, it...wasn't enough."

Rooney flaps a hand through the vision of the redhead, which I dissolve obligingly so he can confront me with nothing between us. "So you bought the club I worked at, injected me with some spirit tracker without my consent, and..." He looks me up and down, notably unsure how to sum up what happened next.

"I stole the club from the previous owner," I say first, for honesty's sake. "But that wasn't until after I'd marked you, before you left the club. And once I found you, I—" The next admission makes me wince, because after the days I've spent leaning more about Rooney's mindset, I know upfront it won't sound as romantic as some might think. But I don't deserve an audience with such a feisty young spirit if I can't be honest. "I designed myself for you. Everything I could be, tailored to what your mind told me you'd want."

"That's insane," he deadpans.

"I don't ascribe to human definitions of sanity."

Rooney bites his lip before tipping his head. "Fair enough." He rubs his damp face, expression turning suspicious when I dispense a paper towel, but he accepts it readily enough. Dabbing thoughtfully at his eyelashes, Rooney leaves me to squirm. It's not until he's crumpled the towel and thrown it at the over-full trash can, that he once more levels me with his attention. "And what now? Are you here for the rest of my life, then?"

"If you want me to be."

"What if I don't?" he presses, voice sharp. His finger jabs firmly into my chest, chin tipped up defiantly. "What if I tell you to leave me the fuck alone, that I don't need to be saved by anyone, *including* some puffed up cosmic stalker who became obsessed with me after one fuckin' kiss?"

My hands are shaking. Another unfamiliar feeling. "Then I'll leave."

"Leave me alone?"

"No. I'll leave Earth. I'll find my way out of this dimension and return to the edges of the universe to continue as my species was intended."

Rooney frowns, his pointed finger relaxing until his palm settles over the human heart that only beats because I've told it to. "But that'll kill you eventually, won't it?"

"I suppose so, although we don't see that as death; more an evolution. It'll be quite a long time before my being matures that far," I say as a form of consolation. "You need not keep that on your conscience, Rooney."

"I don't have a fucking conscience," he bites out. His hand balls into a fist, knocking against my chest once. "I'm a nasty sonuvabitch who doesn't give a fuck about how my choices or actions affect anyone the fuck else, least of all myself. I don't care about you, and I sure as goddamn hell don't care about *me*."

Curling my much larger hand around Rooney's fist, I take a step forward until I feel the heat of his frustration and rage in every harsh exhale. "As difficult as it may be to believe that a selfish, inhuman being such as myself can care about anything but my own interests, please believe that there is nothing I would not sacrifice for you, Rooney. You are the only being I've ever been drawn to and I don't believe there'll be another after you."

Rooney's lips part, but after seconds without sound, he presses them into a tight line.

"You should take the rest of the night off," I suggest.

He shakes his head. "If you've been stalking me you know why I can't do that."

"I'm your boss," I say with only a hint of a tease. "I'll make sure what happens is what needs to happen to keep you comfortable."

Pulling his fingers out of my grasp, Rooney adjusts his ponytail so it covers the nape of his neck once more—I can't help but note that he hasn't demanded I remove the opal yet. "I need to get back to my shift. I'll...we can talk afterward. Yes?" The hard look he levels me with indicates this is some sort of test, the nature of which it's not difficult to guess.

"Alright," is all I say.

Rooney pins me in place for several moments more, before his shoulders relax and he nods. "Okay then."

I sidestep, opening the door and gesturing for him to exit the bathroom. The changing room is, fortunately, mostly empty. Rooney takes two steps forward, rests his weight against the doorjamb, and then with a stubborn set of his jaw, whirls upon me and seizes my tie. He yanks, jerking me downward, and I oblige him by following the gesture without an iota of resistance. So immediate is my obedience that I don't pause to consider what he might want until his red-bitten lips collide with mine.

The kiss is brief but explosive, leaving me reeling long after Rooney's withdrawn. I want to chase him, because the reminder of how intoxicating his essence is has left me in a state of desperate shock, but I force myself back.

"See you in a couple hours," Rooney says, then with a smirk, he fixes his posture to radiate his usual don't-give-a-fuck confidence and stomps out of my reach.

THE REST OF ROONEY'S SHIFT PASSES IN A BLUR. I WATCH HIM ENTERTAIN THE MEN, allowing more of my being to linger inside him, reminding us both of our blooming connection. Thorny and tentative, yes, but for this man I'll bleed myself dry of anything I can offer him, so long as he stays within my atmosphere.

When the time finally—blessedly—caresses the shoulder of two a.m., something out of the ordinary happens: the woman, Nova, approaches me with a set jaw and blazing eyes.

"We have a situation," she tells me.

At first I blink back at her, wondering what business of mine her situations are, until I realize having bought Caution means I *am* the one meant to put out the fires. A brief puff of frustration rises in my chest, but I choke it back. Refusing to keep peace in Rooney's place of employment, which became my responsibility by my own choice, would inconvenience him. So, I ask what needs to be handled, and follow her to the source of the commotion, pretending not to be as bewildered as I feel.

The *situation* is a disturbance between one of the pathetic little attendees and a gaggle of wretched wingmen, objecting to the attitude of the young professional being paid to arouse him. Her arms are crossed tightly across her exposed chest, and although I try to sound authoritative, it becomes painfully obvious I don't know how to talk peace into this *situation*.

"If you have better things to do," Nova says tartly, "I could—"

"Yes," I agree before she can finish her sentence. "Are you the manager of this establishment? You are now. Handle this however you see fit." I clasp her smaller hand between my own, dip my head in a polite nod, and make myself very, very scarce. A flicker of my awareness stays behind to ensure I've made the correct call, and I'm satisfied when Nova's surprised expression hardens as she turns back to address the rabble-rousers.

Wonderful.

By the time I've returned to the back room and composed myself, the club officially closes and the remainder of the patrons are shuffled out. I stand aside, out of the way of the dancers as they file in to remove their masks of paint and shimmer, don street clothes, and drag their tired feet through the employee exit.

All the while, I wait for Rooney to appear. He doesn't, though. With each person who departs, I grow more and more antsy, wanting to reach out to find exactly where Rooney is and why he hasn't come to find me. But something stops me. If he hasn't made an appearance, his absence must be deliberate. I don't sense any distress, thus I have no justifiable cause to seek him out other than what *I* want. If I want to make a statement about respecting Rooney's autonomy after all the decisions I've made without his input, I ought to give him...space.

After all these decades on Earth, indulging every whim, I suppose I've forgotten what space feels like.

CHAPTER NINE

ROONEY

I'm sitting on the edge of the stage, watching my feet swing, when Shard finally seeks me out. "I was wondering how long it'd take you to crack," I say with a wry smile, which grows when his expression twitches in what's almost a pout.

"I assumed you needed some time to think."

Shrugging, I allow, "Maybe," and give him nothing else.

Shard sighs. "Rooney—"

I jump to my feet, taking several steps backward toward the pole. "Come here." The stage is a bit tacky from being mopped, which is better than other reasons the black surface might be damp. Shard, the show-off, shrugs his suit jacket off, then rolls the sleeves of his white button-up shirt above his elbows. I lean against the pole, supporting myself with one arm above my head and the other at the small of my back, and do my best not to drool at the strong contours of his forearms.

It may or may not be creepy that this inter-dimensional being was so obsessed with me that he invaded my mind and recreated himself as the man of my dreams, but I'm having trouble being angry about it. Especially when he blurs just slightly, going from standing on the floor to a soft blue mist that stings my eyes. When I've blinked it away, Shard is standing in front of me.

I don't move, don't speak, and when he extends one of his beautiful hands toward me, I don't push him away. Shard cradles my cheek, then steps close enough to drop a kiss on my forehead. The sensation makes my skin crawl—not because it's unwelcome, but rather, I don't know what to do with the intimacy.

Face warming, I give him a shove, groaning when all that meets me is a rock-hard abdomen. Shard takes a step back, obligingly. I yank my phone out from the pocket of my hoodie, which I'd tucked myself into before slipping out of the dressing room while Shard was... busy.

To put us on even ground, I throw my hoodie aside, leaving me in nothing but my little red shorts. The makeup I put over my top scars has faded, rubbed off by friction and sweat. I'm sure my eyeshadow is a smudged mess. And yet as I lift my foot, catching it and bending in a slow stretch, Shard watches me like I've just got done hanging the moon. Still standing on one leg, I open my phone and pull up a music app, clicking shuffle on my Dance Practice playlist. Then I jack the volume up all the way and toss it onto my hoodie.

"Dance with me," I order.

Without pausing, not even half a second to consider what I've said, Shard crowds me against the pole, taking my hips in his big hands and squeezing.

"Just tell me what to do," he murmurs, and gods if that's not the sexiest thing. I *never* get to tell people what to do, not in a context where they actually *listen*.

I ease into the moment, swishing my hips until Shard's grip softens, allowing me to move without breaking contact. Experimenting, I take his hand and wind around the pole on my tip-toes, then teach him how to turn me—once, twice. He perfects it quickly. My phone speaker isn't very loud, but the large, empty room amplifies the sound, kissing the outline of each note with haunting shred of echo.

When I take my first spin around the pole, I expect Shard to move out of my way, but he doesn't. No, his skin ripples, and translucent blue windows open on his torso, so my legs pass right through him when I come around. I'm not sure if it amazes me or makes me nauseous—bit of both, maybe, but I'm determined not to get sick, so I stick with awe.

Something occurs to me, so as I flip upside down on the pole and drop my legs into the splits while holding myself by just upper arm strength, I ask, "What do I taste like?"

Shard blinks in surprise, and says, "I don't know."

I frown. "Why the hell not? If you're so into me, why haven't you— How do you know what—"

The pole stops its slow spin when Shard cups my cheek. He kisses my chin, then nuzzles his stubbled cheek against my smooth one. "I already told you, didn't I? You're the most beautiful creature I've ever witnessed. If I taste your soul, I fear it will be the sweetest fragment in all the universe."

"Okay, and?"

"And what if I take too much?" He shudders. "I have no desire to collect anything from you. You're already perfect in your whole."

"That's so— How can you know, then? That you want me, if you don't know what I taste like?" I must be going insane demanding a spectral being eat a part of my soul, like I'm demanding a virgin try just the tip, because you won't know you'll like it if you don't *try*.

Shard grabs my chin. Before my eyes, his oak-brown complexion changes, paling until that comforting riot of blues is visible in his depths. Except this time, I don't feel settled, I feel...*so much more.*

"There will never be another being who captivates me like you, Rooney," he says with an intensity that gives me no choice but to accept what he says as truth.

His white shirt melts away into nothing, exposing more and more blue until there's nothing left of humanity in Shard's features, eyes gone super-nova-white. Waves of dark hair lengthen, color leaching out until the locks are a celestial white, floating gently around his face, framing his strong jaw.

I'm getting light-headed hanging upside down like this, and without me saying so, Shard grabs my shoulders, brushes his lips over both my eyelids, then pushes me upright. The pole resumes its lazy spin, bringing me around and around, my lashes fluttering as I fight uncharacteristic dizziness. It's like earlier when he was inside me, but opposite: I pass through Shard, and I feel what it's like to be suspended in space. Weightless. Iridescent blue tendrils slither from his depths, surrounding me. Cradling me.

"Kiss me," I demand, trying to hop off the pole, but Shard fists his hand around mine, preventing me from letting go. Then he shocks me by tugging himself upward until our torsos are level, his chin dipping so his lips brush my hair. I try to catch them, but Shard pulls away with a laugh.

"Not yet."

"Why?" I feel like a child, whining, begging him to give me something other than floating before me while we turn slowly.

"You don't believe me yet," Shard says like it's obvious. "Dance, Rooney."

So I do. I flip and spin until I'm hot, until my skin is crawling with need, and it's only then that Shard steps forward, pressing me against the pole with his strong chest against my back. We still, the only movement my harsh breathing, until Shard weaves his thick fingers through my hair and tugs my head back until my throat is bared.

Then he claims my mouth like it's always been his.

Something explodes inside my ribcage, guiding my spine into an arch as I open my mouth for more of him. Shard invades me thoroughly, precise sweeps of his tongue around mine, not feral but deliberate. As if he's been planning this for centuries. Perfecting himself for this moment, so he'd be ready to pour starlight down my throat. Shard might say I'm a perfect jewel made for him, but he's wrong: I'm suddenly certain, above all else, that this incredible being melted through thousands of dimensional ripples to find me. Because *he* was destined to be *mine*.

I roll my hips back, grinding my ass against him. "Shard," I whimper in a need-drenched voice. I'm not sure how to ask for what I want, because I'm not typically the guy asking to get fucked. I'm not usually being asked either, people just...do it. But not Shard.

"What do you want?" he purrs, his voice resonant.

Definitely not Shard. He'll make me beg first before taking something I don't want to give—although he was determined to give something I didn't want to take. Protecting me from a world that wants to eat me is, well. Interesting, coming from a being I've watched actually *eat* a person.

"I want... you to eat me. Taste me," I insist.

Shard laughs. "Back to that?" Then he hums, holding me in place while his fingers creep down the crease of my hip. I shudder once, then go very still, my breath a hiccuping gasp. Shard doesn't make me beg for it, which doesn't mean he doesn't tease, one fingertip running up the short length of my dick through the tight spandex.

Cool air rushes between my thighs when Shard nudges them apart, exposing how wet I've gotten just from kissing him. The palm of his other hand curves to squeeze my ass, firm and purposeful, massaging the sore muscle. I go boneless and slump against him, allowing room for him to slip under the waistband of my shorts. He strokes the glans of my cock, circling his thumb and rumbling in satisfaction when my hips cant into his grasp. Then he reaches lower, toward my core, where I'm wet and hot and needy.

"Since you asked so nicely," he purrs, "I'll taste you."

Then he drops to his knees, pulling my shorts down with him. Fortunately, he doesn't dematerialize them, just pulls my legs out from each hole while making sure I don't fall over in my haste to be naked for him. Once I'm fully exposed, Shard takes a handful of each of my ass cheeks, spreading them to reveal my holes. The noise he makes is primal, desirous. Neither of us have the wherewithal to hold out any longer: Shard buries his face in my cunt, tonguing inside me with that hot, flexible muscle.

He doesn't leave an inch of skin neglected, switching to rimming me, tongue circling my ass while his fingers plunge into my depths. He fucks me hard with them, bites one of my ass cheeks, and makes a wet, pleased sound when I howl like a cat in heat. I've never been on the *pant someone's name* train, and I'm still not, but only because I can't fucking *breathe*. Shard forces my back to arch until he can lick the underside of my cock, the tip of his tongue flicking over the too-sensitive tip while the pad of his thumb rubs my asshole, dripping with saliva.

I ride his face, a tangled network of nerve endings in critical condition. I almost don't notice when the touches shift from his mouth and hands to...

something else. I look down through teary eyes and see the spectral tendrils wrapping up and down my legs, caressing the inside of my thighs and the back of my knees. One particularly thick tendril, so bright I can barely look at the fractals exposed by its mass, takes advantage of my amazement, quickly wrapping around both my wrists and pinning them above my head, trapping me against the pole.

Shard stands, melded so close against my back we must be overlapping. I'm stretched to my limits, hung like a prize at a fair. He gets a grip on my cock, which barely fills his large hand. That doesn't stop him from using his slick palm to jerk me with single-minded focus. I buck into his hand, chasing the ruthless indulgence he's given me no choice but to accept. I cry so loudly I can't hear myself, a drawn-out yell becoming my whole being. There is no sound in space, so Shard swallows it up.

He pinches and rubs my nipples, which after top surgery lost most sensation, yet I feel his touch like sparks sending electric shocks to my core. I squirm, loving the unfamiliar rainbow of physical sensations. There's a thick, phallic length pressed in my cleft, but Shard makes no move to put it inside me. He rocks it between my cheeks, gasping his pleasure as he propels me closer to mine.

We're racing, I think. Shuttling toward the same black hole, sweet oblivion in sight. One of his tendrils corkscrews its way into my cunt, stimulating my walls with a textured fullness I can't describe. I bear down, putting more pressure on the phallus between my cheeks, feeling Shard's thrusts pick up in time with his furious jerking of my cock.

"My jewel," Shard whispers, in my ear, behind my teeth, spilling into my gut and filling me up, an opaque-skinned bubble about to burst, and only the gods know what's inside.

He doesn't need to say *come for me* or anything else, because that's all I need: The reminder that there's one person in this fucked-up universe who wants me, and that's *enough.*

I come with shattering force, gushing from my cunt as my legs shake in near-painful bliss. Shard shoves his fingers into my mouth, giving me a taste of myself, feeding the scream back into my being so I lose nothing, even while shaking apart. Drool spills down my chin as I gag and suck on those fingers, throating them as if they're his cock, and he responds like my enthusiasm alone is greater than any external stimulation.

"*Perfection,*" is all I hear, multiple dimensions hissing his words back at me so I can't escape them any more than I can the hot come that jets against the small of my back, shooting up the curve of my spine and dripping down my cleft. My legs are wet down to my ankles by the time the crescendo falls.

Shard releases my wrists, and I crumple into his arms the second he's no longer holding me up. He wobbles supporting my weight, but steadies quickly enough, managing to avoid either of us tumbling to the stage.

"Ah, fuck," I groan, dropping my temple against his shoulder. "They just cleaned the stage."

Instead of reacting poorly to my words—*that's* the first thing I thought to say?—Shard chuckles. "I assure you, cleaning a defiled stage is well within the realm of my abilities."

And I'm so exhausted that the only thing I'm able to do is laugh along with him, cradled in the galaxy of his arms.

CHAPTER

TEN

SHARD

I've made up my mind.

"Rooney," I say the moment he enters the dressing room, turning away from my conversation with Nova, which was at its conclusion anyway.

"Chill out, tiger," Rooney says, waving me aside as he walks to his place beside the mirror.

I am a being born from space dust and I've been alive for more millennia than I care to count. Yes, I chose to remain in Earth's dimension, but only for the purpose of studying and collecting experiences I could never access at the farthest reaches of the universe. I do *not* lower myself into a sulk just because a snarky human has denied me attention.

Except this is *my* snarky human, the best one of them all, and I am absolutely sulking at his dismissal when I have been preparing for this all week. Even having given himself to me—in a manner of speaking, as he strongly objects to being, in his words, a "kept man"—Rooney maintains a firm, often caustic, spirit of independence. He doesn't like to be coddled or bullied, even when I'd rather like to coddle him and have instincts that veer dangerously close to bullying. Loving instincts, but still bully-adjacent ones.

So I wait by the door like a good partner, nodding stiffly as the other employees take their leave. Rooney's relationship with me stopped being a subject of gossip when he slapped Sara last month for calling him a— That is, he accused everyone in the room of agreeing with her, then thanked her for saying the quiet part out loud, and demanded anyone who had something else to share stand up and say it to his face. Nova put a stop to the open conflict, Sara quit, and I dragged Rooney back to my apartment to calm him down. Thoroughly. Until he couldn't speak anything but my name and *please*. After that, it didn't have the same thrill, so I became more of a door-stopper than a superior, what with Nova having taken over managing Caution far better than its previous owner.

Which was a not-insignificant element leading to today's conclusion.

Rooney has half a skip in his step when he meets me, wrapped in warm clothes for once, as he learned quickly I wasn't going to compromise on his safety just because he was used to the aesthetic of a tortured artist. Spring will come soon enough, and he'll be able to stomp around in his preferred garb again. I take his hand, warmed to my core as I always am when he's in a good mood and feeling affectionate. Rooney hasn't changed for our dynamic, nor would I want him to, so the shifting colors of his energy and the sharpness of his tongue often have me treading carefully.

I knew that Rooney's baseline disposition wasn't a dealbreaker for me when I first began pursuing him, but then, even a few short months ago, I didn't know what that would feel like, or how a life where I was allowed to witness him untethered was going to look. I enjoy it more than I could have imagined—and, as a being who has witnessed the birthing of new dimensions, I possess familiarity with many wonders.

But none so flawlessly unrefined as the man I now call my partner.

"Let's go home," Rooney says the moment we've turned the corner toward the parking lot.

"No late-night excursions today?" I tease.

"Did you see the heels I was wearing tonight? Gods, *fuck* no. You owe me a foot massage for that."

I wrap my arm around the small of his back, pulling his chest flush with mine. "Did I ask you to wear ten-inch platforms?"

"No."

"Then why am I offering penance for it?"

Rooney smirks. "Because you like me, or something."

I don't have anything to say to that, so I kiss his forehead, then his nose, then finally his lips, slow and sweet. His eyes flutter closed, and for a moment I drag him through a second, two, our kiss frozen in the vacuum of space, before I draw him back down to solid earth and we're standing in our living room.

I had thought it'd be more of an argument to get Rooney out of that repulsive building he was living in, but he made the decision to move here before I'd even brought it up. Small mercies.

Rooney trots off the moment he blinks the stardust from his eyes, leaving me to sigh after him. He disappears into the bathroom to shower, and I pull a plate of fresh sushi out of the fridge. While he's going through his nightly decompression routine, which has become mandatory, I meticulously arrange the sitting lounge: chilled white wine, rose-infused massage oil, and dark chocolate-dipped candied orange peels, which unexpectedly became one of Rooney's favorite treats. But many things about Rooney are unexpected, so I provide the best I can conjure up, and gladly.

Once Rooney emerges from the shower, soft and pink-tinged, with frizzy half-dried hair, the next hour passes in a sleepy haze for him, and an anxious gauntlet of indecision for me. How do I bring this up? Will he see it as me springing it on him, now that it's three in the morning and he'll be ready to sleep soon?

I sense the *take me to bed* energy when Rooney's muscles tense, preparing to pull his feet off my lap. I tighten my grip on them, prompting a curious look; when the thought gets stuck in my matter, he jiggles his leg as a sign for me to get the fuck on with it. Not unfair.

Fighting through my uncharacteristic bout of nerves, I blurt, "I gave Caution to Nova."

Rooney blinks owlishly. "You what?"

"Nova has been acting as the manager for the last few months," I explain, hurrying to get it all out when Rooney raises a brow in the *that's shit I already know* fashion. "My goal in acquiring the club has been achieved, so there was no reason for me to keep it in my possession." Forging paperwork was unbelievably difficult, anyway. Collecting fragments of dimensional detritus while floating in space as a nebulous concept was far easier than *taxes*. Had it been a legitimate business venture, I could have paid someone. Alas.

"So you just gave her the club?"

"I don't have any use for it. After so many years of putting out fires, she deserves the authority, don't you think?"

He shrugs. "Sure. But why are you telling me this right now?" Right to the heart of my plan.

I take a moment to consider my next words more carefully. 'I told Nova not to expect you tomorrow' won't go well. It needs to be presented as a question. An option. Not just about his safety, but my *feelings*, which I'm not yet used to expressing.

"I was wondering if there's anything you'd like to do that isn't..."

"Stripping?" he deadpans.

"Yes."

"Sure, but..." Rooney turns toward the window, the curtains thrown wide. He's become mildly obsessed with the nightly view, although he hasn't told me why. I don't mind. The stars are—were—my home.

"Rooney, my jewel, I think you should quit your job," I finally say, exhausted by my lack of delicate words. "I can offer you everything. Anything you wish, I can provide. I've never had a reason to pursue anyone else's desires, and don't have many of my own. My being has long been an experiment, collecting experiences instead of celestial debris. With you, I could be so much more. *We* could be more."

Then I hold my breath.

Rooney stares at me for a long time, long enough that I begin to squirm like a lovesick youth. Finally, he narrows his eyes and says, "I don't need anyone to save me from my life."

"So you've said," I allow generously. It's a mantra of his.

"But..."

"But?"

"This is about more than me, yeah?"

I tilt my head. "I suppose. I mean, yes." My brow furrows at the simple way he presented the observation. "I want to give you more."

"Alright," Rooney says on a yawn. He pulls his feet out of my lap and stretches, curling his fingers above his head and arching his spine so beautifully I nearly forget what we were discussing until he adds: "On one condition."

Ah. There it is.

"You need to taste me first."

My back goes straight, every muscle tensing. Rooney crosses his arms and shifts to the other end of the couch, hazel eyes blazing with challenge.

"My jewel..."

"Not even a whole bite," he allows. "A sip."

I run my hands through my dark waves of hair. I've never held an appearance for so long, enough to develop familiarity with a body. It's yet another thing that has changed with becoming Rooney's partner. Included among that is, of course, the desire to leave his soul untouched.

Except while it was easy to refuse the first time we discussed it, having been so close with him, the temptation to indulge his request is near unbearable.

"Rooney, I've told you why I don't want to do that."

Tilting his head, Rooney seems to genuinely consider how to proceed, which bodes poorly for me. He's far too smart, especially when the logic is premeditated. "I trust you," he finally says.

I had been expecting more, but those three words feel like a gut punch. Rooney hasn't told me he loves me, and I'm not sure he ever will. Which is fine, because I don't care about the human concept of love. Especially not when my feelings for him veer much closer to metaphysical obsession than something so pure and simple. Thus, 'I love you,' while a cornerstone of human devotion, has little to no importance to me. Trust is something entirely different.

"What if I don't stop?"

Rooney laughs. "What if? I always expected to die young. At least then I won't end up an unclaimed body at the morgue."

The thought fills me with distress and rage. I surge up from my corner of the couch, every particle of my being exploding through my physical form. I see myself reflected in Rooney's wide pupils, nebulae of icy blues swirling within a filmy contour, barely keeping its proper shape. Half of one hand is transparent when I cradle the back of his neck, finding the opal under of his skin to ground myself. Rooney pushes colorless hair from where it's fallen over my eyes and tucks it behind my ear, unafraid of the magnitude of my being.

"When your earthly time comes to its end, I will carry your soul into the stars with me," I swear. "You will be an infant star, and I'll hold every particle of your being within mine until it's time for us to expand. Together."

Rooney fists his hand in the long locks of my hair and drags me close, kissing me with searing heat that brings me back to myself, my shape firming again. When he pulls away, he holds me by the hair so I can't follow. "That's insane, I hope you know. And really fucking awesome, but before you get me to agree to it, you need to give me this. Okay?"

"Give *you* a—"

"I want to be the most important thing inside you," he announces, clear and pointed.

Stunned, I regard him, taking in his sincere expression. He allows my hair to slip from his fingers when I lean in to press our foreheads together. "Alright," I concede. "One sip."

A gentle smile transforms Rooney's face. The nearer I draw, running the tip of my nose down the line of his jaw, the louder his energy thrums. Under his skin. Calling to me. I tuck my face in the crook of his neck, inhaling deeply, smelling him. Intoxicating. Perfect. More radiant than any galaxy, no matter how far-reaching.

Lacking anything else to say, I part my lips the smallest fraction, allowing a breath to caress his skin, disturbing the most infinitesimal particles of what makes him *Rooney*, my jewel, the soul inside the flesh. On the next inhale I allow a smoke-like curl of his essence to pass my lips, running over my tongue like a drop of fresh spring water. It's so exquisite my entire body shudders, overwhelmed by the pleasure of consuming him. I've never taken so little of a soul before, having needed more to keep and examine, but Rooney is an elixir more potent than anything I could collect from anywhere, anyone else.

"You taste like the purest starlight," I inform him, whisper resonating against his skin, now covered in shivery bumps. I rub his shoulders, holding him in place so I can meld half of my being into his, giving him part of myself as well. We blend like a tight harmony, endless singing prisms.

Rooney wraps his arms around my neck and breathes a contented sigh. "How much did you take?" he asks in a sleepy murmur.

A smile barely touches my lips, the slight contact standing fine hairs on end. "Just one sip, as you said."

"Was it enough?"

I nuzzle behind his ear, then scoop him into my arms, keeping our bodies aligned and our souls intermeshed. "More than enough," I answer.

Dark eyelashes fluttering with exhaustion, Rooney spares his own ghost of a smile. "Told you."

Full, enough so I could expand into a dimension for just the two of us, I carry Rooney to bed.

FIN.

ABOUT JEM ZERO

jem zero (they/he) is an autistic transmasculine person who lives with their family in a house built by their great-grandfather. They primarily write queer Sci-Fi/Fantasy with strong themes of love and social justice, and they adore nothing more than giving trans men happy endings.

Further eccentric nonsense can be found on their website & social media, including novels, short stories, and award-winning erotica. They're "jemzero" basically everywhere.

Visit jemzero.com for more information.

CONTENT NOTES FOR ALL STORIES

Please review the content notes and trigger warnings provided for each story in this collection to ensure the best and safest reading experience.

Seed and Bone by Genevieve Brandon

Blood and gore (mild), death, murder, child abuse (imprisonment and neglect), violence against women, physical injury, loss of consciousness, deaths of parents (off-page), wartime setting, child sacrifice (mentioned/off-page), threat of sexual assault (off-page), explicit consensual sex

Her Velociraptor Librarian by Mindi Briar

Brief confinement/claustrophobia, panic attack, bullying (off-page), homophobia (off-page), destruction of egg clutch (off-page), explicit consensual sex

The Kings' Bride by Lisa Edmonds

Blood, grief, loss of parent (off-page), animal deaths on-page, mild gore, confinement (off-page), life-threatening injuries, loss of consciousness, monsters eating people, threat of sexual assault, explicit consensual sex

Bride of the Forest by S. C. Grayson

Chasing, voyeurism, death of a parent (off-page), persecution of witches (remembered/off-page), explicit consensual sex

That One Time I Let the Hero Succumb to His Own Ego and Moved in with the Monster by Elisse Hay

Misogyny, violence against women, visually impaired character, religious references (Greek pantheon), blood/gore, death/grief (off page), lateral violence, explicit consensual sex

Girl Dinner by Kristin Jacques

Cadaver dissection in educational/medical context, monster eating people and human flesh, body horror, medical content, gore, humans as prey, death, altered mental states due to predatory pheromones, mild bullying, physical abuse (brief), sexual harassment by person in authority (brief), explicit consensual sex

Meat Cute by Desireé M. Niccoli

Blood, gore, animal death (bycatch caught in nets), distress/grief, wound tending, monsters eating people, explicit consensual sex

Psychopomp in Bloom by Holly Rose

Explicit sexual content; aftermath of car crash with fatalities; blood; death of spouse (off-page); on-page death of elderly woman (not graphic); non-denominational spirituality (with mentions of goddesses and angels); medical 911 call; grief; funerals; homophobia (off-page), explicit consensual sex

Bride of the Dragon Prince by Megan Van Dyke

Human sacrifice (does not actually die), physical injury, blood, death (off-page/remembered), death of parent (off-page/remembered), death of sibling (off-page/remembered), plague (off-page/remembered), grief/loss, animal death for food, explicit consensual sex

Just One Sip by jem zero

Homophobic slurs, sex work, attempted sexual assault, drug use (both with and without consent), gore, bodily functions (vomit, blood, etc.), mild existential stalking, explicit sexual content and consensual sex